Watching Glass Shatter

Watching Glass Shatter

James J. Cudney

Acknowledgements

Writing a book is not an achievement an individual person can do on his or her own. There are always people who contribute in a multitude of ways, sometimes unwittingly, throughout the journey of discovering the idea to drafting the last word. *Watching Glass Shatter* has had many supporters since its inception in August 2016, but before the concept even sparked in my mind, my passion for writing was nurtured by others.

First thanks go to my parents, Jim and Pat, for always believing in me as a writer, as well as teaching me how to become the person I am today. Their unconditional love and support has been the primary reason I'm accomplishing my goals. Through the guidance of my extended family and friends, who consistently encouraged me to pursue my passion, I found the confidence to take chances in life. With Winston and Ryder by my side, I was granted the opportunity to make my dreams come true by publishing this novel. I am grateful to everyone for pushing me each and every day to complete this first book.

Watching Glass Shatter was cultivated through the interaction, feedback, and input of several beta readers. I'd like to thank Cammie Adams and Kourtney Daugherty for providing insight and perspective during the development of the story, setting, and character arcs. They read several different versions, giving a tremendous amount of their time to help me draft this book over several months. The extended beta reading team, who read a complete version of the novel and provided many suggestions and corrections, also deserve my appreciation: Nicki Kuzn, Becki Silver, Linda Stevenson, Chanel Carter, and Suryasol. I am thankful to a few kind folks who also read many chapters providing helpful comments and ideas that enabled me to refine characters and plot lines: Lisa, Robyn, Cimone, Lina, and Louise.

I'd also like to thank author Melanie Mole for introducing me to my publisher, Next Chapter. Without Melanie's generosity, I would not have launched this book. I am also honored to be part of the Next Chapter team and enjoy working with everyone in this company. Thank you to them for printing *Watching Glass Shatter* and making this lucky guy a published author.

Prologue

Ben uncrossed his legs and hunched forward. Wobbly knees trembled under the mahogany desk as he fought to suppress his plaguing nausea.

"Do you have any specific instructions on how I should handle the matter?" Ira Rattenbury's mellow voice echoed off the thin, panel-covered walls of an office hiding in Brandywine's downtown historic square.

"I hoped you might have a solution. This was a difficult decision." Ben lifted his head from a determined stare at the envelopes he'd dropped on the desk. Uncertain how to broach a troublesome topic, he removed and cleaned his wire-framed spectacles and replaced them on his pale and furrowed face, shuddering at the reflection of graying hair at his temples.

"Altering your last will can disturb your long-held confidences in prior decisions. Do the envelopes contain a change to the estate's division among your heirs?" Ira shuffled through the paperwork strewn across his desk.

"No." Ben inhaled the scent of the sandalwood candle Ira's secretary lit outside the frosted glass office door, its pungent burn reaching his unprepared nose.

1

Ira's face crinkled. "Did you acquire new assets we need to account for?"

"Nothing since we spoke last year." Ben's hands pressed atop the leather organizer tapping an unknown rhythm incapable of soothing the erratic hesitation in his voice.

"I want to do anything I can to help. Maybe you should tell me to whom the envelopes belong. It's quite a fine and delicate parchment, early twentieth century. I'm assuming the contents are of significance."

"Yes, the stationery was a gift from my wife years ago. I apologize. I don't mean to be unclear. Regret terrorizes even the strongest of men..." Ben flinched while peering out the window at a mother pushing a baby carriage along the main street, unsettled by the grinding whirr of traffic passing by a few feet away. Someone, other than him, needed to know what he'd done all those years ago.

Ben knew it was time to confess his sin especially after watching so many people ripped from existence around him. His oldest friend recently died of a heart attack on the golf course, mid-swing in front of him, as they finished under par on the last hole. The image of the five-iron and golf ball gliding through the air, both landing several feet away on the dewy grass, as his friend fell to the ground, still haunted Ben. Fear of his own mortality had been cultivated that day.

Ira pushed back his leather seat a few feet, stood, and adjusted the pocket on his linen coat. "I understand your difficulty. If this contains material of a sensitive nature, I assure you, I will personally handle the matter. No one else in my office will know of our conversation."

A wince formed on Ben's face when the chair's heavy legs scraped across the wooden floor. "Yes, I insist only you administer my estate going forward." Ben's long fingers waded into the bowl of coins on the desk. "You've a promising future ahead of you, Mr. Rattenbury."

Ira nodded. "I value our relationship, Ben, if I may. After all these years as your attorney, we should dispense with the formalities." He handed Ben a glass of aged brandy from the thick crystal decanter sitting on his marble sideboard. The intoxicating smell lingered in his nose before descending upon the rest of the tiny office.

Ben accepted the tumbler with tense, whitened knuckles and swallowed a healthy pour. The warm liquor soothed him as he pushed the chair further back from the desk. "Yes, please call me Ben." He stood and walked toward the arched window, focused on the narrow floor-to-ceiling corner bookshelf. His fingers traced the crackled spines of the law books. "I knew the day would come when I needed an ally I could trust, someone removed from my family who wouldn't... hold an obligation to... reveal my indiscretion to them."

Ira nodded, swallowed the remains of his drink and sat in his chair. "Tell me what's troubling you, Ben."

"Both Olivia's and my parents have passed away in the last few years. I've inherited responsibility for this family as its new head." As he paused between thoughts, Ben listened to the wind's hollow interruption whipping through the covered porch outside the glass panes. "I need to face the consequences of a decision made many years ago. Perhaps in the future, I'll want to tell them myself, but for now, my family will better handle the news if I'm already dead and buried."

Ben shared his story with Ira, who offered a smile when Ben seemed unable to summon the proper words. "I will do my best to handle this exactly as you wish."

By the end of their conversation, Ben grew confident he'd chosen the right man to administer his final wishes. "I appreciate your discretion in this matter. In addition to delivering these envelopes upon my death, I have one more task which requires your assistance."

"Certainly."

Ben removed from his coat pocket a piece of paper containing a name and thrust it toward Ira. Dogging remorse and pain percolated within his hand's visible tremor.

Ira studied the translucent parchment. "Who is Rowena Hector?" A dutiful concern in his voice pled with Ben for a deeper explanation.

Ben turned away from Ira unwilling to let him see the salty drops materialize in his eyes. "You must learn everything you can about Rowena upon my death and not beforehand. I expect Olivia will ask for guidance based upon what I revealed in the letters. Please convey this decision tortured me for years, and that I struggled with choosing the coward's way out."

Chapter 1 – Ben & Olivia

Present, Memorial Day Weekend

Sitting in the backseat of his steel-gray Mercedes-Benz sedan, Ben switched the mobile phone to his other ear and removed the seatbelt out of his way, loath to strap himself in for any length of time. When its band rested tightly across his chest, he struggled to breathe, preferring instead to trust in his long-time chauffeur's driving abilities more than a piece of nylon fabric hinged to a pulley. "I'm in the car heading toward you. I should arrive in twenty minutes."

"Still happily married to the woman of your dreams?" Olivia's lyrical voice echoed on the phone.

"Ah, my beautiful Olivia. The last forty years have been amazing. There's so much ahead of us and still to come."

"I love you more than yesterday."

"But not as much as tomorrow." He played along enjoying their frivolous banter.

"Please get to the party soon. It's not any fun when I'm dancing a rumba by myself. Remember when we crashed into the instructor while taking those silly dance lessons, and she yelled at us for being fools? Oh, I never laughed so hard."

"Ha, yes! We are quite the pair. No wife of mine should ever dance alone. At least not while I can prevent it." Ben glanced through the car window, surprised by the speed of the muddy water cascading down the mountains as his chauffeur took the exit to their country club in Brandywine, Connecticut. "I believe tonight is the first time the whole family has been together since last Christmas. Am I right?"

"Yes, they're all here now reminding me so much of the *you* I remember from our early days." Olivia sighed and waited for Ben to respond.

Ben's thoughts drifted while lightning crackled in the sky, and rain pounded the black-tarred roads around him. "Time flies by too quickly, Olivia."

"You've got a few months left, then you'll retire and have nothing but time to be a grandfather and a father doling out advice. Even if they don't want to listen to us. They never do, do they? Wishing you could turn back the clock. At least we can finally take our trip to Europe..." She paused. "Are you still there, Ben?"

Ben snapped from the storm's hypnotic trance upon hearing Olivia's rising voice. "I'm sorry. Recalling their antics over the years distracted me. I don't know how we survived five boys."

Ben heard her beautiful snicker–about to tell Olivia he loved her–when the car swerved as it neared the final exit on the slick asphalt curve, unaware traffic had come to a full stop ahead. He dropped the phone from the unplanned change in direction, grabbed it from under the front passenger seat, and raised his head.

Ben's heartbeat and breath paused significantly longer than usual, enough to recognize the encroaching overpass column directly in his purview and to accept the impending fate laid before him.

Whoever said life flashes before one's eyes in your final moments never lived to truly describe it. In Ben's case, although they only lasted ten explosive seconds, those moments managed to include all sixty-nine years of his existence, each image punctuated by a blinding flash of pure white light and deafened by the harsh snapping sound of an old-time camera shutter.

CRUNCH. Grinding squeal. Bright light glimmers in a dark vacuum.

The enchanting depth of Olivia's cerulean blue eyes the night they first met at the opera. Their wedding day when he truly understood what it meant to find one's soulmate.

SNAP. Utter blackness, followed by a perforated vibrant glow.

The Thanksgiving feast spent at the hospital when his sister-in-law, Diane, broke her foot trying to avoid dropping the turkey on Bailey, their ten-year-old Shiba dog. Seeing his granddaughters nestled in tiny pink blankets when his sons brought them home the first day.

POP. Sharp, dark void. High pitch release of pressure, then a translucent shining flash.

The white-water rafting adventure on the Snake River in Yellowstone National Park where his boys rescued him from falling into the cold water only to stumble upon an angry moose searching for dinner. The final family portrait taken the prior year when everyone wore shades of black and white for a retro-style Christmas card setting.

BOOM. Screeching whistle. Bright light fades to total darkness.

The parchment letters which held the secret he kept from Olivia, pawned off on his attorney to handle once anxiety and fear defeated any chance of Ben telling his wife the truth in person.

The car hydroplaned atop a few inches of the warm, pooling rain and crashed into the steel overpass. The collision immediately torpedoed him through the front windshield, shattering what was the well-lived but haunted life of Benjamin Glass.

A final burst of the bulb's filament into jagged shards.

* * *

Despite Olivia's tendencies to lead and control, she'd little ability to plan Ben's funeral services on her own. Diane recognized her sister's fragile grip on reality teetered on the edge, volunteering to go with Olivia to the funeral home to manage most of the phone calls, selections, catering, and organizing.

Choosing Ben's burial clothing served as the only funeral activity Olivia handled without any help. After pocketing an hour's worth of sleep and waking up alone the morning after the accident, she accepted his death was anything but a dream. The restless night highlighted a comfort she didn't know how much she had relied until stolen by fate. Olivia thrust her tired body out of their bed, walked to the closet, and pushed a slew of hangers across the sleek metal rod reminiscing while passing each suit as though every year of their lives disappeared before her weary eyes. She searched for the one he'd worn to the Met's opening opera the prior year. After weeks of shopping that summer, she'd finally convinced him to expand his horizons with a new designer, selecting a modern-cut, three-button black wool suit adorning him better than any other had fit in the past. Even Ben had admitted she chose correctly. And he'd rarely admit so, given she'd laud it over him teasing Ben for days. They enjoyed their game of one-upmanship over the years, but now days later, she knew it was lost forever.

The final burial service ended thirty minutes earlier, and although everyone else had left, she stayed behind for her own last goodbye. Olivia's memory focused on the somber tones that had serenaded the lowering of Ben's casket six feet into the ground. Once the skirl of the bagpipes blasted its sorrowful resonance, Olivia, standing a few feet from Ben's freshly open grave, could no longer thwart the wrecking ball that planned to decimate any remaining strength. The slow, melodic sound sliced away at the newly loosened threads once tasked with keeping her heart intact and sheltered from acknowledging a widow's pain. Her battered eyes betrayed any remaining fortitude she'd stored deep within her body, and as the chords of "*Amazing Grace*" resounded from the chanter pipe, the cords of her soul, once intricately woven into Ben, ripped from Olivia's chest. The flood of tears from her stinging red eyes trailed her cheeks as she walked to the car leaving behind a single set of prints that marked an unknown future.

As she stepped off the cemetery's grassy path, she pulled a black cashmere sweater closer toward her shivering skin to halt the biting frost growing deep within her bones. Ben always said her true beauty glimmered when she wore black and gray, complimenting her on the elegant silhouette against her ivory skin and dark sable hair. She kept her shiny locks shoulder length, usually tied back with a clip, and although gray had appeared the last year, the varying shades were regal and striking on her patrician face.

Olivia pressed her palm to her chest and lowered her head until she'd emptied a few layers of grief. She opened the car door and slid across the back seat next to Diane.

All that remained before her impending post-Ben world began was to tell her driver he could leave the cemetery, but uttering those words felt impossible. As if Diane sensed the struggle within her sister, she leaned forward and motioned to the driver to start the car, allowing Olivia a few moments to accept the beginning of her new life. While the car served as a false protection from the reality waiting outside the doors to its passengers, it also evoked a budding nostalgia.

"I'm so sorry, Mrs. G. He was a good man." Victor had been her driver for twenty-five years taking her to each child's pediatric appointments, all her charitable foundation work, and every dinner with friends and family. "I'll take care of you today, Mrs. G." He checked the rearview mirror and nodded when he saw Olivia's eyes, a quiet acknowledgment she'd heard his words. They sat in silence as Victor released the brake and inched the car away from Olivia's latest prison.

Olivia and Diane had come from a poor upstate New York family where they shared a bed until they were nine years old, later pushed out of the door to work as housekeepers by age thirteen. Their parents told them only enough money existed for one to go to college, even if they could secure a scholarship to pay for most of it, and Olivia earned the lucky windfall. Diane believed school held no importance to her appearing content to remain in the small comforts of her home. Supporting her sister seemed easier for Diane than choosing her own path in life, focusing on anything but what she ought to do for herself.

"It was a beautiful ceremony." Diane relaxed into the car seat. "The cherry tree you planted alongside the grave was touching, Liv. You've created a lifetime of memories for your family."

"Is everyone else at the house?" Olivia pressed her fingers to her temple, pacified by the warm blood swimming through each one under her clammy skin.

"Yes, they're setting up lunch. Only your boys will be there. We've spent enough time with friends and neighbors. I even asked George to stay away, so I could help you without worrying about him."

George, Diane's soon-to-be ex-husband, had attended Ben's funeral service and conveyed his sterile condolences to Olivia. Though he'd been married to Diane for thirty years, George barely knew his wife's family, not ever having an interest in other people's children nor any of his own. Diane had finally grown tired of his cavalier attitude and vigilant penchant for ignoring their marriage, requesting a divorce earlier that spring.

"That was a good idea. You really should have dumped that unfortunate man years ago." Olivia placed her hand on Diane's noticing the age spots more prominently displayed on her sister's than her own. Her voice stammered, but she held firm until finishing her thoughts. "Thank you for everything you've done for me these last few days."

Despite being a few years younger, most people assumed Diane was at least a decade older than Olivia. She'd grown out her hair the last few years and tightly braided it to her lower back, wearing the same dress as she had to her nephews' weddings and other recent funerals. She hated to spend any time fussing with her appearance. "It's a shame Ben's brother couldn't make the funeral."

Ben was the youngest of several siblings. When Olivia called her brother-in-law, he could barely even speak on the phone from the impacts of grief and his aging mind. His children stopped in for the wake but chose not to stay for the graveside burial.

"No, his family has withered. Ben only had us left. It's unbearable for our children to go through this agony. You first focus on your own pain but watching them suffer steals all remaining breaths."

Diane fumbled with the clasp on her purse and handed Olivia a tissue. "And without any warning. It's awful, but you'll know how to help them through it."

"I can see the pain in Ethan's eyes, but he's strong and will grieve privately. He'll miss Ben the most. Ethan's always been so focused on spending time with all of us, his grandparents... oh, I can't..." Olivia dabbed her eyes with the tissue.

"It's such a shame to lose his father when he's so close to becoming a doctor. Ben would have been so proud when Ethan fulfills his dreams."

Olivia nodded. "Matthew had to tell his daughters their grandfather died. They're too young to understand, but it was dreadful for him to show them Ben's casket. He keeps talking about all the father-son weekends fishing and camping at Lake Wokagee. They'd planned another one this summer."

"They loved those trips. Well, maybe not all of them."

"That's true. Theodore has alienated himself from us even more than usual the last few months."

Theodore was Ben and Olivia's eldest son, and though she would always call him by his proper name, everyone else chose Teddy. Ben had groomed him to take over the law practice at the end of the year, coaching his son on how to act as a stronger, more respected leader and to become a less antagonistic man. Teddy's actions were always packaged with a rough edge, and the tone of his words and speech pattern sounded robotic. Although Teddy had shown up to football Sundays and movie nights, interacting with his family always resembled more of an obligation rather than an enjoyment.

The car turned passing the corner where Ben had always dropped off the boys for the school bus in the morning on his way to work. A few heavy drops fell from Olivia's eyes. She let them roll across her cheeks, reluctant to grant them total control. She imagined Ben lining each son side by side, inspecting his loyal soldiers, and patting their heads as he christened each one ready to begin his day.

"At least Caleb is back for a few more days." Diane rubbed her sister's shoulder. "You'll get to spend more time with him."

Caleb had only agreed to attend the anniversary party the prior weekend after much pressure, but he stayed in Connecticut for the funeral to grieve for his father's passing. Olivia once thought Caleb would stay home with her and Ben when they grew older, but abandoned hope when he disappeared to Maine ten years earlier.

"Caleb's hurting. I know my son. I wish he weren't all alone. He needs someone to lean on… a girlfriend, a wife. The guilt over living so far away must be consuming him."

"Caleb is strong like you in so many ways holding back to protect himself from the intensity of it all. I'm sure he's got friends to look out for him. What about Zach? Are you still worried he's using…"

Olivia interrupted. "He drove back to Brooklyn last night for work. I heard him arrive early this morning. Zachary's actions are always unclear."

Olivia thought Zach often spiraled out of control when he left his five-year-old daughter in her and Ben's care unsure of what trouble he'd engaged in. She and Zach hadn't been close the last few years, and despite a few attempts at a reconciliation, it always proved futile.

"Five boys without a father. We should have had more time." Olivia leaned forward and reached a hand to the front seat to sturdy herself. Her head sloped toward the floor of the car when her voice cracked.

Diane rested her head on her sister's back. "I know, Liv, but you'll support them. You'll remind them of Ben, and they'll find a way to get through their grief. It takes time. Pain is different for everyone. You need to replace it with memories of something positive."

Olivia summoned memories of Ben's marriage proposal when he'd arranged a private afternoon lunch in the southern nursery of Connecticut's finest botanical gardens. Dressed in a heather gray knee-length chiffon silk dress with sleek embroidered violet straps wrapping around her neck, Olivia meandered the slate stepping stones to a patio shrouded by voluminous twenty-foot cherry trees. Ben stood underneath their cascading flowering branches, shadowed by the umbrella sky of brilliant pink, red, and white hues, holding a single sprig of cherry blossom. On the far corner of the patio, before the grafted trunks of the cherry trees met the pristine, freshly-mowed green lawn, a four-piece string orchestra crooned romantic melodies. When Olivia stepped inside the trellised gazebo, she smiled at the fresh-cut lilies, reminiscent of the bouquet he'd brought her on their first official date. A waiter poured them each a glass of Dom Perignon, and as she reached for the champagne, the thick edges of the goblet pressed into Olivia's fingers. She inhaled the scent of the sweet liquor and shivered at the shower of a bubbly effervescence dancing on her face. The quartet played Roberta Flack's "*First Time Ever I Saw Your Face.*" Ben dropped to one knee. Olivia's hands trembled until Ben took one into his own. As the strings of each instrument blended immaculate harmonies and the musician's lyrics rumbled in the background, the reverberation through the wooden floor of the gazebo poured into her.

Ben's words still fluttered today in Olivia's ears... *Will you do me the honor of becoming my wife... to complete the picture of the future I've wanted... ever since the day we met at the opera...* even in the car moments after Ben's burial, when realizing she wouldn't ever again see his face.

Olivia acknowledged Diane's comfort with her eyes as the car pulled onto their street. "I'm unsure how to do this... to start a new life without him by my side. We were together for over forty years. The boys have all left home. I'll live here on my own now. I'll eat breakfast alone every morning. I want to crawl into bed and close the door to my new life." Olivia's breathing quickened as she panicked and shook.

"Calm down, honey. You need to relax and breathe. You're not alone. I'll help every day if you need me. We can stay outside until you're ready."

Olivia considered her sister's suggestion wiping tears from her eyes and clutching her chest. Her sanity told her she didn't need to return to the house. Not a single part of her was ready for this new widow phase where she woke and fell asleep alone in the bed she'd shared with Ben for so many years.

"At least this misery ends tomorrow when we read Ben's will and hear his words again. It should offer some closure and help me decide my future path."

Chapter 2 – Olivia & Ira

Ira would normally hold a client's will reading in his own office, but given this had the potential to wreak havoc, Ira chose what he thought best for Olivia. He'd only met her once when Ben included her in their family's estate planning decisions.

Ben's personal study reminded Ira of his client, given it held an air of old world charm, historic beauty, and cozy memories. Ira sensed Ben's presence in the room imagining him with an after-dinner cordial in one hand, a cigar in the other, and a symphony recording playing in the background. To the left, an expansive seating area circled around a beautiful stone fireplace under twelve-foot cathedral-domed ceilings. To the right stood a large traditional oak desk near the over-sized bay windows with an original Tiffany lamp on its corner.

Olivia held a striking yet maudlin pose as she sat upright with her legs angled toward the fireplace, posture clean and crisp with an arch matching the back of her tall, wing-backed leather chair. She held a cup of tea in her hands atop a fine silver-rimmed china saucer and stared calmly at him. Ira assumed she'd been crying recently as her swollen eyes refused to hide behind whatever makeup she'd applied as a wishful cover.

"Mr. Rattenbury, meet my sister, Diane." Olivia pointed to her left and placed the cup on the table. "It's eleven thirty, we should start."

Diane poured chamomile and raised the porcelain teapot toward him. "Would you like a cup of tea, Mr. Rattenbury?"

"Yes, how kind of you." Ira watched the other members of the family take their seats. "I'm pleased you could attend today. Ben included you in his estate, often speaking fondly of you when he'd come visit me."

Diane blushed and handed him the tea. "I'll miss Ben more than I know how to say."

Teddy, the eldest son, and his wife, Sarah, sat on the couch across from the oak desk. Teddy's hair had turned salt and pepper even though he'd barely entered his early thirties. His wide-set green eyes sparkled when the sunlight blasting through the front window landed on them. Teddy fussed with his collar settling on leaving the top button open, and his awkward face scowled.

Sarah, thin as a rail, displayed a bird-like appearance. She had ash-blonde hair closely cropped to the sides of her face, a charming southern accent, and almond-shaped green eyes she hid behind. Ira placed her at forty, almost a decade older than her husband, and while some might consider her pretty, she also appeared worn, tired, and faint.

Ira nodded and shook their hands. "Nice to meet you both. You have my condolences."

Sarah's neck craned forward. "Much obliged."

Teddy did not respond. A frown still occupied the better half of his face.

Next to Teddy sat Caleb with wavy dark hair and olive skin, different from his parents. Perhaps reminiscent of the relatives in the various family pictures scattered around the room. Caleb's eyes appeared heavy and distant as though he wished he were anywhere but in that room at that moment. Ira reached a hand toward him. "It's good to meet you. Your father spoke highly of you. I'm sorry we haven't gotten to meet before this weekend."

Caleb shook his hand with a firm grip, his eyes looking past Ira toward the window. "I appreciate it, Mr. Rattenbury. I'm not home often, but my father mentioned you on our calls."

Olivia smiled. "Caleb designed this room for his father many years ago. Ben proposed a mid-century modern motif for his study. I never saw the room until finished, but Caleb has always had good judgment. And he loved and respected his father."

"It's very impressive. You're an architect?" Ira lifted his head.

Matt, walking toward Ira, interjected before Caleb had a chance to respond. "Yes, my younger brother plays with his little drawings all day long. And by younger, I barely mean so by only eleven months, but he never could keep up with me. Right, Cabbie?"

Caleb twitched at his hated nickname recalling the tortures his brothers inflicted on one another over the years.

Matt was neither tall nor short, but his witty personality and energetic demeanor compensated for his indiscriminate height. He wore brown stubble across his cheeks and well-defined chin, and dark bags loomed under his eyes, as if he hadn't slept in weeks. "Caleb hates when I call him Cabbie… it goes back to our golf days when he ran up and down the course trying to catch any player who'd give him a chance at the ball. Breaking news… he never did!" He shook Ira's hand and backed away, his dimples shining far across the room.

Caleb cocked his head smiling at his brother over the childish banter. "Let it go, Matt. We all know you're the sports hero in the family. No need to overdramatize today."

Matt crumbled a napkin and threw it with deft expertise at Caleb. "I'm just joshing. It's a grueling day for all of us, Cabbie." He ran his fingers through his thick chestnut hair, his muscular arms thrown above his head. The napkin landed in Caleb's half-empty glass of seltzer. Matt's fists pounded the chilled air, and he shouted *goal,* as the dunk sprayed drops of seltzer and ice across Caleb's perplexed face.

Matt's tone dropped flat when he looked back at Ira. "We appreciate you coming to the house. My wife wandered upstairs with our girls. We thought it best not to have them at the will reading. If we need Margaret, I can run upstairs to get her."

"No, it's fine. We can talk to her afterward if anything comes up. Ben's will is straightforward when it comes to what he chose to leave for everyone." Ira shifted his weight as he leaned into the desk.

Matt nodded and took a seat after punching Caleb in his right arm. A token of affection or mischanneled grief.

Ira glanced next at the youngest son whose youthful glow could challenge any teenager. He had a lanky, wiry frame, bore a thick head of reddish-blond hair, and boasted several freckles on his ruddy complexion. "You must be Ethan. Your father's pride was evident over all the work you've accomplished at the hospital. Boston University, right?"

"Yes, sir. My second year of medical school is almost complete. Pleased to meet you, Mr. Rattenbury." He quickly took a seat on a chair closer to the window, on the far side of the grandfather clock, while his gaze constantly checked on his mother.

Ira's eyes opened wide. "We're missing someone... Zach?"

Olivia's eyes darted around the room. "He was in the hallway a few minutes ago. Let me go check." She stood and angled toward the door.

Diane placed the teacup back on the table, looking out the double doors, and motioned to her sister. "Liv, he's walking down the stairs. There's no need to search for him. "Zach," she yelled. "We're in the study."

Zach walked through the open doors with his daughter, Anastasia. "I'm here, no need to find me. I was just checking on my girl." He picked her up, swung her from side to side, and she giggled with an innocent laugh. When he put her down, she closed both the doors with a flourish as though she'd known it was time for privacy.

Zach, clad in acid-wash jeans and a black t-shirt with bare feet and dark wet hair, was ruggedly handsome. He kept a trim beard set across his squared chin and high cheekbones as well as two visible tattoos. One on his arm where an artist had drawn a green and pink vine running from Zach's left wrist up to the back of his neck. On his right forearm, a pair of black and white dice danced, along with a few colored playing cards, the ace and the king of hearts. The red had begun to fade, not unlike many other things in his life.

Olivia's lips pursed as her voice grew harsh. "Zachary, it's not a good idea to have her here with us. Margaret could watch her upstairs with the other girls. Would she mind, Matthew?"

Matt lifted his head. Something he fiddled within his pocket had been distracting him. He mumbled "Huh?" as his eyes pressed together, and his neck jutted to the side.

Diane took her grandniece from Zach, gently brushing the girl's wild copper locks while placing Anastasia on her lap. "I'll watch her. There's tea in the pot if you want a cup."

"It's helpful for her to absorb the family dynamics, Mom." Zach walked to the sideboard. "No, too hot out for tea. I'm gonna pour a glass of brandy. Anyone else need liquid courage?" He carefully emphasized the word *liquid*.

Sarah and Teddy exchanged glances, their eyes shifting back and forth across the room.

Olivia kept silent, but Ira could tell by her rising, wrinkling nose, she was ready to summon a rattled angst at her son's behavior.

Ira spoke to clear the strain. "Since we're all here, I can begin."

"Yes, I agree with you. Thank you, Mr. Rattenbury." Olivia motioned for everyone else to sit.

Ira stifled a laugh considering Olivia appeared to view the reading of the will as her marionette show despite knowing he maneuvered the strings for the rest of the afternoon. A few minutes later, Ira completed delivery of the basic premise of the will, when he drafted it, and what the next steps would include. When everyone nodded with their understanding, he continued.

"Let's discuss the specifics of the estate. I will cover a few items we should handle before anything else, when it comes to distribution of assets. And now, the following is directly from Ben's will: *To my beloved sister-in-law, Diane, I leave the sum of two hundred thousand dollars disbursed as soon after my death as possible. Diane, you have been like my own sister, and you have always taken care of this family as if it were your own. I should take care of you. You need to find happiness. You need to live the rest of your life as you want to live it, not as someone else forces you to do so. Think back to our conversation after your mother died, and you will know what I mean. Do not accept what stands today. Find your own adventure in life."*

Diane's eyes welled at the depth of Ben's appreciation for their friendship over the years. She glanced at her sister with eyes hungry for acknowledgment. "Liv, did you know he was gonna do this?" Her voice strained, and she gently tapped her chest.

Olivia's lips curled in the corners forming into a gentle smile as her cheeks grew pink. "I did. I didn't know how much, but we wanted to take care of you should anything happen to us. You deserve the opportunity."

Ethan stepped forward and hugged his aunt. "He loved you. This seems right."

Diane placed Anastasia on the floor in front and sat back into the chair fumbling to find its arms. "Please, continue. Don't mind me." Her hands clasped together across her mouth and nose. Her eyes darted back and forth across the room settling on disappearing into the family portrait on the far wall.

Ira nodded and noted he was reading directly from the will again. *"To the three charities of Olivia's choosing, I leave the sum of one hundred thousand dollars. Olivia, helping others has always been your passion. You have been a driving force behind so many positive causes. I am confident you will know how to divide this money to benefit the greater good of Brandywine and of Connecticut."*

Olivia nodded looking toward the ceiling, her fingers and palm resting on her chest. "Thank you, Ben."

Ira continued. "For clarity, Ben and Olivia drafted the next piece of the will together, and I assure you they were in full agreement on the following proceedings: *For the remainder of my assets, I leave our house and property to my wife, Olivia, to live in and/or use as she decides along with a monthly subsidy to use for any upkeep and maintenance, contingent upon Olivia or a member of the family retaining ownership of the property. The subsidy payments have been set aside for a ten-year period. For any investments, cash, and/or equity to our names, we shall equally divide them with fifty percent allocated for Olivia and fifty percent allocated and divided equally between each of my five sons, thus being ten percent each."*

Ira stopped speaking while his eyes swept across the room. The lack of shocked expressions assured him they'd expected this division of assets. "As of earlier this month, the total monetary value of these assets, which we will divide as previously noted, equals twenty million dollars, meaning Olivia will inherit ten million, and each of the boys will inherit two million dollars, net of taxes, payable within the next two months as I liquidate the accounts."

Olivia broke the silence in the room. "Boys, your father and I considered putting the money in a trust for when each of you turned forty, but ultimately decided to release it while you're younger and can enjoy it."

Each of the five boys managed some form of a nod. Ira knew from his many conversations with Ben they'd all been careful with money. Even though the family had grown further apart over the years, this was the fair approach.

Olivia nodded. "Good. We have enough money to take care of ourselves and families. We were lucky, and he was a remarkable husband and father to do this for us. Please continue, Mr. Rattenbury."

"As always, you're a shining example of grace, Mrs. Glass. Yes, to continue, the next discussion includes the law practice Ben owned along with his two colleagues, Mr. Jason Wittleton and Ms. Nora Davis. For those who are unaware, Ben had sixty percent ownership in the law practice, and his two partners each owned twenty percent. They are minority owners but are comfortable abiding by the terms set forth in this will regarding Ben's interests. Ben had been transitioning the firm to his eldest son, Teddy, with plans to transfer the daily administration by the beginning of the new year. Should Teddy continue to assume full responsibility for the daily administration of the firm, he will represent the sixty percent majority of the Glass family's share, making the firm's decisions; however, he should divide any of the firm's profits among all five children. Given Teddy will handle the running of the firm, he will inherit twenty percent and the remaining four sons will each inherit ten percent, disbursed annually by the firm's accountant. Should Teddy decide not to keep leadership, the first right of purchase goes equally to the two co-partners. Ben hoped the firm would stay in the family, but he recognized circumstances could change. He wanted provisions in either case. Do you have any questions?"

Matt spoke up, clearing his throat and puffing his chest. "Since I handle the accounting for the firm, I can explain any details you need. But I've got this one in the bag. I've already spoken with Mr. Wittleton and Ms. Davis, and they understand we need time to process and decide on any changes." His hands moved as he talked, as though his excitement and pride fought for the top-dog trophy. "They trust me to handle daily operations. We've been paying profits from the firm on an annual basis, usually in February. It's a minor adjustment if we're only changing the percentages and not selling. We're golden."

Olivia interrupted, her voice cutting through a growing tension. "Of course, we're not selling. Theodore has wanted to follow in his father's footsteps since he was a young child. Within a few weeks, he will assume leadership with his new partners' guidance expected from time to time."

Teddy's grim expression, as if he'd grown discontented in the conversation, captured Ira's attention.

Sarah, upon noticing her husband hadn't responded, chimed in. "I reckon y'all need a lil' time to figure this out." She bristled with a nervous energy, her pallor suddenly a bluish green.

Teddy nodded in agreement. "Yes, we'll address it soon. There is no need to get into those details today. Let's move along, please."

Sarah and Zach locked eyes. She reached her hand to Teddy's shoulder, but his entire upper body flinched upon contact.

Zach rubbed his hand across his stomach as a nerve in his left forearm sharply twitched waking the vines crawling on his skin. He stood to pour a second brandy, shaking his head the entire time he walked over to the sideboard.

Olivia cleared her throat. "Do you need another one right now, Zachary? It's not even noon."

"Yes, Mom, I do. It's been a long day. I don't usually hear my father's will being read, thank you very much." He dropped two ice cubes in the art deco glass and swiftly swallowed. "Good stuff, Dad." He toasted with a flick of his hand toward Ben's desk.

Olivia summoned Ira's attention. "Do you have anything else we need to discuss right now? Or should we take a few days regarding next steps and reconvene as a family at the end of the week?"

Caleb jumped up, his voice cracked as he spoke. "Mom, I need to get back to Maine soon. I can't stay through the end of the week."

Before Olivia could respond, Diane chimed in. "Let's not worry about it right now. Today's an exhausting day. There's way too much for any of us to get through in one sitting. We'll figure it all out."

Olivia nodded at Diane, appearing grateful to her sister for holding the peace.

Matt agreed. "I need to check on the Yankees game. They should play any minute. Time to kick your boys' asses, Ethan."

Ben had once told Ira about the long-standing rivalry over which of Matt's and Ethan's teams would win each season; it covered all the major sports and created many fierce battles of loyalty across the family. The Glass men had been solid supporters of all the New York teams, but when Ethan moved to Boston, his allegiance went with him, as did their father's.

Ethan smiled. "Red Sox rule. No chance for the Yanks, brother."

Matt and Ethan stood, assuming the will reading had ended. Both walked by the sofa and were about to open the doors to exit. Matt had his hands pressed to Ethan's shoulders either to jump on him or hug him.

Ira couldn't decide what Matt would do, but he had expected no trouble up to this point with Ben's requests. The next part had kept him awake the last three nights preparing for a potential confrontation. His palms grew sweaty despite the years of experience he had in delivering difficult news. Ben had become a friend the last few years, and Ira experienced more empathy for the Glass family than for other clients. He cleared his throat and steadied his hands on the desk.

With eyes focused on Matt and Ethan, he spoke. "We have one more matter to discuss. Gentlemen, if you wouldn't mind sitting for a little longer. I have a final message from your father he asked me to oversee."

"You need me to stay, too?" Matt questioned Ira as he slid the phone back into his pocket, his lips pursed and dismayed. His ample sigh perforated the room.

Ira nodded at Matt noticing Olivia's head tilting in his direction.

Olivia's lips formed into a narrow slit. Her eyes pierced at him as sharp lasers penetrate the fog. "Mr. Rattenbury, we've covered the house, the estate, the law practice, and the charitable donations. What else do we have to review?"

Ira withdrew two envelopes, leaned toward Olivia, and placed them in her shivering hands. "We need to discuss these, Olivia. Ben wrote them a few years ago, and he asked me to deliver them in the event of his death."

Ira's eyes glanced across the rest of the room with a determined focus. "But he clearly specified what he wrote in these letters does not change the terms of his will. He explicitly wanted them handed out *after* the will reading finished."

The grandfather clock loomed in the background, the noon hour arriving with the loud crash of twelve cymbals. Olivia's skin blanched an unnatural shade of white. She clutched her chest, and the jitter of her legs caused the teacup to rattle against the saucer.

"Do you need a glass of brandy, Mom?" Zach took the teacup from her hands.

Olivia sighed. "Yes, I would like one now. Thank you." Her hands rested atop her knees to steady them.

Zach poured two fingers worth of Remy Martin, dropped off the glass in her cold hands, and moved toward Diane to retrieve his daughter. "Interesting. Open them, Mom. Maybe Dad's got another son who's planning to knock on the door."

Olivia dropped the glass, already empty of its contents which had begun settling her nervous stomach. Her rapt eyes followed the glass as it rolled across the carpet landing at Ira's feet.

Diane lunged, offering her sister a cocktail napkin. "Zach, don't say such a thing. Your father would never cheat on her."

"I was only kidding, trying to lighten the mood in here. We all know how much he loved her. My bad. He didn't keep secrets from us. From you."

Olivia picked up the glass and dabbed at the brown and green basket weave carpet with the napkin, as her eyes and hands deeply focused on the task. "Of course not. I knew you were joking. It shocked me, that's all. Please explain, Mr. Rattenbury. This is unexpected." While she controlled her quaking legs, her neck and head still faltered.

Ira continued. "Yes, prior to opening the envelopes, please do let me provide a few more details. Several years ago, Ben arranged a meeting with me to discuss an amendment he wished to include in his estate. Ethan, you'd recently graduated from high school and Olivia, yours and Diane's mother had just passed away. Ben spoke about the importance of family and how ensuring you all knew how much he cared for you directed his every decision. He handed me these two envelopes. One belongs to you, Olivia." He paused, pushing himself to say the final words. "And one belongs to his son."

The room was silent for fifteen seconds until Teddy clenched his jaw and interjected. "Don't you mean sons? He has five sons."

Ira waited a moment to allow the family time to react but had no choice not to continue as all eyes focused upon him—some with doubt, others with a discerning glower. "He meant son. Even I do not know specifically what he wrote in these letters. He asked me to deliver the first one to Olivia. When she finishes reading the letter, she will know what to do with the second one."

Zach's eyes rose, and his cheeks lifted with each word. "But which son? Mom, open the envelope. This doesn't make any sense."

Ethan stayed silent. A hint of a boyish smile, full of innocence and adoration, focused on his mother.

Matt sent a text message, holding very little interest in the discussion.

Teddy spoke, dismissing everyone else's input. "What silliness. Our father didn't play games. What purpose does this business about final letters serve, Mr. Rattenbury?" Teddy shifted his lower jaw, his teeth scraping against one another and sharpening for a readied feast.

Ira chose not to reply hoping Olivia would know how to control her son.

Caleb stood and shuffled to the window, his shoulders hunched forward. He appeared angry or afraid of the contents of the second envelope. His eyes pressed tightly, and his lips mumbled incoherently.

Olivia spoke, her voice was deliberate and soft with each phrase. "Let me open the envelope, boys. I have no idea what this means, but I'm sure reading the letters will clear any confusion."

Diane walked over and sat on the chair's arm placing her hand on her sister's shoulder.

Ira spoke again. "Ben had one other message which I should deliver to Olivia after you've all left. He intended for the boys to give her time to read the letter on her own."

Teddy again objected. "No, we will not leave the room. It would seem to me we're all in this together. Give them to me." His hands reached out toward Ira, stopping an inch away from his wife's nose. Sarah jerked backward with a distinct gasp of familiarity.

Teddy's right cheek twitched as his top teeth pressed further on his jaw. Ira was determined not to let Olivia give Teddy the envelopes.

Caleb spoke, surprising his brothers, with his back toward his family as he faced the window. "Dad wants Mom to read them alone. We need to give her time."

Zach disagreed. "No, she needs to open it and tell us what's going on. Come on, Mom. Let's get to the juicy details." He slid his hands together, lifting his brow several times.

Matt had stopped playing with his phone but tapped the table beside him, fixated on the spinning needles of time on the grandfather clock.

He shrugged his shoulders and bobbed his head a few times. "I need water. Maybe you should open it without us. I want an intermission."

Ethan stared at the floor, absorbing the impact of what happened around him. "It's up to you, Mom. If it's between you and Dad, you should read it and decide if you need to tell us his last message."

Zach and Teddy continued fighting, each raising their voice while arguing unsuccessfully over the best next steps. Teddy would not let up. His voice strained, eyes stretched wider than normal, and a hollow tone grew more pompous with each response.

Olivia stood, her hands pushing down against the invisible yet stagnant air. The shrill sound of her voice emanating across the room told them she'd had enough. "Boys, we've all had a horribly rough week, and I can't handle the disagreements. Your father died. I miss him so much, and we should honor him by supporting one another, not behaving like silly little children throwing temper tantrums. Please give me time alone with Mr. Rattenbury."

Diane took Anastasia from Zach, as he poured another brandy, and left the room. "I'll wait outside if you need me, Liv."

Zach took a sip. "Need another, Mom?" When she declined, he took the bottle and left the study with feet stamping the floor as if he marked a return path in each stride.

Matt had already disappeared up the stairs notifying everyone it was time to check the scores and read to his girls.

Teddy and Sarah walked out together; Sarah ripened near the point of illness. Teddy tried to whisper as he pushed Sarah through the doorway, but his voice carried across the room for everyone to hear. "This letter reeks of useless nonsense."

Ethan gently touched his mom's hand, telling her he loved her, and looked over at his brother. "Caleb, are you coming?"

Caleb nodded. "Yes, in a minute. I wanna talk to Mom."

Ethan exited the room and joined his aunt and niece in the hallway. His relaxed posture and innocent eyes stood out, the only son focused on protecting his mother and not worrying about himself.

Caleb's eyes grew darker and heavier by the second. "Mom, I'm not sure what Dad wrote in the letter, but maybe it's nothing. Maybe you shouldn't read it."

Olivia kissed her son. "Caleb, it's the last communication I have from your father. It's the only time I'll ever again hear his words. I must read it. You go on. I'll find you a little later." She squeezed his hand.

Caleb hugged her. "Goodbye, Mom." After a long stare back, he dropped his head and pulled the heavy wooden doors to the study shut as he left the room.

Olivia sliced the envelope's seal using the silver opener with the Glass family crest sitting on Ben's desk. She pulled out the contents and spoke to Ira. "You mentioned you had one more message for me? I'd prefer to know before I read my husband's letter."

"Yes." Ira noticed the skin under her eyes had grown darker since he first arrived. "Ben asked me upon his death to locate a woman named Rowena Hector. My associates are searching for her based on the brief details Ben offered to me at the time. I know little of her nor what he put in the letter. Do you know anyone named Rowena Hector?"

Olivia's eyes grew wider and her lips thinned out. "I do not, but I'm about to discover what secrets my husband has kept." She unfolded the parchment with a delicate ease and stared at its contents. "I recognize his penmanship. He had distinct round and tall O's whenever he wrote out my name."

> *Dearest Olivia,*
>
> *If you're reading this letter, my time has come, and I've left you for whatever lies before us in this great voyage we call life. I assure you, had I any choice in the matter, I would never leave you. I'm grateful you'll have more time with our boys to raise the intelligent and strong men we discussed ever since meeting at Turandot.*
>
> *Our life together has been something I treasured every day and night. Whether it was you and me courting or showing*

our sons the wonders of Yellowstone, it was always special to me. No other man has been as lucky as I to have such an adoring wife, an idyllic home and family life, and five caring, respectable, and genuinely good sons.

Our sons have been the center of it all. As each of our boys came along, I learned to love with more depth and power, and to understand how to recognize such amazing gifts as blessings. I also realized not everyone in this world has been as privileged as we have been, and for that, I'm compelled to reveal a secret I should have confessed when it happened many years ago.

I know what I'm about to tell you will come with great shock, and it has the ability to change the dynamics of our family. My reasoning came from a good place years ago, one where I only cared to bring you as much happiness as I could deliver. When you told me you were pregnant, I felt fear, shock, and joy at the same time. While I was nervous about the changes it would bring to our lives, I eventually grew to believe it was our destiny. And I desperately looked forward to you having the baby.

Unfortunately, it wasn't meant to be. You were exhausted after giving birth to each of our sons, often under heavy anesthesia and pain medication. I watched you sleep for a few hours each time admiring your beauty and serenity. But shortly after our son was born, he stopped breathing and didn't survive.

At the same time, another woman had given birth to a baby boy. She was a young girl who couldn't care for the child. She had only been in this country for a few months. Knowing such incredibly intense pain and despair at losing a child, I didn't want to bring the same horror to you. I reacted quickly and convinced the girl we would provide the right home for her new baby. I gave her money to get her life started. She left, and I never saw her again. Her name was Rowena Hector.

I considered telling you and formalizing adoption paperwork, but I feared what might happen if we'd gotten the authorities involved. Rowena worried they wouldn't let her stay in the country if she formally gave up her rights to the child. I handled this in a risky manner, especially when a family law attorney should know better. I foolishly focused on the devastating loss if it didn't work out doing it the right way.

I know you may disagree with what I ask of you next, but it was my decision back then, and I must now correct the path I chose. Nothing will ever replace you in his heart, but our son deserves to know the truth, especially since I'm gone. I need to absolve myself of this guilt and sorrow, despite my approach branding me a cowardly man. I beg forgiveness and for you to understand I thought it better at the time to spare you the pain of losing a child and to find a way to take care of a new life by giving a baby a home with two loving parents. When we meet again, I will do everything in my power to show you it came only from love.

I've written another letter to our son—and I do mean our son—as we raised him from birth through his journey into becoming an adult. He'll always belong to us, but he should have the opportunity to decide if he wants to meet his birth mother. Ira will search for her, and if he finds her, I want you to give our son the second letter, so he can hear from me how and I why I made this decision. If Rowena Hector has died, I leave it to you to decide whether to tell our son about my actions or pretend this never happened.

And now, the hardest part. You're undoubtedly curious which of our sons I'm speaking of. When you've found Rowena, and are ready to give the letter to our son, please read it before giving it to him. I beg of you not to open it until you have found Rowena. I hope someday courage will conquer cowardice such that I tell you in person and destroy this letter, but for now, this was the only way I could confess. Until we meet again, my darling Olivia...

Ben

Chapter 3 – Olivia & Diane

Despite summer's early attempt to burst on to the scene, the weekend ushered in dark clouds and a cool, heavy rain. For Olivia, the tattered noise of drops pounding against the window were simply another item she added to the growing list of reasons why she couldn't sleep. Olivia opened her eyes and breathed in her surroundings. The vibrant sun rose above her backyard as though nothing bad had happened. Everyone around her would start another normal week. Except for her. The empty side of the bed sent pangs of grief to Olivia, but it was the bitter letter she wanted to incinerate that had pushed her over the edge. She'd already read it too many times since becoming aware of its existence, praying it would change each time the words passed her doubting lips.

When the letter was first mentioned, she thought Ben had pulled a trick to encourage her to laugh instead of cry over his death, a comfort she wanted to rely on, but she knew Ben would never use the boys in such a seedy manner. He might have jokingly confessed to hiding another wife or losing their money, but he would never fabricate a story about the boys. If he wrote the words, they must be true. He'd never lied to her before, except, he had.

Ira rang twice to speak with her, but she declined his calls, even after some of the boys pushed her hard to quell their fears over Ben's last letter. Olivia had been whirling not only from her husband's death, but the secret he revealed from the grave, bound to wreak havoc on an already burdened family bereft of their leader. Anger intensified over Ben's selfish decision. She'd lost a child, and no one allowed her any time to mourn. A baby who died without ever recognizing its mother's arms around him, treasuring any opportunity to know love before the world forgot he existed. Salty tears filled her eyes and painful questions plagued her head.

What happened to the baby? Was there a burial? How did no one realize it? Does anyone else know? Who grieved for my lost boy?

Olivia's parched throat screamed evolving into a loud and guttural wail. It echoed off the bedroom walls, sending her body into tormented convulsions of frustration and rage. Her hands shook and searched for something to throttle, finally settling on the closest object in her path.

Diane rushed into the bedroom. Olivia ripped apart Ben's pillow and cried in rampant distress. Diane hugged and cradled her sister in her arms. Their sticky, sweaty skin pressed against one another in the hopes two were more prepared to fight off misery's lecherous grip.

"He's gone, Liv. I know you're hurting. I'm here for you. Let it out."

"I'm not crying because he's gone. I'm crying because of what that jerk did, what he took from me. How could he do it?"

"Oh, Liv. You don't mean it, honey. Ben was taken too soon from you. He didn't cause the accident. That's just your anger talking."

Olivia kicked the pillow away and jumped off the bed thrashing and jostling Diane from her path. "I'm not talking about the accident. I need to get out of this house."

Diane sat motionless on the bed watching as her sister released intrusive pain and pent-up emotion. "Talk to me. What's going through your head? Is it grief over something in the letter?"

Olivia paced the floor, pulling out locks of hair as she ripped a silver flower clip from her head and threw it across the room.

As it whizzed by Diane's face and slammed into the bedpost, three of its metallic petals splintered and cracked, each one disintegrating on its flight to the floor. A final crashing sound emanated against the foot of the nightstand, resulting in Olivia dropping to her knees with eyes full of fury and lips full of venom.

Olivia begged for a hug, and she crumbled into Diane's waiting arms. "I'm not ready to tell you everything Ben wrote in the letter. I need to figure out what it means and what I must do now. He lied to me."

Diane rubbed her sister's back to calm her. She pulled Olivia's hair together in a bunch and away from her eyes. "Why don't we get breakfast, and you can tell me whatever you feel comfortable telling me right now. One mistake doesn't erase forty years of a good marriage."

Olivia smirked. "Forty years of a good marriage? It may have been happy at one time, but it swarmed full of lies. You don't understand what he's done, Diane."

Olivia slipped away from the embrace and walked to her bathroom kicking Ben's mangled pillow to the side. Feathers glided through the emotionally-charged air to the carpeted floor as she treaded on to wash away the tears. When she entered the bathroom, she could only find his terrycloth robe, still hanging on the back of the door, unused since the morning of the anniversary party. The musky scent soothed her as she searched for any memory to bring her relief.

Olivia sniffled and breathed in deeply recalling the day she'd met Ben forty-two years ago. After the New York law firm where they both worked had won a few high-profile cases that summer, they received an invitation to Puccini's *Turandot* performance at the Metropolitan Opera House. Once entering the ornate hall, Olivia stood in the foyer searching for someone she knew to watch the crowd with before the performance began. The room boasted wide and open spaces with endless gold-plated ceilings holding sweeping silk draperies against the thick white marble columns. Bowls of fresh purple and yellow freesias uncurled their soft petals against each of the pillars, and the peppery strawberry scent drove Olivia's senses dreamy and gleeful. She glided toward the West entrance, stepped up the glossy set of stairs and quickly lost her footing. As she leaned to the left narrowly missing a waitress carrying hors d'oeuvres, a man caught her arm, and she fell against him, jolting at the charge of electricity surging through her body. Although an office romance might damage her career, it didn't stop her from pursuing Ben. Olivia graciously thanked him for saving her from an embarrassing fall, and her eyes stared into his for a moment longer than she'd expected. It was that night at the opera when they'd shared their first kiss. It was brief, a goodbye kiss after the performance ended, and his masculine scent fashioned a chill down her back. She'd worn three-inch pumps and still had to stand on the tips of her toes to reach his lips. When they pulled away from hers, a wave of euphoric serenity chased out everything around her except for that moment with Ben. She would never forget the kiss, not even in his death.

Diane rested on the disheveled bed for a few moments longer analyzing the situation. As she became distracted by guessing the unknown contents of Ben's letters, she thought back to a conversation they'd had several years earlier...

"*Are you all ready for the party this afternoon?" Diane asked.*

"*Yes. I'm an old man since the last kid ran out the door in search of greener pastures. How is my favorite sister-in-law?" said Ben.*

"*I'm your only sister-in-law, at least on my side of the family, you old coot. Tell me something I don't already know.*"

"*I can't imagine having anyone else I'd want as my real sister more than you. And I include my own sisters.*"

"*I'll accept it. You've been such a good husband to Liv all these years.*"

"*Join me for a drink in the study, Diane.*"

"*Sure, but nothing too strong for me today. I'm sure Liv has tons of tasks for me to focus on this afternoon. I'm probably in charge of cooking, entertainment, and clean-up.*"

"*Don't let your sister tell you what to do. You need to relax. You're not their mother hen... Oh, I'm so sorry. I didn't mean to say such cruel words.*"

"*Don't fuss about it. George didn't want kids. It's not in the cards for me.*"

"*Forgive me for saying it, but you need to leave that louse and put yourself first for once.*"

"*I know he isn't friendly and doesn't often do much, but he's provided for me all these years. It's not like he ever hurt me or anything along those lines. Besides, if I'd left him years ago, what would I've done... adopt a child on my own?*"

"*Adoption is a rewarding and fulfilling path. All children need a good home with a loving parent. You would have been a terrific mother, Diane.*"

"*Said the man with five of his own boys. I'll consider it, but as of now, I've no intention of leaving him after twenty-five years of marriage.*"

"*I can respect your decision, but you need to focus on yourself and your own future. I told the estate attorney that same thing when I saw him yesterday. Since the boys are all grown, I wanted everything properly buttoned-up for whenever something happens to me in the future.*"

"*You're being vague and morbid. That's abnormal.*"

"*It's been a rough couple of years for this family. So much change has been happening. I simply want to prepare for whatever else may occur. I'm getting older. Not handling the stress as well I used to.*"

"*But we're a strong family, and we'll get through it. You're good at taking care of everyone.*"

"*I wouldn't go that far. I've made questionable decisions along the way. I'm afraid to disappoint Olivia.*"

"*Are you worried Liv won't agree with your decision at the lawyer's office?*"

"*Not exactly.*"

"*Liv can be a force when she wants to be. She's certainly set in her ways.*"

"*Strong-willed like her mother, but that shows why I love her so much. You'll need to support her if anything happens to me. She never lets herself get close to anyone else besides you, and of course, the boys.*"

"*That's true. She still hasn't warmed up to Sarah or Margaret.*"

"*The ladies she works with at the charities are purely business connections. On those rare occasions when they tried to bond, competition surfaced above anything else. Remember the incident with the fashion show?*"

"Oh, I remember it. Betty and the girls wouldn't talk to her for weeks. They still hold a grudge every time some fool suggests another fashion show. Poor Liv… she didn't mean to be so loud, it just came out. She's always been a victim of her own sharp tongue."

Diane jolted from her memory when Olivia closed the shower door. As memories of the fashion show incident disappeared from her mind, a laugh supplied the energy she needed to leave the bedroom while Olivia finished dressing. Years ago, Olivia had volunteered to lead a designer's charity ball and needed to find several women to model a new clothing line by Ben's client's wife. When the client's wife offered to let Olivia's friends walk the runway, Olivia's response said it all. Unfortunately, she delivered the response while at a press release event where a news crew recorded her saying "None of those ugly cows would even fit in this couture. It would be as if we asked Miss Piggy to model a new petite line of muumuus." Her sharp voice and snooty demeanor were prominently displayed on *News12* for the next three days, on the hour, every hour, and not even Ben's firm, nor his client's corporation, could have it pulled.

Diane shuffled downstairs to the kitchen to prepare breakfast. She switched on the coffee, having already prepared it the night before. Grabbing a quiche out of the refrigerator, she sliced two giant wedges and put them in the broiler to warm up.

While the coffee dripped, Diane set two places at the breakfast nook in the corner, her favorite spot in her sister's home. When she'd stay over to watch the boys, they always wanted to eat in the kitchen. Olivia and Ben usually served meals in the dining room preferring a formal atmosphere. Diane favored the ease and comfort of squeezing into the padded benches and chairs in the corner of the kitchen. The table overlooked the gardens in the backyard, always full of vegetables, fruits, flowers, and birds emanating warmth and offering intimacy. The boys would get toast crumbs all over the seats and spill orange juice on the floor. Diane enjoyed taking care of the boys and even cleaning the mess. She hadn't been blessed with warm and inviting memories in her own home, saddened when most everyone else took them for granted.

She checked the quiche savoring the golden-brown crust and bubbling gruyere, her nose tempted by the comfort it offered. The over-sized kitchen held several sprawling islands full of top-of-the-line cooking equipment, china—both fine-dining and regular daily use—glasses, silverware, and serving dishes. Olivia collected both antique and modern kitchenware inheriting their mother's love of food but not her culinary skills. Most of the items went unused except for the core stock; however, Olivia enjoyed having beautiful toys around her.

As Diane placed the dishes on the table, Olivia entered the kitchen. She'd pulled her hair into a bun, and while her face still blistered a blood red, the puffiness had receded.

"Thank you. I know I'm not making much sense," Olivia mumbled.

"It's okay. I'll cut you slack for another day or so. Then I'll force you to live again. Do you wanna talk about the letters?"

"Yes."

"Pour the coffee. I'll take out the quiche and sit at the nook in a minute. We should eat in the kitchen."

"That's a good idea."

Diane arranged two floral placemats on the table, added a fork and knife for each of them, and unfolded two cloth napkins, as Olivia wouldn't use paper ones. She and their maid, Louise, once had words about it. Louise no longer worked for Olivia.

A few minutes and several bites later, Olivia started talking. "Something happened years ago, and Ben handled the situation on his own. He never told me until this letter."

"Ben was good at handling situations. He knew how to be practical and keep things from getting out of control."

Olivia tossed her head to the left side raising her cheeks and eyes toward the ceiling. "He may've been a little too good. And before you ask, no, he didn't have an affair or kill anyone."

Diane giggled. "Oops, I didn't mean to laugh, Liv. Affair? Murder? Seriously, that's not the Ben we both know."

"You mean *knew*." Olivia glanced at her sister, and they shared a brief recognition of their collective loss.

Olivia continued. "But what he did was serious, and it has consequences. I need time with Ira. It affects one of the boys. I'm not sure which one it impacts."

"This doesn't make sense. Was Ben upset with one of the boys?"

Olivia shook her head. "No, but before I can give Ben's letter to my son, whichever one it is, Ira needs to do research to figure out exactly when this… situation… happened. Ben kept a secret from me, but wants me to fix the problem. I don't know how he did it. I'm so angry with him." A few tears formed in Olivia's eyes.

"Can you forgive him?"

"Maybe in time. But right now, if he weren't already dead, I'd kill him myself." Olivia released an accidental, exasperated chuckle as she glanced toward her sister.

Diane smiled in return. "Laughing helps, doesn't it, Liv?"

"I suppose I could say yes, a little." Olivia grinned and poked around at her fruit bowl.

Diane had removed the grapefruit, knowing her sister couldn't stand the bitter taste. She was usually one step ahead of Olivia these days. "You need to call Mr. Rattenbury and figure out what to do. Then you can move forward and finish what Ben wanted you to handle."

"After I talk with Ira, I want to spend time with each of the boys before I find out who Ben's letter belongs to… before everything changes. I'm going to stay with each of them for a few days this summer."

Diane reached for her sister's hand. "No matter what Ben's letter says, Liv, they'll always be your boys, and you'll always be their momma. You may fight and argue, but in the end, that's all it is, a temporary fight."

Olivia smiled. "Not always. Not if I lose one of them."

"Nonsense. How are you going to lose one of your sons? I don't know why such a fuss, but I'll listen when you're ready to talk." Diane dropped the dishes in the white farmhouse sink, and her eyes fixed deep into her sister's. "How about instead of losing someone, you gain someone? What if I move in with you the next few weeks to help you and the boys through everything?"

Olivia nodded. "I don't want to be alone. I'd like that. We need some changes around here."

Chapter 4 – Caleb

After finishing college years ago, Caleb had been driving around the coastal mountains on the highway connecting Northern Maine to Canada when he stumbled upon a stunning piece of property nestled behind a hidden lake. He fell in love with the land's sweeping beauty, comforted by a peace he hadn't experienced since early childhood. On the south and west sides were untouched plots belonging to an elderly man who had no interest in selling or building, nor had he stepped foot on them in decades. To the east lived a charming young couple who had planted a flourishing orchard separating their property from Caleb's land. The northern border held a long, winding entranceway packed with thick, tall, hundred-year-old fir trees. It created a perfect shield to the outside world—a shield Caleb had grown dependent upon since his move to Maine.

Every flower and bush in Caleb's sprawling backyard absorbed the intense glare of the scorching sun that week after he returned from the funeral. He inhaled the lilac blooms as they rode the backside of a breeze across his porch. Lifting a glass of iced tea, he smiled when a familiar face came into view. "You look good working up that sweat."

Walking up from the vegetable patch, Jake smiled back, while wiping a few drops of sweat from under his right eye. He wore cut-off denim shorts, dirtied Reebok high-tops, and had slightly pink skin on his chest and back where his shirt should have been. Jake threw his gloves at Caleb. "Shouldn't you be helping me, Ousier?"

"You have a new nickname for me every time I turn around. It's more fun to watch *you* work." Caleb smirked as Jake reached the porch.

"I'm teaching you a few of the important things you missed growing up." Jake bent lower and kissed Caleb, tugging the back of his neck. "Mmm... I love this mug."

Caleb smiled once his lips freed up cleaning the smudge of dirt Jake left behind when wiping his eye.

Jake's short blond hair covered dark roots reminding Caleb of the boys he lusted after at the beach years ago with their closely shaved punk styles narrowing on the sides but spiking up in the top front. Dark glasses stood out on Jake's narrow, oval-shaped face offering hints of sexy professor by day, bad boy by night.

"Nicknames are my calling card. Ouiser was *Steel Magnolias*. You can be a little cranky sometimes, like Shirley Maclaine." Jake sat on the bench next to Caleb and poured a glass of iced tea. "And you can watch me all you want, but don't think for a minute it means you earn any credit this time. You may have designed this garden, but it lives and breathes due to my hard labor over the years."

Caleb had met Jake on the day he closed on the house, five years earlier, when he'd stopped for a celebratory drink at the local wine bar. As he turned to sit at a stool, he bumped into Jake sending a glass of chardonnay onto the stranger's neck and shoulder. As his eyes traversed the full length of Jake's tanned and toned body, a familiar longing grew deep inside. Caleb leaned in close, drawn in by the woodsy scent pouring off Jake's skin, and was tempted to lick the buttery wine off his neck, sensing his heat inches away. Reality struck, and Caleb backed away, recognizing he stood in a public bar where straight-men still outnumbered gay ones by twenty to one. The final push arrived when Jake inadvertently brushed Caleb's inner thigh while catching a napkin as it fell from the table. Jake feigned clumsiness, but Caleb had known a flirt when he met one. They stared into one another's eyes for a few hungry seconds and without even speaking, locked hands and left the bar silently understanding the animalistic urges between them. Once outside, Jake pushed Caleb against the brick wall of the building, the cool stones a direct contrast to the heat between them, and roughly grabbed his willing waist. Holding him steady at the neck with one hand, he licked the shell of Caleb's ears working his way toward his chin and finally landing on his lips. Caleb returned with a kiss, their bodies pressed against one another with the pulling force of magnets knowing a special connection had sparked.

Within six months, they'd fallen in love, and Caleb had asked Jake to move in with him, bonding over their mutual love of architecture, landscaping, and renovating old farmhouses. Their most recent project included expanding the garden to include a walled herb section across from the orchard. Anticipation grew over the future scent of rosemary and basil wafting into the kitchen while they cooked Sunday meals. Jake, an elaborate and ingenious cook, could prepare a beef bourguignon that would rival Julia's any day of the week.

Caleb winked and leaned his head against Jake's shoulder as they sat on the bench. "So, my mother called. She's coming to visit next week."

"How do you wanna handle it?"

"She wants to spend a week with me this summer. She's planning a trip to my brothers, too. I guess she wants to talk to each of us about the future. I couldn't say no to her."

"Of course. I'm still shocked she's never visited in the ten years you've been here."

"It wasn't easy. They tried a few times, but between my dad's work schedule and my mom's volunteer commitments, it didn't pan out. I guess I could've tried harder."

"Don't be too hard on yourself. You're always traveling to client sites. You're not always home. And it's difficult to tell your parents you're gay."

"I should have brought you with me to the anniversary party. Now you'll never get a chance to meet my father."

"We talked about it and chose not to take the focus off their celebration. But he had the accident. It all happened so fast." Jake drew Caleb tighter against his chest with his right arm rubbing the tense muscles in his shoulder.

While Jake knew a funeral bordered on insanity as an appropriate time for an introduction to Caleb's family, the inability to stand by his side to soothe the pain and tragedy of losing a parent had destroyed him. Jake also hoped to grow close to Caleb's family, especially since he retained no relationship with his own anymore.

"I know. We can't change the past. But we need to decide what to do with the future."

"I'll support you however you need. If you want me to meet your mom, great. If you wanna spend the week with her on your own, I'll find some sugar daddy to take me in for the week." Jake enjoyed teasing Caleb, but he also knew how to foil the pressure of painful memories weighing on him. "We'll figure it out. I know you're going through hell right now, hon."

"Sugar daddy? I don't think so… you belong to me even if you *are* a pain in the ass. We've got time. She won't arrive for a few more days."

Jake put on his gloves to head back to planting. "Come with me to the garden, and let's put in the new stones for the herbs. Manual labor might take your mind off your troubles for a while. And tonight, we're gonna watch that new spy movie, you know, the one with the British hottie you wanna shag."

"You do know what I like…" Caleb used his best English accent. "I'll walk down in a minute, just want to finish my drink."

Jake wandered the path to the garden to continue working. "Make it snappy, Ms. Davis. I'm the nicest goddamn dame that ever lived, but I won't wait forever."

After Jake left, Caleb opened his wallet and slipped out the black and white picture of his family from a prior Christmas stored there to remind him of his old life back home in Connecticut. As much as he loved his new life in Maine with Jake, a huge piece of him had yearned for honesty with his family. Although Caleb's family remained in the dark, he'd known since early childhood he was gay, but also too scared to tell anyone.

After entering his teenage years, he fought hard to hide every erection he couldn't control when his classmates changed for swim practice in the locker room. One weekend, he learned of a movie with a shirtless Ryan Phillippe that drove girls crazy. Caleb later bought *54* at the local electronics store, hiding the package in his baggy cargo pants so his brothers couldn't find it. Thinking he'd been alone one evening, Caleb loaded the DVD on his laptop and watched several scenes over and over again, too afraid to search for porn sites in fear his brothers would check his recent computer history. After a few minutes into the flick, he no longer questioned the sexual desires deep inside his body. As he laid in bed, his jeans and shorts pulled to his ankles, watching Ryan grind against someone on the dance floor, Caleb pretended Ryan's hard body enveloped him. He'd pulled the front part of his shirt over his head, wrapping it tightly around the back of his neck, as he liked the way it increased the size of his upper body. Just as Caleb had found his high holy nirvana, the door busted open, and Teddy walked in shouting at his brother for eating the last sleeve of Oreos. Caleb kicked the laptop off the bed. It landed near his brother, setting itself on pause, revealing Ryan's tight ass for all to see. Caleb couldn't stop his nirvana from exploding and quickly grabbed a pillow to cover himself, while Teddy screamed, "Are you whacking off to some dude?" Matt and Zach arrived home from the movies at that moment and walked in as Caleb slunk under his covers. Teddy showed his brothers the laptop and called Caleb *Ass-Munch*, resulting in all three teasing Caleb for weeks about getting hard to some naked guy. They later admitted to thinking he'd jerked off to Salma Hayek's tits, but for a two-week period, inconsolable horror had terrorized Caleb, resigned that his brothers had discovered the secret. He also hadn't ever again eaten an Oreo, not even when they began selling the new kinds with different flavors.

Instead of dealing with the growing need to physically touch another man, he directed his attention to escaping his secluded reality. At fifteen, he took an after-school job working for a neighbor who owned a landscaping business. He also worked summers at the town clerk's office processing construction permits for building outdoor additions, decks, and gazebos. By eighteen, he'd left for college at an unknown architecture school in Maine where he finally earned the opportunity to explore the lust he'd been having since Ryan's eight-pack abs set his world afire. After his first physical experience when he was twenty with another guy (his best friend's roommate), Caleb knew he couldn't return home and live a lie. He chose to move away rather than divulge the secret to his family. He'd even left behind his high school friends and found a new circle of people to get closer to at college, never replacing the intimacy he once cherished with his family when younger.

Caleb jolted from his memory when he heard Jake's voice.

"Put the picture away and let's talk for a little while, Gloria Swanson." Jake jogged back up to the porch. "I knew you couldn't stop your obsession with the letter."

"I know. As much as I want to, I'm not ready for her to know."

"What are you afraid of?"

"My mom can be difficult. She tends to react poorly before considering what she means to say. I've been through enough with my father's death already. I don't want to deal with another loss right now."

"Loss? Do you expect her to disown you like my parents did me?" Jake's family banished him when he came out after graduating from college, forcing him to stay in Maine, rather than deal with his family's homophobia.

"My dad may have been okay, but my mom can be judgmental. She has this idea of how things are supposed to be. And if reality doesn't match up, well, then, she..."

"People change, Caleb. She lost your father. Maybe she won't react that way now. I doubt she'd wanna lose a son right after losing her husband."

Caleb's bond with his father surpassed those of his brothers during childhood. His father had always talked to him about the importance of being a gentleman and an honest man. Whenever he'd caught Caleb telling a fib, Ben never punished his son. He would listen to why he lied and ask what he'd learned from being dishonest. He'd always told Caleb that secrets were dangerous and had a way of bursting out in the end. It seemed important to Ben that his sons learned how to accept the truth—to be open and honest about their feelings.

Jake ruffled Caleb's hair. "I know you miss your dad. Maybe you should talk to him if it provides relief. I know he can't respond, but maybe you'll have a breakthrough."

"The guilt over our lost time the last few years is overwhelming. He never knew about you. Or how happy you make me."

"I'm sure he knows now. I may not be religious, but once you die… your memories and steadfast beliefs transform, don't they? Death sets your mind free. Gone are the hang-ups and crazy crutches you once firmly held." Jake rubbed Caleb's shoulder to comfort him.

"He may have told her the truth about me in his letter."

"You never read the letter. You don't know anything yet."

"My mom still has it. She hasn't said anything. I left her house after the reading of the will and went to his grave. I haven't been able to ask her since visiting him. I stood at the cemetery staring at the fresh dirt and temporary stone with his name… it was the first time I cried over his death. Everything came rushing back from when I was a child."

When the lawyer had mentioned the two envelopes from Ben, it unleashed a panic in Caleb over realizing his differences from everyone else, bringing to the surface concerns his family would reject him. It had brought back all the things he'd fought hard to suppress the last decade—the restless nights, churning stomach, and unsettling sensation of skin crawling.

"Even if he told her, your mom loves you. I've heard the messages she's left you. I've seen the cards she sends for your birthday. You need to give her a chance."

"I need more time. I'm so glad you're helping me figure it out."

They walked the steps to the garden to finish working when the phone rang. Caleb dashed back toward the kitchen, read the caller ID box, and cradled the extension.

"Hey, Zach. What's going on?" Caleb spoke into the handset. "Slow down, you're not making any sense…"

Pulling the phone away from his ear, he whispered to Jake who had followed him to the kitchen. "It's my brother, Zach. He's drunk. He's slurring something pretty fierce."

Caleb continued. "Zach... chill. I can't understand what you're saying... what? You did what?"

Jake laughed as he listened in on the conversation. "Ooh... this ought to be good."

"Zach, you're joking. You seriously crossed a line." Caleb held his hand up to cover Jake's mouth, then pulled the phone back to his ear. "Does Mom know?"

Jake slipped next to Caleb and kissed his cheek. "Finish yard. Five minutes. Deal with family drama. Or I will." As he walked away, he mumbled. "Your poor mother... she has no clue what's coming her way with you troublesome Glass boys."

Chapter 5 – Zach

Neon glow sticks invaded the large open space producing the only light on the dance floor. Hundreds of twenty-somethings dressed in as little as possible, approaching the edge of ecstasy, pulsed to the pervasive rhythm reverberating off the club's walls. The Atlantis Lair was an abandoned warehouse a group of bored millennials had converted into the latest hot spot in Brooklyn. The weekend started early Thursday as the clock struck midnight in the club where patrons gripped bottles of beer or plastic cups filled with vodka and overly sweet and sticky mixers.

A Latina waitress stepped to the third platform in the corner and waved at the DJ. Dressed in a one-piece glittered black nylon retro bathing suit, Tressa and her conspicuous image were uneasily dismissed. "You need somethin', Echo?" She tossed her jet black curly hair to one side and raised her voice to shout over the fervent boom of the bass drum.

"Yeah, a break. Think the boss will mind if I let the machine do the work for a few minutes?" His black denim jeans served as a second skin to his trunk-like thighs and powerful calves as he twisted around the glass window to see her.

"Nope. He's in the back with the other jackasses planning next month's parties. Take a ten-minute breather with me. I need a drag."

He set the next two tracks and slipped out the back entrance with Tressa. A white ribbed tank accentuated the curves of his broad shoulders and well-defined chest. Chunky black boots clunked across each concrete step lifting his apple-round ass from side to side.

As Tressa lit up, she tried to grab it, but he maneuvered a few inches too far ahead. "So, how's Anastasia doing, Zach?"

When the streetlamp's glow descended on his bulging biceps, his tattoos, bathed in dim light and dark shadows, came alive. "My girl is good. She turns six in a couple of weeks." He twisted off the cap of his Diet Coke, tossed two white tablets in his mouth and swallowed. "Thanks for calling me *Echo* in front of the others. Kind of want to keep my real name on lockdown around here, babe."

"No problemo. And her mother? She still tryin' to get back in the picture?" Tressa exhaled a perfect smoke circle that floated above her head and disappeared into the starry city skyline.

Zach had managed to keep Katerina, Anastasia's mother, out of their lives for the last two years. She lived in a rehab clinic most of the year but had recently sprung herself claiming to have kicked the addiction to crystal.

"Katerina came by last week. We talked. She wants shared custody with no supervision required. I can't do it. Not after last time."

Tressa placed her hand on his hip. "Good plan. That chica is loca."

"Si, muy loco. Extra loco." His mouth sneered, and his eyes opened wide.

Zach finished his soda and tossed the bottle across the sidewalk to the receptacle a few feet away. It bounced off the rim and knocked itself to the bottom causing a girl in gothic garb walking across the street to hiss at him. He grabbed his crotch, as if to tell her to screw off, but she'd already turned the corner.

"So how you doin' with your papa's death? You mentioned they read the will this week?" She adjusted enormous cleavage that wished it could burst beyond the stretched-out nylon fabric keeping it captive.

Tressa and Zach had been close since he started at The Atlantis Lair several years ago. They'd slept together a few times until the true extent of his personal issues surfaced, telling him she didn't need more trouble in her life. They agreed to stop screwing around and just be friends, but she still flirted with him and talked about his tattooed body and hard ass. She'd also sworn off men for a few months and had recently begun dating a lesbian bartender, deciding to explore her bisexual side in the meantime.

Zach smirked. "Yup. And it was ridiculous. My dad left my mom a letter and told her to read it alone."

"That's sweet." A forced, fake smile appeared as she lit a second cigarette before offering one to Zach.

He declined. "You know liquor is my only vice these days."

She nodded. "You shouldn't even drink if you're tryin' to stay away from it all."

"It's weird. The lawyer handed my mother a second letter, and she's supposed to give it to one of my brothers or to me—we don't know. She hasn't said a word since the will reading four days ago," Zach spat out. "It pisses me off. My dad has a message for us, but she won't share it."

Zach had frequently reminded his mother she couldn't keep the contents of the letter a secret and demanding everyone should have a chance to read them. When she said no, he erupted on her, citing her selfish behavior over the years. She and Zach had engaged in an intense fight, resulting in him storming off to places where people truly cared about him, as he put it to her that day.

"Have you told her why it's important to you, papi? Maybe it was personal, and she's still grieving over his death." Tressa previously told him she lost her father as a teenager and how she still thought about him every day, especially right before bed when silence paralyzed her mind and she needed comfort.

"She called today and left me a message. My mother wants me to stay at the house in Connecticut at the end of June for Anastasia's birthday, just the three of us. She plans to bitch at me for leaving my girl with them when I'm here. You know, I still haven't told her where I work. Her intuition tells her I drop my kid off and get wasted as a tribute to my past. She hasn't realized I'm done with the drugs and the partying."

Tressa perked up. "Zach, you're the top DJ in New York right now. You're hotter than anyone else in the industry. You're why this place packs full of millennial douches every night. Your mama might understand if you told her what you're trying to do with your life."

Zach shrugged. "Maybe. I can't stop thinking about my dad. I miss him. I still can't accept he was alive last week and later died in some fucking accident. I don't get it."

Tressa stroked his forearm where the pair of dice met the playing card, gently pulling at the short hairs, as she did to relax him when they used to share a bed. "Shit happens, guapo. It sucks. I've been there. It takes time. I'm still not over my papa dying, and that happened ten years ago. You need to talk about it more."

Zach shut his eyes for a few seconds and cleared his head. "He was a good dad. He didn't give me crap about my choices. I know he wanted me to finish school, but after Anastasia came along, I had no desire left for college and studying. I needed to use my creativity. That's why I did coke for so long. It kept me from having to deal with everything else in my life. But he always pulled me back in. Did I ever tell you he pushed me to rehab?"

Tressa shook her head. "You rarely talk about those days anymore."

"My Aunt Diane babysat Anastasia for a weekend to give me a break. Desperation clung to my body, willing me to party with my friends and forget my life. We were out for twenty-four hours when we crashed from exhaustion. When I got home, my father stood outside my building. He knew I was wasted. He'd been calling me for hours, but I didn't have my phone. Anastasia learned how to walk on her own and took a dive off my aunt's back steps. She wasn't hurt but got scared and wanted her daddy. My parents couldn't reach me, and my dad drove to the city, waited at my apartment until I came home, and saw what was going on."

Tressa grabbed Zach's other hand, telling him the second track had taken over inside. They only had a few more minutes left to talk.

"I wanted to see my daughter, but he wouldn't let me go on my own. He told me I had to check myself into his friend's rehab facility and get better first. Damn, I miss him."

Tressa nodded. "He was a good papa. What did you do?"

Zach smiled and laughed loudly. "What could I do? I knew he meant business. If I didn't get help right then and there, it'd have been far worse in the long run. I went inside and showered. He let me call Anastasia to tell her I needed to take a trip for a few weeks, drove me to the facility, and registered me for in-patient treatment. I've been off drugs since that day. But I won't give up my liquor."

Tressa hugged him. "And it comes full circle. Look at how good of a papa you've been to your daughter. Papa and mama, hon. Maybe you should give your mama a chance since he's gone."

Zach groaned. "I've been considering it. Maybe my mother and I need a come-to-Jesus meeting. I can't take the bitchy attitude."

Tressa laughed. "Have you told her about the LA producer coming to meet you later this month? Maybe if you told your mama that you put your life back together, have a steady job, been focusing on music again, and stopped dealing and using, she may back off?"

"Perhaps, but now's not the right time. What if the producer doesn't believe my music leads anywhere? I need to prove to myself, and I guess to her, that I can be successful at writing songs. She never supported it when I was younger. My dad might have come around, but I'll never know." Zach massaged his temples. The bass needled on his last remaining nerve, and the Tylenol hadn't yet kicked in.

Tressa pulled him closer, kissed his cheek, and hugged him tightly. "Te amo, amigo. Te amo. We'll get through this." She scraped her cigarette across the pavement and tossed it into the trash. "Vamos, you got a few more hours to go inside. And this little mamacita needs huge tips tonight."

Zach grabbed Tressa's arm and ushered her through the door. She shuffled across the steps and he walked to his booth, noticing he had two texts from his brother and one from Katerina. He first responded to Katerina.

Zach: *Stop bugging me. I told you I'm getting a lawyer.*

Kat: *I want to see my daughter.*

Zach: *No way. Not having this convo again.*

Kat: *You'll regret it. She needs her mother, too.*

Zach reflected on his situation for a moment, realizing he needed to find a lawyer but also didn't want to ask his family for a handout. He read his brother's messages.

Caleb: *You okay? What was that call about?*

Caleb: *You were pretty messed yesterday.*

Zach: *Yeah. Listen, 4get what I told you.*

Caleb: *That you screwed up that bad? Then why did you tell me?*

Zach: *I don't know. Been 4eva since we'd talked before yesterday. Had to tell someone.*

Caleb: *But her? Why?*

Zach: *Yeah. I know. I'll handle it.*

Caleb: *Pickles is gonna lose it. It'll send him over the edge.*

Zach: *No doubt. He can NEVER know.*

Caleb: *We all have secrets.*

Zach: *What does that mean?*

Caleb: *Nothing. Forget it. Now we're even.*

Zach: *Sure. Like that hilarious cicada incident.*

Zach laughed over his brother's mysterious message, but then became alarmed when his mother's number rang on the phone. He picked up.

"Hey, Mom. Got your voicemail. Sure, I'll take a few days off to stay with you at the house in a couple of weeks."

"Oh, good. I have a lot to talk to you about. I wanted you to know the importance behind my request."

"Yup. I get it and will call you tomorrow to plan Anastasia's birthday party."

"I'm going to call Theodore in a few minutes. I need to be certain he is ready to take over your father's law practice. I know he's capable, but he needs to learn how to build more open and trusting relationships with his employees. This firm remains the last thing we have left of your father. It's his legacy to you boys."

"Mom, I'm sure Teddy knows it. I got to get back to work."

"Work? You know, Zachary, you need to be more..."

"Enough, Mom. I can't do this right now."

Zach hung up and turned off his phone before taking control of the DJ equipment.

Everyone in my life is fucking nuts. I need to get my daughter away from these people.

Chapter 6 – Teddy

Teddy turned off the hot water faucet, pushed open the heavy glass door and grabbed a plush green towel from the bar outside the shower. After stepping through to the white tiled floor, he dried his pale and lanky body. One to follow explicit routines, he started first with his face, followed by his thinning hair, and worked his way to his size twelve feet.

Despite only being thirty-two, Teddy's body already showed signs of aging—his knees clicked when he walked, his shoulders stooped forward, and his skin took on a yellow hue. Never one for the gym or eating well, he cared little about his health and spent most of his time at the office working late nights. A typical dinner consisted of a bag of chips from the vending machine in the office kitchen and a gyro from the truck staying open late in front of their building—no vegetables—just loaded with creamy sauce and an extra packet of salt. The halal food cart vendor knew him by name, having a to-go package ready each evening at nine o'clock.

Teddy wrapped the towel around his waist below his sharp, protruding hip bones, and swiftly ran his fingers through his graying hair. While pulling out the razor blade and shaving cream, his father's face reflected back at him in the mirror. It scared Teddy so soon after his father's death. His body shifted in the mirror as if to jump back several years. He welcomed the interruption when his phone buzzed with a text.

Ethan: *On a break from my shift. Just checking on you.*

Teddy: *I'm fine. Heading to work. You?*

Ethan: *Good. Thinking about Dad. Remember when he brought Bailey home?*

Teddy: *Bailey? The dog?*

Ethan: *Yup. He loved that puppy. As did you.*

Teddy: *That was a long time ago.*

Ethan: *I'm adopting another Shiba.*

Teddy: *Okay. Why are you telling me? I'm not dog-sitting.*

Ethan: *Just don't want to lose contact since Dad's gone.*

Teddy: *I miss him, too. We'll be okay.*

Ethan: *You ready to become partner? Dad prepped you well.*

Teddy: *I can't talk now. Got to go.*

Ethan: *Can I call you later? I need advice. Something happened.*

Teddy: *Do it over the weekend. Got a bunch of meetings today.*

Teddy dropped the phone and pulled the razor across his chin, nicking the cleft, and sending a steady, viscous stream of warm blood dripping down his neck.

When he had been a young child, Teddy's parents both worked at the law firm. He spent most of his time with his grandparents, who adored him, but it also meant he spent little time with Ben and Olivia. Over time, Teddy received little emotional caregiving as each new baby had claimed priority for those moments. Once he could talk, his father showed more interest in his first-born son and took Teddy with him to the office for a few hours each week to give Olivia a break from so many young children at home. Teddy became obsessed with the first words he learned to read from his father's divorce agreements. Though odd for a child so young to understand words such as "uncontested" and "arbitration," it came naturally to Teddy. Near the end of grammar school, Teddy openly talked about people getting divorces and standard custody arrangements. His peers' confused faces comforted him, knowing he had surpassed them all. But he never acknowledged them as his peers—even his classmates were inferiors.

Most of his life revolved around making decisions other people expected of him. When he turned fourteen, his father pushed him into the mock debate club to strengthen his ability to take command and to develop leadership skills. His mother enrolled him in a public speaking class at the local university to build his confidence and stage presence when he turned sixteen. In the summer before he left for college, Teddy interned in his father's law office scribing meetings and researching financial records and land deeds. His father selected Yale as Teddy's undergrad and law school, it being his alma mater and a source of many happy memories. None of those were options Teddy had any opportunity to discuss. Teddy wished he could use the skills he learned on the debate team to counter his parents' decisions with his own well-planned requests, but in the effort to turn Teddy into his father, Teddy lost the ability to focus on his personal needs.

While cleaning the blood and re-applying shaving cream to his cheeks, Teddy noticed the lines forming around his eyes and mouth. He changed blades on the razor and began the ritual over again. Start first with your neck, as his father taught him.

In the last few months before the accident, knowing he would retire soon, Ben scheduled meetings three times per day with Teddy. In the mornings, they would discuss the day's caseload to cover employee issues and communication skills, both of which frustrated Teddy. He'd little desire to talk to his colleagues unless needing an answer about a case or canon law. Opposing counsel in divorce arbitrations and settlements always feared him, but while Teddy could settle a bitter divorce case with mellow ease, managing his colleagues and a firm on his own felt unnatural.

For lunch, Ben would pick a different client, bringing Teddy along to build his son's relationship skills. Teddy's least affinity included the lunch meetings, as they rarely served any purpose. His father would do the talking, asking about the client's state of mind, post-divorce plans, and support structure. It was too personal for Teddy. He admired and respected his father for caring about the client's well-being, but to Teddy, his job as the client's attorney required a focus on securing the best deal possible in the divorce. The client had responsibility for the emotional survival upon splitting from a spouse.

Promptly at six each evening, Ben held the third daily meeting to review his earlier accomplishments and offered instructions to Teddy on what he needed to complete by the next morning. Ben showed his love for his first-born son by teaching him everything he knew to achieve success in family law, but for Teddy, its sterility had become the only way he knew how to live.

Teddy rinsed the razor, splashed warm water on his face, and dried off his cheeks using the towel around his waist. He left the bathroom and walked toward the bedroom to dress before driving to the office. As he sifted through the closet, Teddy located his Friday suit in its usual spot, freshly pressed, as he requested. Sarah always collected his dry-cleaning on her way home from the hospital each week.

Teddy had met Sarah through his brother, Matt, and sister-in-law, Margaret, at a holiday party they'd thrown many years ago. Sarah, a recent arrival in Connecticut, had started working at the hospital as a pediatric nurse where she delivered Margaret and Matt's first daughter. After a Glass family summer barbecue, Sarah and Teddy went on a double date with Margaret and Matt, and although no sparks manifested for Teddy, time ticked away to select a wife.

While searching in his closet for a tie, Teddy recalled the day he asked Sarah to marry him...

"It would seem to me since we've been dating for three months, maybe we should make this permanent," Teddy said.

"*Matt and Margaret did take the time to introduce us. It was kind of them, especially since I don't know many people around these parts,*" Sarah said.

"*True. What do you think of me?*"

"*You're smart. I reckon you work a lot. You must not get a lot of free time.*"

"*My father expects me to take over the family law practice in a few years. Do you enjoy being a nurse?*"

"*I love working with babies, that's why I moved north for this job. I don't much relish working the overnight hours, but maybe it will change in the future.*"

"*I work late most nights. We'd have time on the weekends together, but we wouldn't see each other much during the week.*"

"*True. I also haven't met anyone else in your family besides Matt.*"

"*I don't spend a lot of time with the rest of my family. I've got a few younger brothers, but they live further away. Matt already has a daughter, as does my other brother, Zach. Do you plan to have children?*"

"*I want a few kids. My parents passed away, and I don't have any brothers or sisters. So... it's just me.*"

"*Well maybe we should get married. I'm already ahead of my brothers in so many other areas, it's time I surpass them as far as a wife and kids.*"

"*Are you proposing to me, Teddy?*"

"*It would seem so.*"

A high-pitched beeping noise jerking Teddy from his memory indicated Sarah arrived home from her hospital shift and deactivated the house alarm.

In the early part of their marriage, Teddy and Sarah had struggled to connect. In time, Teddy became more than the mechanical and stoic man Sarah had married leading to emotional intimacy in their relationship. She'd begun to motivate Teddy to consider alternative options besides what his parents had instilled in him since childhood. Once Teddy had admitted his true passions, Sarah pushed him to talk to his father about the future of the firm. Teddy had planned to have that conversation, but Ben passed away and Teddy forcibly directed his attention back to the firm. His anger and arrogance reappeared more quickly than it had once dissipated, adding to the strain of his weakening marriage. Teddy hadn't realized his relationship declined at home, but Sarah knew she'd slipped further away each day that passed.

Teddy pulled on his boxers, crossed the parquet floors, and called out, "Sarah, is that you?"

Sarah confirmed and climbed the winding staircase to their bedroom in the south corner of their colonial-style house. She'd spent most of her shift walking the hospital floors, hitting at least twelve thousand steps per day on her Fitbit tracker. While Teddy couldn't care any less about exercise, Sarah's focus energized with every step she took. She'd been training to run the NYC Marathon that upcoming November, still bitter she'd missed the last one due to Teddy's work schedule canceling their trip.

As she came around the stark white landing, Teddy, standing in his starched, checkered boxers, kissed his wife. "Good morning. How was your shift?" He bent his hands backward, enjoying their crackling noise.

"I am exhausted, but the Abbotts finally gave birth to the triplets. It's pretty amazing what a woman's body can handle." Sarah untied the drawstrings on her pants, letting them fall to the floor. Stepping out one leg at a time, each limb glided as though she danced a ballet when leaning forward. "By the way, your mother called me today."

"What did she call you for?" Teddy's voice held a gruff tone. He knew his mother distrusted and barely tolerated Sarah. It would be unusual for her to call at all, nonetheless at work.

"She wants to spend a week with us for the Fourth of July. She asked me to take time off and mentioned you closed the office for a few days around the holiday. Why didn't you tell me?" Sarah fussed with the roses in the vase on her dresser twisting a few dried petals off the flowers with a bobbing tenacity.

"I am closing the office. The courts are closed a few days, and my father's partners are taking their vacations. It seemed to me we'd have a light week. I forgot to tell you."

"They're your partners now, Teddy." Sarah reminded him of burdens he preferred not to discuss, as she whipped her head around to face him. "Have you decided to tell her about selling your father's practice to Wittleton and Davis?"

Sarah stripped off her blouse, leaving her in nothing but a pair of white cotton panties and a padded pink sports bra. She stepped toward the dresser and pulled out a box of crackers from the drawer snapping open the plastic packaging with nimble fingers.

Teddy walked closer to her, his body flushed as he rubbed her neck with wishful hands. "No, I haven't decided yet what I want to do. I'm still processing my father's death. I can't disappoint her."

"It's not about disappointment. It's about choice." Sarah's voice chirped at him as she pecked at a soda cracker. "Your father forgot to teach you how to be a friend, how to listen, how to love... You were never given the option as a child. But you're not a child anymore, Teddy."

"I couldn't do this for another thirty years. You've convinced me to focus on other parts of life it would seem I might enjoy. I wish I could have talked to my father before he died. Now I have to talk to my mother." Teddy continued massaging her neck, sliding his fingers beneath the straps that left uneven marks as they pressed into her shoulders. Knowing her ticklish nature, he took caution to be gentle near her underarms.

Sarah's shoulders relaxed as she hung her head lower. "We did much better at fixing us before everything happened. We need to get back to that. Taking over the firm won't let it happen."

"I know. I hear you. What did you tell my mother about spending time with her?" He lifted her bra and pushed her toward the bed.

"I said yes. She's your mother. She lost her husband for heaven's sake. I couldn't say no, at least not without her hating me even more." Sarah shrugged her brow, redirected his hands away, and followed it with a soft kiss on his lips. "Give me some sugar before you leave."

"Let's not talk about it right now." He grabbed her neck and pushed his lips further on to hers.

Sara pulled away. "Aren't you fixin' to get to work?"

"Yes, in a few minutes. I have other things in mind to occupy our time." Teddy pushed Sarah on the mattress while pulling down his boxers, standing naked before his wife. With pursed lips and a rising erection, he whispered to her. "Would you happen to have any idea of what I have in mind?"

Sarah smiled. "Yes. If my momma were still alive, she'd tell you she could see your Christmas right now. But I'm done ovulating this month. I reckon we should save it?"

They'd been trying for a year with no success, even narrowing the specific times they could have sex and for how long and in which positions. It had become more of a task to check off on a list rather than a romantic or loving exchange for Teddy. They'd wanted to have a baby for years, desperately clinging to the rocky pastures of their marriage, growing further apart with each failure. He'd spent too many nights listening to Sarah cry herself to sleep over hitting her forties, still not having children, watching the clock tick away, each second pricking his skin as a reminder of every futile attempt.

"It would appear you win. How long do I have to wait?" His obnoxious voice growled while he pulled up his shorts. As he finished, he gripped his hands together and produced several loud pops in a row.

"Probably on Sunday. I'm sorry." Sarah pushed him back toward the closet to put on his clothes. "I'm still hoping to find other ways to get pregnant."

Teddy finished dressing, grabbed his briefcase, and left the bedroom. "Luck is on our side this time."

He descended the stairs into his office on the first floor where he drew open the curtains and switched on the overhead light. The room brightened with a white glow as he breathed in fresh paint wafting off his canvases. On the walls were his recent watercolor series focused on inclement weather changes. He'd been watching the impacts of all the strange storms in the area decimating trees and beaches, and he captured on canvas the various changes throughout the months. He admired the destruction as it energized him to know he could snatch it and manipulate it as he pleased in his artwork.

On Sundays, while Sarah slept before heading to the hospital for her shift, he would set up his easel and supplies in the backyard and paint the changes as he interpreted them. He hoped to catch the sun begin its slow and colorful descent each evening, displaying a secret, beautiful danger lurking in the depths of the incoming moon. Art amplified his passion, not family law.

He recalled the letter his father left behind at the reading of the will, assuming it had been connected to his future inheritance of the law practice. He'd been angry when his mother had subtly informed him she didn't have the wherewithal to talk about the letters at any point during the last few days. Teddy hadn't been able to accept her cavalier answers, as he called them, and kept pressing her to let him read both. Olivia begged him for a few more days to which he agreed without any understanding of the stammer in her voice, noting she could have the weekend and later telling her it contradicted his better judgment.

As he shut the front door, he decided it was time for him to apply more pressure before delivering the decision to sell the law practice.

Chapter 7 – Matt

Matt had always been proud that his mother would tell everyone he'd been her perfect little boy during childhood. He had everything from looks to body, intelligence to friends, wit to charm—the proverbial golden child. And as he grew older, it became a priority to ensure others saw him as meeting and exceeding high expectations, always on top and winning first prize. When he chose not to follow in the wake of his father's and older brother's golden legal pathways, and instead to seek an MBA in the finance world, Matt knew he'd saddled himself with an uphill climb and no option to plateau.

Matt met Margaret while studying at business school. They married several months afterward and had three daughters—Melanie, Melissa, and Melinda—within the first five years. Margaret, a former runner-up in the Miss Connecticut pageant, maintained a strict beauty and exercise regimen, training at the gym at least four times per week. She styled her curly, golden hair weekly at the salon, wore bright and cheery makeup, and her outfits were immaculate despite having three young children who could often be a little messy. Matt still referred to Margaret as the beauty queen who stole his heart, while their relationship resembled the definition of pure love, including plans for a total of six children.

As Matt glanced at the time on the TV, noticing many children's toys and books scattered around him on the floor, Margaret stood from the sofa. They finished watching a video on the new kindergarten school they'd chosen for their oldest daughter. After weeks of discussion and interviewing at seven different schools, they agreed on the Madison Academy, which turned out to be the most expensive of everything they'd visited. Matt still didn't believe there were any concerns with the public schools in their town, but Margaret usually got her way.

"I know it's an expensive school, but it stands out as the best option for Melanie. It will give her the right education from the beginning, and she'll be safer than in the public system. I've heard nightmares from your mother about teachers with little experience and administrators who don't know how to do their jobs. We want the best for her, Matt." Margaret placed both hands on her hips.

Matt leaned forward on the edge of the couch to kiss his wife good-night when he heard and felt the crush of Cheerios on the floor beneath his bare feet. "D'oh. I'll clean those later. Are you sure you don't want to get a puppy for the girls? Think of how much less cleaning you'd have to do." He smiled and tilted his head, his dimples glowing somewhere between irresistible and adorable. "And yes, we made the right decision on the school. We'll find the money." Though he searched for his most convincing voice, it came out somewhere between a pleading child and a gluttonous dieter. His feet continued to tap the floor with frenzy.

"Won't the inheritance from your father pay for school? I can ask my parents if you are worried."

"No, we agreed you could be a stay-at-home mom until the girls are full-time in school. You don't need to talk to your parents, Margaret."

Although a tight situation, they'd planned to re-evaluate in the future if Margaret needed to get a job or if she had her hands full at home with the kids. Margaret met her end of the deal as his three daughters were well-behaved, intelligent, thoughtful, and affectionate. He couldn't renege on their deal this early, despite his rising fears.

"Check *Facebook* before you go to bed. I took the sweetest photo of the girls at the mall today. Two hundred likes already!" Margaret cupped her hands around the back of his neck, pressed her lips against his, and kissed him goodnight. "Don't stay awake too late watching the game. You have a breakfast meeting with Teddy tomorrow to go through last month's books."

"Yes, we're meeting at the Club to talk through it. Teddy the Robot had no time during the week, so he pushed it until Saturday morning." He stood and waved his hands in the air emulating the Tin Man from *The Wizard of Oz* until he laughed so hard he fell back into the couch. "It'll be the first time he and I work together on the law practice finances. My dad never transitioned those pieces to Teddy before the car accident. I'm sure it'll be a fun meeting. Kind of like a root canal. That jerk can act so condescending."

"You're so cruel to your brother." Margaret's spider-like eyelashes fluttered above her hopeful eyes. "I'm taking the girls to swimming lessons and dance class in the morning. Can you also write a check for the landscapers? They'll be here tomorrow, and I forgot to pay them last week."

"You betcha." His left eye twitched a few times until his fingers pressed into it for relief. "My brother deserves it. He's been such an ass at work lately. I'm gonna put a whoopee cushion on his chair Monday morning."

"You're such a child sometimes, Matt. Do I have to punish you like I do the girls?" She tapped her fingers on the coffee table as she straightened a few magazines.

"Yeah, punish me. I can suggest a few good ways." He bent forward, shaking his head, and panting his tongue. "I'll come to bed shortly, just want to check out the game. Oh, I forgot. My mom called today to ask if it would be okay if she stayed with us for a few days in July. She wants to spend time with each of the crew to figure out her next steps."

Matt knew Margaret had little patience for her mother-in-law. Olivia often tried to tell Margaret how to raise the girls, accusing her daughter-in-law of being too flexible in her parenting approach. Matt always refused to choose a team. He told them both they had good ideas and wouldn't commit either way. It annoyed Margaret, but she told Matt she understood he had only chosen to be respectful of his mother to avoid a fight with her.

Margaret pushed the rocking horse back into the corner and headed toward their bedroom down the hall. She stopped at the door, her nose and upper lips raised. "Sure, but we're leaving for Disney soon, so she needs to work around our vacation. How long will *The Queen* be here?"

"Ha! No clue. I told her you were in charge and would sort it out." He winked. "I know you don't always get along, but maybe things will change since my dad's gone. She does care for you." Matt tried his best to persuade her, bringing forth his sure-fire win, puppy-dog eyes, and a set of pouty lips.

Margaret sighed. "Okay, let's have her over on the Sunday before we leave, and she can head back home when we go to Florida. I guess I'll need to clean tomorrow. I can't let her find a single ounce of dust, or she'll tell you I'm a bad housekeeper."

Matt smiled. "You're a doll. I'll help you tomorrow night. And don't worry about everything looking perfect… remember, she'll be with Teddy and Sarah for a few days before she comes here. It'll be a vacation to spend time with you compared to her visit with the Robot and his little magnolia."

Margaret laughed. "I don't get it. I understand your mother might think Sarah and I took her sons away, but does she really want you guys to remain alone the rest of your lives?"

"You know my mother. No one measures up for her boys. She hated Zach's ex-girlfriend… what's her name… Katerina… and encouraged him to lock her in the rehab facility. Ethan told me she convinced him to keep his girlfriend back in Boston rather than come to Connecticut for the funeral. That's probably why Cabbie hasn't ever brought around a girl. He's the smart one," Matt quipped, with eyes squinting as he nodded his head.

Margaret smirked and took the scrunchie out of her hair. "I suppose you're right. She has been generous with the girls and even sometimes with me. I wish she wouldn't be so stubborn and judgmental. And by the way, that's not why Cabbie… ugh, now you've got me saying it you little weasel… Caleb hasn't brought around a girl, Matt. I'm pretty sure he's got another reason."

Matt lifted a brow. "Well, you can spend quality time with my mother when she stays over next month. And as for Cabbie, no one ever knows with him. I barely get a text from him now and again. I'm kind of hoping Dad being gone will force Caleb to spend more time with us since he came back home for a few days. I miss my brother. Dad took him and me fishing every summer when we were young. Cabbie and I were so close. I don't know what happened."

"You haven't mentioned your dad all day. I can't imagine what you're going through... I'd be such a mess if I lost my father." Margaret walked back toward her husband and crouched on the floor beside him, one hand on his knee.

Matt considered his wife's question, realizing no one had asked about his mental state with everything going on. Everything focused on helping his mother and keeping the law practice operational until he and Teddy talked through next steps. "I miss him, doll. I saw him every day at the office, and we'd spend time together on the weekends with my mother and the girls. I don't know what the future holds without him. Our team has lost its captain."

"You were close to your dad. We've given him three grandchildren... probably made him realize it was time to retire and spend the rest of his days with you monsters." She rested her hand on his, tickling and rubbing his palm while slanting her eyes over her word choice. "Monsters. Ha."

"True. I should have spent more time with him talking about being a dad. He and I had so much in common. I could call him on the phone to ask a quick question, and he always knew the right words."

Matt thought back to the last time he'd talked with his father before the accident. His father had asked Matt to join him for a drink at the Club since Teddy was meeting with a client for the first time on his own. Ben didn't want to head home yet and hoped Matt could keep him company and keep his mind off Teddy's first meeting with their biggest client. Matt had declined to deal with a personal matter and regretted his decision, but he couldn't change it now.

Margaret nodded and stood, her fingers lingering on his wrist. "He knew how much you loved him, Matt. I have total confidence in you to be a good father, just as he was, and those are big shoes to fill. I miss him, too. He always watched out for me even when your mother gave me the cold shoulder."

As Margaret walked down the hall to check on the girls, she yelled "*Goodnight, hon*" and headed to the bedroom, leaving Matt to question how his wife would survive a week with his mother. He knew at the root of the disdain lurked their similarities—neither one would ever acknowledge it. But he also valued his balls, planning never to tell either of them what he really thought.

He'd also been concerned that his mother asked too many questions recently. She cornered him a few days after the funeral, mentioning his erratic obsession with fielding calls and text messages throughout the whole ordeal. Matt knew he hadn't looked well, especially when he wavered from high to low depending on the conversation and time of day. It was also peculiar for him to disappear during family conversations and get-togethers, or not regularly shave, even in the worst of circumstances. He'd hoped she thought it was just the grieving process and wouldn't delve any further into what else had been going on in his life.

Matt flipped the channel to the Yankees game hoping they'd finally pitch a no-hitter that season. He needed to bust Ethan's chops about it, as rubbing his team's wins in his brother's face brought him extreme joy. Always in good fun.

He leaned back into the couch and grabbed the report he'd finished working on earlier in the day before he left the office. Matt wanted to ensure it was ready for his brother's input. Matt had only joined the family law practice earlier that year, as Ben had finally gained confidence his son amassed enough experience to handle larger accounts. Although Ben had offered to let Matt take lead on the family law practice's and its associated charities' finances, he still required an outside accounting auditor review them quarterly. Another reason he wished his father was still around. Matt was frustrated dealing with Teddy's arrogance and frigid temperament when it came to the law practice.

When they previously disagreed about setting billing terms for Teddy's client, even though precedent noted Matt was right during their weeks of arguments, the final response from Teddy was a note given to his secretary to hand deliver to Matt: *"It would seem to me I make those decisions around here, Matt. Please set the terms as I already explained. Discussion closed."* Matt later dropped several chocolate laxatives into his brother's lunch that afternoon, stealing the idea from their brother Zach. It was the only way he could retaliate on an equal playing field.

Matt laughed aloud when he recalled the two biggest events occurring at the office the afternoon he'd finally got revenge on his brother. First, the entire secretarial pool took bets on why Teddy left at two o'clock, the only time they'd ever seen him leave the office before anyone else. Teddy's own assistant came closest when she suggested he left to put on his big boy pants for a client meeting, not realizing he'd spent the entire time nearly destroying his shorts. And second, everyone kept blaming the new file clerk as the one who left the nasty smell emanating from the men's bathroom, causing the girl from Human Resources to pass out in poor Ms. Davis' arms. Neither woman could glance at one another since that day, especially when the HR woman awoke with her face buried in Ms. Davis' ample breasts. Despite the woman being his father's business partner, and maybe even his own boss, Matt still couldn't stop himself from checking out Ms. Davis' healthy rack on occasion.

Though Matt was doing well for himself as an accountant managing the books for a few other law firms in Connecticut, other than his father's practice, he hadn't landed any other influential accounts. Ben had planned to introduce his son to colleagues who owned firms closer to New York City where Matt could build a name on his own. But they hadn't gotten around to it, as mentoring Teddy to take over the family practice had stolen the priority the last few months.

Matt once again flipped through the monthly report tabulating the incoming revenue and growing operating expenses. Many of the firm's assets had fully depreciated the prior year leaving little to zero write-offs for him to include. At that rate, the firm wouldn't achieve their profit margins. He was certain his father hadn't mentioned these facts to his two partners. Matt placed the report on the table deciding he needed more time before talking with Teddy about the finances at the firm, given he had a few other pressing matters.

He watched the Yanks win the game despite giving up two hits—he threw the pillow at the TV. "You're better than this, boys!" After turning off the TV, he grabbed his checkbook to pay the landscapers. Scrolling through the online register on his laptop, he perused the upcoming bills. The mortgage was due in a few days plus payments on the new van they'd bought to accommodate three children's safety seats. And they needed to put an extension on the house to add more bedrooms, as the girls barely squeezed by in two small rooms. Matt couldn't think about money anymore and decided to call his brother to check in.

"Hey, Matt. What's up?" Ethan said.

"Yanks and the Knicks won tonight. Boston's a pathetic loser. Again. Third time this week. You pick the worst teams."

"Dude, you are ruthless. We're gonna catch up. It's my year. I know it."

"Sure. I've got a dinosaur to sell you, too. So, what's going on?

"Eh, I'm exhausted. Working way too much, but it'll all come to-gether. I have a few days off next week and hope to take Emma away for a long weekend."

"You serious about her?"

"Yeah. She's the one. I need advice."

"That's cool. Be careful she doesn't get pregnant, man. Kids are ex-pensive!" Matt perused the credit card statement containing all the sports groups and social clubs Margaret had selected to cultivate each daughter's physical and intellectual abilities. Margaret believed if they offered more options, each girl would determine her own strengths and latch onto the right hobbies and talents. By the end of each month, they'd spent all their remaining disposable income on the girls with little put away for future savings.

"I'm not ready for kids. I'm still finishing school, Matt. Hopefully, one day."

"Don't wait too long to propose. Dad's gone. I'm worried about Mom." Matt thought about his daughters who would grow up without ever getting to know their grandfather. He'd relied on his father's advice about everything in his life.

"Mom's strong. I spent time with her after the will. Hopefully, Dad's left her enough money to support herself. I'm a little worried about the letters. I hope it's nothing serious, like over losing the money or anything."

"You think? No, I'm sure it's fine."

"We'll see. I need to ask you something." Ethan's voice held a quiet longing for someone to listen.

"Listen, I gotta go. Talk soon. Love ya, man." Matt's financial distractions took up residence once again in his mind.

"Matt, I need to talk to you. Got a few minutes?"

Matt never heard him and hung up, pacing the room. He'd forgotten about the letters the attorney had mentioned, which prompted him to worry over his own inheritance. Matt and Margaret hadn't even thought about college for the girls and would soon have to pay for private school for their eldest daughter. He wanted to have more children, especially to have a son, but it wasn't financially possible in their current circumstances. He preferred water torture over participating in that conversation with Margaret, as it quickly approached time to plan the next kid to stay on their schedule.

Though it would be difficult, he needed to expedite getting his inheritance. He had a balloon payment due on the loan he'd taken out the prior year for the family van. It was too late to call the attorney to get a status on the timing for his share of his father's estate. He decided to call Teddy in the morning to cancel their meeting on the firm and ask him to close on the estate with Mr. Rattenbury as soon as possible. The auditor's meeting could wait.

Matt's eye twitched as he opened his briefcase and grabbed the bottle tucked into the inner pocket. He convinced himself he should take two more to sleep better that night. It had worked the last few evenings and the entire week of the funeral. He'd only blacked out one time after taking the pills, and no one else knew a cop had once found him passed out in a ditch by the side of the road not too far from where Ben had crashed.

Chapter 8 – Ethan

Ethan crossed State Street to Faneuil Hall to order breakfast for Emma on the way home from his overnight shift at the hospital. The deep and heavy bags beneath his twenty-three-year-old eyes revealed a long night in the ER had occupied his time. It was his fifth consecutive night at the hospital since he'd returned home from the funeral, and he needed the next twenty-four-hour down period to recuperate both emotionally and physically.

Paying for two egg sandwiches, bananas, and a raspberry scone, he pocketed the change from his favorite brunch restaurant, ran his fingers through his thick hair, and set off toward the bike rack across the street to pedal home to the apartment he shared with his girlfriend. Emma, who had graduated from college with a degree in music education, had been preparing a fall ensemble for the school where she finished her student teaching. After generating renewed interest in the failing chorale program with an enthusiastic and interactive approach, she had been offered a job as Boston Prep's Chorale Assistant Director, a position she was more than happy to accept.

He and Emma had dated for two years before moving in together at the end of the spring semester the previous month. He'd wanted to find a new place rather than keep either of their apartments since both leases came due, but Emma was over the moon to decorate his loft. He'd been lucky when he first moved to Boston and found a sweet deal, as the owner had converted it from a former baking factory. On most days, he could still catch a whiff of its yeasty, buttery smell—an instant comfort to his senses. Given his long hours at the hospital, Ethan suggested Emma take full reign to decorate their apartment. All he'd accomplished since moving in a few years prior was to buy furniture, install a few curtains on the oversized windows and add a couple of rugs to the cement floors to warm up the place in the winter. Emma had recently purchased paint colors, and her excitement bubbled over in anticipation of showing him during breakfast.

Ethan crossed back over State Street to locate his two-speed bike and head toward their loft twenty blocks away. Traffic was sparse early in the morning, but tons of runners roamed the streets. Tossing the sandwiches, bananas, and scone in his backpack, he hopped on his bicycle and joined the traffic pattern heading west. As he rode through the street, his mind drifted to his family. He still woke most mornings with watery eyes and a knot in his chest, saddened over how much he missed his dad.

As the last of the boys, Ethan benefited the most from his dad's experience as a father. When Ethan arrived, Ben had the right balance of mentor, teacher, friend, and confidante. He was more open-minded and accepting with Ethan, especially as Ethan was a good five to ten years younger than his brothers. His father would always tell him he wanted all his sons working with him at the family law practice, but knew practicality came before reality. And when Ethan's wide-eyed welcoming approach to the world branded him the apple of his father's eye, Ethan earned the liberty to do whatever he wanted in life, always having his father's respect and love no matter what path he chose.

When Ben unexpectedly died, Ethan was comforted to know it occurred from an accident and not a disease that ravaged and ripped apart his father's mind, as it did during his grandparents' final days. But not having an opportunity to say goodbye to his father before he passed was also difficult. By the time Ethan became a teenager, his brothers had all left for college. Ethan found ways to spend extra time with his parents and grandparents, hoping to create strong memories by joining his mother's charities and volunteering with her on holiday mornings to work at soup kitchens. He learned golf, so he could play a few rounds with his father on Sunday mornings at Willoughby Country Club. His friends would often tease Ethan, calling him *'momma's boy'* and *'daddy's boy,'* but Ethan didn't mind. He loved his family, holding no fears in showing it or spending time with them.

Ethan stopped his bicycle at the light as it turned red at the intersection. His mind suddenly became distracted by memories of his late paternal grandfather, William Glass. He recalled the winter when he turned fourteen, and his grandfather, who had turned ninety, built a wooden gameboard they could use to play Scrabble...

"Ethan, my boy, you need to hold the sandpaper more tightly if you want to get an even surface. It's about consistency and focus," Grandpa William said.

"Like this?" Ethan asked.

"Exactly. Put your elbow into it. As smooth as a polished floor, son."

"Thanks, Grandpa."

"How's the family tree project coming along?"

"Good. Dad gave me information on Grandma since she's no longer alive, but I need to know a little more about you."

"Go ahead, shoot."

"Dad's got three older brothers and four older sisters, right?

"Yes... kiddo. Your dad is the youngest."

"What else can you tell me about them?"

"Not much more to tell. Not much more I remember..."

"When did you and Grandma get married?"

"Oh, sixty years ago, Matty."

"I'm Ethan."

"That's what I meant. How's the table leg coming along? Let me look."

"Okay, I'm done with this one."

"Very good, Teddy. You're learning."

"But Grandpa..."

"Let me go tell your grandmother how good you're doing."

"But Grandma passed away."

"I know she did. I said your father, Ethan."

A honking SUV behind him pushed Ethan from the diversion as he pedaled his way back home reflecting on his grandfather's failed health. Soon after finishing the table, Ethan's grandfather was diagnosed with Alzheimer's disease and unable to live on his own. Ben chose to move his father, William, into the family home in Brandywine, which meant Ethan saw him every day. Since his grandfather was confined to his bedroom in the last few months, he and Ethan played scrabble each afternoon when school ended and checkers before bed. All on the gameboard they built together.

Ethan recalled sitting by his side at night watching his grandfather breathe, hoping each new medicine would have a dramatic impact, but it never happened. On several nights near the end, his emaciated grandfather grew angry and scared, jumping out of bed, screaming for his wife who'd been gone for many years. Watching his grandfather go through the torture of not recognizing family members, fighting with nurses over medication, and forgetting how to eat deeply impacted Ethan.

Shortly after William passed away, Eleanor, Ethan's maternal grandmother succumbed to the same disease, but she passed away quickly. Ethan and Eleanor shared the same passion for researching the family's history and finding as many treasures and records as possible. He tried to teach her how to use the computer, but she couldn't remember how, even before she got sick. On many occasions, Ethan had to re-enter the data about their ancestors into the software program, as she kept overwriting each person with someone else's birthdates and marriages. He finally got wise to her mistakes and kept backup copies, so he only lost a few days' work from time to time. The passing of his grandparents, as well as the emptiness of the family home, affected Ethan as deeply as his parents. Fear and melancholy compelled him to maintain a sense of stability and continuity within the family, even if it was only him and his parents most of the time. While it was traumatic for two of Ethan's favorite people to die within a year of each other and not have his brothers around every day to lean on, it inspired him to map his career path with accelerated speed. He enrolled in Boston University to get his undergrad degree and doctor-ate in geriatric medicine. He was determined to cure the disease, to improve his patient's lives, and to ease recoveries.

Ethan's left arm signaled as he gripped the handlebar with his right hand, turning onto his one-way street and pulling near the front of the loft at the end of the block. He locked the bike to an open slot on the outside rail and strolled toward the building's side entrance. He lived on the third floor and enjoyed walking the stairs rather than riding the elevator. As he hopped the last one, his phone vibrated. Ethan clicked accept and read the message from his brother.

> **Matt:** *Red Shits lost again, kid. You got no chance at the World Series this year.*
>
> **Ethan:** *The slow and steady turtle's gonna win this race.*
>
> **Matt:** *Ha! Crawl back in your shell. Hell will freeze over before you score.*
>
> **Ethan:** *Don't be so sure. I got a good feeling.*
>
> **Matt:** *Seriously? If you diagnose patients like you pick teams, I'm never coming to you. Not even for a cold. Maybe hemorrhoids. Yeah. You can fix those for me, Doc Loser!*

Ethan ignored his brother's last reply, inserted his key in the door, rolled the heavy metal into the wall and stepped into his apartment. Emma stood on a stepstool in the kitchenette behind a cupboard door, her cut-off denim shorts covering all but the lower semi-circle of her tempting cheeks as she reached for plates on the top shelf. The bottom of his Boston University t-shirt tied around her waist given it was at least three sizes too large, presented an alluring treat for Ethan where it landed on her mid-section.

Emma retrieved the plates and stepped down the ladder adjusting the set of chopsticks stuffed inside her auburn hair to keep it pulled back and off her face. She stared back at him with milk-chocolate eyes as her petite frame and long, shapely legs danced across the floor in comfortable ballet slippers. Her eclectic yet girly style always brought a smile to Ethan's face, especially given how beautifully any article of clothing she wore flattered her body.

"Breakfast first. Then you need to peruse the colors I picked out for the walls. You'll love them, for sure." Emma spoke with a child-like intensity.

Ethan pulled off his sweater, poured two cups of coffee and grabbed the milk and sugar for Emma. He preferred his coffee black, needing the rich and bold flavor and thick, mud-like consistency to wake him each day.

Emma unpacked the treats he selected for them and sliced the scone in half. One half crumbled over the table as she separated the pieces, causing Ethan to tease her. "You make some of the biggest messes." She lit up, as always, with a stunning smile and expression, filling Ethan with warmth.

"Well, if you don't want any of the scone, I can finish it myself." A suggestive desire accompanied her words as she licked the pastry.

"Nonsense." He swatted at her hand as she ran around the table. "Give it to me now or pay the price later." His French accent always made her laugh.

"So, you want me to paint the walls, chartreuse? That's what you're saying?"

Ethan caught up with her, boxed her against the single row of laminate kitchen cabinets, and grabbed both her wrists above her head.

Emma giggled when he finally let her go and placed half the scone in his mouth. He bit off a piece as more crumbs landed on her neck. He bent and sucked them up in one swoop with his lips.

"You're such a pig." Emma grabbed her phone and took a photo. "*Snapchat* time."

"That's a *no* to chartreuse, whatever color it is… let's see what you have to say now." Ethan shoved the rest of the scone in her mouth. The camera, turned in the wrong direction, flashed as it took a picture of the ceiling.

She grabbed her cup of coffee, swallowed, and blew him a kiss. "That was good, for sure. Thank you. But let's eat our sandwiches and look at the swatches. I will run to the paint store this morning to buy whatever we agree on."

Emma and Ethan finished their breakfast, considered the options, and selected a slate gray, violet, and mint green combination for the main room in the loft which would match the natural flooring they intended to keep intact.

Ethan used a moment of silence to tell Emma about his recent discussion with his mother. "My mom's looking to come visit in a couple of weeks."

Emma smiled. "Really? I definitely want to meet her."

"I know you were upset you couldn't come for the funeral."

"Yeah, but you were caught in the middle."

"I wanted you by my side, but I understood what my mother meant. You wouldn't have met her at her best. And I'd have been busy with the funeral services and chatting with all my Dad's friends and colleagues."

"I guess. I would have been overwhelmed. Just don't like thinking she doesn't approve of me."

"Have an open mind. You two haven't even met. She's not all that scary."

"I know. But I want your mother to like me."

"She will. I plan to keep you around for a long time."

Emma and Ethan spent a few minutes of alone time in the bedroom before she left for the paint store, promising to return in a couple of hours while he caught up on sleep.

As he cleaned the kitchen, Ethan sent his brother a text.

> **Ethan:** *Glad I saw you last week at Mom's. You need to come home again.*
>
> **Caleb:** *I know. We need to spend more quality time together.*
>
> **Ethan:** *Maybe another fishing trip?*

Caleb: *That'd be great. When?*

Ethan: *I'll check with Matt and Zach. But soon.*

Caleb: *Zach's got his hands full with some girl.*

Ethan: *He's always got his hands full of some girl.*

Caleb: *Ha! Maybe the Robot will come this time.*

Ethan: *Teddy won't go. He's too busy with Dad's firm.*

Caleb: *True. You ask Teddy. I'll ask Matt.*

Ethan: *No deal... you talk to Teddy, I'll talk to Matt. I need to get even with him.*

Caleb: *Wimp. Fine. I'll ask the Robot.*

Ethan entered the bedroom, pulled his Looney Tunes t-shirt over his head, and dragged his cargos to the floor. As he stepped out of his tennis sneakers, a card fell out of the pocket of his pants. Ethan gathered it and slipped it beneath the wool blanket his aunt had quilted for him.

Pulling out his mobile phone, he deftly punched in numbers while gazing around the room. When it connected on the third ring, a nasal voice spoke.

"Excelsior Jewelry Repairs. Marty speaking. How may I assist you?"

Ethan pulled the phone closer to his ears. "Hi, it's Ethan Glass. I wanted to check on the item I left with you last week."

"Ah, Mr. Glass. I planned to call you this afternoon. It's an exquisite piece. Did you say it belonged to your grandmother?"

"Yes, it's been in my family for generations."

"It's a beautiful piece, worth quite a bit. Are you sure you don't want to sell it?"

Ethan chuckled. "No, definitely not. I'm going to propose to my girl-friend. But it needs cleaning and sizing."

When Ethan arrived home for the funeral, he'd spent time with Diane talking about Emma. They'd had a strong bond most of his life, especially after his grandmother passed away. When he told his aunt that he found the right girl, Diane pulled out her mother's engagement ring and gave it to him. Guilt brewed inside Ethan when his Aunt Diane had gifted it to him, but she had no children and Olivia wore an engagement ring from his father. The rest of the boys had already been married or didn't show any interest in family heirlooms, but Ethan always had. Diane told him his Grandma Eleanor felt emphatic it belonged to him whenever he'd fallen in love.

Marty added, "I can do it. No worries. Just drop off one of her rings later today so I can get a size comparison. You can pick it up in a week." Marty hung up.

Ethan smiled, remembering his grandmother and the anticipation of proposing to Emma. His family could use good news—and he could use good news, too.

Ethan dialed a second number on his phone and waited several rings before anyone answered. When it finally happened, Ethan quickly sat up in the bed. "Hi, this is Ethan Glass. I'm calling to check on my test results. Do you know if Dr. Kane is available?"

A voice on the other end of the phone told him to hold on. Three excruciating minutes later, Dr. Kane showed up. "Ethan, I'm glad you called. Can you come into the office this week?"

Ethan's grip on the phone grew tighter. He stopped breathing for a few seconds as pressure built in his head. "I'd prefer you tell me the news on the phone, Dr. Kane."

The doctor paused for a moment. "I have the results of the biopsy we ran on your tissue sample. It would be best if you came onsite for this conversation, Ethan."

Chapter 9 – Olivia

Olivia spent most of the week planning her trip to visit each of her sons, asking Victor to bring her to Caleb's Maine home as the first leg of her adventure. As she marked off items on her list, Diane called to her from the hallway.

"I'm back, Liv. Where are you?"

"Up in the bedroom packing for the trip to Caleb's." Olivia stared at her long, camel-colored cashmere winter coat purchased on her New York City trip to see the Rockefeller Christmas tree with Diane the prior year. "How cold does it get in Maine? I suppose I need to bring this heavy coat."

Diane rounded the corner across the room and stood in Olivia's bedroom doorway as her sister inspected the clothing. "You may have been the one to go to school and work at that fancy law firm, but sometimes you lack basic common sense, Liv. They don't get snow in June. You don't need a heavy coat. Take your long red sweater, the one you wore last week when we visited the cemetery. You may need it one or two nights if he's too far into the mountains."

"Let's not quibble. I've never been to Maine. Maybe I should ask what I can bring." Olivia combed through a pile of shoes.

"You don't need to call Caleb. Don't be nervous. He's your son. You're finally getting to see where he's been living all these years. Your time is better spent on figuring out what you wanna accomplish while with him."

Olivia pushed a few dresses out of the way and tapped the king-size bed. "Please sit here with me. It's time I told you about something."

Diane sat next to her sister and clasped her hands in her lap. She noticed Ben's dirty coffee cup still lingered near the alarm clock. "It's been two weeks since he died. You haven't sorted any of Ben's clothes, and his favorite mug is still on the nightstand. Isn't it time to do a little cleaning?"

"Yes, but it's the least of my concerns right now. You wanted to know what's in the letter." Olivia willed herself not to get sidetracked over how much she missed Ben, despite the anger consuming her. "One of the boys is not my son. My biological son." Her hand gripped her chest while her despondent eyes fell to the floor boring a hole through the carpet.

Diane tilted her head to the side and scrunched her eyes, her voice hollow and hesitant. "I don't understand."

"I'm not sure I do either." Olivia grabbed her sister's warm and comforting hand. "After I gave birth, the baby didn't survive. Ben stood by the nurses when they tried to save the baby, but he died while I was all drugged up. They couldn't do anything for him. I lost a child, Diane."

Diane's hand dropped to her chin and covered her mouth. "Why've you never told me before?"

"I didn't know. Don't be a stupid old fool." Bitterness clung to her words.

Diane pulled back from the unexpected reaction, careful to let the venom squeak past her.

"Another woman gave birth to a baby at the hospital. She had been searching for a respectable couple to adopt the child. Ben gave her money, and the nurse switched babies, I guess, before anyone else found out."

"That's crazy," Diane said. "How did you not know it?"

"I was knocked out from the anesthesia with all five boys. Giving birth was never easy for me, Diane. I know you haven't ever had a child before. Let's not act ridiculous as well as simple-minded."

Diane sat speechless for a few seconds deciding whether she should fight back. She settled on being the bigger person. "I know you don't mean that. Let's not act ridiculous as well as nasty. Continue."

Olivia paced the floor for a minute, then broke the silence. "It happened quickly. I'm not certain which one he's talking about. I've read the letter repeatedly, but he left me no clues. He didn't say much else, just addressed the second letter to our son and told me not to open it until Mr. Rattenbury found the birth mother."

Diane shifted on the bed, her gaze focused on Olivia. "The estate attorney? He's looking into this for you?"

Olivia's voice grew frail and muted. "I talked to him yesterday. The woman's name is Rowena Hector. She moved here from Scotland to have the baby. Mr. Rattenbury will research immigration and hospital records during the years when Ben and I had the boys. He's certain he'll find out what happened to Rowena, and then we'll decide what to do next after we have enough information to proceed."

"So that's why you want to visit the boys before the lawyer finds Rowena. You wanna spend time with them, before you find out one of them isn't your biological child."

"Yes, it's all I can concentrate on." Olivia' voice fell lower than a mumble, as her eyes closed and blocked all traces of light. White knuckles pressed hard into the handle of the half-packed luggage.

"But you're still their mother no matter what happens, Liv."

"I know. It doesn't change anything, except it does. What if Rowena wants to meet her son? What if he wants to meet her? I just lost Ben. I don't want to lose a son, too." Tears rained down Olivia's flushed cheeks.

Diane's chest constricted as she walked over using her sleeve to wipe Olivia's tears. "Nonsense. Don't try to predict the future. Take this one step at a time. They've been your sons for thirty-two years. Nothing will take it away."

"I suppose," Olivia whispered as she walked toward the bathroom to grab a tissue, passing a mirror on the closet wall. "I'm looking older,

Diane." She cleared her throat before continuing. "Actually, I'm just looking old."

Diane sat in silence processing all she'd heard.

"What would you do, Diane? I'm angry with him, but I can't bring myself to read the other letter. He wanted me to wait until we find Rowena. If we can't find her, maybe I'm not supposed to ever read it. Then nothing would change."

"Ben was practical. I can't say if this was or wasn't the best decision, but he decided it years ago. And you can't change what happened. It was important enough for him to finally be honest." Diane paused to collect her thoughts as the curtains blew across the window from the racing wind. "Think of the burden he must have carried all these years, knowing he's been keeping this secret from you. Consider what it took for him to write down this confession and give it to someone else to deliver to you upon his death."

"Him? What about me? Why did I have no choice in it?"

"He raised someone else's child as his own and never told you because he didn't wanna hurt you. He never treated any of the boys differently. He was a father to all of them."

Olivia nodded. "He was a good father."

"Maybe he planned to tell you someday himself and not via the letter. He didn't expect to die in a car accident. He lost his chance to be honest with you. Maybe it was taken away from him in the end."

Olivia listened to Diane's words as the whirr of a lawnmower's engine blazed outside her window. It soothed her mind as she sat against the bed bargaining with an unknown debtor for ownership of her future. "No, the fool had years to tell me. I can't waste any more time guessing why he did it or why he chose to tell me in this manner. He did. It's done. And I have to fix it." She wiped her face dry, tossed the tissues in the corner wastepaper basket, and drew a deep breath.

Diane placed a hand on her heart. "What'll you tell the boys when you visit each of them? They're gonna ask what's in the letter."

"I'll be vague, play down its importance. It's not lying if I'm waiting a little longer to get the full story. I need all the facts before I destroy my son."

"Will you still tell him the truth if Rowena is dead?"

"I don't know. Don't push me. I need to figure out how to reconnect with each of my sons to decide... what the hell my future will be without Ben. I am more than his wife, you know."

"Yes, I know. Don't take it out on me. I'm not your personal punching bag." Diane nudged Olivia with the palm of her hand. "Let me give you a few minutes alone. I'll make us some lunch."

While Diane left, Olivia sat on the gray recliner in her bedroom corner lifting the foot bench to rest her tired legs. For years, her identity was mother and wife. She'd quit her position at the law firm when she was pregnant with Caleb, as working a full-time job, raising several boys, and maintaining a house and home bordered on impossible. After Ethan had arrived, she and Ben found the solution to augmenting her roles as mother and wife in their family. She joined the local ladies' social leagues and charities gradually taking on more responsibility until she became the chair of several committees and a director on a few boards for children's health advocacy. Olivia grew energized by her new roles when many corporations sought her out to collaborate on social awareness campaigns and non-profit humane causes close to her heart. When Ben died a few weeks ago, she'd lost her ability to focus on all the activities that had once filled her days. Her friend, Betty, stepped in to keep things afloat until Olivia could return.

As she focused on the clothes strewn across the bed and the clanging sound of Diane preparing their meal, Olivia's mind returned to guessing which of the boys Ben had written about in his letter. She found reasons why it could be any of them, each one more bruising than the last.

Could it be Theodore since Ben knew she wouldn't be able to accept losing her first-born child? Theodore was different from them both, unable to share intimacy or express real emotions. While she and Ben weren't overly affectionate around the boys, they tried to always kiss each other hello and goodbye, a loving touch of a hand across the other's shoulder when passing through a room. Something had been holding Theodore back for most of his life, and Olivia worried his DNA dictated his lack of affection.

She worried the letter could be about Matt as he didn't resemble either of them, but she was certain Matt inherited her own father's facial expressions. Whenever Matt was excited, his entire smile grinned ear to ear and his eyes bulged. He'd rivaled their dog, Bailey's, boisterous shake whenever he got wet, just as her father did whenever he'd fallen in the pool given his fears over swimming. Matt and her father even shared the same rapid wiggle in their upturned noses whenever they told a white lie. But Ben knew how much Olivia wanted Matt, and when she almost miscarried in her second trimester, he promised her no one would take away their baby. Maybe it was Matt given how sick she had been during those last few months before giving birth to him.

Caleb was a mystery, pulling away when he became a teenager, more than any of the other boys and more than Olivia thought normal at his age. Teenagers always grew more private during their awkward years, but Caleb never found his way back from them. Maybe Caleb internalized the missing link to her and Ben, unconsciously moving his life in a different direction. But he also had a penchant for gardening and watching the beauty of nature blossom like she did. They'd talk for hours over planting vegetables, spend afternoons reading gardening books, and disappear on weekends to visit local nurseries when he was a young child.

Zachary had always been a handful getting into every possible type of trouble. He knew right from wrong, but he made poor decisions. She and Ben, like the rest of the boys, had a practical approach to life where they were future-thinking in everything they chose to do. Zachary lived each day as he wanted to, ignored consequences, and never felt compelled to follow suit with the rest of the Glass family. Perhaps he inherited a different set of hopes and dreams from another pair of parents. But she was certain as much as Zachary tried to be as different as he could from everyone in the family, he and Ben shared an identical walking pattern, with a slight favor of the right leg often forcing them to veer to the side. And before Ben's hair grayed, she'd often mistake them for one another from far away.

Olivia bonded most closely with Ethan in the last few years, given she spent the most time with him as a child. She had him all to herself while the older boys were away at school, developing a strong mother-son bond. Ethan had researched the entire family tree and knew over twenty generations of the Glass family. He also showed an innocence and naivety unmatched by anyone else in their family, never revealing an angry bone in his body. Maybe he came from a much simpler family who never even thought about the fears that saturated her and Ben's restless nights.

If she kept this up, she'd find herself committed in an institution like Ben's brother. Olivia wasn't sure how much longer she could hold on without breaking down in front of the boys, which was the last thing she could let happen without having all the facts.

Please, Mr. Rattenbury, make this go away soon. I don't want to lose any of my sons.

Chapter 10 – Caleb & Olivia

Caleb stepped onto the second-floor platform as he came off the back staircase, rounding the corner toward the bedroom. He stopped in the hall and watched Jake from a distance, his body leaning against the doorjamb.

The master bedroom was their private oasis. Merging their sometimes-differing styles, as Jake was prone to pop culture and modern art while Caleb preferred more traditional styles, was easy for once. They both wanted the room to have a natural transition from the outdoors but also appear comfortable and cozy. Nestled in the corner, a Cherrywood mantle they'd built themselves adorned the bluestone fireplace.

Jake lifted the suitcase onto the chest and shut the zipper looking around to verify he packed everything. His eyes met Caleb's at the doorway. "I didn't hear you come up. How long have you been standing inside?"

"Just a minute. I enjoy watching when you don't know that I am. That's when I capture your innocence." Caleb flirted with his eyes before kicking off his running shoes.

"I'm always innocent. You're the one with the guilty conscience," Jake said. "I'm packed."

Caleb thought back to the day Jake moved into the house. Jake had taken extra care not to disrupt anything or leave boxes in the open. Caleb soon realized Jake didn't acknowledge the house as his own. As the weeks passed, Caleb removed his older pictures from the wall and donated furniture he'd considered ready to replace, even though it was only a few year's old, symbolic of their lives joining as one. Once Jake noticed Caleb had cleared the place for him to decide together the style of their shared home, he relaxed and welcomed every minute of it.

"You look good, but you'd look even better if you took off those clothes," Caleb replied.

"Exactly what I had in mind."

When Olivia crossed the Maine border, the trees stood taller, and the setting sun drenched the limitless sky with a beautiful blue and purple hue. The reflection off the coastal sea and the sweeping views and massive cliffs in the western backdrop encouraged a sense of serenity around her, especially the clean fresh air as it blossomed in her nose.

Olivia adjusted the silver band on her left wrist and glanced at the time on the glass faceplate. Too many people relied on cell phones to track time, and they ignored the need to wear a watch these days. For Olivia, the watch you wore revealed a bold statement. If you selected large and showy, you were an attention seeker. If you chose a digital timepiece, you had no respect for history. If you didn't wear a watch, you weren't detail oriented. Olivia's timepiece, a 1940's Waltham silver and diamond antique watch, was a gift from her grandmother on her eighteenth birthday. Today, she wore it around her wrist as a badge of courage to give her the confidence she needed in seeing Caleb for the first time in his own home.

She wasn't due to arrive at his place for a few more hours, but Victor hadn't encountered any traffic, putting her just a few minutes away. She planned to surprise Caleb by arriving early to take him out to dinner. Victor exited the highway and turned onto the final one-lane road leading to Caleb's house.

The muscles in Caleb's throat contracted restricting his air flow. "Are you sure you don't mind staying at the hotel while my mom visits? I know we agreed it best if I spent a few days on my own to check if it was the right time to tell her about you, but you own this place, too."

Jake said, "I know. And we decided together. I won't be far away, so if you choose to tell her, I can run right over and do a song and dance for my entrance."

"Please don't."

"What do you think? A little Britney? Gaga? Maybe I'll go old school and pull out some Barbra?"

Caleb ambled toward the bed and threw a square burgundy pillow at Jake. As Jake tried to block it, Caleb tackled him, and they fell on the shag rug. "You will not do a song and dance for my mother."

Jake moved his lips toward Caleb's and whispered. "I won't do a song and dance, but I am going to do something else before I leave." He unfastened Caleb's brown and blue plaid button-down shirt, unhooked his belt, and pressed his mouth against Caleb's pulsing neck.

Caleb moaned, curling his toes at the touch of Jake's fingers, and let him continue on his path. "Open for business, sailor."

As the car traversed the long driveway, the enormous green balsam fir trees leading up to Caleb's house reminded Olivia of the holidays. Ben always ensured they had a twelve-foot Christmas tree in the hallway foyer, as it was her favorite season. Victor parked the car and helped Olivia with her bags. As he lifted out the last piece, Olivia summoned pride and comfort over the massive house standing before her. Caleb had built his dream home, the one he talked about as a teenager every day and night. Its brilliance as picturesque as any painting she'd ever seen, still carrying his signature look of ornate beauty and natural elegance.

She stepped to the open porch handing Victor a generous tip. "You don't need to stay. Caleb expects me and that's his Jeep." She pointed to the side of the barn.

"You gonna be okay, Mrs. G? You were awfully quiet the last leg of the drive."

"Yes, I'm just remembering Ben. He would have wanted to visit with me. I'll call you if I need anything else before the end of the week. Thank you, Victor."

Victor shut the trunk and started the engine. "Be good, Mrs. G. I'm glad you took the trip up here. Mr. G. would have loved this part of the country."

As he drove away, Olivia inhaled with a deep breath, pulled the red sweater closer to her body and sensed an intoxicating burnt hickory smell reminding her of childhood campfires.

Jake twisted his arm out from under Caleb's back and stood at the edge of the bed. "I better go shower before I head to the hotel. I should get your scent off me, you know."

As Jake walked to the bathroom, Caleb shifted toward the fireplace, grabbed the poker, and pushed another piece of hickory in the hearth. "I'll pour a couple of glasses of Malbec before you leave. It's the one we bought at the Mendoza Vineyard with those locals who thought we were from Australia."

Jake winked at him. "We've already been down-under twice today, Mr. Jackman. Even I could use time to refuel."

Caleb ignored Jake's banter and awful Australian accent. He grabbed a pair of sweats from the bottom drawer tossing on a t-shirt and light jacket before heading toward the staircase. Their bedroom sat on the second floor, but the kitchen and wine room were on the first.

Olivia took one last breath and pressed her chilled hands on the iron knocker of the wooden door before her. She pulled back, surprised at its heavy weight, and pushed forward with her entire body against the last restriction that kept her from reconnecting with Caleb.

As the thunderous sound echoed behind the house's exterior walls, anticipation over the visit filled her mind. Caleb didn't tell her *not* to come, but he hadn't appeared too thrilled with her request to spend a week together in his remote Maine home. It was time to talk to him about finding a wife and settling down. She'd force him to understand why it was necessary.

Jake rinsed his hair one last time and rotated the copper knobs stopping the pulsing rainfall above his head. As he grabbed a towel, the boom of the front door knocker echoed in the house. Drying off his body, he shouted to Caleb. "Is someone at the front door?" He tied the towel around his waist, swatted at the steam near his eyes, opened the bathroom door, and headed to the hallway.

Caleb had finished pouring the second glass of wine when he heard both the front door and Jake's voice. "Yes, someone's here, probably a delivery. I'll check." He put the bottle of Malbec on the counter and took a sip of the wine.

Passing the dining room, Caleb took a right into the main hall and placed the wine goblet on the antique Edwardian console table by the stairs. Jake descended the stairs in only his bath towel, pausing when Caleb appeared closer to the door.

"You're dripping on the floor." Caleb smirked at Jake.

Jake smiled while he bent over scanning the front window to see who stood at the door. "I can take the towel off to dry the floor if Mr. Blackwell doesn't approve of my outfit."

"No. I need to answer the door. Go put clothes on."

"I dress for the image. Not for myself, not for the public, not for fashion, not for me."

Caleb squinted at him. "Explain."

"Marlene Dietrich. A bit of a dominatrix."

"Maybe no lessons right now. You'll tempt the delivery boy." Caleb grinned at Jake, swung open the door and looked out, first noticing the black suitcase on the steps followed by a red blur flash by him. His eyes moved upward to his mother's excited grin and red crocheted maxi cardigan flowing in the wind. His right arm stiffened, his teeth sliced across his tongue, and all clarity disappeared from his head.

Jake pressed down another step. "Babe, who's here?"

Olivia looked first in Caleb's direction. "I'm early, no traffic..." Her eyes darted from Caleb to Jake, who stood a few feet behind her son, stunned when his towel hit the floor, exposing his naked body.

"Oh Lord," Olivia gasped.

"Put something on, Jake." A mix of embarrassment and humor carried Caleb's voice. He attempted to block his mother's view of Jake.

Jake stepped forward to reach for the towel, suddenly losing his grip on the handrail, his feet reaching the drops of water falling from his skin. Within seconds, his legs gave way and his body slipped on the final step sending him a few feet forward landing in front of the *Welcome* rug where Olivia stood. When he came to a full stop, with his naked body sprawled across the foyer and his legs spread wide apart, Jake closed his eyes and tried to hide the faint glimmer of a smile.

Olivia tried to turn away, but her eyes locked in on the metal bars piercing Jake's nipples, and when she lowered her head to avoid staring, they landed on his waist. "Penis. Cover your, oh, what on God's green earth is going on," she stuttered. "That must hurt... are you okay?" She bent further down and pulled straight up, her head whacking into Caleb's face on the return.

Caleb, shaken from the blow, couldn't find the towel and decided to rip off his own jacket, throwing it on top of Jake to cover his critical parts. All he could do was mumble something unintelligible and shield his mother's eyes.

Jake said, "I'm not hurt. But I could use a hand."

As Caleb leaned toward him, Olivia caught sight of a red bite mark on her son's upper neck, unsure what just occurred. She glanced back at Jake, threw her hands to her eyes, and backed out the door. "Who is this? What kind of..."

"Mom, where are you going?"

"I'm early. I should... called. Let me... a quick walk. You probably... a minute." Olivia's voice faltered as she wandered the wood-chipped driveway in no obvious direction.

Caleb's skin flushed tomato red, his body full of rising heat and sheer embarrassment. He couldn't summon his voice and couldn't decide whether to run after his mother or check on Jake. "I, she... you..."

"Quit acting like a southern republican conservative belle and help me up, Miss Bankhead." Jake's voice pleaded with Caleb as he attempted to hold back his laughter. "Well, at least she knows you're gay. Check one box off the list. Should we consider her knowing I've got several body piercings, and her son gets turned on when I bite his neck as the extra special bonus news? Just wait until she finds out you're the..."

"I've had enough of you. Let me go find my mother and fix this. I love you but go next door please!"

Jake's sheepish grin turned devilish.

It melted Caleb's heart as he jogged the wood-chip pathway to remedy the situation. He ran back for a quick kiss before searching for his mother.

* * *

After an awkward introduction between Jake and his mother, Caleb sent Jake upstairs to dress. Not the best way to present your mother to the man her gay son lived with. Whether fear or embarrassment drove the exodus, the incident sent Jake running to the hotel sooner than planned. He exited out the back door and left a note for Caleb to call him later that evening, apologizing and laughing in unison over the entire situation.

An hour later, Caleb and Olivia sat across from one another at a local Italian eatery near the base of the mountain range. A Canadian transplant had purchased the old mayor's home and asked Caleb to convert it into an after-hours bar and club with a Tuscan theme, complete with live vines bearing dainty white flowers that meandered the walls and crawled through the ceiling rafters. Caleb's pride in his work shined, as he wanted to show something to his mother he'd designed.

Olivia's silence hovered around the corner table in the restaurant when they sat. Caleb insisted on having the conversation with his mother in public, as he knew she'd restrain her emotions and practice civility. He didn't want to have an argument in his home, especially given he'd managed to keep it private for the last few years.

Olivia spoke first, as she unfolded the cloth napkin in her lap. Her lips puckered as if she'd tasted too much lemon in her water glass. "*Architectural Digest* should feature this place and your house, Caleb. You have an incredible talent, and I'm proud to be your mother."

Caleb responded in a cautious tone. "I'm glad to know it, Mom. It was an enormous amount of work, but I didn't do it alone."

"Does Jake live with you?" Olivia hesitated with each word stumbling to determine exactly how to ask the question.

Caleb had decided earlier to be honest with her, given what she witnessed when walking into his house. "Yes, Jake lives with me. How much do you want to know?"

"You're my son, Caleb. I love you no matter what you choose to do with your life. I won't say I understand it or I'm happy about it. It can't be easy living an abnormal life. It's not what I would want for you, but I do want to know more about your new life." Olivia lingered as she chose each word, shifting the fork and knife further away from the edge of the ruffled placemat, then swallowed a heavy gulp of the peppery red wine.

"My life is fantastic, Mom. Jake and I have been together five years. He's a school teacher. We live a pretty quiet life up here." Caleb planned no response to her comment about leading an abnormal life due to being gay. "Not much different than you and Dad."

"I wish you hadn't kept this hidden from me for so long. Have you always been...?" Astonishment percolated over his comparison of their relationships so close to his father's death.

"Yes."

"Is that why you never come home anymore?"

"Yes."

"Did you expect your father and I would reject you?"

"Maybe."

Olivia ground her teeth with increasing pressure. "Don't answer me with one-word responses. Talk to me, Caleb. I'm your mother."

Caleb noticed the couple at the next table perked up when his mother raised her voice.

"Mom, please don't cause a scene. I'm not sure how to respond or how to handle this situation. I didn't expect you to find out this way. I wanted to tell you when I thought you were ready to hear the truth."

"When *you* thought I was ready to hear the truth? What's with the men in this family? I wish you hadn't kept such an important secret from your father and me. I'm starting to hate secrets." Her spoon dropped off the side of the table on the floor.

The waiter wandered over with a rapid focus and brought her a new one. Caleb smiled and waved him away before he interrupted the conversation with his mother. Once it started, Caleb needed to finish it.

He adjusted his posture, setting his back square against the stiff chair. "Selfishness triumphs again for my mother. Don't forget this was my story to tell, and I never felt comfortable. I wish I had an opportunity to tell Dad, but I'm gonna accept I'll never know how he felt." Caleb's heart beat faster as he paused to catch his breath. "Mom, what happened with those letters from Dad that Mr. Rattenbury gave you?"

The dreaded question. Olivia's jaw clenched tighter. "I still have them. I haven't opened the second one. Your father wanted me to share it with you boys in a few weeks."

Caleb's foot tapped against the table. "Did he say anything in the first letter…"

"About you or this?" Olivia jumped in before he had a chance to say it aloud. "No, Caleb. Your father didn't know you were…"

"Gay? I'm glad you aren't telling me it's just a phase. How would he have reacted?" Caleb would give anything to find out since his secrets had been divulged.

"I don't know. Let's talk about something else for a little while. Surely, I need time to consider everything. I simply wasn't expecting this... to learn you're... Not that it's wrong. Just, I didn't know, and I'm... I am only still thinking how much I miss your father."

Caleb recognized the tone. When his mother became frustrated, sometimes disappointed, she'd emphasize words differently... *surely... simply... just...only still...* as if she needed to defend every phrase with some extra word to later provide an escape clause. It would be better to ask again in a few days, when she'd hold an open mind and embrace a conciliatory attitude.

He suggested lasagna, and when she agreed, he signaled to the waiter who watched them the entire time he and his mother sparred, constantly checking on the table. They spent the rest of dinner talking about Maine and his job, avoiding any discussion related to her seeing Jake naked or the fact her son was out of the closet.

When she left for the restroom, he read the messages on his phone.

Jake: *How's Mommie Dearest? Ask her what she thought of me. But don't ask her to eat the cookie, Mother.*

Caleb: *I know that one. Joan Crawford.*

Jake: *Half right, my Padawan. Someday...*

* * *

After a few days, Caleb remained uncertain if he should tell Jake to come back home. They'd chat each night from separate beds in separate places rationalizing the pros and cons. They settled on mostly cons, given she still hadn't been able to talk about the whole situation. She asked once where Jake had gone and expressed concern when Caleb told her he stayed at a hotel. Caleb took her on a few tours of the local sights, showed her the plans he drafted for remodeling the barn, and chatted about his brothers.

By Monday morning, enough time had passed, and he brought up the subject again. Caleb woke early and suggested a walk to the farmer's market to buy fresh eggs to cook omelets. Olivia's eyes shined for the first time since she'd arrived, which encouraged him to move forward with his plan. They took a long walk down the hill, arriving at a few produce stands near the valley. Her ability to keep pace surprised him, but Caleb knew she might struggle on the way back up.

"Can we talk now, Mom?"

"Talk about what, sweetheart?" Olivia perused the cartons of brown and white eggs. "Do you have a preference?"

Caleb was tempted to respond he preferred Midwestern men with cute dimples and accents, but he convinced himself it might be too soon to inject humor into the situation. "Brown eggs create better omelets. I want to talk about Jake."

"Jake's nice. I don't know him, so I can't say much. Those piercings must hurt. I've never seen one up close before. What are you putting in the omelet? Do we need any cheese? I haven't had brie in a long time." While her eyes focused on the farm stand, her words seemed less than committed to the conversation.

"Fine. Get some brie. They don't hurt. They feel good. But I don't want to talk about Jake's piercings. I want to talk about Jake." Caleb walked closer to her and placed his hand on her shoulder. "Mom, please. You came all this way to spend time with me. Shouldn't we talk about this?" His eyes relaxed and silently pleaded with her to listen to him.

"Caleb, I'm not ready." She tossed a bunch of tomatoes back into the bin, not having enough focus to find the right ones. "I came here with plans to ask you to move back home. To ask you to spend the summer with me and figure out my future. Your father died. I thought I still had you. But I don't have you. I probably haven't had you for years. I'm scared, Caleb. I don't want to live alone." Her eyes welled.

Caleb pulled her aside and hugged her. He hadn't thought about her grief. After she found him with Jake, all he could focus on was coming out to her, telling her the truth, and finally freeing himself to avoid the divisive trap that hovered between necessary seclusion and inherent honesty. But he'd forgotten she lost her husband, and he'd lost his father.

"You haven't lost me. And you haven't lost anyone else. That's what you're afraid of? Don't forget you have Aunt Diane, too. She called yesterday to check on how you were doing. She wants to be here for you."

Olivia held her son's arm for a minute, her eyes fixated on the landscape surrounding them. "I'm afraid of all these secrets." She stopped herself before saying anything else.

"Mom, it's one secret. I'm gay. It doesn't change anything for you. It's my life. How does this impact you?" Caleb pushed back with rigid force. He stepped to the side to let a young girl pay for the items in her basket.

Olivia grew silent for a minute listening to the chatter of the market around her. "You're right, Caleb. I know this is about you. I have my own life to manage. Give me a little more time, and we can talk about getting to know Jake. Will that be okay?"

Caleb shrugged his shoulders and stepped to the register, recognizing the cashier had listened to their entire conversation. "Sure. I can give you more time, but since we've opened this door, we can't ignore it. If you want me to spend time back home, you have to accept this part of me... you have to accept Jake as part of my life." Strength settled in Caleb as he said those words. He missed his family, but the battle lines had been drawn over who controlled him. Jake would always win.

Caleb paid for their groceries, ignored the odd looks he received from the farmers, and walked back toward the road, hugging his arm around his mom's shoulder. It had been a long time since they'd shared a realistic and honest conversation.

* * *

Caleb left the next day for a meeting with a client he couldn't reschedule, as he was close to securing work for the next six months for his entire office. While boarding the plane, he texted Teddy.

Caleb: *Ethan and I are planning a fishing trip. Interested?*

Teddy: *When?*

Caleb: *This summer.*

Teddy: *I'll think about it.*

Caleb: *Come on. Dad's gone. We can't drift apart.*

Teddy: *I know he's gone. I have the firm to protect. Remember?*

Caleb: *Isn't Matt helping?*

Teddy: *Not his job.*

Caleb: *We should all go.*

Teddy: *I told you I'd consider it.*

Caleb: *It's important. Ethan wants you to go.*

Teddy: *And you don't?*

Caleb: *I didn't say that. Just meant all five of us need to go.*

Teddy: *I'm busy. Another time.*

Caleb: *You can't ignore us.*

Teddy: *And you're one to talk? Haven't you been gone for a decade?*

Caleb: *That's not fair.*

Teddy: *Oh, poor Caleb says it's not fair. Try sticking around to support the family before bitching.*

Caleb: *Why are you starting something with me?*

Teddy: *I'm tired of you getting away with leaving reality for the rest of us to deal with.*

Caleb: *Fine. Don't go. I don't care.*

Teddy: *Go crawl back in your security blanket, baby brother.*

As Caleb idled in his seat aboard the puddle-jumper, he turned his phone off and let his mind drift to a conversation with his father years earlier...

"*Are you sure you cannot stay another few days, Caleb? Your grand-mother just passed away, and your mother could use your shoulders to lean on now that the funeral is over,*" Ben said.

"*I wish I could, Dad. I loved Grandma a lot, and I wish I could stay longer, but I've got a complex deal brewing back home, and no one else can handle it,*" Caleb said.

"*Ah, you don't understand the problem. You disappeared. Always have something else going on. You're alone up in Maine. No one to help you with the business. No special someone at home to keep you warm at night. I worry about you, son.*"

"*I'm fine, Dad. Really... I'm super busy. I don't have time for a social life or a wife.*"

"*I never said wife. I meant someone you could lean on, someone to encourage a smile after a long day of work. We all need love in our lives.*"

"*I should go, Dad.*"

"*I know when my son has no more use for his meddling father... just know this, Caleb... I love you no matter what happens. You'll always be my strong, intelligent, bold, and brave son. Whatever you choose.*"

The pilot's voice on the speaker startled Caleb from his memory, and he pulled his seat back into the upright position realizing the plane neared the landing strip.

What were you trying to tell me, Dad? Did you know all along? Damn, I miss you.

* * *

Olivia stayed behind at Caleb's house keeping busy by tending to the garden and cooking dessert for when he arrived home. She would be leaving the next day and wanted to do something special for him to show her gratitude for spending the week with her. They'd spent a few nights talking about his father recalling the weekends camping at Lake Wokagee and the family football games in their backyard. She grew stronger even if each memory made accepting Ben's death more difficult than the last.

While Olivia sliced apples for a pie, the house phone rang. She expected a machine to answer it, but it kept ringing. On the tenth ring, she walked to the table in the hall, wiped the sugary fruit juices off her palms, and cradled the receiver to her ear. Caleb had an old-fashioned rotary-dial phone connected on the console table by the stairs. "Hello."

"Hello, is Mr. Glass available?" an excited voice said.

Olivia at once thought of Ben, raising her hand to her heart. It was the first call she'd received that produced a direct reminder of her late husband. "Um, no…"

"Neither of the two Mr. Glass are available? Caleb or Jake Glass?"

Olivia nearly dropped the phone at the question. She focused on the grandfather clock in the corner watching the second hand slowly tick by for an eternity. "I'm sorry, did you say Jake Glass?"

"Yes, Caleb's husband. I need to speak with him."

"No, Jake left. May I take a message?" Olivia's heart pounded in her chest. *Husband. Caleb is married to Jake. He never told me he was married.* Olivia momentarily forgot someone else dangled on the phone until the voice spoke again.

"Yes, please. Tell them to call Chester at the adoption agency as soon as possible. I may have great news for them."

Olivia dropped the phone receiver to the base without even acknowledging Chester's request. She stared at the clock, her heart beating in unison with its chimes pounding in full force around her.

My son is adopting a baby?

Olivia raced toward the vintage liquor cabinet in the living room and grabbed a glass from the second shelf. She lifted the bottle of scotch from the tray, her hands quivering as she clinked the rim of the bottle against the crystal snifter. Finishing off the first one with a single swallow, she poured a second, willing the slow burn to creep throughout her insides.

Why do you all keep so many secrets from me?

Chapter 11 – Zach & Olivia

Bright light cascaded across Zach's hazel eyes as he tossed to his left side summoning instant regret over not shutting the curtains when he'd arrived home. The morning sun drenched the room as Zach yawned and pushed the clingy cotton sheets away from his body. He'd only strolled in from work a few hours earlier and had barely slept given the bed no longer offered him the same comforts it once did in youth.

Whenever he'd stayed in Brandywine, he slept in his childhood bedroom on the third floor. Since Zach was the noisiest of their boys, his parents had given him the attic which meant he was the last one awake in the morning. He'd divided the space into his sleeping area, tucked into the roof peaks, leaving the rest of the room for his music, keyboards, and drums.

Stepping over last night's jeans and black tank top, he rubbed his eyes and looked toward the wall clock for the time. He reached for clothes, inhaled a tequila-and-cigarette odor, and threw them in the corner with the rest of the pile. The downside to his job, besides the late hours, was the permanent filth of ashtrays and saturated liquor bottles. He located a fresh pair of Nike running shorts and a V-neck t-shirt in his duffel bag and checked his phone.

No messages. Good, no drama today.

Anastasia sat at the kitchen table watching a *Dora the Explorer* video on her iPad. Diane and Olivia stood nearby flipping buttermilk pancakes and scrambling eggs on the griddle.

"What time did Zachary get in last night?" Olivia's lips squeezed together, her mind still processing the trip to visit Caleb.

"I'm not sure. I tucked Anastasia in around nine and fell asleep soon after. I didn't hear him get in."

"I need to talk to him about these late nights. It's not good to keep carting her back and forth between here and Brooklyn. Anastasia never knows where she's sleeping each night."

"Zach's schedule hasn't had an impact on her. She loves her time with Grandma and Auntie D," Diane cooed as she tickled Anastasia's belly.

"It's unhealthy. She's a five-year-old impressionable child who starts school this fall. She needs a routine. And a mother. Since Katerina's worthless, it's up to me to provide the maternal connections. Zachary should move back home so she can go to the Madison Academy with Melanie in September. I hope he's not planning to send her to some school in Brooklyn."

"Liv, don't be too hard on him. He's a good father." Diane plated three chocolate chip pancakes for Anastasia, poured syrup on top, and refilled her own coffee mug. "You've been ornery ever since returning from your trip to see Caleb. Were you able to convince him to move home?"

Zach walked the first set of steps and shuffled left checking if Anastasia still slept in the small room next to the library, but she did not. The cicadas buzzed in the trees beyond the house, more active this year than in the past. He laughed remembering the time he dropped hundreds of dead exoskeleton shells in Caleb's backpack one morning before they left for middle school. Unfortunately for Caleb, when he went to open his bag to put his books in the locker, he screeched and drew more attention to himself. When the bag fell to the ground, dozens of dead cicadas poured onto the tiled floors in front of half the school. His friends teased him for weeks after the incident sneaking behind him and buzzing in his ears. Caleb also earned two days' detention for disturbing the hallways, unwilling to rat out his brother for fear of what being a snitch would cause him.

Zach walked into his father's library where various law reviews and journals filled the chestnut brown shelves as well as collections of encyclopedias and many American classics. Ben also included a special section for his first and second edition mystery novels. Reading was never a passion for Zach, but knowing they were his father's favorites caused him to sample the stories every so often. As he meandered the shelves, he noticed a *Sherlock Holmes* second edition on the top shelf. It was his favorite book series prompting Zach to recall sneaking into the library to read a few pages late at night when everyone else had slept. The room was usually off limits to the boys when they were still young given the immensity and value of the collection their father had amassed. Not until years later did Zach learn to appreciate their beauty.

Curiosity over what his mother would do with the room since his father's death crossed Zach's mind. It had been a month, and she still hadn't removed a single item of his in the house. After being sufficiently nostalgic, he continued into the hallway and descended the staircase to the first floor. His pocket vibrated, prompting him to check on the annoyance. It was Sarah, Teddy's wife.

This can't be good.

Olivia lifted her head from the stove and shot her sister a sideways glance from across the room. "No, Caleb's not going to come home. I don't want to talk about it."

"You don't want to talk about a lot these days, Liv." Diane pressed her sister attempting to get her to crack and to refrain from being so stubborn.

Ignoring Diane's comments, Olivia plated the eggs and set the dishes on the breakfast nook. "How are your pancakes, Anastasia?"

Anastasia grinned. "Yummmy."

"Please put away the iPad while you have breakfast, sweetheart." Olivia directed her granddaughter who pressed the pause button and put it on the bench to her right.

Diane swallowed a swig of coffee, thanked her sister for the eggs, and ate her meal. Olivia excused herself indicating she planned to wake Zachary.

Zach pressed accept on the keypad. "Sarah, haven't I already done enough for you? To what do I owe this... pleasure?"

"You're ever the charmer, Zach. I reckon I owed you news."

Zach considered his response. He'd recently been caught off guard by Sarah and found himself in the middle of quite a situation. "You certainly owe me something, but we agreed never to talk about it again."

"We did agree, hence why I'm calling you. Don't fly off the handle now. I will never mention it again after today."

"Fine. What do you want, Sarah?"

"It worked. I'm pregnant."

Zach choked on his own spit and repeated "You're pregnant?" As he balanced his feet against the cold floor, Zach saw his mother standing nearby.

Shit.

Olivia rushed back to the kitchen tripping over her own feet at the speed she'd undertaken. A dangerous curiosity lurked in her mind over whom Zachary had been speaking with, but she also knew it was uncouth to eavesdrop. She thought he'd said someone was pregnant, growing angry that he'd knocked up another girl.

"Is Zach awake?" Diane wiped the syrup dripping from Anastasia's fingers.

"Yes, he's on the phone in the hall. I'm going to fix him eggs." Olivia contemplated the mess he'd gotten himself into this time.

Diane stood and put the plates in the dishwasher. "I'm going to see Margaret and the girls. I'll call you later about lunch. Be kind to Zach, Liv."

Diane left the kitchen as Zach wandered in. She raised her eyes and cocked her head in Olivia's direction, then pointed her thumb toward the ground before heading up the stairs.

Zach took it as a warning for him to beware of his on-edge mother behind the doorway. The family had developed a code for interpreting Olivia's passive-aggressive behavior.

"Good morning," he grunted. "Where's the coffee?"

"Did you have a rough night, Zachary?"

Zach crossed the tiled floor, kissed his daughter's forehead, and slumped in the chair across from her. "No. Please don't start with me this early."

Olivia fussed with her right earring, a diamond hoop Ben had given her for her birthday several years ago. Her face flushed. "Zachary, I'm not starting trouble with you, but we do need to talk. That's why you agreed to stay here for a few days, right? Anastasia turns six years old tomorrow and starts school in two months. You can't keep bringing her back and forth between here and Brooklyn. How are you planning to give her more stability when you don't come home until six in the morning?" She placed a hand on his shoulder. "I'm not trying to be difficult. I want to help."

Zach swallowed the pile of eggs he'd put in his mouth. He considered for a moment blasting her with anger over her constant judgment, recalling Tressa's advice to tell his mother what was going on. When Anastasia giggled, he began gesticulating his arms and hands in an erratic beat. "Mom, I get you don't agree with how I live my life. We've talked tons of times before. What do you expect I'm doing when I leave here?"

"I hope you're not still on drugs. Are you still on drugs?"

"No. I haven't been on drugs for two years. I'm working."

"What kind of job could you perform at three in the morning?"

"Tell me, Mom. Tell me one passion I've loved my whole life that maybe I might want to turn into a career?" His ears flushed as his voice grew enraged.

"Since you dropped out of college and decided not to get your law degree?" Olivia threw a white cast-iron frying pan into the dishwasher. The loud noise clamored against the kitchen walls.

"Why is it always so difficult for us to have a decent conversation?" His fist pounded the table as he rested his head against its cool surface.

Neither Olivia nor Zach noticed Anastasia rising from the bench. She stood in her pink and white *Paw Patrol* pajamas next to her father and tugged on his arm. "Daddy, don't yell at Grandma. She made me pancakes."

Zach and Olivia looked at one another and back at Anastasia. Zach stood, picked up his daughter, and swung her in his arms. "I'm sorry, baby. Grandma and I are only talking. Everything's okay. We're not yelling. Why don't you take Dora into the den and sit on the couch? I'll be inside in a minute."

Anastasia hugged him and walked over to Olivia. "Grandma, don't be mad at Daddy. He misses Grandpa, too." She pushed open the swinging door and left the kitchen.

Fighting with his mother, Anastasia's precocious insights, and the news Sarah had conceived as a result of their impromptu connection, finally defeated Zach. He couldn't hold back the frustration, his eyes widely spread ready to leap from their sockets, and the pressure cranking up his throat, ready to spew venom at anyone challenging him. *Go ahead Mom, just start in on me again...*

Olivia unfolded her arms and grabbed ahold of her son. "Zachary, she's such a smart little girl. Maybe I'm being too hard on you."

Zach embraced his mother, worrying he'd break her ribs from his grip, and instantly recalled the days when they were much closer. Sometimes she knew when he had enough. With his face buried against her shoulders, and his body relaxing, he mumbled, "Mom, I've screwed up really big this time. Sarah's pregnant, and it's my kid."

* * *

Zach took a nap after telling his mother what had happened with Sarah. While asleep, he dreamed of a conversation he had with his father the day Anastasia was born...

"*Congratulations, son. You've joined the ranks of fatherhood. We're a small group in this family so far... just Matt, you, and me. And he only beat you by a few weeks,*" Ben said.

"*Thanks, pops. I'm a bit freaked out. I don't know how to raise a baby, especially when Katerina's already talking about getting her first crystal fix,*" Zach said.

"*Are you sure she stayed sober the whole time she was pregnant?*"

"*Yeah, we had a deal. She promised to stay clean as long as I agreed to pay for everything. I was a hawk watching its prey to ensure she didn't drink a drop. It took every cent I had.*"

"*You know I'll give you money if you need it, but we've talked about that before. You want to earn your own money and won't accept a penny from me. I understand. Just know it exists whenever you want it.*"

"*Thanks for understanding and respecting my wishes. I guess that's what being a dad means, huh?*"

"*Being a father is a difficult thing, Zach. It takes time to figure out what kind of dad you want to be. I wasn't a respectable father to Teddy those first few years. I learned as each day went by, and eventually, it finally dawned on me. I just had to love you boys and be a good role model. The rest will soon fall into place.*"

"*But I've got a daughter. I can't teach her how to be man. What do I know about raising girls?*"

"*Maybe your mother can help. You need to focus on fixing that relationship, and the one with your daughter will come naturally. I believe in you, son.*"

"*Pops... I know you want Mom and me to sort shit out, but she's on my case too much, especially since I need to focus on Anastasia.*"

Zach's body jumped out of his restless slumber when his daughter yelled his name from the other room. He slipped out of bed, sweat pouring off his face and neck and checked on her. Hunger drove her discomfort and she wanted a snack. After getting her settled, he called Caleb.

"What's up, Zach? I'm getting off a plane to meet with a client. Everything okay?" Caleb inquired.

"I told Mom I slept with Sarah."

"I still don't understand why you did that to Teddy."

"Well... it's complicated. I'll tell you when you come back to visit."

"That may be a while. Mom was just here."

"How did it go?" Zach said.

"She kind of walked in on me and someone. It didn't go so well."

"It's time you stopped hiding this secret. All's fair, I told you mine. What's his name?"

Caleb choked. "What did you say?"

"You heard me, Ass-Munch. Ha, I still laugh over that day. You didn't realize I knew you were gay?"

"Ummm... No, I mean... How did you know?" Caleb rested against the airport counter as he exited the ramp. Now two people in his family knew he was gay.

"Damn this family and our secrets. Do you want the long answer or the short answer?"

"Short answer for now. I've got a client waiting for me."

"Tuesday evenings are gay night at The Atlantis Lair, the club where I DJ. I often need to politely decline the male guests when they flirt with me. After the first few times, it wasn't clear why they reminded me of you. It was fucking weird. Every single time, something just made me picture you. Eventually, it hit me. Caleb's also gay."

Caleb relaxed learning someone finally knew, but it was too much for him to handle all at once. "I need to go. Quickly... what was the long answer?"

"You used to call out Ryan Phillippe's name in your sleep. As well as talk about his ass. A lot. Like every night when you were a teenager."

"No. You're messing with me."

"Nope. I didn't have the heart to burst your bubble, Cabbie. I figured you'd tell me when you were ready. That's when I moved into the attic bedroom. So, you could do your own thing without me knowing. I thought it was just a creepy phase. I mean, seriously, you were obsessed."

"Did anyone else know?"

"Not a chance. You're pretty good at keeping quiet. I'm just pretty good at figuring it out. That's why I made up shit about Salma Hayek's boobs, so Teddy and Matt would leave you alone. And Caleb... it's totally cool. We're all on the Kinsey scale somewhere. Personally, I seem to have a thing for..."

"Stop. That's enough."

"You don't want to hear my fetishes?"

"No. But, Zach, I'm glad you're cool with it. Listen, I wanna come hear you DJ one night."

* * *

Zach stayed with his mother for another three days planning a festive get-together for Anastasia at the local amusement park. Several friends from her pre-K class came with their parents to glide on the swings, play in the arcade, and fly in the rotating car and spider rides. Olivia grew more confident in how her son parented his daughter watching his every move at the park to monitor his learning and growth. She wished Ben were with her to see their son following in his father's footsteps, but her eyes grew unfocused and unable to weep anymore.

Zach also brought his mother up to speed on his ex-girlfriend's release from the state rehab facility and her threats to sue for custody of Anastasia. He and Katerina had never arranged any legal agreement stating Zach gained full custody. She'd verbally relinquished control a few years ago, forced to let Zach raise their daughter after being remanded to the rehab facility as part of a court decision for selling crystal meth to teenagers. Since Katerina served her time, had been released on good behavior according to her counselors and sponsor, and received a clean bill of health, she wanted to slither back into her daughter's life. Katerina didn't seek full custody but had requested a shared agreement without a requirement for supervision on her visits with Anastasia.

Later that evening, Olivia poured a cup of green tea for each of them as they sat in the study on the comfortable sofa near the fireplace. She suggested calling his brother, who could provide a recommendation for the right lawyer on Zachary's case.

"Mom, I can't ask Teddy to fix my problems, knowing the whole time I slept with his wife," Zach pleaded. "Do you think that highly of me?"

"Zachary, you may have explained why you and Sarah slept together, and I suppose I can even understand it on some level, but I don't know how we're going to get past it as a family. Couldn't you have donated your... you know... not actually sleep with her? You have to tell Theodore what you and Sarah have done. You can't let him raise a child he doesn't know belongs to you."

Olivia rustled her fingers together, determined not to let history repeat itself. She couldn't tell Zachary why it was so important until Mr. Rattenbury found Rowena Hector. *Is this going to be a repeat of Ben's actions all those years ago? Maybe you and Theodore aren't even brothers.*

"I know, Mom. I made a bad decision. I thought it was the right thing to do at the time. I had been eating dinner with them when Teddy was called away to meet with a client. We'd been drinking, and Sarah told me what happened with their failed attempts at getting pregnant. Yadda yadda yadda... clock ticking... blah blah blah... we joked about having so many brothers in this family, was it even a difference if one of Teddy's brothers got her pregnant instead of her husband. I suggested she ask Caleb, since he lived so far away and didn't have any children. We were being funny. It's so messed up."

Olivia choked on her tea foraging for a proper response. "No, it wouldn't have happened with Caleb."

"It was a joke at first, but we kept drinking, and one thing led to another, and it just happened. We regretted it instantly and agreed never to speak about it again."

"And it was only the one time?" said Olivia.

"Yes, once before the funeral. That's why I was a little awkward for a few days. I didn't know how to react to her. I mean, come on, Mom. Who sleeps with their brother's wife? Do you see why I can't ask Teddy?"

"I do, but we can't let Katerina push you around. I'll talk to Theodore when I visit him after you return to Brooklyn. I'll ask him to find the right lawyer." Olivia assured her son she knew how to solve his problem.

"You can't tell Sarah what I've told you. This has to stay between us, Mom," Zach begged. "We've had enough pain with Dad's death and my on-going battles with Katerina. Don't drag everyone else into this, too."

Olivia closed her eyes and concentrated on conjuring better memories. Three weeks ago, her life was a shade away from normal, at least until the villainous hand of fate intervened. She became a widow. Her sister requested a divorce. She had a gay son. Another slept with his brother's wife.

If they really are brothers. How did I not recognize any of this happening around me, Ben?

Chapter 12 – Teddy & Olivia

Teddy and Sarah lived in Northeastern Connecticut in an historic town with less than five thousand residents, closer to the Rhode Island border. Sarah had wanted a home that evoked Southern charm, echoing the types of places she'd grown up around in the South. A few weeks after they'd become engaged, they soon purchased a large colonial home recently remodeled by the previous owners.

Despite her son and his wife living less than twenty miles away from the family home, Olivia wanted to stay over at Theodore's during the week she spent time with him. It was useless to go back and forth when they needed to plan the upcoming family Fourth of July barbecue. Teddy tried to convince his mother they should cancel the festivities this year given Ben had just passed away. Olivia conceded to having the party at Theodore's home and inviting only the boys and their families rather than the whole extended family.

Olivia arrived on Sunday morning and remained parked outside her son's home preparing herself for an awkward visit by practicing her yoga breathing. Although Zachary had continued to plead with her to keep his secret, Olivia needed to compel Sarah to confess to Theodore what she'd done. Given she arrived a few minutes early, Olivia pulled a compact from her handbag and powdered her flushed cheeks. With an untenable ache in her stomach, she expelled warm air from her mouth and told Victor to wait a few more minutes until she was ready for her son. She smoothed the silk scarf against her chest, popped the door handle, and pushed out of the car while dialing Theodore. She wasn't going to surprise another son by arriving early and needed to ensure fate wouldn't revel in a second round of torture.

Sarah sat at the circular kitchen table, her feet and legs woven and crossed underneath her, listing groceries for the upcoming party. Teddy walked through the mudroom door announcing he'd finished scraping and cleaning the barbecue. "It looks brand new, and it seems to me it will be ready to use for the party on Tuesday." After dragging the chair back a few feet from the table, Teddy interlocked his fingers, flipped over his hands, and cracked several knuckles.

Sarah frowned pulling back her blunt-cut hair and enclosing it with a clip on the side above her right ear. "You know that noise annoys me. Please stop carrying on. Your momma should be here any minute. I have sliced ham and salads to snack on, and I'm brewing sun tea on the porch."

Teddy cracked one remaining knuckle that hadn't yet released and stood from his chair, jaw locked in place. "Done now."

"How will the conversation about the law firm go?" Sarah's nose wrinkled with annoyance over his deepening ticks.

Sarah and Teddy had spent the week finishing their discussion on what to do about Ben's law practice. After weighing the pros and cons, they decided it was time to execute a change in their lives. With the money they would inherit from Ben, they could afford for Teddy to stop working. He could begin to focus on his interest in painting. Sarah even argued they'd have additional money once they'd sold the practice to the other partners, which brought Teddy closer to agreement.

The final pro putting their decision in favor of selling the practice came when Sarah told Teddy she was pregnant. A few weeks earlier, Teddy had woken up to a strange note on his bedroom night table. He'd later learned all the details, including how she'd come home early from a hospital shift and tip-toed into their house while Teddy slept. She framed the results and wrapped them in the morning's paper, knowing the first thing Teddy did when he awoke was to read the daily news while sitting in his favorite chair on their back porch. She had poured his coffee, set a few slices of buttered toast on a plate, and arranged the gift so it sat on the table near his regular chair. The note had told him to find a surprise waiting for him on the porch. He hadn't been aware she was hiding behind the door watching him look around. A scowl overtook his face, initially annoyed at her games, until he noticed what she'd left on the table.

Teddy opened the newspaper and caught the heavy silver picture frame falling toward his lap. When he saw the stick read *pregnant*, he jumped from the chair, spilled his toast onto the floor, and turned around to find Sarah standing behind him with a glowing smile. His annoyance dissipated replaced by a cautious and optimistic grin.

As he sat waiting for his mother to arrive, Teddy nodded at his wife. "It seems to me she won't be happy with my plan to sell the practice, but I'm hoping that'll offset when we tell her to expect another grandchild." A few minutes later, the phone rang. "Speak of the devil…"

* * *

A few hours later, Teddy paced the carpeted living room floor, darting back and forth in an unknown circular path, absorbing several shocks from the static electricity beneath his feet. His mother went to unpack in the bedroom, and Sarah left to purchase groceries at Costco. Teddy planned to talk about the law practice that afternoon. He preferred not to have the discussion with his mother, but the sooner he started it, the sooner she would get over it. It wouldn't help to hold back until the end of her trip, plus the excitement growing inside him over the baby ached to burst from his skin.

Teddy had intentionally planned to leave out the conversation he had with his brother, Matt, the prior week, where he learned the firm barely held financial water the last year. He planned to go through the books with the outside accounting firm after the holiday once the second quarter closed. If they had potential losses, he'd deal with it at that time and not beforehand.

Teddy recalled Matt asking him if it were possible to expedite releasing their father's inheritance. It was odd Matt pushed for the process to happen so quickly, but Teddy also knew Matt needed to keep his life tidy and orderly, bordering in obsessive behaviors. He'd promised to call Mr. Rattenbury this week but hadn't been able to do so with everything going on. He located the cordless phone extension and dialed the lawyer, who answered on the second ring.

As he sat on the ottoman, another shock zapped Teddy while he rubbed his foot across the carpeted floor. He enjoyed the sensation as it jolted him back into power. "Mr. Rattenbury, it's Teddy Glass. I don't intend to trouble you on a Sunday, but I was curious as to the status of my father's estate."

"Good afternoon, Mr. Glass. It's no trouble at all. I spoke with your brother a little while ago."

"My brother. Which one?" Teddy's eyebrows arched high.

"Matthew. He called with the same question this morning."

Teddy's mind clouded over, annoyed he misunderstood his brother earlier in the week over who would call the lawyer. "I appreciate you taking both of our calls. I'm sure it would be easier for me to call him, but since I have you on the phone, it would seem to me you should tell me now."

"There is no need to call him. I can repeat the conversation. I have a few more papers to file and then Matthew can work with the bank to set up the individual accounts. I expect it should be ready in four weeks. I will need your mother's signature on a few forms."

"She's here with me, I'll let her know. Is that all, Mr. Rattenbury?" Teddy tried to hang up, but Ira interrupted.

"Matthew was a bit... how shall I say... eager... to expedite these proceedings. I do hope he understands it takes time to obtain a death certificate, probate the will through the state, and certify the transactions. I'm working as quickly as I possibly can."

Teddy's concern grew deeper given Matt's comments about the practice having a sub-par financial year and his urgency in closing on the estate. He thanked Ira and disconnected the phone.

Once Sarah arrived home, Teddy unloaded the packages.

Soon after, his mother entered the kitchen. "I'm settled. The room looks lovely. Did you purchase a new quilt for the bed? I don't remember the magnolia pattern." Olivia's disinterested voice filled the air.

Sarah smiled. "No, it was my momma's. I found it in the closet the other day when I was fixin' to clean out the spare bedroom and thought it would look nice."

Olivia attempted to hide her frustrations with her daughter-in-law. She'd never been close with Sarah and thought the woman was beneath Teddy. She was a nice girl, a little too direct and a bit too boring. "It's such a pretty color, and I've always said it's good to have a treasure handed down from older generations."

"Yes, I agree, Olivia. Would you care to sit in the living room? Teddy and I have a few items we ought to talk about with you."

"I have an issue I ought to talk to you and Theodore about as well." *You little tramp.*

Teddy led the way to the living room where he and Sarah sat on a mustard-colored leather sofa.

Olivia chose the single chair sitting across from them. She sat with her back held high, shoulders arched, and head poised to command. "Perhaps I will start?"

"It would seem to me I should to go first. I've made a decision about the practice," said Teddy.

Olivia waited, her feet tapping the carpet as she swallowed several times. *Oh, they don't want to tell me Sarah's pregnant yet.*

"Dad has built a respected, well-organized, highly-praised and remarkable practice. He and his partners have spent significant time mentoring me these last few months on the ins and outs of its administration. I enjoyed spending time with Dad each day watching how brilliantly he managed his career. When I consider everything that he's accomplished and all he's done for our family, I couldn't be prouder to be his son."

Sarah's lips curled upward, and she rested one hand on her belly, even though the fetus was only a tiny speck growing inside her. She'd pulled a blanket around her, spread her arms out around her on the sofa, immersing herself the comforting nest she'd built.

Olivia loved hearing about Ben's strengths and admirable character. Her blue eyes danced with excitement at her son's words. She ignored the hint of concern beginning to grow over his tone and word choice.

Teddy paused, relaxing his clenched jaw. "Dad taught me many skills over the years, but he taught me the greatest lesson in his death." Perspiration gathered under his arms and in the creases of his elbows. He clasped his hands, his knuckles a translucent white.

Her son's every word, blink, and breath impacted Olivia. Despite his profuse sweating, she hadn't seen this type of confidence from him in a long time. As much as she rooted for him to be his own man, she feared what he was about to tell her. "Your father was a good man, Theodore. His death taught us all a valuable lesson." She looked away, chastising herself for letting her emotions dominate her, inconsolable over how much she missed Ben.

Sarah leaned in closer to her husband and gave him a light peck on the cheek. Rubbing his arm, hovering near him, she focused her eyes across the room at Olivia. "I didn't know Ben as well as you both did, but I respected him these last few years. I reckon he was proud of Teddy for all of his accomplishments."

Olivia's stare plunged deep into her daughter-in-law's eyes. Sarah was never after the family money. It was apparent Sarah loved Theodore, though obviously not as much as Olivia loved him. She couldn't understand how Sarah could sleep with Zachary and hurt Theodore in such a sickening way. Olivia needed time alone with Sarah to comprehend what had been going through her daughter-in-law's mind when she dragged Zachary into the mix.

Teddy grabbed his wife's hand and dropped the bombshell. "I've decided to sell the law practice." His shoulders relaxed as the words left his mouth.

Olivia struggled to find words as she grasped the arm of the chair, her right thumbnail leaving a permanent indentation in the leather. Losing Ben proved hard enough, but to accept their son would choose to sell off his father's legacy. She barely mumbled a "why?" and sunk into the back of the chair, sensing defeat creep throughout her nervous system.

Sarah's eyes darted away from Olivia and focused on a few loose carpet threads. She held onto Teddy's hand with a few steady pulsing grips. "Go ahead."

"I want to paint. I need a break. And it would seem to me I should choose my own destiny." Teddy developed a fully-risen self-assurance in his voice replacing his previously demanding tone with a careful, but determined, poise.

Olivia excused herself after Teddy's revelation claiming to have a migraine. She stumbled against the bookshelf and knocked a delicate glass swan figurine off the shelf as she tried to leave. She never even noticed it fall before shutting the door to her room.

"After that display, I couldn't tell her about the baby. It would send her over the edge," Teddy said.

"It was the easiest excuse your mother could conjure rather than stay and have a real discussion about the future. She's incapable of caring about others." Sarah's voice was full of angst as she moved to the floor and stretched her legs.

"You don't have to be mean."

"That's the truth. It ain't mean. I'm proud of you for finally telling your mother what you want to do. It's long overdue." She moved to a squatting position, balanced on one leg, and rotated her arms in giant circles about her sides. Exercising calmed her.

"I suppose." Teddy's jaw shifted as he looked down the hall at the room where his mother slept.

They ordered dinner, but Olivia stayed in her bedroom and only came out for a glass of water. When Teddy attempted to have a conversation, she held her head and said it needed to wait until her migraine disappeared.

* * *

On the morning of July 4th, Teddy drove to the store to buy propane for the barbecue. While out at the store, Matt texted mentioning he couldn't attend the party as two of his daughters ran a fever. Teddy was at first annoyed because he wanted to ask his brother why he kept pestering Ira Rattenbury, but then felt at ease, realizing it would give him more time to talk with his mother about the baby and selling the law firm, especially before he had to tell his brother he may soon be out of job. While driving home from the gas station, Teddy thought back to a conversation with his father right after graduating from college...

"My first-born entering law school. I'm proud of you," Ben said.

"Yes, I'm following in your footsteps, as you've always planned, Dad," said Teddy.

"Someday you'll take over the family practice, and hopefully your brothers will be alongside supporting you to the top. I know you're ready to handle it all, but you need to do something about your attitude, Teddy. You're always angry. You never relax, and you need to learn how to build an intimate connection with someone."

"That's not important to me right now. I want to get through law school and get on with my life."

"But you need friends to guide you along the way. You need to empathize with your clients to earn their trust."

"Hey, Dad... do you ever get a break from the office? You seem pretty involved in every decision. Don't you get bored or tired?"

"Certainly, but you only get to the top by working hard. I knew ever since I was a young kid I wanted to have my own law practice. I never wanted to work for someone else being subjected to their every whim and fancy. You'll desire the same once you observe the intricacies of the legal system working by my side. Once you're ready, I'll retire and pursue my passions, and so will you when you have children in the future."

"Did you ever consider working in something other than law? Something more creative?"

"No. Law has always been my passion, Teddy. Just like you."

The driver of the car behind Teddy beeped its horn jarring Teddy back to reality. "Wait a damn minute, I'm moving." Teddy crunched together his fingers as he turned the steering wheel with brutal force, causing the tires to screech. *Not like me, Dad... not like me...*

While Teddy was out, Sarah set up the furniture on the back lawn and hung a few decorations.

Olivia surprised Sarah when she walked toward the house to get plates and napkins. Dressed in sassy blue dress pants, a red and white chiffon dress shirt, and an American flag silk scarf tied around her neck, Olivia blocked Sarah's entrance. "Did you encourage him to sell Ben's practice?"

The scowl on Olivia's face, looking as though she had stepped out of a catalog for bitchy mothers-in-law ready to pounce on their victims, irritated Sarah. "Are you feeling better, Olivia?"

"Please answer the question, Sarah. I want to know if this was my son's idea or if you pushed him into it." Olivia kept her arm on the doorframe to ensure Sarah couldn't get by.

Sarah backed away a few steps and motioned to Olivia to sit on the porch chairs. "I know you don't care for me as much as the day is long, and you never thought I was good enough for your Theodore or for your family. What I don't know... is why." Sarah stood with arms set on her side as she rattled off each complaint—an eagle spreading its wings as wide as possible, swooping down on its prey. "What have I ever done to you besides love your son and want the best for him? Is this because I'm not a good ole' Northern girl? Or because I'm older than him?"

Olivia listened. The grimace receded as she sat on the wicker chair, but her eyes blazed harder on Sarah. "Don't be silly. Keep talking... quite a little rant you've started."

Sarah exploded. "For the last six years, you've tolerated me, acting perfectly civil when we're together. You've never said a bad word to me, but your anger seethes beneath the surface, infuriated as you suffer through Teddy's choice to marry me. I don't understand it. I love him. He loves me. We make each other happy. I reckon I'm the one who's helping him realize there's more to life than working eighty hours a week. I've given him hope for a different future. One where he has a chance at being happy and enjoying life. Don't you want that for your son? Or do you want him to turn into his father and drop dead from all the stress you've put on him."

Olivia stared at her daughter-in-law as bullets shot from her eyes with no chance of missing the intended target.

Sarah lost all her breath upon finishing the release of all the pressure building up inside. Even a steam pipe blows the cover off a manhole at times. The color drained from Sarah's face, stunned at her own words, not expecting them to leave her mouth. "Oh, I'm sorry, Olivia. I didn't mean to say that about Ben." She reached for her mother-in-law's hand, but rejection, as though the hand of the Satan himself had offered assistance, shot back with all-too-familiar ease.

Olivia nodded at her daughter-in-law and stood, while clapping, one hand half cupped around the other, as though she wore her good satin theatre gloves. "Quite a performance, Sarah. You should have been an actress. Have you gotten that all out of your system?" Olivia's rage amped up another notch. She knew Sarah didn't hold all blame, but her daughter-in-law had tempted Olivia with a direct bullseye to aim her fury. And her patience waned from the whirlpool forming around her, its gravity more than she could fight.

Sarah leaned back against the wall. "Is that what you really believe about me?"

Olivia shrugged one shoulder and wrinkled her nose. "I don't know anymore. Should I believe you're a doting wife as you say? Or are you a trollop who sleeps with her brother-in-law to get pregnant?" Olivia snarled, as she fought back tears forming in her eyes.

Sarah's face whitened, her eyes turned dark and beady. As her legs grew weak, she gripped the door frame. "How do you know?"

"Does it matter how I know? Isn't it enough to simply know?" The tears won cascading her face. "If you want to be part of this family and you love my son, help me understand what the devil could possess you to do such a heinous thing. Lying about a baby, dear God."

Sarah revealed to her mother-in-law all the events that had transpired the last few years. She explained how much she and Teddy wanted to have children, but so much time had passed without it happening. Sarah talked about Teddy's low sperm count and his bouts with depression over the terror of disappointing his father throughout the years. She challenged her mother-in-law over not recognizing how assuming a larger role in the law practice pushed Teddy to lose weight when he had none to lose. She highlighted his pallor and skin growing duller, the heavy bags under his eyes, and premature gray hair aging him at least another ten years. And she exposed his hidden talents and dreams to paint, noting how it was the only time Sarah had ever seen him happy and excited.

Olivia listened to Sarah's pleading, telling her daughter-in-law she found it hard to accept. "As his mother, I would have known if he had any of those wishes or problems. He's just foolishly daydreaming. All men do it." She crossed her arms and looked down the bridge of her nose at her daughter-in-law.

"I'm not sure you would know, Olivia. I reckon you don't recognize a lot of things going on right in front of you. I screwed up when I slept with Zach, but if I tell Teddy now, he will be heartbroken, and I don't know what he'll do. I didn't sleep with Zach because I was attracted to him or I wanted to cheat on Teddy. I wanted to make Teddy a father. And yes, I encouraged him to sell the practice because I reckon it's what he desires. I only want to give him what he deserves. I love him."

It took her a minute, but Olivia acknowledged Sarah had made a valid point. She opened her mouth to respond, then noticed Teddy had returned from the store and was walking up the back path to the porch.

"It seems to be looking good out here, ladies. Nice work! Unfortunately, Matt's girls are sick, so he canceled. It'll be the three of us, Aunt Diane, and Anastasia. It would seem Zach disappeared to Brooklyn, working again." He smiled as he dropped the propane tank next to the grill.

Sarah walked inside to splash cold water on her face hoping to hide the obvious impact of her mother-in-law's inquisition.

"Did I say something wrong?" replied Teddy.

Olivia walked over to Teddy and grabbed his arm, her own shaking with each word. "Theodore, you do know how proud your father was of you, don't you?"

"I suppose so. He never told me he was proud. Are you okay, mom? What's wrong with Sarah?"

"And do you really want to be a painter, Theodore?"

"Yes. It's important to me. Why are you asking these questions?"

"And you're excited about this baby with Sarah?" A mascara-stained tear trailed the slope of Olivia's left cheek.

Teddy's heart sank as his mother peeled away layers from his usually impenetrable coating. "Sarah told you about the baby?"

Olivia nodded.

Teddy's teeth shifted across one another, clicking and grinding, and his hand rested on his chest as he closed his eyes with careful ease. "She and I have been trying to conceive a baby forever. It finally happened this time."

Olivia attempted to kiss his cheek, but he pulled away and cocked his head to the side, unwilling to let her pierce the thick Teflon coating covering his body. "I'm going to check on Sarah. What did you say to her?"

"I'm proud of you, Theodore. I'm proud of my son."

Teddy peeled her grip off his body and walked into the house to find his wife.

Olivia stood, ignoring his rejection, questioning for how long she could continue to call him her son, fearing this all led to a painful and dramatic conclusion. It hadn't stopped with losing her husband, but with each visit to the sons she thought she knew so well, the stakes grew in spades. The tiny fractures surrounding her family, ones she expected fixable without even lifting a finger, were deeper crevices and dangerous fissures about to unleash huge consequences for the entire family.

When will this drama end, Ben? How dare you leave me?

Chapter 13 – Matt & Olivia

Matt and Margaret owned a three-bedroom starter house that the prior owners had converted from a bungalow. They lived a few neighborhoods away from Matt's parents but in a well-established block with a few acres of property including plenty of room to expand in the coming years. They'd paid more for the house than they wanted to at the time because living on the right side of town held a necessary prominence for Margaret.

Shortly after Olivia arrived, Margaret said, "I'm glad you had a nice time at Teddy's. Matt should be home in thirty minutes. He texted me when he left the office. You'll be sleeping in Melanie's bed, and she'll sleep on an air mattress in our room."

"I hope it's no trouble, Margaret. It was imperative I spent quality time with you and Matt this week, and I didn't want to drive back and forth each day from my house. Perhaps it would have been better if you all came to stay with me for the week." Olivia had tried that tactic once before, but Margaret fussed over packing the girls' clothes and toys as they had tons of games, books, and videos to keep them occupied during the day.

After everything that had occurred the last few weeks, Olivia anticipated a few quiet days with Matthew and his family hoping he'd provide her strength and ways to better handle the situations with Caleb, Zachary, and Theodore. Matthew was generally the most practical of her children, which assured her this trip would put everything back on a proper course.

"It's no trouble at all, Olivia. It'll be cozy and give us more time to talk about the plans Matt and I have to build an extension on the house. We're going to need more space soon." Margaret pushed away an *American Girl* coloring book and juice bottle to the side.

"May I assist with dinner?" Olivia noticed the glow shining on her daughter-in-law's face.

Matt pulled off the highway in his blue Volkswagen Jetta turning into the apartment complex behind a gas station. Billy Joel's "*We Didn't Start the Fire*" blasted on the radio, and Matt crooned the chorus each time it came on. After arriving in the lot, he parked in the back corner, pulling out his phone to send a text. While typing, a relentless knock persisted at the window.

He jumped back in his seat and noticed a young kid with an eyebrow piercing and skull cap leaning against the car next to him. The kid signaled for him to roll down the window.

Matt hesitated at first, then pressed the button and stopped the window after it left a six-inch gap.

"You Matt?" The kid's enlarged pupils darted back and forth.

Matt nodded, tapping his foot against the center console. "Yup." As he looked the kid up and down, two key facts hit him. One, the kid was just a teenager. Two, he had a long piece of metal strapped to his forearm near where his fingers grasped the loop in his jeans. Matt contemplated pulling away faster than his favorite pitcher's speedball. *What the hell am I doing?*

Sensing Matt's glare and tension, the kid shifted his weight and reached in his other pocket ensuring Matt saw the knife he'd been carrying. It wasn't just a metal strap. "I don't got all day, man. You bring the money?"

Matt grabbed the bills he put in the cup holder. "Yeah, right here." *Damn, I'm gonna die in this car.* "How old are you?" He bit his lower lip, chewing on a piece of skin to keep his teeth from chattering.

"Does it matter to you how old I am, dude?"

"Just curious, a bit young to do this kinda..." Matt thought back to when he was sixteen practicing football, analyzing stock reports, and playing video games.

The kid leaned forward against the Jetta staring through the window gap. "What do you do for a living, Matt?" His knuckles tapped the car door. His stare stirred Matt's fears.

Matt shifted toward the passenger seat and locked the door with his shaky fingers. "Why do you need to know?" *Don't provoke him. He's got a knife.*

The kid reached through the six-inch gap and took the money from Matt's hands without even touching the window glass or door frame.

Matt realized this was second nature to the kid. *I can take him if he starts a brawl.*

"Exactly. I don't need to know what you do for a living. And you don't need to know how old I am. Thanks for the cash, Mattster." He flipped the bottle he pulled from his pocket into the passenger seat and walked away. "Enjoy the meds, bro. You won't know what hit ya."

Matt closed his eyes and breathed out heavily. *I need to get the hell out of here.* He flung the car into reverse and sped out of the parking lot.

Margaret drained the boiling water out of the pasta into the sink, the steam fogging the window above. "I brought a few bottles of chianti. It might go nicely with dinner. Shall I pour you a glass while we wait for Matthew to get home?" Olivia set the table searching for any shift in her daughter-in-law's body language.

"No, not for me. I've had a bit of a headache all day, and red wine makes it worse. Pour yourself a glass, please. I keep the opener in the top drawer."

"Can I get you any Advil or Tylenol?"

Margaret shook her head, the golden curls bouncing off her slender neck. "I'll ride it out, thanks. Did you see the pictures I posted online today? The girls were playing with Anastasia at the park. I got one with them all on the swing set."

"No, I don't have an *Instagram* account. I've been a bit busy the last few years."

Olivia was convinced Margaret was pregnant again. No wine. No medicine. Glowing.

Margaret mixed sauce into the spaghetti and checked on the girls through the wall opening into the living room where they watched a puppet show.

Olivia sampled the wine and pressed on. "Matthew is such a perfect father to the girls. I'm confident he'd be just as good with a son. It's a bit ironic I had five boys but only have granddaughters and no grandsons so far." A vein in her temple pulsed when she said five boys, causing her to consider that Matt might be the one Ben referred to in his letter.

Margaret dropped the slotted spoon onto the stovetop and opened her mouth to reply, but Matt suddenly unlocked the door and passed through the side entrance to the kitchen. Margaret's face relaxed, displaying relief at the interruption and giving her a chance to reorient the conversation.

After kissing his wife, he looked over at his mother. "It's so good to see you both. It's been quite a day. Let me go change, and we can eat." As he walked by fiddling with his jacket pocket, his fists pulled together in a compact ball.

* * *

After several days of playing Grandma, Olivia went for a drive to give some thought to what she'd seen at Margaret and Matt's house. She was certain Margaret would be revealing a pregnancy soon enough from everything she'd seen and heard. After about an hour, Olivia stopped at the playground near the corner of their house hoping to find Margaret and the girls, as she didn't have a key with her to enter their home.

As she walked toward the playground area, Olivia noticed the girls jumping into the sandbox to play. Before she could get close enough,

Olivia discovered that Margaret was not alone. Sarah had just approached from the opposite side. Olivia stood, partially hidden by the telephone pole, listening in to their conversation.

"Thanks for meeting me. I reckon I needed to talk to someone who understood how to deal with that woman. Bless her heart," Sarah said.

Margaret hugged her. "Absolutely. I needed the break myself. *The Queen* is out for a drive. It's awful how suddenly Ben passed away, but she's worse than usual."

"Tell me about it. I'm still sore from her verbal lashings." Sarah ripped open a bag of chips. "I'm craving salt today. Have one."

"You probably cried it all out from her visit. At least yours ended. She's still with me for a few more days. I'm not sure how long I'll survive without fighting back."

"I fought back this time. I've been so quiet over the years letting her attitude go without ever pushing back. I couldn't do it this time. She attacked me over some issue between Teddy and Ben."

Olivia glanced over at the girls observing Melanie protecting her younger sisters on the swing. She'd not inherited that watchful eye from her mother. If she had, Margaret would have known Olivia stood just a few feet away. Annoyed at her daughter-in-law's words, Olivia tried to understand their perspective.

"But the girls love her. I guess she's just protecting her sons and grandkids," Margaret said.

"And we ain't worth a hill of beans? She has to cut us some slack."

"I know. Ben kept her in check all these years. I'm afraid for what's to come."

"We'll get through this together. I'm fixin' to find a way to butter her up."

"At least we have each other. Come on, let's go play with the girls. I wanna get a few pics of them all. It'll take our mind off Olivia. She's supposed to meet me at the house in a little bit."

Olivia reflected on the conversation she'd just overheard. Neither said anything too untrue, but their words were still hurtful. She'd been trying to be more open-minded, but it wasn't going to happen on her own. Everyone needed to give a little, especially Sarah who'd been the more troubling one at the moment.

* * *

A day later, Matt retrieved the drawings he'd received from the architect who had designed a first draft of the house expansion plans. He sat on the couch in the den near Olivia, fidgeting with the rubber band that held the schematics together. It snapped across the room narrowly missing his mother's face. As he unrolled them on the coffee table in front of her, Olivia noticed the architect's name in the lower right-hand corner.

"Matthew, why didn't you ask your brother to design the extension? Caleb would have done them for you. Your father would have been so proud to watch you boys work together."

Matt looked up, curious how his father would interpret his recent parking lot actions. "I don't know. Caleb's not around, and we only met with the architect once. These are preliminary based on our first conversation. I might ask Caleb to eventually review them."

"You're adding four more bedrooms?" Olivia noticed the distracted look in his eyes as he scanned the room around them. "Matthew?"

Matt's attention was stuck on his conversation with Ira Rattenbury earlier in the week, frustrated it would be close to a month before the attorney settled his father's estate. When Olivia called his name, he re-focused. "What did you say?"

Olivia noticed his brow appeared moist, and his eyes still darted back and forth. "I asked you about the bedrooms you're adding. Do you feel well, Matthew? Your complexion is a bit faint."

"I'm fine." Matt's voice raised several octaves higher as he jumped up. "Just tired. Worried about the game tonight."

Olivia paused but couldn't wait any longer. "Matthew, is Margaret pregnant again?"

Matt stopped pacing the living room and hurried toward his mother. "Did she tell you she was pregnant?" His chest squeezed all the breath from his lungs. His right hand twitched uncontrollably.

Olivia stood pushing the drawings to the side, so she could pass by the table. "Matthew, you don't look well. Let me get you water." She walked to the kitchen and filled a glass from the tap.

Matt reached in his pocket and opened the bottle. He poured out two pills and swallowed them with the glass of water his mother handed him.

"What are you taking, Matthew?" She reached for the bottle.

He retracted his hand as though it held the solution to all life's problems, and he held the only elixir left on the planet. "Nothing, something to settle my stomach. It's been a little off lately."

"Give me the bottle, Matthew."

Matt sensed his entire body tense and shake. *Could Margaret be pregnant again? We can't afford another baby right now.* His heart rate sped up a few extra beats per second. He needed to relax. Matt slipped into a trance.

Olivia took the opportunity to seize the bottle from his hands, noticing his rapid heartbeat and guiding him to the chair on her left. "You need to sit."

"Leave it, that's mine. Stop interfering." Matt's words spilled from a sharp, venomous tongue. His hands tried unsuccessfully to grab hold of his only remaining cure. At the last second, when reaching for the bottle of pills, his open palm landed on Olivia's chin, smacking her backward into the sofa. He stared at her uncertain how he'd lost all control.

"I'm so sorry, Mom. It was an accident. I didn't mean to hit you." His rough voice pitched low as he hung his head in shame. Nothing but the fervent whistle of a train barreling on its tracks with no set course echoed somewhere in the distance. It soothed Matt as his body flushed hot and cold with a debilitating force he couldn't control.

As Matt sank into the chair, his mother shrank back into the couch, cupping the side of her stinging and blotchy red face. After she caught her breath, Olivia searched the contents of the bottle. "Matthew, it's missing the prescription details. Where did you get it from?"

Matt looked at his mother and then at the floor. He had lost control. He needed to talk to someone. "I don't know his name. I bought them off Craig's List. I met some kid in a parking lot. What does it matter to you?" He covered his face with his hands and bent forward over his lap. Dizziness plagued his head, and the nausea overwhelmed his remaining grasp on reality.

Olivia sat back on the couch letting out a gasp as all energy escaped from her body. She dropped the bottle into her purse and rested a hand on her son's shoulder. "Matthew, I don't know what's going on here, but obviously you need to talk to someone. I'm here. Tell me what's going on." Olivia's voice held a rigid tone as she attempted to regain control.

* * *

Olivia spent the next few days with her son trying to understand what happened to the boy who once appeared to have a perfect life. As she talked to him, she learned perception was part of the problem. Everyone else had looked in from the outside picturing a happy couple with a beautiful family, a well-kept home, plans to expand, a challenging but rewarding job, and years of future happiness blossoming as the days passed.

No one had seen the buildup of paralyzing pressure over the last decade filling every cell of Matt's body until he became so tightly wound, the energy had nowhere to dissipate. Gaping fissures in his newly punctured body armor surfaced allowing any control he hoarded to escape his grasp. Instead of talking, he pushed the concerns deeper inside, but it only caused a ripple somewhere else. His body ticked like a furious time bomb, and no one had been tasked with defusing the sparking timer before he detonated.

She agonized at the thought of losing him, believing the same ferocity had amassed control inside of her. By the end of the week, she'd learned her son had been alternating between anti-anxiety pills and various stimulants trying to maintain a balance, so no one would know what happened. She worried about the legal ramifications given the pills he took belonged to other people, not to mention he'd bought them off the internet.

Olivia had known of Zachary's addiction to coke in the past, but Ben had handled that situation. He'd never told her the details though she knew her son was in a rehab facility for a few weeks, as the signs in the preceding months were evident. With Matthew, it was different as he didn't have a drug problem, at least it didn't appear so to her. He had an anxiety problem and used drugs to hide it. Olivia's lack of experience left her blind to handle the situation, but she assumed Ethan or Zach could offer proper advice.

* * *

Matt went for a walk reflecting on why he neglected to tell his mother about the financial issues with the law practice. He only explained he had trouble keeping up with personal expenses. While walking, his mind drifted back to the last conversation with his father about the firm's financial situation...

"Dad, got a minute? I need to chat with you about an issue before the quarterly meeting with Ms. Davis and Mr. Wittleton," Matt said.

"For you, absolutely. But only a few minutes... I'm taking Teddy with me to the Goddard luncheon to show him how to handle tough clients."

"You guys are spending a lot of time together lately. Maybe I could join you at the next one, too?

"Let me get Teddy set up to manage the firm at the end of the year, and then you and I can talk about your future, son."

"Okay. I'll wait on the sidelines a bit longer. About the meeting next week... we're gonna miss the forecast this quarter. We're down ten percent from prior year's earnings."

"Ten percent? We are pretty close. We'll make it up next quarter. Goddard will win big in this settlement."

"But next quarter's goals are even higher, Dad. We might be off our game a little this year. You've been working with Teddy more on..."

"We'll be fine, Matt. Just pull together the numbers, and I'll look at them tomorrow. Then you can take them to Teddy for his input. I need to go. I'm sure you can handle this one."

"But Dad..."

A bicycle crossing his path jolted Matt out of his memory as he stepped into the street.

I really could have used your help right now, Dad. This team needs its coach. I miss you.

* * *

Matt and Olivia finished their conversation the next day. "Mom, please don't talk to Ethan. I can fix this. I will talk to Margaret about the changes we need to make. I don't want everyone to know what's going on. It's the last thing keeping me strong enough to handle the situation. I don't want everyone to cast me as the failure. Please let me do this my way."

Olivia hadn't seen her son beg this way before. Even as a child, he accepted when his parents told him *no* to any of his requests or wishes. He rarely asked for much, but he'd never been this desperate. He'd always been a rational and level-headed man.

"Matthew, I don't know how to help you myself. Ethan will know what to do. We don't have to tell anyone else, but you can't hide this from Margaret. She needs to know what's going on. I know it in my soul she is pregnant again, but she hasn't told you yet. You're scared of losing the house, but you're planning to build an extension. You can't afford another baby, but you're paying a fortune to put the girls into the best schools. I can help you with money. I can help you with the house. I can't help you with stopping the pills and coping with anxiety. We need professionals."

* * *

Olivia arrived home in the evening with an immediate need to rest given each visit to her children delivered a powerful blow to any remaining strength she had left. She'd even doubted her skills as a mother, curious if the contents of Ben's letters served as punishment for her weaknesses and inability to recognize the deep splinters in her family's facade. A debilitating pain persisted when realizing her children's lives had fallen apart as much as her own. She flipped through tons of family photo albums searching for the moment when each son's path went off course. Some had been keeping secrets from her for years, yet she knew she held partial blame. As she flipped through the books, she noticed many of the pictures were missing uncertain if she'd lost or misplaced them.

As she lay in bed, Olivia's mind wandered despite the exhaustion lurking on the surface and deep within her body. When Ben passed away, her world turned upside down leaving her to face the future on her own. She and Ben had pondered so many plans for their future after he retired from the practice. They'd planned an elaborate vacation to Italy that autumn where they'd bask in the Tuscan sun, sail along the blue Amalfi Coast, and immerse themselves in Italian culture, renaissance, and history. Experience *La Dolce Vita,* the beauty and sweetness of life while doing nothing. Now she would be figuring it out all on her own, not to mention solving the predicament Ben had put her in with his decision to switch her child with a stranger's baby all those years ago.

Olivia had hoped that as she spent time with each of her sons she'd get a clearer picture of her future as well as figure out which one wasn't her child before the lawyer located Rowena Hector. She never expected to discover each boy veiled a secret just as Ben had. She felt confident placing her hopes in Ethan to find resolutions to the situations, especially Matthew's problem. Olivia located the phone and dialed Matthew's mobile number, desperate for assurance he'd improved since she left the day before.

"Hi, Mom." Matt stepped into the bathroom and shut the door.

"Matthew, I'm calling to check on your progress."

"Better since we talked. I'm heading back from a run. It cleared my mind." He zipped open the pouch on his windbreaker.

"Good. I know you don't want me to tell anyone, but I'm worried about you. You need to get help."

"I know, Mom. I will. I need a few days to prepare and decide how to tell Margaret. We talked a little tonight. You're right. We're having another baby. The Yankees won. Things are looking up again for me. It'll all work out." Matt turned on the cold water.

"I suppose I should say congratulations even if it doesn't comfort you with the warm and fuzzies. You'll figure it out, but you need to avoid any dependency on those pills the next few days. I'll talk to Ethan when I arrive in Boston. I'm taking the train tomorrow morning, but I won't tell him I'm asking for you. I'll tell him it's for a friend."

"I appreciate it, Mom. Listen, I need to take a shower and tuck in the girls. We'll talk on the weekend."

Matt clicked the end button on his phone and checked his reflection in the vanity mirror. A man with tired red eyes and an empty stare peered back. He opened the spare bottle he'd retrieved from the windbreaker, cupped his hand under the faucet to capture a few drops of water, and swallowed two more pills.

Just a few more days...

Chapter 14 – Ethan & Olivia

When his mom suggested she should visit him in Boston, Ethan jumped at the chance to finally have his mother meet the girl he'd wanted to propose to. On prior occasions, he was certain his mother's jaw had unhinged in preparation to swallow his sisters-in-law in one bite. Despite his mother's wavering standoffish and overly-direct attitudes, given what he'd witnessed with his brothers' wives, Ethan knew his mother's overprotective nature eclipsed every other aspect of her personality. It still left him concerned for Emma, who couldn't hurt a mouse, invoking curiosity whether she could hold her own against his mother.

Emma and Ethan finished packing their suitcase in preparation for staying at the hotel with his mother while she visited. Even though the loft's size could accommodate Olivia, between painting and searching for more furniture, staying in ill-prepared quarters wouldn't suffice for his mother's visit. Ethan's mom offered to rent adjoining rooms at The Ritz Carlton, which meant they'd have plenty of space to relax and enjoy a mini-vacation. Both were excited to stay somewhere fancy especially given their need for a break from busy schedules.

Ethan took the week off from school and kept limited rounds at the hospital, so he could spend a good part of the time with his mom. Emma split the week and planned to stay the first few days at the hotel to visit with Olivia, but she also needed to fly back home for a quick trip to Cleveland to catch up with her family before her teaching position started the next month.

"Are you ready to meet my mom, Emma?"

"Yes. I'm excited. I hope she likes me."

"She will love you as much as I do." He slid the front door open.

"Let's get out of here. I'm for sure going to relish a few days away from the smell of paint."

"You're heading straight to the hotel to check in while I meet her at the train station, right?"

"Yup."

Ethan slipped his feet into his favorite gray loafers and grabbed the keys off the gold tray Emma's parents had bought for them on their last visit. He loved meeting them and understood where Emma's purity had come from. They barely knew him but already treated him like their son. It convinced Ethan they'd be a good support system for Emma, especially if he changed his mind about proposing to her based on the news he'd received from the doctor earlier that week.

Olivia peered out the train's window as it passed through the final stop before her Boston arrival. Victor needed a few days off to check on his family, which prompted Olivia to take the train to Boston. She sipped her tea and thought about how to bring up the conversation with Ethan concerning his brother's addiction to various pills. She had little knowledge what Matthew took, but Ethan would certainly ascertain his brother's devil.

Her mobile phone chimed. She still needed learn the phone's features and hadn't gotten familiar with the different sounds. After realizing it wasn't a call, she read a text message.

> **Caleb**: *I should come home for Dad's birthday next month. Maybe we could all spend it together since this is the first year he's gone.*

Olivia knew it would be good to have him home for a few days, but she was surprised he wanted to come back so soon. Her phone's dancing little dots told her he'd written another message, admiring the ease at which she could hide behind the internet's protection, but worried her son had sensed her discomfort when it took her so long to reply. It chimed again with a harrowing persistence.

Caleb: *Perhaps it would be a good time for me to bring Jake.*

Olivia had momentarily forgotten about Jake, her son's secret husband. Her body still loitered in shock knowing he'd gotten married without telling his family. Olivia's often old-fashioned ignorance conjured awkward images and complexities over the fallout of two men getting married. It felt wrong, but she wasn't sure if it was simply her inexperience talking. The phone call from the adoption agency kept replaying in her mind. *Are they really trying to have a baby?* The phone chimed again.

Caleb: *We can stay in a hotel if it would be easier.*

Olivia looked across from her at the two men sitting together on the train seat. They were closely seated suggesting that her mind question if they were a couple. It hadn't occurred to her when she first sat on the train in Connecticut but getting Caleb's text challenged her to consider the option. *Are any two men sitting close to one another a couple? Do I need to learn gaydar? How do you tell if they're just friends? Or more? Is it different than when a man and a woman are dating? What kind of wedding did they have? How do you raise a child in that kind of household? Who makes the bed in the morning if you don't have a housekeeper? How do they get intimate? Oh, Lord. I can't think about him having sex after what I saw. Piercings on his...*

Olivia considered talking to Ethan about Caleb's news, part of her reluctance to let herself accept her new son. Ethan might have insight she hadn't considered given his background in medicine and science. She texted back.

Olivia: *Let me think about it. I'll call you tomorrow. I love you. Mom.*

With each of her sons having problems and secrets, and a few of her own, as well as she multitasked, she needed to focus on Ethan. He would find the solution for each of the disasters.

Ethan stood in the train depot a few feet away from where passengers would disembark. He'd told his mother to call his cell phone when she arrived, so he could find her. Ethan knew she was a little nervous being on her own in Boston. He flipped a coin to occupy his idle hands while waiting for her train to arrive. The last time his mother had visited Boston occurred with his dad when they attended Ethan's graduation. He wasn't ready to introduce Emma to his parents, as they had only been dating a few months, and he didn't even know if the relationship would last. Over the last year, he had become certain he'd met the woman he would marry, but he took his time to let their relationship evolve naturally, given they both still had to finish school. While he'd told his parents about Emma, and they acted enthusiastic, an actual introduction still hadn't occurred.

As the passengers fluttered about the station, Ethan's mind drifted to the last conversation with his father shortly before he died...

"Hey, Dad... I need to ask you a question," Ethan said.

"What is it, my boy? What can your father help with?" Ben said.

"I'm in love with Emma. I'm gonna ask her to marry me."

"How long have you been together with her? We haven't even met this girl."

"Two years. She's moving into the loft with me next week."

"How do you know you love her?"

"I wake up wanting to grow old with her. When I smell her perfume, I remember the comforts of home... when I was a child and felt all warm and fuzzy. She cares for and protects me... and well, you know, I want to be with her all the time. And when she's gone, something's missing. Part of me disappears, replaced by a sense of emptiness until she's back in my arms."

"It sounds like you love her. But before you propose to her, maybe your mother and I ought to meet her?"

"*I'd love that. Maybe I could bring her to your anniversary party at the end of the month? And if you and Mom love her as much as I do, maybe I'll propose to her while we're home.*"

"*Go for it, son... life is too precious not to take a few risks every now and again. You're a smart young man, and if you found the one... bring her home to meet us.*"

As the announcer called the arrival track for his mother's train, Ethan broke free from his memory while the train pulled into the platform.

I wish you could have met her, Dad. I know you'd have loved her, too.

Everything had changed after the conversation with his father. Ethan developed intense headaches, preventing any ability to concentrate sometimes culminating in dizziness and nausea. At first, he thought a merciless stress had overwhelmed his body assuming it would go away while life calmed over the summer. On the day before his father's accident, Ethan had been walking rounds at the hospital when a blinding pain in his right temple hit him. He passed out while taking a break in the hospital lounge, alone except for another medical student who quickly caught him and helped him sit. Ethan worried the hospital might force him to take a sabbatical if they learned he'd been unable to manage the workload or had any impactful medical issues. He had been tracking a tight schedule and didn't want to lose any time to meeting his goals. He'd no time for a serious illness.

Ethan's symptoms improved on the drive to Connecticut for his parents' anniversary party, but he still visited a new doctor back in Brandywine where they wouldn't connect him with being a medical student in Boston. He'd expected to learn he had developed a thyroid problem or that a constricted flow of oxygen to his brain caused the frequent dizziness—all treatable conditions. After a few trips to the surgeon and several rounds of testing, he'd learned differently.

Ethan saw his mother among a few hundred weekend travelers shuffling off the train. He met her at the end of the platform sharing a warm embrace. They headed to the hotel and met Emma in the lobby for cocktails, hoping it would ease the introduction.

Ethan knew Emma was naturally gifted at relaxing people. She was good with children and beloved by his patients at the hospital. He had brought her on weekend rounds to give his sicklier patients a chance at smiling. While he had a benevolent bedside manner, it was often Emma's sweet nature and calming stories that enabled his patients to experience a few positive moments in the last months of their otherwise difficult lives.

* * *

Ethan and Emma took Olivia on several tours of Boston during the first few days of her trip. Ethan thought his mother and girlfriend had connected but feared misinterpreting the facts until he finally overheard them talking on Emma's last morning before her flight back home to her parents. He'd been dressing in the hotel bathroom as they chatted.

"Emma, you're such a beautiful and intelligent girl. I understand why my son loves you."

"You're so sweet, Mrs. Glass. Although I miss my parents and want to see them, I wish I could stay here with you. The last few days have been so fun. I worried about meeting you this week."

"Please call me Olivia. Worried, why were you worried?"

"Well, first, I'm so sorry about Mr. Glass. I never met him, but Ethan has talked about him with such admiration and love, almost as if I had time with your husband. But I worried because I can't imagine losing a husband. Ethan and I have only been together for two years, but I, for sure, would be devastated without him, you know, since we're together. And you were married for forty years. I couldn't possibly hold myself up as you have this whole week. I give you props. You're a strong role model for us girls."

"Emma, my dear girl. My life has been difficult, especially the last few weeks. I've learned more about my family since Ben's death than I did the entire time I've known them. And not one day has passed since I lost Ben when I haven't woken or gone to sleep crying, or both. I'm learning people put up walls and nothing is ever as it appears to be. All much faster than I can handle. Sometimes it's less about getting angry over a situation when you can't change it but figuring out a way to deal with it directly. I have a few of those I'm facing right now."

"You totes made my point. Your husband died less than two months ago, and you're already learning how to grow from it. You still have so much you need to do in your life to protect your family."

"Yes, apparently I do."

While Ethan took Emma downstairs to the lobby to catch a cab for her trip to the airport, Olivia ordered room service. Ethan wanted to stay in that night which made it easier for Olivia because she could privately talk with him about Matthew's problems. She'd already decided she could trust him with Matthew's secret, especially given she couldn't solve it on her own.

Ethan arrived a few minutes later. "I'm back, Mom."

As he entered the room, she noticed his withdrawn eyes and pale skin. Olivia shivered at the invasive red lines that dominated the weakened blurry whites of his eyes. "Good. I know you were worried I may be a tad ruthless with Emma, concerned over my relationship with Sarah and Margaret. I need to relax and give everyone a chance. Emma is a delightful girl, but I have a different topic we need to discuss before dinner arrives."

Ethan walked over to his mother, throwing his arms around her neck. "I'm sick, Mom."

Olivia hugged Ethan. "Oh, I can cancel room service if you're not hungry."

"No, Mom. I'm really sick."

Olivia's motherly instinct assumed control, and she knew what he meant the second time. The hurt and pain with each prior sons' secrets combined into a single basket of horror, leaving her kicked deep in the gut and unprepared for anything else around her. She grabbed hold of her son, her brooch piercing through his white crew neck t-shirt to the skin from the force of her grip. As she pulled back, droplets of blood pooled on his chest. As a larger one formed, it separated from the fabric of his shirt, descending, and gliding to the ground through the stagnant air. Its lava eruption burned her when landing on her bare right boot, and its resounding splat penetrated her core. She had a momentary fright at the blood accepting that it isn't always thicker than water, especially if you don't share blood with that son. She desperately needed to locate Rowena Hector.

"Tell me what's happened, Ethan. Tell me what's wrong." Her voice quivered as if she'd already lost him.

But it didn't matter what he said. The same haunting dark cloud loomed around them corralling her family in a den of despair. The skin on her neck and arms bristled. Her throat parched and swelled stealing her ability to breathe. A heavy weight pushed down on her body echoing quicksand driven by an unrelenting curse. The same paralysis tortured her a few months before when she heard no response from Ben on the phone the night of their anniversary party.

Ethan replied, "I have a rapidly growing brain tumor, and the doctors give me less than three months to live."

* * *

Ethan slept for a few hours in the hotel room's queen-size bed. Olivia had no desire to climb into her own bed. Instead, she sat in the comfortable extra-wide chair across from him the entire time he dozed rising once only to answer the door when room service arrived.

When morning broke, Ethan rustled in the bed and opened his eyes. "Have you been sitting by my side the whole time, Mom?"

"You need to eat to keep up your strength. I've ordered breakfast."

"Thank you. I am a bit hungry. Did you think about my questions from last night?" He rubbed a few specks of sand from his eyes.

Ethan and his mother had spent the rest of the prior evening talking about the test results and second opinion he sought after getting the initial diagnosis. He'd met several specialists who all came to the same conclusions. He would survive until perhaps Labor Day when his body would begin to deteriorate from the condition with a rapid vengeance. They pleaded with him to focus on building his support structure and informing his friends and family what he'd learned. Only a week had passed since the final confirmation from the doctors, but he hadn't yet stopped going to school or the hospital. In their conversation the prior night, Ethan left his mother with a couple of questions before falling asleep: *Should he tell the rest of the family about his condition? Should he ask Emma to marry him? Should he end the relationship and keep the love of his life from watching him die?*

Olivia spent the whole night considering her response. And more of her own questions. *Why was such an innocent, beautiful boy going to suffer? How was she going to deal with losing a son and a husband in the same year? What if Ethan was the boy Ben had secretly switched with her dead baby? And what if this was punishment for Ben's decision?*

Ethan's skin flushed. His hair was pasted against his scalp not unlike Olivia's memories of him as a baby in her arms. The earnest smiles and wistful eyes of the boy she'd raised, healing his boo-boos, cooking chicken soup when he stayed home sick from school, and convincing him the first crush would always be the hardest, were long gone and never to return. Of everything she'd confronted in the last few months, this was by far the most painful. When she embarked on a course to spend time with each of her sons, she never expected to end up in a place of far greater devastation.

Ben made the choice to switch babies. Caleb chose to hide his true identity from his family. Theodore chose to sell the family practice. Zachary chose to sleep with Sarah. Matthew chose to take the pills and go into extreme debt. But her baby, Ethan, didn't choose to get sick. He didn't choose to die. He chose to channel his grandparents' suffering and his own pain into becoming a doctor who could heal people. Who would heal him? She closed her eyes and silently wept ensuring he couldn't see any tears, knowing her duty as his mother dictated a staunch barrier that protected her dissipating grasp on the imminent decline of the Glass family.

"If you love her, Ethan, you cannot keep it a secret. You need to give Emma the option of staying with you or leaving on her own before it gets worse. You can't play with someone else's life. Let her choose."

Chapter 15 – Olivia & Diane

"I appreciate you calling with an update, Mr. Rattenbury. As you can imagine, the last two months have been difficult since reading Ben's letter. How much longer before you expect to locate Miss Hector?" Olivia sat in her bedroom chair distracted by the rain falling outside her window steaming the panes with muggy dew. She hoped he'd unearthed more answers by now, especially since initiating her plan to reconnect with each of her boys.

"We're much closer, Mrs. Glass. I found her hospital records and her entry into the United States. I confirmed a subsequent move to Michigan, but I've yet to determine where she ultimately settled. I'm still not certain if she resides in the United States, returned to Scotland, or perhaps passed away."

Olivia fought the desire to ask him what year she arrived in Connecticut as it would reveal to her which son was destined for sharing an unforgiving shellshock with her. She'd held firm by hiding the second letter to avoid any attempts at prematurely opening it. Having the answers that you seek at your fingertips, but a deep-rooted inertia holding you from appeasing that demanding curiosity, took its toll on her body. Her face had transformed into Diane's the last few weeks—at least two more fine lines around her lips appeared each time she looked in the mirror.

"I understand, Mr. Rattenbury. How much longer do you anticipate? My husband's seventieth birthday would have been in a few weeks, and I want to tell my sons about this mess he's left us in."

"I can't promise, but two more weeks should suffice while I determine Miss Hector's current status." Ira concluded their conversation.

* * *

After completing fifty laps in the pool the following morning, Olivia dried her body, poured a glass of iced tea, and sat in the lounge chair on the deck realizing the summer heat had finally settled in the Northeast. Her mind drifted to happier moments with Ben at the opera. He had known she enjoyed their special moments together where they could forget work, let the children enjoy an evening with their grandparents, and treasure a few minutes reminiscing about their past. Ben chose different seats each year to give them a new view, a new experience, and a new hope. It was his way of showing her each successive season was also a beginning for them. Over the years, his imagination was the quality she most valued in him, followed closely by the genuine connection he shared with her whether it was the gifts he chose, the way he made love, the compliments he bestowed upon her, or in how he adored his family.

Diane stepped onto the pool deck. "Ah, there you are, Liv. I didn't expect you to find you lying out in the sun." As she stepped closer and out of the glare from the sun, Diane saw her sister's strange expression.

"Liv, what's going on?" Diane sat on the chair next to her. "You've been to all the boys and told me practically nothing about Ben's letters. From the beginning, please. Let's have girl-talk like we did when we were children." She poked her sister's ribs, needling her more than necessary.

"They're all a mess. And it's my fault."

Diane's face held a puzzled expression. "Hmmm… talk to me."

Olivia painfully explained everything she'd learned on her visits to her sons, ending with the final conversation with her youngest. "Ethan is dying from a colossal tumor that's about to devour his entire brain." Olivia tried to stifle a burgeoning chuckle, but it rippled out, fixated on pushing her sanity one step further away. "The Glass family has become a caricature of who we once were."

Diane's mind processed the news Olivia delivered, beaten and burdened with each blow. Olivia never joked about anything. No matter what happened. "Holy Mary, Mother of God, I don't know what to say. Is that everything?" Her voice wavered, high and low pitches each trying to steal the spotlight from the other, neither quite adept at success.

"You mean besides Ben dying and learning one of my sons isn't really my son? I suppose that's enough for the summer." Her hand covered her lips to hold back the hysterical emotions that had begun percolating near the surface. She curled into a tight ball rocking back and forth on the lounge chair unable to stop herself from shaking. She knew she'd lost the fight when Diane refused to back down.

"You're actin' crazy, Liv. Are you about to have a stroke?"

"No, it's not a stroke. I'm not okay, but what else could go wrong? Does God exist? Is he laughing at me? What else could go wrong in my life?"

Olivia screamed at the top of her lungs, long and piercing, scattering a few birds out of the trees above them.

Diane covered her ears as she rushed over to her sister. She at first went to cradle her and provide comfort, but a wave of energy consumed Diane, and she instead shoved Olivia into the pool. Diane's hands trembled as she watched what she'd done, releasing the pressure from a seventy-year-old radiator valve long overdue. A gasping hiss rose above the pool's gentle waves.

As she sunk to the pool floor, Olivia found relief forming within her body from finally telling someone else what had transpired. Kicking her feet with the swiftness of a school of fish escaping a shark, she shot to the surface and swam to the edge for safety.

"Was that necessary?"

"I'm sorry, Liv. I... I... thought it would help. You were so intense." Diane's eyes shined as though she suddenly realized everything Olivia had spewed. "Did you say Ethan is dying? What do you mean *dying*?"

"He has a brain tumor. The doctors can't operate given its location, and it's growing at such an alarming rate. They expect him to lose motor functions within six weeks. They don't give him any longer than October."

Olivia stepped out the pool and dried herself off before revealing the painful details of her last few weeks' spiraling disaster. Confusion settled in her weakened mind when she tried to understand how a mother couldn't recognize her son was gay, but she also feared what others might say about her. Although she'd worked with many gay men in her charities and social groups, it was different. They were acquaintances whose lives were none of her business, but Caleb was the son who didn't trust his parents enough to have an open conversation. Her hands and chest shook when she realized she might have said something insinuating she hated gay people. She couldn't lose Caleb, and if it meant Jake came with him, she had to consider learning how to be more accepting and tolerant.

While Zachary sleeping with his brother's wife came as a surprise, the continued series of rash behaviors was not new given all the many poor decisions he selfishly made in his life which had always lead to disastrous consequences. As much as she loved her granddaughter and had no desire to give up Anastasia, her birth still changed the course of Zachary's life. He could've been a great lawyer and more successful if he waited until he grew older to have children. She'd never been able to convince him to move back home and stop whatever nonsense occupied his attention in Brooklyn. Zach teetered on the cusp of a necessary change which was apparent every time he listened to her suggestions or talked about the methods he used to teach his daughter.

Theodore would be heartbroken upon learning Sarah carried another man's child, but it might change his decision to sell Ben's practice. Olivia hoped he hadn't already spoken to the other partners, as she needed time to convince him following in his father's footsteps could still be the right outcome for his future. Theodore might have thought he wanted to paint, but his lifestyle wouldn't allow him to raise the baby if he decided to stay with Sarah. Although Ben left each of his sons a decent amount of money, Olivia knew it wouldn't be enough to carry them through an entire lifetime without ever working again. But she also understood if Theodore's passion was becoming an artist, she had no business squelching the fires that burned within a young man's heart.

Margaret's pregnancy would push Matthew over the edge. Olivia had barely convinced him to stop taking those pills when she stayed at his house. She still needed to determine how to get him the proper help, certain she'd scared him enough to stay away from self-medicating for a few more days while she unearthed what to do next. She couldn't burden Ethan with his brother's problems given the seriousness of his own health. Images of her youngest son dying from a brain tumor in less than three months pummeled her.

By dinnertime, Olivia and Diane had finished a few bottles of wine, barely managing lucid conversation without slurring or nodding off. Shortly after the sun set, they both drifted off into a deep slumber.

Diane awoke the next morning to find she'd fallen asleep on a chaise lounge on the pool deck. Olivia slept in a similar chair to her right, her eyes still shut as drool slipped from the left corner of her mouth.

"Liv, wake up."

Olivia stirred as a sound resembling a cross between a starving brown bear and an electric can opener emanated from her lips.

"We fell asleep out on the patio." Diane put a hand to her head with a determined force acknowledging the painful impact of the prior evening's activities.

"What? We're out where?" Olivia pulled herself into a sitting position. She laughed at the sticky Velcro noise when her skin pulled away from the chair wincing at the sight of the layer of skin left behind. "Damn it! That hurts." Despite the burning sensation creeping along her skin, she let out a loud guffaw.

"What? Do you think it's funny? My neck and back ache as though a truck plowed into them. I won't be able to walk right for a week." Diane stood and kicked the chair with enough force for it to shoot across the patio and land in the pool. She laughed when it reminded her of Olivia's unexpected tumble the night before.

Olivia stared at her sister with an urgent need to focus her eyes on something stationary. A parched throat weakened her body and a pulsing ache throbbed inside her left temple. "You won't be able to go out in public either. At least not looking as bad as helter-skelter."

"What's wrong with you? You won't be able to walk when you get up either. I can't believe we slept outside all night."

"Diane, you should see yourself right now. Your face has a stripe across your eyes and nose from lying in the chaise. You're an American flag. No, a raccoon. That's it. You look like a rabid raccoon with those eyes."

"I'm so glad you find this funny." Diane stared at her reflection in the water. Several narrow stripes blistered across her face from the pressure of the chaise lounge straps while she slept. "You're right. I could pass for a rabid, and hungover, raccoon. You caused this. How much did we drink?"

Olivia tallied the bottles while holding her head from crashing into her shoulders. "I count three wine bottles. Plus, a half-empty bottle of vodka on the table."

"Maybe we're just having a nightmare."

"An awful one. But at least I look better than you do." Olivia winked.

"I'm glad to hear you laughing. We'll get through this. I don't know how anything else could possibly happen to this family right now. We've hit rock bottom worse than ever before."

"From your lips to God's ears. Haven't I had enough surprises for a lifetime? No more please…"

"Amen, sister."

"I never imagined we were so far off track. We all have our little quirks and issues, but this is a disaster. How could I be so ignorant and foolish?" Olivia pressed her fingers in the bags under her eyes, hoping it would release enough pressure for her to move forward with the day. "Diane, did you take photos out of my albums? I noticed the other day I was missing some."

"No. I haven't seen them in years. Where could they be?"

"I don't know. How odd. But one thing I do know… someone needs to take charge of the Glass family and put us back on the right path."

"As soon as I'm no longer a wilting flower forgotten in the scorching sun, and I put medicine on these burns, I'll help you figure out how to do it."

Olivia and Diane lifted one another off the chaise lounges and headed back to the house to prepare for the day. Olivia showered and dressed reflecting on what brought her strength in the past. She'd managed to live most of her life as what she hoped was a good sister, mother, and wife. She accepted she'd told a few little white lies—everyone did—but never anything to harm people. She'd told Diane several times she liked her husband, even though he was one step above a lazy oaf. Few people cared for their in-laws, at least in her experience. She'd convinced Ben he hadn't put on too many pounds despite the four pant sizes he'd jumped in the first two years after their wedding. Everyone gained a few pounds, what was the difference? He lost the weight eventually.

She never kept a disruptive secret or told life-altering lies in her sixty-seven years. She was a truthful woman and valued morality in those closest to her. Sometimes she spoke too honestly, too direct, but it was no different than the color of her eyes or the shape of her feet. Changing such attributes never crossed her mind. Could she be less hard on her children? Should she extend more love to her daughters-in-law? Would she find a way to have a relationship with a son-in-law? Maybe she could accept some of these changes if she applied focus and adopted an alternative mindset.

But how would she tell her son that she wasn't his real mother? What did having an adopted son mean as opposed to having a biological son? Was it really any different? She raised him. She had been his mother for his entire life. The muscles within her crippled heart constricted, pinching every nerve in her body as the guilt roamed wildly throughout her mind, convincing Olivia it would change everything in their relationship. What would happen if Rowena wanted to meet him? But far worse, what would happen if he loved Rowena more?

Olivia didn't have any answers to her questions, nor did she have the energy or confidence necessary to find them at that moment. Did it even matter? Was the real impact of Ben's death and revelation an impetus for her to re-evaluate her relationship with each son? Before any of this happened, she'd thought she was close with each of her children, but now feared she hadn't been that good of a mother. Secrets and lies tore apart her family ever since she'd heard the name Rowena Hector through the appearance of the letters. She needed to excise every hidden truth and nasty, covert darkness that lurked within her family's façade into the open, so everyone could heal.

As she left the bedroom, Olivia ignored the dirty cup still sitting on Ben's nightstand, its importance far less than anything else in her life these days. Time had arrived to arrange for her sons' return home to honor Ben's memory on what would have been his seventieth birthday, but also so she could rebuild the bonds between brothers. She needed to stop obsessing over the letter and determine how to help her sons fix their problems. The letters had become an unfortunate crux to lean on, a red herring for what loitered among her years of ignorance... a rabbit hole to get lost in... and she was too old to play Alice.

Chapter 16 – Caleb

Caleb's exit from a downtown office building rivaled a speeding ambulance. A restless hand covered his thumping heart, as he stopped short before crashing into a group of tourists.

Jake chased after him. "We could be dads in less than a month. I was scared Caitlyn wouldn't love us. Or choose us."

Caitlyn, an eight-month pregnant young girl, was anything but interested in motherhood. She'd been working on her graduate degree when the unexpected pregnancy interrupted her life. Her solution—search for a loving gay male couple to adopt her baby, as they would be the best parents who could provide all the necessary things for a child growing up in the modern world.

Caleb smiled as he stood catching his breath from the winded dash on a street in South Bangor, where they'd met with the adoption agency. "Of course, she would. You're the most caring and loving man I know."

"So are you. She loved us both. Chester even confirmed we were the most ideal couple, unlike any they'd ever met before."

"He did."

"You were unusually quiet inside. Are you having second thoughts? We talked about this, and you wanted to move forward."

Caleb's eyes met Jake's. He owed him the truth. "I'm not sure. With everything happening this summer, I'm a little worried."

"Is this about what happened with your mother?"

"No, my father."

"Him dying in the car accident?"

"Yes, I mean no. It's about how to be a dad. I don't believe I know how to be a dad. I thought I did, but what if our kid doesn't respect me or thinks he or she can't talk to me about important stuff. I'm not certain my parents did their best. Maybe I won't either."

Jake sunk his hands in his jean pockets fumbling to find the keys. "Caleb, you've always said they were good parents... just sometimes they were not easy to talk to. You were the one who chose *not* to tell them about being gay. Your mom is coming around a little, each time you talk with her..."

"Stop right now, babe. I know I screwed up. It's always been me. Fear stopped me from telling them I'm gay, and now I'm afraid to adopt my own child. I need to accept myself. I need to tell myself I'm worth it, and I'm good enough."

"You're not in this alone. I'm half responsible."

"What if that's how I am with our kid? I don't want him or her to suffer because I have a hard time with my emotions."

"Don't you think you've been open with me? I know you've been as honest as you could possibly be. We've had lots of conversations about our parenting beliefs and passions. You've bonded with some of the people here who weren't too friendly with our kind at first. You've connected with your aunt about the real you."

"I know. I'm not sure what my issue is." Caleb closed his eyes bobbing his head to keep focused on one problem at a time.

"I do, you jackass. You've always thought that's what everyone sees when they look at you. Just another gay man, but that's stupid. You're a man. You're an architect. You're a great crossword player. You suck at sports. You forget to put the lid back down on the toilet. You put empty cartons of ice cream back in the freezer. You buy me the perfect gifts for my birthday. You love watching old car shows. And oh, yeah, you're also gay. It's just one piece of who you are. Not the most important piece."

"Are you seriously gonna bust my balls?"

"Yes, I like those balls, Ms. Minelli. Don't you remember I had it pretty damn hard coming out to my parents? They rejected me. They don't care if I ever go back to see them. Your family are good people who want to support you. You have to learn to accept who you are and forget the rest. I'm one hundred percent certain you'll be a great father. We'll be great fathers together."

"Maybe you're right. Maybe it's last-minute jitters."

"When's the last time you spoke with your mom?"

"She left a voice mail yesterday to confirm I'd visit for my dad's birthday next week." Caleb unlocked the Jeep. "Get in. We have to drive to the restaurant in ten minutes for dinner with my client."

"Did you ask your mother if she had concerns when I come with you to Connecticut?" Jake hopped in the passenger seat and pulled the door shut.

"Not yet. I'll call her tomorrow. You made a lot of good points. I guess I need to do some intense soul-searching."

"I love you. I always have. I know what makes you tick. I know when you need a good swift kick in your ass. Take your time. You've got a few days. I'm not worried." Jake leaned over and hugged his husband. "After all, tomorrow is another day."

"*Wizard of Oz?*"

"Scarlett O'Hara. *Gone with the Wind.* At least you've got the right decade this time."

As he passed through the hall, Caleb raced the steps and caught the phone before it transferred to voice mail. Though he and his aunt had begun to grow apart since he moved to Maine, they'd always had a strong bond, sometimes even more than Caleb had with his own mother.

"Aunt Diane. I've missed you. What's going on?"

"I'm doing well. Your momma's okay. She's sad to plan your daddy's birthday party, but part of me thinks it's helping her heal."

"I'm glad you're around for her." He stepped into the kitchen, poured a cup of coffee, and took a swig.

"So, tell me, Caleb. When do I get to meet Jake?"

Caleb choked, spitting out the coffee and watching it fly across the kitchen counter. "Uh... Jake?"

"Yeah, Jake. Your, uh... secret... uh... husband?"

"Mom told you? She didn't tell me she had announced it to everybody." Caleb's stomach retracted further inside his body. He leaned against the sink, bracing himself for more discomfort, certain she'd rip into him for keeping the secret from her for so long.

"I'm not just anybody. Yes, your mother told me what happened on her trip. But relax. She hasn't told anyone else. She needed to talk to someone who could listen to her side of the story. I've always known, Caleb."

Caleb poured the last of the coffee into his cup. "You have?"

"Yes. I've known since you came home from college the first Thanksgiving. Well, that's a lie of the devil. I've always thought so since you were a young child, but I wasn't sure until you came home that weekend."

"That's the one when you went to the hospital after tripping over..."

"Bailey. Yes, I was so distracted trying to decide whether to tell you I knew, I didn't see the dog. Poor thing. At least he got some turkey."

"Damn. Zach figured it out. Now you. Are you upset with me for not telling you?" He regretted not talking to her the last few years, but he also knew how close she and his mother were, unwilling to put his aunt in an awkward position.

"I could never be upset with you. I know this is hard. Your mother can be a little difficult to handle sometimes. Your father would have been fine. We never talked about it, but he didn't have a spiteful or hateful bone in his body. Not that your mother does either, but she takes things too personally. She'll come around."

"How did you know?"

"You told me, but not with words. Before you left for college, you closed up tighter than a clamshell. You'd only talk about school or your job. You stopped discussing anything too personal and seemed afraid to have an opinion on anything. When you came home that

Thanksgiving, I noticed a newfound comfort inside you over your life choices. At first, I thought you matured, then you mentioned a few friends—never any girl's names. I could tell you finally accepted it, but you weren't ready to tell anyone."

"I tried to tell you. Mom interrupted."

"I know, I remember. I felt bad, but you left soon after, and I didn't wanna push you."

"You could have. I would have been honest if you asked me."

"It wasn't my job to ask you. It was your job to tell me. Just like it was your job to tell your parents when you felt comfortable."

"She's always been a little upset at how close you and I have become," Caleb said.

"I've only been filling in while you decided how to tell her. I know what's she's going through, Caleb. When your grandfather died years ago, I couldn't talk to anyone for months. I couldn't think about anything but him. I'm sure your mother is impacted the same way right now."

"Do you mean because my dad died?"

"No, honey. It's not about death. It's about loss. She's trying to understand what she's lost among all these changes. First your father passes, and she is alone sooner than she expected. Then she learns you've been keeping secrets from her. She's scared that she failed to be a good mother or did something wrong when you were a baby."

"She didn't do anything. I've always been gay."

"I know that. You know that. She's never been around anything different than her. It's instinct for her to find something or someone to blame. It may be the wrong approach, but it's natural."

"Do you believe she's changed? Grown from losing Dad?"

"I haven't seen this version of Olivia since we were teenage girls. There's a different kind of fight brewing inside her. One that still wants to win, but maybe knows how to play a fair game now."

"So, I should give her a chance?"

"Yes. If she's raised such a caring and amazing guy, I'm sure she's got the same genes in her. It's just taking a little longer for you to see it."

"Thanks, Aunt Diane. I appreciate it."

"Good. Trust me. I'm older and wiser. Hurry up and bring this man home to meet me."

"I know. I asked Mom if I could bring Jake with me when I come home next month."

"And what did she say?" Diane sighed.

"No response yet. I will ask her again."

"Don't ask her today. Wait 'til tomorrow. Let me talk to her today. We had a good moment this week where her mind opened to a few possibilities. She needs time."

"Are you sure? I don't want to drop you in the line of fire, Aunt Diane."

"I'm positive. Let me figure out how to approach this with her. Email me a picture of Jake. I want to see how cute he is. Something tells me you picked a good one, honey."

Caleb laughed while glancing through the window. Jake dropped bright red peppers into a wooden bucket in the outside garden, lavishly skipping and dancing for his husband's amusement. "Yeah, maybe I did."

Later in the day, as Caleb stood in line at the downtown village deli to order lunch, an email from his mother arrived.

Caleb,

I hope you're having a good week. I'm preparing for the birthday party. It's easier than I thought it would be. I'm excited about all the gifts and the food your father would want to have at his party. I know you were worried about the letter he left us, and you probably think he wrote it to you because of your lifestyle. Don't confuse the two things. We can talk more when you get here. I almost left you a message the other day, but it's easier for me to write down my thoughts than say them to you on the phone.

I'm not ready to tell you I accept your choices. And I don't mean choosing to be gay. I know enough to believe God builds us all differently. I'm referring to your choice to hide it from your family all these years. I'm putting myself in someone else's shoes more often these days. You have your reasons, and someday maybe we can talk more openly about them. For now, I want to move forward and learn from it.

Anyway, the point of this email is to tell you it's okay for you to bring Jake. I want you to be comfortable when you're here. And I'm assuming you'll relax if Jake comes with you. Please go slow with me, Caleb. I can't learn to accept all this change at once. You should both stay at the house with me. Come a few days early so we can figure out how to tell your brothers. Write back and let me know you received this email.

Love,

Your mother

* * *

Across the room later that evening, Jake sat in the recliner reading a book on adoption laws. When the phone rang again, he answered the call.

Jake's eyes sparkled. Caleb imagined it was how he looked on Christmas mornings as a child. Jake put his hand on the phone's speaker. "It's the agency. Caitlyn chose us to adopt her baby. She really chose us. If we still want a baby, this one belongs to us."

Caleb closed his eyes and prepared to respond, the whole time hoping he'd decided correctly. It was important to stop disappointing the ones he loved, but he also knew he needed to be honest about what he wanted. After all, both his father and Jake had taught him to be honest about the fears and desires lurking within. And sometimes waiting a little longer was the best thing for everyone involved.

Chapter 17 – Zach

Zach arrived at The Atlantis Lair fifteen minutes before the DJ booth required his artistic command. The crowd hadn't yet picked up, as the late-nighters kept their pensive distance until at least midnight. He stopped at the west bar and pawned a Diet Coke off the lesbian bartender he'd met earlier in the year. He'd made the mistake of hitting on her his first day at the club, nearly losing his testicles that night. After a few months, they'd grown to appreciate each other's satirical charms.

Tressa stepped toward Zach. "Some little shit celebratin' his twenty-first birthday just ordered a pussy cocktail. Who has a vodka and cranberry as their first legit drink?" Her voice rode side saddle on the high pitch of the beat playing in the background.

"Exactly. Should be Absinthe followed by a hit of X. Those were the good days," Zach said.

Tressa smirked. "Good days? From what you've hinted, you don't remember the good days, Echo."

"Yeah, I remember enough." Zach winked.

"Cut the crap," Tressa interrupted his insolence as she counted her tips. "You've been done with that shit for years. Don't ruin your sobriety by reveling in it again. It's bad enough I let you have a few drinks sometimes. So, how's the crazy going back at Casa Glass?"

"The usual. I spent the week with my mom earlier this month. She wants me to move back to Brandywine with Anastasia, even thinks I need to create a more stable home life for my girl. I took your advice and tried to tell her about my music." He smirked. "It didn't go so well."

Tressa stuck her finger in her mouth and faked a vomit noise. "Drama sucks."

Zach's phone vibrated against the wood trim on the edge of the bar. "Fuck me."

Tressa replied, "We've been through this before. Done with your dick. Even if you've got a monster..."

"Abundantly clear, princess. It's Pickles, and I don't want to talk to him." Zach backed up with his hands held above his shoulders.

Teddy had earned the nickname Pickles when Zach learned of his brother's childhood obsession with sneaking into the kitchen late at night to eat an entire jar of sweet and sour pickles, initially claiming it a one-time occurrence when Zach had caught him. Their maid, Louise, let it slip one afternoon that she'd been buying several jars a week for months. Zach coined the new name and tortured his brother for weeks.

Tressa grabbed the phone. "Echo's line. How's your gherkin?"

"Echo? Gherkin? Do I have the wrong number? Hello, Zach?"

"No, you got the right line. Just the wrong name, Pickles."

Zach grabbed the phone from a highly entertained Tressa. "Hey, Teddy, what's going on?"

"Who's Echo? And what's up with the woman who answered the phone?"

"Ignore her. She's a friend who's hard up for dick."

Tressa smashed a cherry in his ear reveling in her latest masterpiece, minor payback for all they'd been through.

"You have some nice women in your life, brother. Tell me, how's Katerina doing these days? Have you gotten any other girls pregnant?" Teddy said.

Zach stood stunned for a minute, wiping cherry juiced from the side of his neck admiring and fearing the way it had resembled blood gaping from an open wound.

"Don't start with me, Pickles."

"I've been calling the family all day with my good news. Sarah's pregnant. Or maybe you knew that already?"

Zach's concern over his brother figuring out what happened between him and Sarah grew quickly. "What's going on? Why would you say that?"

Zach held his hand over the phone and called to the bartender. "I need a shot of bourbon. Please!"

"That's good news, right?" said Zach, to the sound of silence meeting him on the other end of the call, still uncertain how much Teddy knew.

"Of course. I haven't said much to you guys, but we've been trying for a while, and it finally happened. It's good news."

"Congratulations. Sarah must be excited." Zach's body weight relaxed against the bar.

"Yes. We've known for a couple of weeks, but she wanted to wait until the doctor checked her out. So far, we're good."

"That's awesome. Listen. I just got to work. I need to jet. I'll see you at Dad's birthday party next week." Zach motioned for another shot and hung up the phone.

The bartender dropped a larger glass of bourbon on the bar's sticky countertop. "Have a double on me. Sounds like you need it."

Tressa walked back to the bar and slammed the tray. "Little shithead expected me to give it to him for free on his birthday." She grabbed Zach's bourbon and downed it. "I need this more than you."

Zach blinked his puppy dog eyes, and the bartender poured him another glass before walking to the other side of the bar.

Tressa said, "Why does your ass need a double?"

Zach checked the time. Five minutes before he clocked in. "Smoke break, let's go." He grabbed Tressa's hand and led her to the street.

Once outside, he explained the situation to Tressa as she lit up muttering about the kid who tried to cop a feel for his birthday.

"Zach, I'd kill you if you were still my boyfriend."

"Yeah, you make a better friend than nag... though I do miss bury-ing my face in those tits. Brrr... At least I don't have to listen to you bitch at me all the time." His voice was full of painted-on exuberance.

"Listen to me, papi. I kicked your ass once before, and I'll do it again if you keep bein' a little bitch boy. You've gotta stop doin' this shit to yourself. I'm on your side, but seriously, this is messed up. That's your sister-in-law, Zach." She grabbed his ear and yanked. "So, your brother doesn't know, right?"

Zach rubbed his tingling ear. "No. She won't tell him. He called to tell me they were pregnant. He thinks it's his baby. He was pretty happy."

"Sounds so. Now what?"

"Well, my mother wants me to tell him what happened. I kind of told her the secret when I slept over at the house. I told you serious shit happened."

"What do you wanna do?"

"I don't know. It's done. What's the harm at this point? We share the same DNA. There's nothing between Sarah and me. A parent is the person who raises you, not your biological father or mother. Case in point... Katerina. She's not Anastasia's mother even though that bitch gave birth to her."

Tressa shrugged. "I get it. How's that situation going?"

"My mom found me a good lawyer who's filing paperwork to en-sure the custody arrangement is a permanent one. He's gonna serve Katerina the papers next week."

Tressa dropped her cigarette in Zach's shot glass and headed back to the club. "We gotta get inside. Your shift starts."

* * *

The next day, Zach woke at Olivia's place where he'd left Anastasia overnight while he'd been working. He'd slept for most of the after-noon until hunger pains twisted in his gut. He headed downstairs and found his mother in his father's study with the blinds closed sitting at the desk in the dark.

"Hey, how's it hanging?"

"Zachary, good to see you. It's hanging... low?" They both laughed. "I finished planning with the caterers for the party. Diane and I took Anastasia to visit Matthew and Margaret for breakfast this morning. Have you spent much time with your brother lately?"

"Yeah, I saw the note when I arrived this morning. Thanks for watching her again. No, I haven't talked to Matt in weeks. We don't exactly keep the same schedules."

"Can you find time for him this week? He's been a bit depressed lately." Olivia's hands traced the edge of the desk as though it were her late husband's arm. "Anastasia had fun. She and Melanie get along well. It would be so nice if they attended school together this fall, don't you think?"

Zach ignored the comment about school. "I'll call Matt this week and schedule plans to have dinner. Speaking of depression, Mom. You still haven't told us what was in Dad's letter. I want to know what was in his last message to us. I've let it go for a few weeks, but you owe us an explanation about the second one being for one of his sons?"

"Yes, I do need to talk to you about it. I'm planning to discuss it at his birthday party. I needed to pull the final pieces together, and I wanted to spend time with each of you boys before explaining the letter."

"That's not for another week. Can't you tell me now?" Zach's voice shot closer to a whiny two-year-old in desperate need of a nap. Yelling didn't work last time, so a different approach might get better results.

"No. Please let it go. I'm tired of everyone asking me about it. I've agreed to address it at the party. You can wait a few more days. Let's talk about the situation with Sarah and Theodore. I've thought a lot since our last conversation."

Zach took a seat on the couch across from her and rubbed his three-day-old rough stubble. "I'm barely awake, Mom."

"Just listen to me. I visited Theodore with the intention of telling him what you'd done. Maybe it would come across better from me, but I didn't have a chance to tell him."

"I know. He called last night. He and Sarah are joyously pregnant. I assumed you didn't break the news to Pickles."

"He did? Oh, I didn't realize he has been telling people already. When I left, Sarah didn't want to tell the rest of the family until she was further along."

"He told me." Zach scratched at the tattoo on his arm with the letter opener, his skin crawled with a trepid perspiration over the conversation.

"I did, however, talk to Sarah about your little escapade."

Zach scratched deeper into his arm with the edge of the letter opener. It sliced open the King's crown. He grabbed a napkin from the bar to stop the bleeding. "You did what?"

"It just came out, Zachary. Sarah was her usual obstinate self, and I couldn't take it. I told her I knew about your indiscretion. She tried to get me to understand it." Olivia swayed back and forth hoping to keep her mind calm and her voice gentle. A new part of her routine to accept change.

"Did she help you understand it any better than I did?" he inquired. His eyes blistered with annoyance and fear.

"Maybe. A little. It doesn't change my mind. It's still wrong. And I don't agree with hiding it, but I know it came from a good place."

"As I told you."

"Don't be smart, Zachary. I'm trying to be more understanding."

"So now what, Mom?"

"To be honest, this doesn't even come close to my top priority right now. I haven't decided what to do about your brother. He has other problems to deal with. You all have other problems to deal with."

"I'm not your most important project? Your biggest hardship? God, did the world end while I was sleeping?" He snickered and went to his knees as if he prayed for salvation. "What else is going on, Dear Lord? I have sinned and been a bad boy."

"Nothing you need to worry about right now." Olivia grabbed the back of his neck and pushed him forward, just enough to show a playful side she'd kept hidden even most days when he was a child. "Stop being a fool and visit Matthew for me. I'm seeing our reality with a much more astute set of eyes since your father has passed on. You boys are all grown up. Making many *stupid* decisions, but still grown up."

"Is that your attempt at being funny, Mother? Cause if it is, it's not going over well." He winked at her.

She smiled. "Yes, I suppose my attempt at humor failed. I'll practice some more and be ready for you next time."

Zach threw the bloody tissue in the garbage. "Let's get something to eat before Aunt Diane gets back with Anastasia. I'm starving. Let's hit up a White Castle."

"I may be learning, Zachary, but I am not eating at White Castle."

"Yes, you are."

"No, I'm not."

"We'll see, Mom. Old dogs can learn new tricks."

Olivia smacked the back of her son's head. "I haven't done that since you were a teenager. Somehow seems like things might be back to a little bit of normal around here. Maybe I'm getting some control in my life."

Chapter 18 – Teddy

Teddy waited in the conference room with Ms. Davis and Mr. Wittleton, his father's partners, and two members of the external audit firm who finished conducting the quarterly review of the firm's finances. Matt should have led the meeting, but he'd not yet shown up. Teddy's patience wouldn't last much longer, nor the swollen knuckles he feverishly cracked to keep his mind focused on getting to the end game.

Gwendolyn Pierce, the lead auditor, a mid-fifties brunette in a trim business suit, pulled her glasses away from her large, round eyes, and rubbed the bridge of her nose. "Mr. Glass, unfortunately, I have another appointment this morning and can't wait much longer for your brother to arrive. Perhaps you might lead us through the quarter's performance reports?"

Ms. Davis looked to Mr. Wittleton, and they both nodded while Teddy excused himself for a minute and asked his secretary to call Matt on his cell one more time.

Upon Teddy's return, he continued. "Yes, Ms. Pierce. I do apologize for Matt's tardiness. It's unusual for him, but he's been struggling with our father's death this summer. I'm not as familiar with the numbers as he is, but I can walk us through at a high level."

Gwendolyn interrupted, her nasal voice reverberating off the windows. "To be honest, Mr. Glass, I have already had an opportunity to review them in the last few days. For the most part, everything lined up; however, we have a few specific items to discuss."

Teddy nodded. "Please continue." His secretary poked her head in and indicated she hadn't been able to find his brother. He muttered under his breath something about ineptitude, unsure if he directed it at his assistant or his brother.

Gwendolyn looked down her nose at him. "As you're probably *not* aware, when we met last quarter with your father and Matthew, there were a number of concerning items we'd been researching. The firm's earnings, compared to the prior quarter and the prior year, were off by twenty percent. Additionally, two $10,000 disbursements had no receipts. Your father asked Matthew to review the accounts in more detail and send a summary of what he found. Unfortunately, Mr. Glass passed away, and we never had an opportunity to continue the discussion."

"Has Matt failed to send the details to you since last quarter?" Ms. Davis said.

"Correct."

Teddy scratched the back of his head, digging his nails into a spot behind his ear while biting his lip. His brother's organizational skills had normally matched those of an army general—always on top of situations. "Perhaps he planned to bring them today. Do you have copies of the transactions in question?"

"Of course, we do." Gwendolyn's associate slid a folder to Teddy across the expansive rectangular table. It fell a few feet short of Teddy, and when he stood to reach it, his mouth held an austere frown at his colleagues.

"I suppose we should reschedule for next week, which will give me a few days to talk with my brother and our partners to locate the missing information. No further need to waste my... our time... today. I've heard a few mentions of your concern over meeting the firm's annual forecast as well as being significantly under last year's numbers. If I recall correctly, it seems to me last year we had some particularly high-profile cases resulting in an extremely profitable margin. Perhaps we're comparing two unequal and different years?" Teddy flipped through the folder, unsure what he read, nor interested in continuing the farce without his brother's presence.

Ms. Davis and Mr. Wittleton exchanged glances. Teddy noticed it again on the second occurrence, both resulting in a shared understanding of something that had been going on. An understanding he had not been included in and one that had perturbed him.

Gwendolyn continued. "Correct. However, we *already* adjusted for consideration of the budget and forecast for the current year. Matthew and your father agreed with our findings last quarter and planned several changes this summer. Given you brought on new staff the prior year, it would be best to reduce this overhead in the current year. Additionally, your father had been spending *less* time looking for new business and more time preparing for his upcoming retirement. With minimal focus on new business and the increasing expenses, Teddy, it's not easy to earn a profit. You should know this."

At first, Teddy's frustration with the auditor's comments gnawed at him, assuming she'd been referring to his inability to find more clients and the time his training took away from his father's attention on the business. However, when these issues supported the case for selling the firm, his concerns dissipated. "Yes, you're correct. Unless you have any objections, let's meet the same day and time next week to discuss these changes."

"One more item, Mr. Glass," Gwendolyn interjected, not sensing the tension in his lower jaw that generated a loud clicking noise. "In addition to the two transactions from last quarter we were unable to identify, I located three more for similar amounts in the current quarter's ledger. I'm concerned you may have a more serious issue going on than we initially projected."

Ms. Davis stood. "Yes, I suppose so. We appreciate your valuable input, Ms. Pierce. We will conduct due diligence and notify you before end of the week what we find. I trust we'll be able to resolve this next week when we meet again."

The auditors left, and Teddy looked at his father's partners. "Perhaps we should talk about my brother? I do not have favorable expectations concerning this situation."

* * *

After lunch, Teddy stopped at Yale University's Green Hall Gallery to converse with the admissions officer about a potential Master's degree in Fine Arts, given both his interest in painting and Yale being his alma mater. After thanking the director for the tour, learning about the upcoming semester and confirming the schedule for applying to the art program, Teddy sat on a bench outside the gallery and watched the students wandering the campus.

A young woman sat on the bench next to him. She couldn't have been more than twenty with tightly curled brown hair, dark skin, and a Caribbean accent. The campus comforted Teddy, and he pushed himself to interact with her.

"Hi. I'm Teddy."

She nodded. "I'm Carolina. Nice to meet you. Are you a student here?"

"Not yet. I'm considering it. And you?"

"Yes, second year. I'm in the MFA program. I'm an artist. I draw and sketch."

"I'm a painter." He smiled. "I mean, I'm a lawyer but possibly going back to school again."

"You can say you're a painter if you're a painter, Teddy. Own it. My father's a lawyer. He wanted me to go to law school, but I told him no. He understood. He wanted me to be happy."

Teddy laughed. "My father was a lawyer, too. He never knew how much I wanted to be a painter. I tried to tell him once, but he didn't listen."

"You should try again."

"I wish I could. He recently passed away."

"You can still tell him. I'm sure he's listening somewhere." She lifted her hands and looked at him. "The world is full of people listening. Sometimes you need to believe. Tell me about it. Maybe he's listening right now."

Teddy initially scoffed at the girl's behavior and recommendation, but as he sat listening, the extent of his comfort at that moment shined. The discussion eradicated any tension in his body. His jaw no longer ached. His knees were free of pain. All he wanted to talk about centered around his love of art, painting, and creativity.

"I'm having an early mid-life crisis, Carolina. My father passed away. I'm supposed to inherit his law practice and take on his role as the lead partner." His eyes shined bright, and his grin expanded wider than he'd expected his face ever could. "I don't want to. I want to go back to school and focus on painting."

"I can sense your happiness. This is a fantastic campus. Everyone supports one another. Being an artist means a hard life." She rested a hand on his knee and smiled. "I have a good feeling about you."

Teddy nodded. "I've been worried about that. My wife has been supportive. She's the one pushing me to give this a chance. I didn't realize how lucky I was to have her until just now."

"It was a pleasure to meet you, Teddy." She stood and extended a hand. "I need to get to my next class, but I'm glad I could provide some benefit."

Teddy stood, and for the first time in a long time, the urge for someone's warm embrace lingered. He leaned forward and hugged Carolina. "Thank you. You've had an impact on me today. Maybe we'll share a class together one day."

"We will," Carolina said. "You're radiating a positive aura. I'm good at knowing people. I've got a vibe." She handed him a card. "Call me sometime."

As Carolina left, his phone beeped. Noticing it came from the office, assuming it was his secretary, he picked up. An unusual cheerfulness clung to his body like happiness plastered across a clown's face, more than he had experienced in a long time.

"Yes?"

"Teddy, it's Matt. I've just gotten to the office and realized I missed our meeting this morning. Overslept, up late watching a few games. Sorry."

"We need to have a discussion."

"I know. I should have been present. It was important. We've been having financial issues this year. I've done my research. I have a plan to fix it."

"Yes, those items came up. I'm gone for the day. Tomorrow morning at nine in my office. It seems we should have a different conversation. We need to find the underlying cause of those transactions the auditors have been questioning. I've only just learned about them from Ms. Pierce, but frankly, it's a bit alarming. I expected better of you."

"Yes, exactly. I have an explanation. I know what happened and should be able to fix it. I'll see you in the morning." Matt hung up the phone.

Teddy feverishly pressed the end call button waffling between anger at his brother and excitement over his visit to the Green Hall Gallery.

Things are finally looking up, Dad. Maybe you're watching over me...

* * *

On his way home from work the next day, Teddy stopped by his mother's house to discuss the sale of the firm, but she had left several hours earlier.

"Teddy, I hear congratulations are in order." Diane stood in the front entrance foyer. "I love the look of hope in expectant parents."

"Yes, we're beyond excited. I planned to call this week to let you know. I guess my mother told you?"

"Zach mentioned your news when he stopped by over the weekend. As did your momma, but she's not home right now. She headed over to Matt's this afternoon."

"Speaking of Matt, have you noticed anything strange with him lately?"

Diane shook her head. "I saw him last weekend with Margaret and the girls. We took them and Anastasia to play at the park for a few hours. I didn't get to talk with him, but he seemed rundown. He mentioned he had a cold, and he was out running a few errands most of the time. Why do you ask? Anything you've noticed?"

"I'm unsure. Just a little worried. Do you have an idea when my mother will be back?" He pulled his cheek into the side of his mouth gently biting down and releasing puffs of warm air.

"We're supposed to watch a movie tonight. Maybe an hour? She's having dinner at Matt's place. You should really check on your brother."

"I will see him tomorrow."

"So how far along is Sarah?"

Teddy paused, recognizing he'd never asked that question, silently chastising himself for his mistake. "I'm not certain. We have a doctor's appointment this week. She went to the first one on her own to confirm the pregnancy and surprise me with the news once she was positive. I promised to go to the next one, when we'll find out."

"Good. I'm happy for you. Is Sarah still planning to work nights?"

"Yes, but she'll talk to her supervisor about changing her shifts as she gets further along. I'd prefer she cut back on her hours, but with everything going on between the funeral, Dad's birthday party, and all the changes at the office, we need to figure out the right plan." Teddy considered mentioning his wish to sell the family practice, but he decided to wait until he talked with his mother again. "Oh, I did have a question for you. Has Mom said anything about that letter Dad left for us? I never got a chance to ask her when she stayed with me a few weeks ago, and I was curious."

Diane sorted through the magazines on the table, her eyes focused on anything but her nephew. "No, she hasn't. It's best to leave that subject alone, given everyone's reaction at the will reading. She mentioned something about giving it to you guys at the birthday party next week."

"I should get going. Please tell Mom I stopped by, and I'll call her tomorrow."

"Teddy, you're having a baby. Be happy. Loosen up a little, love."

Teddy forced himself to be gentle with his aunt. He'd seen this side of her many times before, and he usually pushed it away. In this one instance, she had a point. He leaned in, kissed her cheek, and smiled. As he walked out the front door, his phone rang.

"Yes?" he answered while stepping off the front patio steps near the pink rose bushes Caleb planted when they were children.

"Teddy, it's Ira Rattenbury. Would you have a moment?"

"Yes, what can I do for you?" he said.

"When we spoke last, you may recall I mentioned your brother's persistence to address everything in your father's will."

"Yes. Should I assume your call means you've completed the transactions?"

"I'm much closer to being finished, but that's not why I am phoning. Matthew left me two messages today expressing his concerns at the time taken to complete this process. In the second message, he was angry over the situation. Perhaps you could have a conversation with him?"

"Mr. Rattenbury, I appreciate the heads up. Matt has been having a difficult time dealing with our father's death. He isn't his usual self. I will talk to him. Please direct him to me if he calls you again."

Teddy and Ira ended their call. Teddy grew more frustrated and arched his fingers back and forth to relieve the tension enjoying the intense sound each time the cartilage snapped. He didn't want all this responsibility right now. He had his own life to focus on, and it was his time to find happiness. It couldn't always be about his family. *What is wrong with my brother? I will not keep doling out excuses for his incompetence.*

* * *

Sarah and Teddy awaited their first pre-natal appointment later that week bouncing in their seats and bickering with the receptionist about the delay. When the nurse finally directed them to the exam room, Sarah sighed as though it'd been hours and dragged Teddy with her down the narrow hall in triple steps. After a few discussions and the necessary bloodwork, the doctor prepared the ultrasound to confirm the baby's due date. Teddy stood by his wife's side, holding her hand, as the nurse applied the cool gel. The room had no windows and dim lighting, giving it a shadowed effect, which Teddy thought was meant to calm the patients. The darkness aggravated him, but he was more interested in meeting his child for the first time.

"Are you excited?" Sarah said. "I can see it plain as the nose on your face."

"Yes, I've never been more enthusiastic." His eyes shined bright as if it contained every star children wished upon.

The doctor said, "I'm so happy for you both. I know how disappointing the last year has been with the concerns and multiple tests to diagnose if either of you were infertile. I did tell you it would be tough, but not impossible, with Teddy's condition."

Sarah's neck and back tensed as the doctor finished talking. "Let's not talk about it. Let's focus on the good news." She fidgeted with the wires attached to the machine arching over her.

Teddy looked at the doctor and back at his wife with compressed lips. "Condition?"

"Yes, I told you. The last time the doctor thought it was low sperm count preventing pregnancy. I guess not." Sarah tried to sit, but the machine blocked her way. Her body tensed, and the doctor pushed her back down.

Teddy nodded. "Oh, I must have missed that conversation." He paused and momentarily considered what it meant, confused at not having any recollection of the discussion, but quickly remembered she was pregnant and wanted to know more. "Yes, how far along, Doctor?"

The physician finished his exam, peeled off his gloves, and looked at Sarah and Teddy. "I'd say you're right at the thirteen-week mark."

He read the wall calendar and counted on his fingers. "You're going to have a Groundhog baby."

Teddy kissed his wife focusing on a future where a different set of blissful hopes had climbed their way to the top. As he moved away, his mind calculated the dates. "February 1st due date?"

"Yes, sounds right," the doctor said.

Sarah counted her fingers on both hands. "We conceived in early May?"

"Yes, within a few days."

Sarah's face displayed a huge rush of joy and relief bobbing back and forth between her husband and the doctor. "You're certain. May?" Sarah's voice echoed a child begging for candy.

"Yes, there is a margin of error by a few days, but you definitely conceived somewhere between the first and fourth of May, Sarah. We didn't run any pregnancy tests the last two months to give your body a break, hence not finding your news any sooner."

Sarah mumbled aloud in a low voice. "It's not Zach's."

"What about Zach?" Teddy cocked his head closer to hear his wife more clearly.

Sarah pushed the machine away with great force and determination, pulling her husband toward her and hugging him. "Nothing. Forget it. If the creek don't rise. We're pregnant. We did it, Teddy."

"Yes, we did. I told you it would happen. Now we need to find out if it's a boy or girl."

Sarah chimed in appearing unable to contain her excitement. "Let's be surprised, Teddy."

"Whatever you want. I'm just so happy you're finally pregnant."

"We're pregnant, Teddy," Sarah said. "You and I are really pregnant."

Chapter 19 – Matt

Matt stood before the ATM on the corner near the park where he often took his girls to play on the swings silently praying he still had cash left in the account. He entered his pin code and requested two hundred dollars.

His phone vibrated, indicating an incoming text. He read another one from his brother, Teddy, asking him when he'd be at the meeting. He was thirty minutes late at this point, already missing the rescheduled one.

The ATM shuffled behind the slate wall and asked him if he wanted a receipt. It gave him hope money existed in the account if it had asked him that question. He clicked yes.

His phone vibrated again. *Damn it, Teddy. I'll arrive soon. Stop texting me.*

The ATM asked if he wanted the receipt emailed or printed. *Printed. Don't need anyone else seeing it in my email.*

A third message on his phone. This time he looked at it.

Unknown: *Dude. I'm in the parking lot. You got my money?*

Matt punched the ATM willing it to go faster. It spilled out his two hundred in twenties followed by a receipt.

He grabbed his phone and responded.

Matt: *Yes, I'm five minutes away.*

Matt grabbed the bills, stuffed them in his pocket, and ran to the car. As he started the engine, he looked at the receipt. Nineteen dollars and eleven cents—the remaining balance.

His phone vibrated.

Unknown: *Leaving in five if you don't show.*

Matt revved the engine and tore out the exit. He needed to show up in time. He'd run out of pills and had no other contacts to get his fix.

Matt finally showed up at the office by early afternoon, but his brother had already left for the day. He called Teddy and apologized for missing the meeting, glad he didn't have to meet him in person. Teddy set another meeting for nine o'clock the next morning.

Matt also saw a missed call from his wife. He listened to her message overhearing an entire conversation she seemed to have at the grocery store:

"Please try again, I'm trying to reach my husband."

"Credit or debit, ma'am?"

"Debit. My husband said our credit card number was stolen, and I need to wait until the new one arrives."

Among the background noise, several angry-sounding, terse beeps persisted.

"Maybe you got a bad debit card, too, ma'am?"

"He told me not to use credit until he received a new one, but please try it. I have all this food to bring home."

Twenty seconds passed, adding to Matt's growing shame.

"Nope. No good. Let me get the supervisor, ma'am."

"I'm so sorry to hold up the line, everyone."

Another few seconds of silence.

"Ma'am, your card has been overdrawn. It says I need to cut it up."

"It must be whoever stole the credit card numbers. I'm sure it's all connected. Here, try this one."

"No, ma'am. We've already tried two cards. I'm going to need you to step to the side over here, so we can help the other customers."

Margaret sobbed. The back of Matt's eyes instantly began to burn.

"Matt, are you there? Oh, it must have gone to voice mail. Can I at least buy the formula and sandwiches? I might have some cash. My girls need to eat."

A loud click indicated the end of the voice message. Matt's back jolted with uncontrollable spasms over the angst in her voice. She had no money for groceries. He had to fix this situation.

I'm such an idiot.

He reached into his brown leather briefcase and flipped open the top of the bottle he'd just bought off the kid he'd met in the parking lot. Two more would squelch the dragons inside him as part of the downward spiral he couldn't escape.

At home that evening, Margaret pressed Matt about the credit card issue while their family ate dinner at the kitchen table.

"I don't understand what happened, Matt. None of the cards worked. I had to leave everything at the register." Margaret stood to check the temperature on Melinda's bottle. "It was so embarrassing. Where were you?"

"The bank screwed it up. I canceled the credit card after someone stole our number. They're supposed to send me a new one this week. I guess they put a freeze on all the accounts until it's fixed." His feet tapped the center pole in the table. His eyes watched the half-full water glass dance to the edge. There was no way he could tell her he'd been in a parking lot with some sixteen-year-old kid selling him drugs.

"Okay, but I need money this week for the girls when they go on their play date with friends. I have tomorrow's dinner with my sisters. It's my turn to buy for everyone. What should I do?"

"Really, Margaret? Can't you push it off until we fix the bank situation? It will only be a few days." His voice elevated higher with each reply. Condensation around the glass began dripping to the floor, though Matt could do nothing but watch as it teetered a centimeter away from falling.

"I could, but it was awful, Matt. It was so embarrassing at the grocery store today. I don't want to tell the girls I need to cancel this week. Can't I go to the bank tomorrow and take cash from our savings?"

"No, the accounts are frozen. Only I can get any money this week until they fix it." Matt thought about his options. He could borrow against the petty cash fund at the office again, but he'd already set off a few alarms with the auditors over the missing money. *Damn it, when will Dad's inheritance be ready?*

Margaret squeezed her husband's shoulder with one hand while she tested the bottle with the other one. "Can you get cash in the morning before work?"

Matt dropped the fork he used to feed Melissa. His face drooped, and his fist pounded the table. "You're seriously pushing me on this? Fine, I'll go right now. I don't have time in the morning." He grabbed his keys and took off for the garage, not giving her a chance to respond nor recognizing as the glass crashed to the ground and splintered into dozens of sharp shards.

Fifteen minutes later, he unlocked the office door as everyone had already left for the day. He keyed in the combination for the safe and took five hundred dollars hoping it would be enough until the estate formally closed. He flipped on the desk radio and listened to the game, the umpire's strike call against the Red Sox calmed his growing urges. As did two more pills.

* * *

Early the next morning, Matt woke to his daughter, Melinda, crying in the next room. Margaret was already in the kitchen cooking breakfast for the older girls. He played with his daughter for a few minutes enjoying every second of her laughter and beautiful smiles. As he set

Melinda on the white changing table his parents had given them, Matt looked at the phone, realizing he had a meeting with Teddy in a few hours. His brain vetoed having a conversation of any kind, still focused on debating whether his mother had revealed to Ethan Matt's addiction to pills.

Matt texted his brother, Teddy, exerting unnatural force against each key in hopes the message would relay sooner than possible.

Matt: *Hey. Got bug from girls. Feel awful. Hold off mtg til btr? Shld be back 2mor.*

No response for ten minutes which was unlike Teddy. After scrolling through his phone, Matt noticed he'd missed a message from another brother and replied.

Ethan: *I miss you. Come fishing with Caleb and me.*

Matt: *Can't. Swamped.*

Ethan: *Not today. In a couple of weeks.*

Matt: *Sorry. Things are crazy right now.*

Ethan: *You okay?*

Matt: *Fine. Maybe in the fall.*

Ethan: *It'd be good to have us all together again. Fall might be too late.*

Matt: *Why?*

Ethan: *Just is.*

Matt: *We'll figure it out. Just don't count on me right now.*

* * *

By late afternoon, Margaret left their house to drop off the older girls on a play date and meet her sisters for an early dinner. Since

Matt had stayed home, Margaret left Melinda with him. He placed his youngest daughter on the couch to watch a cartoon and turned on his laptop to check the status at work, since he'd skipped out for the day. After an hour of catching up on email, his legs and knees jittered. He'd gone most of the afternoon without taking any pills but had reached his limit on holding off from his saving grace.

He couldn't call out of work again the next day without someone realizing the money had disappeared and asking questions. He tried to reach Ira Rattenbury twice but never heard back. Matt grabbed his briefcase, opened the bottle, and swallowed two pills with a feverish impulse while shutting the bathroom door. He slumped to the floor in disgust over his actions and the situation. He'd surpassed losing control. He had the perfect life organized and designed until a few months ago when money got tighter, and his father began talking about retirement. Matt was suddenly forced to explain where he'd disbursed every cent at the firm, so they could prepare Teddy to assume control of the practice. Since the two partners knew the most about the business after his father, they'd engaged in the discussion and asked detailed questions.

Matt had never stolen anything. He'd borrow from time to time between the petty cash funds and the account where they paid company taxes, as it always had a surplus. When the surplus evaporated, he no longer had access to easy funds. After receiving his bonus earlier that year, Matt used a significant amount to pay back the accounts, but the additional line of income had run out. Now Margaret was pregnant. All too much to handle.

Matt turned on the hot faucet in the shower to steam the room. He needed to clear his mind. He rested his head back against the wall rationalizing his situation in the hopes it could help calm him down. His mind wandered, and within a few minutes, he'd fallen asleep with the shower water running on high and the ceiling vent rattling at top volume.

Olivia pulled in front of Matt's house to check on how he'd progressed since their last conversation. She'd taken the pills away and believed he'd sounded stronger when they last spoke. After learning about Ethan's illness, she chose not to mention Matthew's situation. She never heard back from Zachary after asking him to check on Matthew. Olivia wanted to see for herself how her son was recovering, growing fearful she wasn't equipped to handle the situation.

After shutting the car door, Olivia walked the driveway and knocked on the front door. No answer. She had spoken to Margaret, who confirmed Matt was home, less than an hour ago. When the crying inside blasted through the windows, Olivia wandered around to the kitchen door, racing as though the house were on fire. She knocked on the door and pushed it open shouting "Hello." Her heart skipped every other beat until it settled in her throat. No answer, but she definitely heard the girls wailing from somewhere inside.

Olivia brushed by the kitchen chair, knocking over the jade plant, the one Margaret's mother sent to them as good luck with the renovations, on the table. As she stepped through the hall, the planter crashed to the ground, sending dirt flying across the linoleum floor. It reminded her of every painful truth leaving damage around her.

Turning the corner, she found Melinda lying on the carpet near her crib, with her foot caught between two of the spindles. Olivia screamed for her son and ran to her granddaughter. She'd had enough of pain in her children's lives, and her granddaughters were among the innocent impacted by the entire disaster her life had become.

She was afraid to move her granddaughter in case anything had broken in the fall. Melinda whined with a paralyzing force, and tears rolled down her cheeks. Olivia moved the leg stuck in the side of the crib with gentle ease to determine the extent of any damage. As she lifted Melinda's waist higher to free her leg, Matt came running into the bedroom.

His wet hair pointed in all directions. His face sweat unrelenting and disturbing bulbous drops. His eyes blazed red and grew more and more dilated. "What happened?"

"You tell me, Matthew. I just arrived." The ire in Olivia's voice reminded Matt of the childhood scolding he'd witnessed each of his brothers receive. He hung a heavy head in shame.

They worked together to check Melinda's injuries and surmised she'd been crawling up the side of her crib. She must have caught her leg and fallen backward, trapping herself between the bars, before descending toward the floor. The carpet prevented any serious injury, but the fall had frightened her fragile sense of courage.

Matt responded with a quiver in his voice more obvious than the distraught expression plastered across his ghostly face. "She's not hurt. She scared herself." He cradled his daughter against his chest. After a few minutes, her screams quieted, but the weeping still dripped from her eyes and nose.

"Momma. Want Momma."

Olivia reached for her granddaughter, and Melinda opened her arms. As Olivia rocked her back and forth, Matt put light pressure on her legs and arms to confirm nothing had broken.

Olivia spoke first. "She's fine now, Matthew. Get her a bottle, please."

"Yes. Oh, what did I do? My poor girl," he mumbled, as he left for the kitchen, one hand on his forehead, the other over his mouth. "Daddy's here. Daddy will fix it."

Olivia waited until Melinda was calm and stood her up on both feet to observe how she walked. Holding Olivia's fingers, Melinda strolled toward the bedroom door, one slow and careful foot in front of the other, pausing each step, unfazed by her recent accident.

Olivia cooed. "Such a good girl, Melinda. You're such a good girl. Let's go watch *Paw Patrol*. Come on, baby girl."

Olivia sat her granddaughter on the floor in front of the TV and turned on her favorite show. Melinda loved watching Ryder and his cartoon dogs save the world. Olivia found the vacuum and fixed the planter she had spilled in the kitchen while Matt warmed his daughter's dinner. When it was ready, Matt fed his daughter and she soon fell asleep lying next to him on the couch.

"Are we going to talk about what happened here, Matthew?"

"Yes. I screwed up. I only wanted to clear my head for a few minutes, and I guess I fell asleep. It's never happened before. It won't happen again."

"Yes, you're damn right it will never happen again. Did you talk to Margaret?"

"Not yet."

"Are you still taking those pills, Matthew?"

He did not respond.

"Matthew, we're both too old for me to tell you what to do to fix this. It's one thing to risk your own life, but when you endanger your child's life, it has to stop."

"I know, Mom. I know. I can't stop on my own. I tried. I can't keep up with everything I need to do. I can't afford this house anymore. I took money out of the law firm's bank accounts. I can't pay it back."

Olivia kept her feet planted on the floor, as if she stood in cement, and held her narrowed eyes squarely set on her son. He needed to understand her message. "You're going to let me find someone to get you on track, Matthew. Do you understand me? I am done accepting excuses from everyone."

He nodded this time. "Please help me get better, Mom. My girls are too important to me. If I ever did anything to hurt them, I couldn't go on."

"Don't even say such a thing, Matthew. I have little left as it is."

Chapter 20 – Ethan

It was the first day of classes for Ethan's new rotation at school where he should have studied anesthesiology and phlebotomy. As he entered the office, he could smell the chemicals the maintenance staff used to wash the floors the previous evening. The antiseptic odor seemed appropriate for the tone of the conversation he'd been playing on repeat in his mind all morning. He intended to keep his message relatively curt. He needed to thank his advisors for placing their trust and time in him over the last year. He wanted to let them know due to medical reasons, he could no longer continue his studies. And he hoped to assure them his medical condition, which he'd only recently discovered, had in no way impacted his decisions while working for them in the hospital. He was afraid they might express concern over his prior judgments when treating patients.

Ethan listened through the closed door as they discussed his exams, papers, journals, lab work, and various interactions at the hospital in the last few months.

After telling his mother and meeting with his doctor to establish a treatment plan for the next few months, Ethan's first priority had required elimination of the key activities consuming his days—medical school and training at the hospital. He had known there was an urgency to tell his brothers and to let Emma know what he'd learned about his grim future but deemed it necessary to clear off all the nonemotional connections before telling those to whom he was closest.

The door to his advisor's office opened. An older Chinese woman poked out her head. "We're ready for you, Ethan. Please join us."

He walked toward the couch in the seating area to the right of her desk and sat. His advisor and the assigned physician already both positioned themselves in chairs directly across from him—their usual location during his quarterly meetings.

"Ethan, you scheduled this time with us to discuss something about the upcoming academic year; however, more pressing matters have come to our attention."

"Yes, I have an issue we need to discuss."

His advisor reached out and placed her hand on his knee. "We know about your diagnosis. And may I say on behalf of both of us, and on Boston University, we're humbled to have enjoyed the time we've had with you over the last few years. We're also deeply saddened by the news. May I hug you?" she asked.

"You're the first two people I've talked to about this, except for my mother. Unless you count when I went to my father's grave to tell him, but since he's already gone, I suppose that doesn't count." Ethan smiled, recognizing her genuine concern rather than simple professional courtesy. "Yes, you can hug me."

And she did. Ethan swallowed hard and fought back the lump growing higher in his throat. "I'm not even going to ask how you know about my illness. With such little time left, I'd only scheduled this meeting today to inform you I would be leaving Boston University."

Ethan finished meeting with his advisors and talking about his condition. They guided and encouraged him to confide in his family as soon as possible. He thanked them for everything and soon walked off in a silent vacuum on the campus where he'd spent the last five years of his life, knowing he'd never step back on its comforting landscape again.

* * *

As he pulled to the curb noticing all the spots were taken, Ethan hopped off his bicycle and carried it up the steps into his building. When he arrived in his loft, he locked the bike and admired the new curtains Emma had installed while he was away for the afternoon.

"The curtains look fantastic, Emma. Just like you."

She stepped back from the window and nodded her head in agreement. "They are amazing, as you thought they would be. I'm so glad we selected these instead of the green ones."

"I'm so glad I selected you instead of... well never mind." He'd met her roommate the same day as he'd met Emma several years ago, and almost went out on a date with her that first week, too. Luckily, Emma returned his call first and stole his heart.

Emma scrunched her eyes close together and displayed a slight pouty face. "You better not finish that statement, Ethan Glass. I'll call your mother and tell her you're being mean to me. She might love me even more than she loves you since we've met."

"I'm starting to believe that may be true. Hasn't she called you every day this week?"

"Yes, she has. Don't get me wrong, I'm glad to bond with her..."

"But?"

"I'm not so sure why."

"You never know with my mother. Just be happy. Are we still on for dinner tonight?"

"Yes, we're definitely on. I need to run errands for a few hours, but I'll meet you at the restaurant at eight." Emma kissed her boyfriend goodbye and left the loft.

Ethan pulled out the folded-up paper from his wallet and verified his checklist of tasks to do that evening before he asked her an important question.

Checking the time, Ethan verified he had a few minutes before he needed to meet Emma at Le Joliet. He'd selected the restaurant as it was her favorite French bistro in all of Boston. Ethan booked the chef's table in a private room off to the side where the chef would personally deliver each course to his guests, tempting their palates with his latest inventions.

Ethan dialed his mother, and she answered on the first ring.

"Are you ready for tonight?" Olivia told him about the day his father had proposed to her under the cherry trees in the botanical garden, evoking in her mind the scent of lilies and image of Ben on one knee. Such a comfort would never be forgotten.

"Yes. Everything is set. I have Grandma Eleanor's ring in my jacket pocket. The hostess knows to sneak it into the chef who's gonna deliver it with the appetizers. Are you sure I'm doing the right thing, Mom?"

"Yes, I'm confident she will want to marry you. I've spent many hours with her on the phone the last two weeks, Ethan. She's become a daughter to me. She cares for you so deeply."

"Does she know I'm going to propose tonight?"

"She didn't let on anything to me when we spoke earlier. Did you love the curtains? I told her to go with those and not the green ones. She emailed pictures to me last week, and the green ones were awful."

He laughed. "Yes, they looked great. I'm glad it will be a surprise for her tonight. But this is hard, Mom. It's not a normal proposal."

"No, there's nothing normal about it. There's also nothing normal about this situation. You're supposed to have so much life ahead of you. It should be me, not you." Exasperation stole the perimeters of her weakened voice. Her hands shook as she tried to maintain her emotions.

"We can't change it. We have to accept it. I'm not wasting any of the time I have left." Ethan's voice remained calm and encouraging.

"I know. I'll stop. We still need to have more conversations. Did you tell the school today?"

"Yes, they know. They were very caring and pushed me to recognize the good work I've done to date, concerning, you know, the things I won't be able to finish."

"That's their job, Ethan. They're your advisors. They want the best for you, too. Just as your family does. I have something to ask of you, Ethan." Her voice quivered as she spoke.

"What, Mom?"

"I want you to come back home. I want you to live at the house with me. With your brothers."

"I see."

"I want you to come for your father's birthday party next week and stay here until..."

Silence filled the room for a painful ten seconds that felt more like a hundred hours in dark and blistering hell.

"Until I die? You need to say it, Mom."

"Yes, until you die." Idle fear resonated in Olivia's voice. She calmed her tone and continued. "And you must bring Emma. She belongs here with us."

"I will think about it, Mom. I haven't planned that far ahead. I'm taking it a few steps at a time. I ended my ties to the university today. I'm telling Emma tonight and giving her the option of marrying me or of leaving before I get sick."

"She will choose to marry you."

"I hope she will, too. You will need to be available for her afterward. Her strength is a façade, not a certainty."

"You have no idea how much strength people have until they're truly tested, Ethan."

* * *

Ethan sat at Le Joliet's high rectangular marble chef's table waiting for Emma to arrive. Everything was in place. He'd told the chef to pick the menu needing one less task to hold responsibility for. While he wasn't nervous, Ethan couldn't sit still. He'd started to notice minor tremors occurring in his extremities the last few hours. It was an early symptom, his doctor warned him.

Emma arrived and walked toward their table. Ethan sat in the higher platform section of the split-level room and could watch without any obstruction as she entered. She wore a glimmering purple satin dress that fell just a few inches below her knees. A thin black braided rope, with the two ends gently resting on her slim hips, lay delicately cinched together around her waist, enticing him, and flaunting her perfect figure and ivory skin. Her shapely legs glided across the floor toward him. She'd chosen the diamond earrings and necklace her parents had given to her for graduation, and as she walked past the chandeliers in the main room, the jewelry sparkled and danced around her radiant expression. A butterfly clip pulled her hair tightly to the sides of her head casting an exquisite regal appearance. A few auburn locks cascaded over the mesmerizing eyes he often found himself lost in.

"You look stunning, Emma."

"I am stunning."

"Maybe we should go home right now."

"Is that what you wanna do, Ethan?"

"Yes. I mean no. Later. Not right now. Let's sit." His face bubbled with a devilish grin that remembered its remaining life was brief.

After the waiter dropped off their drinks, Ethan knew it was time to tell Emma about his condition. He didn't want to tell her, but he had no other fair options. He thought about taking her to the doctor to let a professional explain it. He even considered asking his mother to deliver the news since she'd become close with Emma. Ultimately, he knew it was his responsibility, and if he only had a few more months left, he was determined to follow through on all the normal steps a couple would take when getting engaged. First, he needed to tell her he was sick, and then he'd be ready to pop the question in the most romantic way possible, given the limitations of the future.

"Emma, there's something I need to talk to you about." He reached for her hand.

Her trembling fingers fell against his cool, shaky grip.

"I learned surprising news recently. It has a huge and unexpected consequence for my future. For our future." He paused to search her rich brown eyes losing himself second by second in the fireworks that were the specks of green waltzing around them from the candlelight on the table.

She smiled and squeezed his hand. "I'm listening."

"I visited the doctor a few weeks ago after I had a couple of dizzy spells and passed out several times at the hospital during rounds. I never told you about them, as I didn't want to acknowledge it was serious."

Emma, eyes glassy at the unexpected directional change in the conversation, attempted to pull her hand back, but Ethan wouldn't let go.

"Ethan, you're scaring me." Her face fell a few shades paler than a harsh winter's white storm.

"I know, but I don't have any other way to tell you. The doctors ran several tests. I checked with another specialist and scheduled a second round of tests. They came back with the same results."

Emma's shoulders shivered as the chill surrounding the table nipped at her skin.

Ethan's fingers had jagged icicles running through them. "I have a brain tumor, and the doctors can't do anything to fix it. If I attempt surgery, I won't survive. At best, the doctor gives me three months. At worst, I may only have a few weeks left."

"Please tell me you're joking." She stood appearing desperate to find herself anywhere else but in the restaurant at that moment. The table shifted from the pressure her body placed upon it. Choosing between locating an escape route or flipping the table across the room, tore Emma into pieces.

No smiles, no laughs, not even a breath of air emanated from Ethan's mouth. Emma yanked her hand back and pushed both to her lips, biting her nails and willing her eyes not to betray what surfaced in her mind.

"Emma." He stood and walked to her side of the table. "Emma, I'm not joking." He wrapped her in both arms. The warmth of his skin overtook the coolness of hers.

"There's nothing to be done?" she whispered, as she stood against him.

He turned her stiffened body around to face him and stared directly at her sullen expression. "Nothing."

While they stood holding one another entrapped in a moment few people ever have to experience, the chef dropped off their appetizers and discreetly walked away careful not to disrupt what should have been the happiest moment of a woman's lifetime.

Ethan grabbed her hands, placing them in his. "I have adored you for the last few years of my life. And regardless of what I learned from the doctors in the last month, it was always my intention to ask you something important this summer. I still want to ask you because I can think of nothing I would want more than to have you by my side for whatever time I have left. But I could never pressure you under the circumstances."

Ethan reached back toward the table and lifted the silver domed cover where his grandmother's wedding ring lay atop a porcelain dish.

Emma steadied her body against the back of the chair, her mind caught between the potential for sheer joy and the painful weight of the truth.

"It would make me the happiest man alive if you would stand by my side Emma, for however many weeks or months I have left, as my equal, my friend, my companion, my support, and my wife."

He pulled her hands toward his lips with one arm and kissed them, and his other retrieved his grandmother's engagement ring.

"If you choose to become my wife, we will live as happily as we can together until I'm gone. But I must give you the opportunity to protect yourself from a future where you will watch me die. I will not ask any questions. I will not pressure you. I will not be upset with you. I love you beyond anything I can explain in words. I want only for you to be as happy as you can be for the rest of your life. And if that means you want to leave right now and never see me again, I understand."

He released her hand after placing the ring on her finger, forgetting his fears, and stepped back toward his seat, his eyes not once leaving hers.

"Emma, knowing everything I dropped on you these last few minutes, I want to give you the opportunity to decide for yourself if you want to marry me."

Chapter 21 – Olivia

Olivia walked toward the bedside table admiring the new frame with Ben's picture she'd set on it the day before replacing the long-dirtied coffee mug. As she fiddled with her notes containing her talking points for Betty to assume control of their philanthropic responsibilities, the phone rang. Olivia checked the caller ID and collected the phone to talk to the attorney.

"Hello."

"Good afternoon, Mrs. Glass. This is Ira Rattenbury."

"I expected your call today. Do you have news?"

"Yes, I finished my investigation and met with Miss Hector myself earlier in the week."

Olivia breathed in each whisper of air that stole her remaining courage. She was filled with utter disappointment upon learning Ira had been successful. "So, she is alive?"

"Yes, living in Michigan. Rowena moved away after the baby was born and took a job at a manufacturing company where she still works, believe it or not."

Olivia sat on the bed with her eyes closed. *I choose to believe not.*

Her toes scratched against the carpeted floor pushing the woven threads from side to side, knowing she would soon discover how much of her life would once again pivot toward another unexpected arc—a consistent pattern the last few months. Initially, she'd hoped the woman had passed away years before, so she wouldn't have to face the consequences of Ben's decision. She had already decided if Rowena had died, the secret would stay buried as there would be no sense in destroying her family if her son would never be able to meet his birth mother.

As the weeks passed, and Olivia had spent time with each of her sons, part of her wanted to meet the woman who had abandoned her baby, uncertain if it were to thank her or to throttle her. After observing the pain harboring within each son, Olivia had developed, and at times encouraged, a morbid curiosity that it would have been better if Rowena Hector could become part of their lives to correct the sins of the past.

The silence on the phone stung as she prepared to ask the question. "Does she want to meet her son?"

* * *

Olivia pushed the prior day's conversation with Ira Rattenbury as far away as she could. She turned to Diane and said, "At first, I felt it odd to celebrate Ben's seventieth birthday... since he'd only passed away a few months ago... but when each of the boys encouraged me to look for a sense of closure and to find a way to move forward, I knew throwing a party was the right decision."

Olivia placed her hands on the back of the chair at the breakfast nook. She'd chosen a soft white sleeveless dress with an empire cut and let her hair fall with a gentle ease around her shoulders, rather than tied back in its usual restricted state. No shoes on her feet, minimal jewelry, a necessary change of appearance as she set the course for her future. "Are you ready?"

"I'm always in the mood for a party." Diane snickered.

"Given all that's happened, I need to bring everyone together and find a way to heal our family. We've shattered into too many directions, and I'm sick and tired of wobbling on the edge of a cliff, one step closer to falling over every time I learn a new secret about my family."

"It's been rough, Liv, but things are getting better. Are Caleb and Jake sleeping in?" Diane joined her sister at the table.

"No. Caleb took Jake for a drive around Brandywine to show him where he grew up."

"Are you okay with Jake being here?"

"Yes. They arrived so late last night I only had a few minutes to talk with them before Caleb ushered him off to sleep. We haven't found an opportunity to discuss how to introduce Jake to the rest of the family."

"I'm sure you'll figure it out before everyone else arrives. When are you expecting them?"

"I've asked everyone to be here at three o'clock today. I've also decided what to do about Ben's letter. It's about time I took control of the situation."

Diane watched her sister closely. Ever since they were children, Olivia's domineering personality clouded each of her relationships. She had insisted on being in charge of their school groups. She'd constantly told Diane how to dress, which classes to enroll in, or what to read. It suited Diane, as she'd hated choosing on her own. Olivia often assumed it was why Diane had stayed unhappily married for such a long period. While Olivia tried to govern the relationship that she'd built with each son, it always fell one rung short on the ladder that connected each of their lives.

"You've always been a good leader, Liv."

"It's taken me some time and several acts of patience to understand Ben's death. It never made sense to me, and you know I've never been one to accept that actions just happened. There had to be a reason he was in the car at that moment. A reason it occurred before he could enjoy retirement. A reason it unfolded before he could tell me about Rowena himself and not through a ridiculous letter." Olivia pushed her plate away waving the envelope at her sister.

"I know what you mean. Sometimes things happen for a specific reason," Diane said.

"The family had fallen apart. None of us trusted one another to talk about our problems. We had no idea what was happening around us and never would have until too late. That's why the accident happened when it did."

"To wake us up?"

"Yes. To show us we've been blindly living our lives without ever stopping to consider what we're doing. We never discuss our emotions and concerns with one another. We decide in a vacuum, or we don't decide at all and let situations go for far too long. You would have lived the rest of your days as an unhappy wife catering to a life of subservience had Ben not pushed you to end your marriage."

Diane glanced across the vast expanse of the table focusing on the hope appearing in Olivia's eyes for the first time in months. "You're right. It's hard to accept that the motivating factor for any of us to move on, or for you and the boys to change, was if Ben died. That's unfair. He was a good man."

Olivia nodded. "Sometimes our choices dictate a path or a destiny we cannot change. Ben chose not to tell me what happened with our baby. He chose not to tell me my child died. Look at what's happened. I learn another son has an inoperable brain tumor, and I have to watch him die with no ability to change the outcome. What if Ben told me our baby had died, and we chose together to switch children with Rowena? Maybe Ethan wouldn't be suffering those consequences now. Maybe he wouldn't be dead in a few months. I'm not saying one thing caused the other, but what if it were destiny for me to lose a child... and this is karma?"

Diane comforted her sister. "Liv, we'll never know what would have happened if Ben took a different path. This is where we are now. You gotta decide how you want to handle the situation. You can't test fate and get a different future just because you don't like the first outcome. What're you gonna do with everyone this afternoon?"

"I'm going to be a leader. I'm going to fix everything. I'm going to do what any good mother would do to protect her family."

* * *

Hours later, Ethan's taxi dropped him off in front of Olivia's house. He paid the driver, stepped out of the back seat, and walked toward the trunk to grab the bags. He had several suitcases packed given he planned to stay for whatever amount of time he had left in his young life.

Matt and Margaret soon arrived. Matt's nerves danced with adrenaline, his skin percolated a sour sweat, as though he hid behind the doors of a closet that a burglar was about to open. Olivia hadn't yet told Margaret what happened with her youngest daughter, but Matt knew his mother wouldn't keep it quiet much longer. Diane let them into the study to the right of the front hall foyer.

Sarah and Teddy walked the side path having parked in the back entrance to steal a few moments of solitude before any drama began. Sarah's face glowed with excitement hoping to talk with Olivia about Teddy being the baby's real father, but Olivia hadn't been able to find time the last few days. Sarah also wanted to tell Zach about her baby's paternity, even though they agreed never to speak about it again, as her news meant they could pretend it never happened—removing nearly all guilt over what they had done. There was no need for her husband to know what occurred with Zach at this point.

Teddy walked toward Matt to discuss the financial situation at the law firm, since Matt had artfully avoided him the last few days, leaving them unprepared for the upcoming meeting with the partners the following week. While Teddy's anger grew evident in his determined and deliberate stride, it exploded with noticeable fury in the hard-set grimace displayed between his clenched jaw and narrowed eyes. Just as he began to admonish his brother, Olivia entered the study.

"Hello. I'm so glad everyone could attend." As her eyes traveled the room, she monitored Diane, Matt and Margaret, Teddy and Sarah, and Zach, each standing around looking for a clear sign of the future to come.

The front door opened, and Ethan called out. "We're here." Emma followed soon afterward, hiding her left hand in her pocket so no one would notice the engagement ring until Ethan was ready to tell them she'd said yes to his marriage proposal.

While his brother walked into the study, Caleb led Jake down the steps. "And so are we." A nervous strain accompanied his voice.

Margaret was the first to notice Jake. She mentally gave herself a high-five for being right in recognizing he could be secretly gay.

Diane jogged over to Caleb anxious to catch his attention. "Jake's even cuter than the picture you sent me. Yum."

Caleb hugged his aunt and whispered, "Back off, he's mine."

Zach grinned, exuding sheer relief today's focus would no longer center around his actions. His brothers could take front stage where they belonged.

Olivia, energized and ready to take control, jumped in. "Excellent, everyone's here. Let's sit. I have many topics I want to talk about to-day before we celebrate your father's life. First, we need to welcome Emma and Jake. They are both new to this family, and I'm sure you are wondering who they are. All will be revealed soon. Please let me say a few words first."

Everyone took their seats. Olivia leaned against the desk toward the front of the room where she could maintain a clear view of everyone. She relaxed her shoulders, rested her hands clasped together on her lap, and began the speech she'd rehearsed earlier that morning. It was going to be her marionette show this time.

"It was important for me to have the whole family together for Ben's birthday. It has been hard for me to accept his death, especially today, knowing he would have been seventy years old and only a few months away from retirement." She paused to sip her tea. "But I have to accept it, as do each of you, and move forward with a life different from the one I'd expected. I resigned from my positions with the charities this week. Betty will take over. It was time for me to begin my own re-tirement."

A few surprised expressions appeared, and some family members said congratulations.

"I miss your father, boys. Just as I'd miss my own breath if it had been taken from me like he was. We spent over forty years together as husband and wife, as best friends, and as parents to each of you. We loved each of you since the moment you were born, through your childhood, and especially as each of you grew into the man you are today." She paused and looked around the room noticing Emma hiding her hand behind Ethan's waist. Jake appeared to study everyone's face, mentally comparing them to pictures he'd seen or descriptions he'd heard, given the lack of any formal introductions to Caleb's family. Olivia knew they thought she failed to notice what really happened around her in the past, but she'd always known enough.

"Some of you gave us lots of gray hair." Her eyes focused on Zachary, as she recalled the highlights of many historical arguments, but also their recent progress.

"Some of you raised yourselves and ran toward your own extraordinary goals and dreams." She glanced at Ethan and Caleb, comforted by memories of their good natures and loving personalities.

"Some of you stayed close to your father and joined the law firm to stand by his side." She looked back toward Matt and Teddy, gratified and honored over all their accomplishments.

"I'm proud of you all for everything you've done, for the grandchildren you've given us, and for the strong and honorable men you've become. I know there have been times when it appeared as if your father and I were disappointed or upset with you. We only wanted the best for you, to challenge you to achieve greatness in your lives. Over the last few months since your father passed away, I've learned parents cannot always protect their children from what the world dishes out. Sometimes the inevitable happens. Sometimes people make poor decisions. Sometimes the truth hurts." Olivia observed each of her children's reactions, noticing the tense, arched shoulders in some. Relief filled other's expression. Her own mind battled finding strength and controlling her tears.

"Since your father's gone, it's my responsibility to protect this family. As much as you're all grown men, you're still my children, and a mother needs to protect her young. When your father died and left me those letters, all the resulting changes swiftly opened my eyes to everything around me. I had become distracted by my work with the charities, in my social obligations, in my drive to tell you boys how to live your lives, unwilling to see reality. I had failed to recognize what happened in each of your lives. And what happened was much more important than what I had wanted for you."

Olivia fiddled with the set of pearls around her neck, twisting each perfectly round orb, comforted by the tightness they claimed around her. She took a few seconds to prepare for her next steps, focusing her eyes on the floor beneath her, recalling the times her sons crawled across the carpet to reach their father sitting behind his desk. The moments when they first stood and walked into her arms. The days when they brought their own children back home to continue the traditions of growing up in the Glass family. "It is time to remove the barriers holding us all back from being honest with one another. We need to learn to forgive ourselves, and others, for the mistakes of the past. We need to focus on the future."

She paused and tilted her head toward Caleb. "Caleb, I want to start with you. When you left Brandywine on your own and built that beautiful home in Maine, I had always thought I'd done something wrong to push you out. I was angry you stayed away and had only visited on Christmas. I'd never realized what went on underneath the surface. I apologize if I've ever been closed-minded or not recognized everyone is different. I take the blame for not creating an environment where you felt comfortable enough to tell us what was going on. I've lost years being open and honest with you. I've lost years getting to know the real you, while you've been pretending to be someone you're not. We can fix it today. I want to get to know you and your husband. I want Jake to be a part of our family."

"Always be a first-rate version of yourself, instead of a second-rate version of somebody else," said Jake.

Olivia said, "Judy Garland."

Jake smiled. "We're gonna get along famously, Olivia." He turned to Caleb as his cheeks grew a rosier shade of red. "I love her already."

Caleb's eyes opened wide, his pupils dilated pools of jet black ink. "Mom, I don't know what to say. I'm glad you want our family to be different, but how did you know we were married?" Caleb reached for Jake's shoulder.

Jake sat back mesmerized by the events occurring before him. He knew Caleb's family could be intense, but his expectations underestimated the drama scale of the Glass secret revelations.

"At your house. You received a phone call the day I left, and the man asked to speak to Jake Glass. It became obvious before long." She walked over to Jake. "Welcome to the family. I want to get to know you better, especially if you boys are going to adopt a baby." She reached forward and hugged him, not noticing the pure look of surprise on his trepid face. Or not really caring. He belonged there now.

Caleb's mouth dropped a few inches as did several other people's expressions in the room. He grew tired of the surprises launched upon him in his father's study that summer.

Diane's face lit with joy as a child brought a blessing in her world, no matter how it came to pass.

"What?" Caleb spit out his drink, spraying a fine mist across the room. "You know about the adoption? Do you know everything we're doing?" His voice both whined and laughed.

"I know way more than anyone thinks I know." Olivia backed away from Jake, her hands twisting once again at her necklace.

Jake said, "Yes, we're going to adopt a baby when he or she is born in a few weeks. I appreciate everything you've said. And I want to be part of your family."

Ethan leaned forward. "Caleb, Jake, congratulations. I'm happy you found each other. I wish you had told me sooner, but I understand it's a process and takes time to get comfortable sharing it with your family. Be prepared as this generation has only produced girls."

Caleb said, "Yes, it's a bit strange. Mom and Dad had five boys, but so far, they only have granddaughters. I appreciate how happy you are for Jake and me. Does anyone have an issue with it or want to talk about it? Teddy, Matt?"

They both shook their heads detecting a shared and connected discomfort sitting in the room, listening to their mother's words and worrying what else she may reveal that afternoon.

Matt's desperation for another pill peaked, but his mother had taken the last bottle he had bought earlier in the week. And the kid he purchased them from the last few times wouldn't return his phone calls after Matt called him a dirty scumbag for raising his prices.

Margaret spoke up. "My brother is gay. I also suspected you were, but I didn't want to say anything until you were ready. Congratulations on the adoption. That's exciting news. It will be great your baby will have lots of cousins around to help him or her out. And speaking of cousins, Matt and I have news."

Olivia interrupted. "Margaret, before you finish that thought, maybe I could continue with a couple more items? I'm sorry, I have a few important messages I need to get out in the open." As she stepped forward, her fingers tugged at the pearls to give herself room to breathe.

Margaret sat, dismayed at her mother-in-law's need to prevent her from revealing her news. Matt had agreed earlier they could tell the family today. "Of course, Olivia."

"Thank you. I'm glad we're able to be honest today so that Caleb could introduce Jake to our family. It's imperative we learn from Ben's death, stop holding onto secrets and understand how to communicate with each another without the walls holding us back."

Olivia raised her eyes toward another son. "Theodore, when I visited with you a few weeks ago, I could tell something changed inside you. Whether it was your father's death or Sarah's pregnancy, you became someone different from who you were in the past."

Sarah's hands shook. Olivia wouldn't dare mention Zach and the baby. She needed to find a way to stop her from talking, so she could tell her the baby was Teddy's.

Margaret jumped in. "You're pregnant? I'm pregnant, too. Oh, when are you due?" She could barely contain herself.

Matt realized Margaret had broken the news to everyone about their new baby. He never told Margaret that Sarah was pregnant, given everything going in the last week. He was happy but scared of whatever would come next.

Sarah stood, forgetting about the dangers lurking around her if Olivia had her way. "Yes, Teddy and I found out a few weeks ago. I'm due in February." She grabbed her husband's hand.

Margaret squealed. "So am I. February 1st." She jumped up and down.

"Me, too." The sisters-in-law hugged, rivaling reunited school girls, lifting the tone in the room a bit lighter and happier.

"Congratulations."

"How exciting!"

"I'm an uncle again."

Olivia let the girls have their moment. The family needed joyful moments among the rest of the news she planned to break today. Letting go of control was part of her future plan, at least once she got through everything she'd arranged for today's events.

The expectant fathers congratulated one another. As they shook hands, Teddy contemplated not talking to his brother about the missing cash at the firm, considering maybe all would be fine based on Margaret's news.

Matt could barely look his brother in the eye concerned over how he'd resolve their open issues at the firm. He was afraid to disappoint his family and couldn't bring his usual chumminess to the table.

Zach's stomach sank afraid of how far his mother would go with her revelations.

Olivia regained control in the room. "It's fantastic news. Anyone else pregnant who wants to share their news?" she joked while rotating the string of pearls around her neck, each sphere pressing into her skin with a powerful force.

All eyes moved with rapid speed toward the only other woman in the room.

Emma blushed and turned to Ethan for a life jacket.

Ethan responded before she had to say anything. "No, she's not pregnant. At least I don't think she is. Are you, Emma?" Ethan had a devilish grin.

While Emma's head shook out a no, her lips formed a Cheshire smile.

"Exactly, I mean, she couldn't be pregnant before we got hitched, right?" Ethan raised her left hand above his shoulders to display her fingers to everyone.

Emma blushed.

Sarah, thrilled that the conversation had turned away from her pregnancy, noticed the ring on Emma's finger before anyone else. "Ethan, did you propose to her?"

Olivia teared up, angry she could do nothing to fix Ethan's situation but resolved to hold her family together despite the impending loss.

"Yes, Ethan asked me earlier in the week, and I've said yes." Drops rolled from Emma's eyes. Everyone in the room thought she cried happy tears, but for Emma, they were not. After Ethan confessed at the restaurant he only had a few months to live, she knew at once she wanted to marry him and be with him until the end. She couldn't possibly leave him despite the circumstances and the fear of becoming such a young widow.

Olivia walked over to Emma and held her close. "Congratulations. I'm so happy for you both." For a moment, they smiled at one another, knowing they would need to support each other through the coming months. They were the two women closest to Ethan, both unready to handle the tragedy soon becoming the focus of everyone's lives.

Olivia whispered in Emma's ears. "Don't say anything yet. I don't want to tell everyone about Ethan until I cover a few other items. I know it's hard, but please be strong for him."

Emma returned to her seat next to Ethan noticing Ethan's knees shaking against hers.

Diane stood behind her and placed one hand on Emma's shoulder. "We need more women in this family. Let's put those boys in their place," she chuckled.

Emma smiled. Ethan kissed his fiancée and attempted to minimize the shuddering which had grown stronger in his right leg over the last few days. The doctors predicted each of these symptoms, but he refused to give into their demands.

Zach interjected. "Look at the great news today. Dad would be so happy with our progress."

Olivia smiled at her son. "He would, but not everything is purely good news, Zachary. We have a few situations we need to talk about as a family before we can move on." Olivia's face flushed red as she swallowed hard against the heat and pressure clinging to her neck and face.

"As I explained, when I saw Theodore a few weeks ago, a change developed within him. Sarah's persistence shined a light on my foolish behavior." Olivia glanced at her daughter-in-law. "Theodore has a few passions in his life he needs to explore. Passions that might conflict with assuming responsibility for the law practice. Passions I never knew of, or maybe I never chose to acknowledge."

Olivia faced her eldest son. "Theodore, it would have brought your father and me great pleasure for you to follow in his steps to become a prominent attorney and take over as a partner in the law practice he built over the last thirty years. You've been working incredibly hard to learn everything you needed to take his place. I don't ever recall asking what you wanted, and we should have asked you. We should be giving you the choice, not telling you what you had to do."

Teddy looked at Sarah sensing relief build around him and desiring everything to work out for once. He glanced back toward his mother. "I needed to hear you say it, Mom. I needed to know you could give me a choice to decide my future. I'm grateful for everything you and Dad have taught me over the years, but I don't want to become a partner. I don't want to assume responsibility for the practice, especially when I'm going to become a father soon. I am tired of exhaustion and fury filling my every day, grouchy with everyone around me because they've disappointed me. I need to shed this steel coating. I've decided to go back to school to focus my energy and my future on something different, something that gives me great pleasure."

Olivia nodded. "I want the best for you, Theodore. Accepting you will sell the legacy your father worked so hard to achieve hurts, but he dreamed of the firm, not you. It has given us many memories over the years, but now it's our turn to focus on our own destinies. I support you in the decision to sell the firm to the partners and follow your dream to be an artist."

Olivia recalled the day Ben came home full of unstoppable glee announcing the bank approved his request for a business loan to start his own firm. She let the memory fade so that she could move on, wistful thoughts still penetrating the surface as she carried forward.

Olivia could tell Matt must have known what Teddy's decision meant. Matt would have to come clean about the money he'd borrowed, and he'd potentially lose his job once the other partners took over.

Matt sighed. "But what about the work I've done for the firm?"

Teddy glanced at his brother attempting to carefully articulate his next words, but his mother interrupted before he could begin.

"Matthew, you've done a great job managing the firm's books for the last few years. In fact, you've been the rock holding together so many ties among this family. But it may be time for you to consider other options, too." She paused, hoping he'd have the courage to talk about his problems, her mind forcing out the images of his daughter dangling from the crib.

Matt sat back silently knowing his wife would have to assemble the pieces he had destroyed. He had no strength left in his body. Withdrawal symptoms had plagued his nerves with increasing pressure each day.

Margaret leaned forward. "What's worrying you, Matt? Do you not want to leave the firm?"

"I'm not sure." Matt's brow released drops of sweat, a salty one landing on his upper lip. He hesitated. "I need time off. I may be under too much pressure."

"Pressure from what, Matthew?" Olivia hoped to get him to talk about his situation, so she didn't have to tell everyone. It was important he admit it on his own.

"From everything. We don't have enough clients anymore at the firm. Dad pulled back to retire. Teddy had little interest in that piece of the business. I kept trying to find ways to balance out the finances, but it's a bit of a mess. We needed to let the new hires go. And we needed to focus on how to win more clients and new business. I can't do it all on my own."

Teddy finally found a chance to speak. "Matt, that wasn't your job. It would seem to me it's the partners' job to handle the administration. You should have told me. I could have tried to help."

"It's not just the firm. I got nervous at home, too." He glanced in the opposite direction of his wife. "Margaret, I'm so sorry."

Margaret raised her brow and cocked her head to the side. "Matt, what's wrong? Talk to me."

"We don't have enough money to afford the renovations on the house. Or the new van. Or all the trips and extravagant spending we do for the kids. I lied about a hacker stealing our credit card information. The bank canceled the account because I haven't been able to pay off the balances."

Margaret reached for her husband's hand knowing she needed to be a good wife. "You should have told me. We can cut our expenses. I thought you did well at work."

"I do, but it's been a bad year. Our bonuses were half what they were the previous year. But that's not all." He hung his head hoping her disappointment in his actions had disappeared in those moments.

Olivia interrupted. "It's okay, Matthew. Let's talk about it. We'll be here for you."

"I took anti-anxiety pills to relax. It was working for a while, but I got too calm and missed deadlines at work. A friend of mine suggested I take a few of his prescription tablets to balance out. After a few weeks, I found myself relying on both and couldn't function unless I popped a couple of pills."

Ethan shook his head. "Matt, you should have talked to me. I could have found better ways to guide you through it. Taking tons of pills is not the way to solve the problem."

"I know, but I was scared. Everyone thinks I'm so perfect, and I always have my life under control. The pressure grew too quickly, and I didn't know how to handle it. I screwed up. The doctor wouldn't renew my prescription anymore because I asked for too many pills." He paused and allowed himself a moment to finish his confession. "I logged online and met some kid off the internet to buy them."

Margaret cried. Diane, closest to her, comforted her with a gentle hug.

"Matthew, you told me earlier in the week you needed a new start. Are you ready to address this problem?" Olivia couldn't mention the incident of Melinda falling out of the crib. It had been more than enough to push her son into talking about the financial situation and the anxiety issues in front of his family. She filled with certainty he'd commit to finding a solution. She also didn't want to scare his wife further, as the accident served as a timely wake-up call, especially since Melinda's fall didn't cause any damage.

Margaret couldn't look or smile back at Matt. She was angry and hurt by his actions but knew the priority she had to face required a tenacity for climbing out of the ditch he'd dug around them.

Matt interrupted when it looked like she was about to say something. "I can't do this on my own. Margaret, I'm so sorry. But I don't want to hide it anymore. I have a problem, and I need help to fix it."

Sarah joined the conversation eager to solve her brother-in-law's addiction. "It's good you're talking, Matt. So many people wait until it's too late and something dangerous happens. You have a new baby on the way. I reckon this is the perfect time to address the addiction, so you can get better and be ready to start over with a fresh mind."

Zach said, "Yeah, Matt. Lots of people face these types of issues. I didn't talk about this with anyone, but back when Anastasia was younger, Dad forced me to deal with an addiction to coke. I entered a rehab facility for a few weeks and was able to kick the habit with his support."

Matt cocked his head toward his brother. "You went to rehab? I knew you used drugs for a while, and you got help, but I didn't know how bad."

"Yeah, I was a mess, but I have been sober for several years. We hide too many secrets in this family. We need to trust each other."

Margaret rubbed her belly. "Matt, we'll fix this together. We'll find a professional for you to talk to and a way to stop this from getting any worse. I need you healthy. I can't do this alone."

Jake leaned toward Caleb and whispered, "And you thought the focus would be on your family finding out you were gay. Your family is chock full of issues lurking behind the surface, and that's not even considering our news. Better than daytime television!"

"Shut your trap, babe, or we'll put you back on center stage." Caleb hit his husband on the arm, the way a cat would bat a mouse, smirking the whole time. "Maybe I didn't know my family as well as I thought I did."

Zach stood, managing the beginnings of a witty smile. "I've heard just about all the news I can take for today. Cabbie confesses he's gay and adopting a baby. Sarah and Margaret are pregnant at the same time. Ethan's getting married. Matt has a problem with pain pills and keeping up at the family firm that Pickles secretly wants to sell so he can become a painter. No offense, Matt, I will teach you how to fight the demons." Zach sighed, throwing his hands up in the air and glancing at his mother. "Maybe we can chill out for the rest of the day, have a few drinks and food, and celebrate our late father's seventieth birthday?"

Everyone laughed in agreement and rose from their seated positions.

Diane nodded at Olivia to acknowledge there was more to discuss, knowing her sister had not revealed everything at that point.

Olivia closed her eyes and continued speaking, tapping one foot against the carpet in a slow and deliberate, circular pattern, hoping to retain her self-control. She pulled at the necklace to keep her agitated hands occupied. "Don't get up yet. I have two more items to discuss before we move on."

Sarah and Zach looked across the room at one another, both having the same thoughts that their secret was about to explode around them. Neither had enough control to stop it.

"I'm proud of my sister for finding the courage to take charge of her life. I'm also thankful to her for showing me the courage to take charge of my life. Not only did she figure out I needed to spend time with each of you, real time where we communicated our feelings and opinions, but she also pointed out it was time I should choose my own path." Olivia braced for the angst and shouting she'd expected would follow her bombshell. "It's time to sell the family home."

Diane gasped. "Liv, you didn't tell me you were gonna sell the house."

Everyone, shocked and concerned, immediately expressed doubts and objections.

Olivia continued, despite their rising concerns. "I didn't tell anyone as I only decided early this morning. It's time I moved on, too. I've lived here with your father for most of our life together, and as much as I will miss being here, it's too big for one person. I need to find somewhere right for me."

She focused on Diane. "I'm taking us on a trip around the world, Diane. We're leaving in a few months to travel to all the places Ben and I had talked about visiting... to learn how to enjoy our lives and how to appreciate each day. But I cannot leave yet. Unfortunately, I have something else I need to do, something a mother should never be subjected to suffer through before my new life can begin."

Olivia stood, lifted her head, and found the courage to finish her thoughts. "The last item I need to tell everyone will bring even more heartbreak."

She moved toward the fireplace, stepping onto the slate tiles cemented before its hearth, her fingers twisting several of the translucent pearls that constricted her airflow as if they wanted to suffocate her. "Ethan has a brain tumor and only a few more months to live."

As she told her family the grave truth about Ethan, the pearls once secured around her throat ripped loose. One by one, they dropped to the slates below, each impact echoing with a sorrowful resonance throughout the room… as she spoke each word… as each tear rained from her eyes… as each blow stole her remaining strength. She could only hear the somber tones of the bagpipe's skirl she'd last heard at Ben's funeral.

Ethan first noticed her falling to the ground, and he jumped up to catch his mother with rapid attention. Her hand caught his, and she dragged him to the floor with her. For a few moments, she sat with her son holding his body with a fierce and uncontrollable instinct, unable to let go. Her eyes sobbed, and her lungs burned. "No, please don't take my baby from me," she cried.

Ethan helped her to his chair, and Emma poured her soon-to-be mother-in-law a glass of brandy, which she drank in the hopes it would cure each pain that ailed her. Once the liquor summoned her hidden strength and fortitude, Olivia found a way to explain Ethan's condition to the rest of the family, including how he would be living at home with her and Emma until the end.

As expected, heartbreaking emotions filled the home and the minds of the Glass family. None of the news they'd learned earlier in the day even held importance anymore, especially not when their youngest had such a brief amount of time left in his unceremoniously innocent life.

Ethan wouldn't allow them to grieve for him. His confidence blossomed, certain he had several more weeks where he'd have all his faculties and capacities to live a regular life before the tumor eviscerated his withering body. He couldn't afford to let himself be a victim but instead insisted his brothers focus on spending quality time with him building positive memories and learning how to take advantage of any remaining moments in each of their lives.

As the family meeting ended, Caleb and Jake took a drive to clear their minds and talk about everything that had happened. Once they'd processed Ethan's news, which was incredibly difficult for Caleb to accept given how much time he'd lost with his brother, they changed their focus to their own future, since they could now be open with Caleb's family. It was the first moment they had been alone since Caleb's family learned about his relationship, marriage, and impending fatherhood.

Margaret drove Matt back to their house to have a private conversation regarding how they'd planned to handle the next steps in procuring the solutions Matt needed to address his addiction. They were distraught over Ethan's news, but it was important they sought treatment for Matt, so he didn't end up in the same awful place. Margaret knew she had to take a lesson from her mother-in-law's playbook if they had any chance of survival.

Diane knew Olivia had one final conversation she needed to have with two of her sons. She found Emma and Ethan standing on the front porch near the rose bushes and asked them to join her for tea in the kitchen to talk about their wedding plans. As hard as it was to consider the limited future they would share, everyone found comfort in Ethan having enough time left to marry his true love, celebrating and creating happy memories to keep with them for the future.

Olivia told Zach, Teddy, and Sarah to stay behind in the study. When everyone else left, and they all sat near the fireplace, she spoke. "I've asked you to hold back because I have one other urgent item I need to cover with the three of you, but it should be handled more intimately."

Sarah, ravaged with fear at where the conversation went, interjected in the hopes she could stop the train from derailing. "Olivia, perhaps you and I could speak privately first?"

"Sarah, hold your horses. Did I get that expression right, dear? I've heard your side of the story, but I've made up my mind." Olivia was determined to address all the secrets, except for Ben's, as her family came first before she would allow herself to deal with Rowena.

"You don't understand. It's important we must speak." A fiery urgency accompanied Sarah's voice.

"Sarah, what's wrong?" Teddy noticed the rumbling of an ache in his jaw, surprisingly relaxed for the last hour.

Zach couldn't sit still. He knew what his mother was planning to do.

Sarah tried pleading. "No, please, Olivia. The situation has changed."

But it was too late. Olivia had spoken at the same time while Teddy's attention focused on his mother's words. "Sarah and Zachary did something foolish. A creative way to achieve your needs."

Sarah sunk back into the couch sensing her entire world ready to crumble. Her heartbeat slowed, and her eyes disappeared into the darkness around her.

"Shit." Zach walked toward the window and opened the closest liquor bottle, the only comfort he could find in the room. He drank directly from the bottle, gulping each swallow as if it were his last. "Mom, let it go."

Teddy's face grew even paler. "I don't understand what you're talking about, Mom."

"Zachary fathered Sarah's baby. They slept together hoping she would get pregnant because you're unable to father children. I'm sorry, Theodore. I couldn't stand by and let you raise another man's child, even if it is your brother's, without being part of the decision. History cannot repeat itself."

Teddy's eyes bulged, and he stared at his wife. "You slept... with Zach?"

"Yes, Teddy." Tears puddled under Sarah's eyes. "I slept with your brother, but you fathered this baby."

Zach stopped in his tracks at those words and rotated his body until she was in full view. "What?" His voice stammered, his shoulders lifted.

Olivia looked confused. "You told me it was Zachary's baby?"

"Teddy and I went to the doctor and learned I'm due February 1st. I was already pregnant when Zach and I slept together. The baby is really Teddy's."

Zach's heart raced. "I'm not the father?"

Sarah shook her head, part of her happy to deliver the news, part of her sad her husband had to find out this way. "No."

Olivia motioned to her son, her gut full of guilt and remorse over everything she forced to happen that day. "Zachary, let's leave Sarah and Theodore alone to talk."

Zach and Olivia walked to the door. Zach thrilled at the turn of events, Olivia despondent she hadn't listened to Sarah's plea.

"No, stay. I'm the one who needs to leave." Teddy pushed by them heading toward the hall. He stopped a few feet away and stared at his wife and brother. As he weighed the consequences of doing the right thing or letting his emotions control his behavior, his body betrayed his mind and won the spar. His right fist pulled back and slammed forward punching Zach's shocked face, landing directly on his left eye, knocking him back a few feet into the sideboard.

Olivia shut her eyes unwilling to take sides between her sons.

Sarah tried to grab hold of Teddy but could see in his eyes it would be a mistake. She retreated to her corner unnerved at the turn of events.

Zach, leaning on the sideboard, watched as his brother took a step closer to him. "Go ahead, Pickles. Hit me again. I deserve it."

Olivia screamed, but she was torn between two sons, right and wrong, the truth and whatever else had happened between them.

Teddy's eyes pierced through his brother, then back toward his wife. "You're not worth it." He rushed out the door leaving his family standing in silence unsure of what would come next.

With a voice full of years that held back her angst and fury, Sarah screamed while rushing out the door after her husband. "You're an awful woman, Olivia. You never listen to anyone else. It's always about you being in control."

Olivia never heard Sarah as her mind was distracted, grateful no one noticed her comment about history repeating itself among the commotion. She knew she'd still had one more conversation with Rowena Hector before she could reveal the contents of Ben's letters. And that would occur in just a few agonizing days. Nothing else mattered until she had her answers.

Chapter 22 – Caleb

Olivia watched and listened from the kitchen window as her son embraced Jake on the back deck, recognizing the love and respect they had for one another as a married couple. Caleb had grown into a caring and loving man, an echo of Ben, and recognizing the son she hadn't seen in years back in her life diverted Olivia's mind toward to the impending crisis. Olivia fiddled with the envelope in her pocket knowing all she needed to do was open it to know which boy's life would change, sizing the repercussions if she learned Caleb was not her child. She'd lost years with him because he never felt close enough to her and Ben to confess his secrets. Since reconnecting, they sewed the first stitch on the patch that would mend their relationship before he became a father. How could she possibly lose him again? She returned Ben's letter to the drawer in his desk in the study and locked it with the key.

* * *

Caleb and Jake stayed in Brandywine for a few more days after the weekend's tumultuous events. While packing their bags, they finished chatting about the implications of everything that had been revealed during their visit.

"I still can't believe you've never been to Connecticut before this trip," Caleb said.

"Nope. Never had time. I want to absorb as much as possible about your family while we're down this way."

"Especially before we have the baby. We'll never get here easily again."

"Speaking of the baby," Jake said.

"Yes?"

"Can we visit with Matt and Margaret tomorrow before we drive home to Maine? I want to learn more about having a newborn. They've got a whole boatload of kids at this point."

"Yes, definitely. You've never been around babies, have you?"

"No, I was the youngest of my siblings and cousins back in Iowa. And even though I'm a teacher, pre-teens are a different sort of nightmare. Being a father beckons quite a more abstract skill set, I suspect."

"You know how to relate to sixteen-year-olds and can mentor those monsters like no other, but we're in for a whole different ball game with babies and toddlers."

"Matt and Margaret will know how to coach us."

"It'll be good to see my brother. I'm still so upset over what he's done to himself with the drugs and the money. He really needs help."

"All the greats turn to some vice at one point or another, babe. Matt's overwhelmed and needs better coping skills. They'll teach him how to handle stress and deal with triggers when he checks into the rehab facility. It'll be good for him."

"You should tell him tomorrow. He needs to hear it from everyone. Since you're still a stranger to him… I mean that in the best way possible, Jake… it'll have a bigger impact coming from you."

"I am a newbie, but I don't want to be. The door is open now. My family wants nothing to do with me, so it's important I get closer to yours. I want to fit in with them."

"You will. Just be careful what you ask for. Once we let them back in, they're in. You saw what happened at the family meeting this week."

Jake laughed. "I did, but it was comforting how everyone cares about each other."

"Yup. So... have you decided what to do about teaching this year? We either need to hire a nanny, or you'll have to stay home. I've got so many projects lined up, I can't easily stop working."

"Are you still thinking about having a second baby again soon?"

"Yeah, it would be great to have our kids close in age. Despite all the drama, I'm glad I had my brothers."

"Well, I guess maybe I should stay home this first year and see how it goes. If we adopt a second baby, we can figure it out as we go. I can take a leave of absence for six months. I've got my tenure already."

"Are you sure? I don't want to pressure you."

"Yes. Remember, we're in this together. I'll take this first year, and maybe you can decrease the projects for next year and take the lead staying home. It's a fair balance. Plus, I'm sure your mother will be up north to visit more often, and she can pitch in."

"And we're gonna want to bring our kid home to play with Teddy's and Matt's new babies. Wow, we're all having children. It's nuts."

"Are you sure it's Teddy's baby?" Jake laughed. Caleb had told him about Zach's drunken phone call confessing he'd slept with Sarah.

"Yes, he texted me this morning. Sarah confirmed it is definitely Teddy's baby."

"You're family's a mess, Caleb."

Caleb placed his hand on his husband's knee, then drew him in for a kiss. After pulling away, he said, "No, Jake. *Our* family's a mess."

* * *

Caleb took a few trips back and forth to Brandywine over the next month to spend as much time with Ethan as he possibly could between his commitments for work and his preparation for the baby's arrival. While back in Brandywine, he and Ethan spent a few days fishing at Lake Wokagee, where their father had taken them as children, attempting to repair the damage and lost time between them. The other brothers couldn't attend, but Caleb was glad as he wanted time to bond with his youngest sibling on his own. At the southern part of town, a few streams emptied into the lake separating the towns of Willoughby and Brandywine, usually a prime location to catch a few bass. They settled on the banks early one morning under an unrelenting sun.

"I'm sorry I failed to be a good brother to you," Caleb said.

"That's ridiculous," replied Ethan. "When you left for college, I was barely a teenager. I understood you had your own life to start. I knew it would be different. Change was necessary."

"We've lost out on so much, and we have no time to fix it." Caleb focused on the line he dropped in the water ten feet out. The fish hadn't yet begun to bite.

"We don't need to fix it. It's not broken. By the way, you're letting the wind carry the line too far away. You always let that happen. I remember Dad trying to get you to be more careful," Ethan joked and patted his brother on his back.

"I know. I never could get the hang of it. Remember how Dad caught those giant largemouths on Labor Day weekend? When he asked me to hold the line, so he could unhook it? And I dropped the pole in the water. I'd never heard him curse so much."

"He was angry, but he also knew you tried. It was never your strongest talent."

Caleb looked back at his brother. "This really sucks. I'm gonna miss you. Even though I wasn't always here, you never left my mind."

"Let it go, Caleb. We can let the anger and the sadness derail us, or we can be happy for the time we had. We can learn from it. You have a kid to take care of in a couple of weeks. Remember what Dad taught us and be sure to teach it to your children. And tell them about me. It'll keep his memory alive for both of us."

* * *

After Caitlyn, the woman who'd selected Caleb and Jake to adopt her baby, went on bed rest for the last few weeks of the pregnancy, Caleb decided she should move into the guest bedroom on the main floor of their house. Having her close would allow them time to talk to the baby each night, as well as to ensure Caitlyn received enough rest and care. Once she gave birth, Caitlyn planned to move back to her own apartment to finish her dissertation and head to the West Coast where she already secured a new job. She would keep in contact with Caleb and Jake in case any medical issues arose after the baby was born, but Caitlyn had wanted to move on with her life and let them be responsible for their child. Shortly into September, Caleb and Jake rushed her to the hospital when labor kicked in. After twelve intense hours, they became the proud parents of a new baby boy.

Caleb called his mother to let her know she had her first official grandson. Olivia was ecstatic and asked if she could visit for a few days. Ethan's health was only just starting to decline despite the occasional trouble he had walking, but Ethan insisted Olivia take a long weekend to meet the new baby. Both Emma and Diane would be around to watch over Ethan.

Olivia arrived in Maine the day Caleb brought his son home from the hospital. As they drove to the front of their house, Olivia met Jake and Caleb on the porch excited to see the newest member of her family. It had no longer mattered that her son was gay, or he had gotten married without her ever knowing. She would have preferred to have been a part of the wedding but convinced herself to let go of what she lost in the past when it came to Caleb. It was the only way to ensure they could have a future.

Jake stepped out of the backseat of the Jeep while Caleb fidgeted over his new family and stopped to check every few seconds that nothing had blocked Jake's exit as he carried their precious new addition. As he neared his mother-in-law, Jake handed his son to Olivia, thrilled to be part of his new family, too.

"Have you decided on a name for this little munchkin?" Olivia tickled the baby's cheek.

Caleb smiled at his husband, and Jake winked back at him.

"Yes, Mom. We're going to name him Ethan Benjamin Glass."

Chapter 23 – Zach

Olivia met Zach in Brooklyn for dinner, surprising him as for once by taking a train into NYC from Connecticut to visit her son. As they sat in a corner booth at the diner, Anastasia played on her iPad while Zach flipped through his phone patiently waiting for the custody lawyer to call back. Olivia noticed the diner packed with hipsters, and while she felt out of place, the happy, younger crowd brought a smile to her face. She'd even chosen more casual clothing the last few days encouraging the freedoms retirement could offer her.

"The bruise appears to have healed well. I wouldn't have expected Theodore to react that way, but then again, I wouldn't have expected you to sleep with his wife. You need to be more careful, Zachary." She chided him while caressing his cheek. "Think about all you're trying to set right. You've done everything you can to prove Katerina is an unfit mother and does not deserve to have any custody other than supervised visits with Anastasia."

"I know, but I need to know it's final. I'm putting everything back together from this hellish summer we've had. Between Dad's death, this custody battle, and the situation with Sarah, my nerves are shot." Zach checked the phone's volume, pressing until it went on high.

"How is the situation with Sarah?" Olivia said. "Have you and Theodore talked since the party?" Her voice no longer held a bitter undertone.

Zach shook his head. "He hasn't returned any of my phone calls. I spoke with Sarah, and she assured me with one hundred percent certainty, Teddy fathered her child. But he can't get past knowing she and I slept together, that we were going to hide it from him if I had been the father."

"He has more than he can handle on his plate with preparing to sell the firm to Davis and Wittleton. I spoke with Theodore this morning, and he expects the sale should be complete in a few weeks." Olivia grew more comfortable with saying goodbye to the legacy Ben had built over the last thirty years. She recognized her future depended on her ability to accept the past.

"Did he say anything about me?"

"No, we didn't talk about you, but I forgive you. Not that you did anything to me, but I've had time to reflect, and I know your heart was in the right place. I've also seen the progress this summer in your own way despite everything that's occurred. You're pulling your life back together by protecting Anastasia and helping Matthew and Ethan get through their own struggles. You're a good father and brother, Zachary."

"Except to Pickles."

"Pickles will come around." She laughed at saying Theodore's nickname for the first time in years. "Let him have a few days to deal with everything. Don't you recall asking me to give you time with Anastasia? Have you thought about my proposal?"

"Yes, but it depends on the results of the custody case, Mom." He checked his phone again, but still no response.

"Let's order food. I'm hungry. Perhaps I should try those loaded burgers with all the toppings. I need more adventure, but I'm not ready for White Castle."

Zach laughed at his mother's sudden transformation. "Are you really my mother? I'm not sure I recognize you anymore."

Olivia smiled, closed her eyes, and breathed deeply. "I hope so."

* * *

Diane took Olivia and Anastasia for lunch leaving Zach home with Emma and Ethan for the afternoon. They played a few games of chess, but by midday, Ethan was tired and retired upstairs to take a nap leaving Emma in the den with Zach.

"How does he seem to you today?" Zach noticed how young Emma looked. Even though they were only six years apart, he'd lived a longer and tougher life. He also knew once Ethan died, it would all change for her. She'd soon have the same distraught expression as the rest of the Glass family, strained and stressed over the damage they'd suffered not only from life but also one another's actions.

"He's good. The headache disappeared, and he finished lunch. He only wanted to rest for thirty minutes, but I suspect he may sleep the whole afternoon. He tossed and turned a lot last night." Emma relaxed into the opposite side of the sofa.

"Do you want to watch a movie?" He noticed the energy dripping from Emma's usual cheeriness. "You look tired, maybe you need to take a nap."

"I am a bit wiped, but I don't want to sleep. Let's watch a movie, something funny. I need to laugh a bit." Emma kicked off her flats and curled her legs into the sofa.

At the same time, they both said, "*The Hangover.*"

Zach laughed. "You dig that movie?"

Emma jumped up. "Yaaas. I love it. It's my favorite."

"Ed Helms is awesome," they both said.

"He slayed it." Emma tossed a throw pillow at Zach. "For your neck. Cute tattoo, for sure. The vine looks so real. What does it mean?"

"You're the first person to ask me that question. No one ever saw past the ink." He smiled at her, enjoying her company, despite the reason she'd moved into the house. "It's a symbol of our family. Each flower represents my parents, my aunt, my brothers, and how we're all part of the same vine, the same tree. We're all tied together fighting for our survival. I understood it right after I knew I would become a father and what family truly meant to me."

"That's beautiful, Zach. You should tell your mother. She'd be thrilled."

As Emma downloaded the movie, Zach fixed drinks. Emma wanted to taste a bourbon and soda.

"I never had one before. It's smooth. Nice follow-up kick," she said.

"Exactly, it's the expensive stuff. Only bourbon I will drink these days. My dad introduced me to it. He used to sneak drinks to me when I'd come home from school on weekends. My mother would have killed him if she knew."

The look between them needed no laughter or explanation. Olivia was a force not to be reckoned with in the past.

And as they settled in to watch the movie, laughing throughout the entire afternoon, they also covered Zach's past with Katerina as well as how Emma and Ethan first met. Zach didn't know much about Emma when the conversation started but quickly understood why his brother fell head over heels for the woman sitting across from him on the sofa. A chenille throw nestled the curves of her body, draped tightly to retain warmth, given the constant chill from the air conditioning Ethan needed on high to keep from a profuse sweat the medication left behind.

"Do you need me to raise the temperature, Emma?"

She shook her head and smiled at him. "Nope, it's nice and comfy under the blanket."

As the movie ended, Zach's phone rang. He had forgotten about the custody lawyer until that point but grew nervous when he recognized the number that called him. When Zach answered, Emma muted the television and walked toward the bar to fix another drink.

Emma watched as Zach navigated his conversation. His eyes grew bright and the side of his mouth curled upward. The way he cupped his hand to his cheek and scratched at his face was reminiscent of Ethan in many ways. Both brothers developed a sarcastic wit and charm about them growing up in the Glass family. While Ethan was more intellectual and pragmatic, Zach more often practiced the art of flying by the seat of one's pants. They both were warm and thoughtful, learning and absorbing it from growing up in a loving family despite some of the barriers that had once existed.

By the time he'd finished the discussion, a grin ran ear to ear across his overjoyed face. Zach hung up the phone and grabbed Emma's shoulders. As he hugged her, the veins on his arms and hands bulged beneath his skin, bringing life to the tattoos that pensively marked his body. "It's done. The judge ruled in my favor. I have full custody of Anastasia. Katerina won't be able to hurt my little girl."

Zach's embraced Emma with fervor enjoying the warmth between them as they bonded. They toasted to the future, but as they finished their drinks, both heard a noise in the hallway. Emma jumped up to check on it, then noted she was going up to bed.

* * *

Zach arrived home having ridden his Harley from Brooklyn early the next morning, sweating from the singe of the sun's rays as it rose above the house and cast a hazy shadow across the backyard. He parked his bike in the garage and went straight for the pool, needing to cool off before his body embraced the slumber he longed for.

It had been a long shift at The Atlantis Lair full of rowdy punks on single's night, where he collected several phone numbers he later tossed in the trash. Upon reaching the pool deck, he kicked off his boots, rubbing his throbbing calves from standing on his feet for over ten hours. Stripping to his black boxer briefs, his hard, sore body ached for the relief of the refreshing water. He stepped into the shallow area, idling at each step, his skin smiling at the sensation of the gentle waves of water as they rippled toward him. He leaned forward and thrust his body into the deeper waters immersing himself in a temporary oasis. When he reached the other side of the pool, he emerged to his Aunt Diane holding two cups of coffee.

"You could do with a little wake-me-up. I put whiskey in it. It oughtta do the trick," she said.

"God, I love you. It was a long night. I needed a swim before catching a few hours of sleep."

"Not if you plan on meeting with the school, you won't."

Zach rubbed his eyes and downed half the contents of the cup. "Shit, that's good. School? What're you talking about?"

"You asked me to go with you to the Madison Academy to decide if it was something for Anastasia. Remember, honey?"

Zach lunged underwater, bubbles percolating to the surface from his stifled screams. When he reached the top, he dried his face, grabbed the stone edge of the pool, and jumped out. "I forgot. Now I understand why you made me the Irish coffee."

"You still haven't told your momma, yet, have you?"

"No. I want to check the place out to see if it's full of rich, white snobby children from rich, white snobby families who only like being around other rich, white snobby people."

"Ha! Don't let Margaret or Matt hear you say that. They just finished enrolling Melanie last week."

"I know. It seems kinda cool. Not a typical private school. They embrace being different from all I've read."

"For once, maybe you and your momma will agree on something. She loves you, Zach. She's been trying real hard to change and let you boys decide on your own."

Zach finished the rest of the coffee, his tongue slurping the last few drops in an exaggerated fashion. "I'm gonna need another if you keep saying crazy shit."

"Really, she is. Maybe she will surprise you one of these days. Your father's death has taught her a few lessons. Possibly just in time."

"Thanks for going with me today. It might be good to get your perspective... not just my own."

"Anytime, sweetheart. I care about you boys... a lot."

Zach walked to his aunt and threw his wet arms around her, laughing as she squealed from the drops of water falling on her skin. "For the record, Aunt Diane, you deserved a helluva lot more than that ex-husband of yours. Maybe I'll find you some hunk at the club next week. You'd be a good cougar… I could see you busting up the dance floor."

Diane stood and moved her arms around her waist. "Like this? I could do the Robot… Go, Teddy! Get your groove on."

They both fell back into their chairs laughing and crying at either Teddy or Diane dancing at The Atlantis Lair.

"Maybe I could hook up with one of them young guys. It's been a long time since this girl's gotten a lil' somethin' somethin'." She smacked her ass with her own hand and winked at her nephew.

Zach closed his eyes and slammed his hand to his forehead. "TMI, Aunt Diane. Way too much!"

* * *

Later that day while Ethan and Emma stopped at the doctor's office for a check-up, Diane took Anastasia to visit Margaret and the girls. Zach, home alone with his mother, updated her on the news from the lawyer.

"It's fantastic news, Zachary. I told you it would work out," Olivia said.

"Yes. And to answer your question from the other day, I have thought about your proposal. I never told you about my other good news. I wanted to wait it out to first see what happened with the custody battle, but since everything seems to have come together for me these days, it's time I share something else with you." Zach beamed as if he'd found the Golden Goose.

"Well, don't keep me in suspense. Out with it, Zachary."

"Do you remember how you've been giving me shit this whole year about my working the night shift and disappearing on weekends? And how you thought I was out getting fucked up again?"

"Don't be vulgar, Zachary. I may have given you a hard time, but we got past all that nonsense with this summer's revelations."

"Yes, but I had a reason for working those crazy hours. I've been launching my music career, and I'm finally getting my chance to shine.

I met with a producer from LA a few times this summer, and he came to hear me at a club in the city. That's what I've been doing nights and weekends. I've been networking and building a name for myself. And it's worked."

"Are you moving to LA?" Olivia' stomach sank fearing the worst if he took her granddaughter far away.

"No, that's the best part. They want to hire me to produce music on the East Coast focusing on the chill new clubs popping up near the Brooklyn canals. I will still have to go to a few nighttime sets, but it'll be a full-time gig where I have my own team, and I get to stay here."

"That's amazing. I'm so glad it's worked out for you. What does it mean in relation to my proposal for you to move back into the house instead of me selling it?"

"It means I'm on board, or I'll give it a chance. Move back to Brandy-wine, and we can enroll Anastasia at the Madison Academy with Matt's girls. Instead of you selling the house, I can move in and take care of the place along with Matt and Margaret. That is if you still think it's a good idea for them to sell their home and move in here to focus on fixing their financial problems, Mom. I'm not promising forever or that it'll even work out, but I'm willing to give it a shot."

"Yes, it is the best decision for all of us."

Olivia hadn't allowed herself to embrace happiness the last few months, but the road before her had started to change before she'd even stepped forward. She placed her hands on Ben's oak desk sensing the letter tease and mock her from the locked drawer. After all the good news Zachary had relayed to her, she wasn't prepared to tell him it might just be a lie. She'd begun to remedy years of anger and endless disagreement with her son unwilling to relinquish it without a fight. She simply couldn't lose Zachary to Rowena now that she'd connected with him again.

Chapter 24 – Teddy

Upon learning Zach and Sarah had slept together, Teddy's newly-surfaced ability to express his emotions and to be truthful with his family began to dissipate. It didn't matter his youngest brother was dying. He couldn't focus on Matt checking into a rehab facility. He had no interest in talking to Caleb and Jake nor meeting their newborn son. He didn't want to be anywhere near his brother, Zach, for fear of what he'd do or say to the brother who had wronged him in such an egregious manner.

Immediately after learning of his wife's infidelity, Teddy spent the following days negotiating with Ms. Davis and Mr. Wittleton, quickly agreeing on a fair price to sell them the remaining sixty percent of the Glass family's law practice. Once they agreed, he worked with a colleague to prepare the papers and presented them to the partners without even running it by any of his brothers or his mother. It was clearly his decision to execute, and he had little interest in getting input from his family. The partners had agreed to forget about the money Matt had taken and would not pursue any legal follow-up. They greatly respected Ben and had wanted to do right by his family. Matt was thrilled as it meant he avoided any embezzlement charges. After the sale happened, the brothers would each receive a useful sum enabling a few of them to move forward with their lives.

Once he'd settled everything, Teddy emailed copies to his brothers and his mother stating his desire to move forward explaining it would be official as of the middle of the next month. He'd given them two days to notify him, in writing, if they had any objections. Otherwise, he'd considered it a completed deal, all within his power based on the terms of his father's estate. The only approach he knew was to treat his family in a purely business transaction, but only this time, it would contain no lunch with the client.

While the papers were in their final review, he needed quiet time where he could reflect on his situation and freely paint without interruption. With the door to his office locked and the rest of the staff gone for the day, Teddy retrieved his art supplies from the closet and worked on his next series of paintings.

* * *

After the two days had passed, Teddy called his mother to verify she read the email, as she sometimes forgot to check her account. Sitting at a local bar near the office, nursing a Manhattan, he waited for his mother to respond.

"I received the email, Theodore. You've negotiated a fair deal. I trust no one has objected to it?"

"Everyone replied indicating full agreement. Even Zach." He observed the bar crowding, and his body twitched in discomfort. He rustled his fingers against the table, pushing them down as hard as he could.

"I ate dinner with Zachary yesterday. He mentioned you won't return any of his phone calls."

"I'm not ready to talk to him, Mom. I haven't even talked to Sarah. I've been sleeping in the guest room if you must know." He spent as little time at home as possible avoiding Sarah and any discussion or confrontation he had no energy to address.

"How much longer are you going to let this go on, Theodore?"

"I've transitioned all responsibilities at the firm to Dad's partners as of this afternoon. I start art school next week. I will need to do something about Sarah in the next few days." He paused before developing an angry tone. "Do you need to know anything else, Mom?"

"I know what they did deeply hurt you, but they had no bad intentions. Theodore... Teddy..."

Hearing his mother call him Teddy, a courtesy that rarely ever happened even as a child, his exterior shell softened. It was difficult managing his anger and frustration, internalizing his father's death, his wife's betrayal, and his brother's foolishness. "I'm trying to understand it. Sarah has wanted a baby for such a long time, and we had been desperately trying the last year. She never once told me I was the problem, and that's the part I'm struggling with above anything else." His fingers slipped off the table, and he rested them on his lap with determined ease.

"That she lied to you or she tried to protect you?" Olivia said.

"Neither. I'm upset she didn't trust me enough to tell me I was the reason we couldn't get pregnant. If she had only talked to me about it, we could have decided together to consider getting a donor or even asking one of my brothers if they would be willing to do it for us. I was given no choice in any of it. I can forgive her, maybe in time, for sleeping with him. Definitely, not right now. I understand they weren't having an affair. It wasn't a betrayal of our love. It was a betrayal of our trust. I'm not sure I can forgive that."

Olivia was in no position to argue with his logic. "Sarah and I talked about it. I know she regrets her actions. I understand why you married her, Teddy. She's a smart woman, even though I said a few bad words in the past. I've recently learned that sometimes you need to go beyond the choice someone made and instead understand the outcome."

"The outcome?" Teddy allowed himself to listen to his mother for once. He knew he needed an ally among the snakes hiding in his family. She was the only option at that point despite not telling him the moment she learned of Sarah's infidelity.

"Yes, the outcome is you are the baby's father. Shouldn't that stand out as the most important reason if you intend to remedy it with her?"

Teddy reflected on her statement, unwittingly releasing the morbid tension from his body when he stretched his limbs and sunk further into the chair. Internalizing Sarah's ridiculous behavior with Zach had distracted him from the astounding news he would finally become a father.

"I need to go, Mom. Something just came up." Teddy hung up the phone, tossed a twenty on the counter, and rushed out of the bar.

Olivia compared her situation to his and found little difference between the two. Could it be fate intervening, so her son did not need to raise someone else's child only because he would soon learn the people he thought were his parents weren't his real parents? Olivia desperately wanted Rowena to arrive in Connecticut, so they could bring this pain to an end. *Why is it taking her so long?*

When Teddy arrived home, he found Sarah resting on their bed. He indicated he was ready to discuss the situation.

While Sarah lit incense to relax them both, Teddy joined her on the bed, pulling the blanket over them to encourage a more intimate conversation.

"I'm sorry." His fingers stretched and rubbed against each other. The sensation had become too familiar to ignore.

"You didn't do anything wrong," she said.

"I did. I forgot to show you how much I love you every day."

"I never doubted you loved me."

"But you didn't trust me enough to tell me I was the reason you weren't getting pregnant for the last few years." Teddy tried to crack his knuckles, but Sarah slipped her hand in his to hold him back.

"I'm not sure it was the only reason."

"What do you mean? Low sperm count caused it." Teddy pulled her body closer to his, her back against his chest.

"True. That's part of it. I reckon there was more to it. You've been a pretty angry, stressed man for a long time. It took me years to break through your walls."

"I said I was sorry." Anger began to fuel the power resonating deep in his voice.

"That's not what I mean. Don't fly off the handle. Let me talk." She reached a hand to his cheek and caressed him.

Teddy looked away. "Go ahead."

"I was angry, too. I reckon part of me worried you and I weren't going to last. You worked all the time. I was never around when you were home. We just couldn't find a way to enjoy each other's company and build a stronger relationship during the first few years. I absorbed a lot of that frustration which takes a toll on a woman's body. What's that expression… don't watch a pot of water or it never will boil?"

"Yes, something along those lines. Are you the pot of water, or am I?"

"I am. We kept trying to have a baby for so long, fixated on it. I also obsessed over whether you would ever change and be more loving and affectionate. Then I stumbled upon your passions earlier this year. I suddenly saw a different side of you, and I realized why I loved you."

"I know. The change was apparent back then, too. When my dad decided to retire, I had to take over the law firm."

"Exactly. Our timing didn't sync up, and you wouldn't tell your parents about your dream to be anything but a lawyer."

"We decided I would tell him." Teddy let her hold his hand again.

"And for a few weeks, I reckon I fell back in love with you, attracted to a stronger, more caring husband. It happened because you started to trust in yourself, and you wanted to focus on your creative outlets. I relaxed, and my body embraced the ability to conceive. I just didn't know it."

"But you slept with Zach. With my brother." Images of his naked wife and brother plagued his mind. He jostled Sarah away and stood from the bed.

Sarah slunk back against the headboard. "Yes, I slept with him, and I regret it. I regret not believing in you, in us. I am angry with myself for being selfish and not talking to you about my concerns and fears. I'm sorry, Teddy. It's all my fault. I should have trusted in us. I'm not a snake in the grass. I'm your wife. You know me. You have to believe I was tryin' to improve our future."

"So, we should blame it on Zach?" He laughed, as his fist hit the wall, bits of plaster clouds wafting from the puncture. "Look, it happened. I'm not happy about it. I'm not going to forgive you overnight, but it shouldn't stop us from realizing we're getting what we wanted... I'm selling the law firm. We're going to have a baby. And it's our baby, conceived from our love."

"So, what do you want to do now?" she questioned.

"You're dumping this on me, Sarah?"

"No, I just meant..."

"You just meant you want me to fix it."

"Teddy, please..." She stood, placing her chest against his back and reaching her arms around his waist.

"I need time." Teddy pushed her away and walked toward the bedroom door. "I came back because I wanted you to know..."

Sarah's wistful expression forced Teddy to recognize the negativity that encompassed them both. His eyes fell to her stomach where for the first time he noticed a tiny bump holding his future, showing him why he needed to find a way to work out the disaster that had become his life. "I wanted to let you know we might still have a chance to fix this."

Teddy left the bedroom noting he wanted to take a walk to clear his head. Before he turned the corner out of the room, he looked back. Sarah's hand fell to her stomach, and she whispered to the baby, "I reckon your Daddy's coming back." Teddy smiled though he didn't know if he believed in happy endings anymore.

* * *

As the weeks passed, Teddy continued to focus on painting in his free time before starting school and closing on the sale of the law firm. On the morning before the firm's transition, Teddy completed the art project he'd started working on shortly after his father passed away, his pride and hope growing stronger as each hour passed, and every image appeared.

While cleaning the brushes, he realized he owed one brother a phone call. He dialed the number and connected on the first ring.

"Hey, Teddy. How are you doing?" Caleb said.

"I'm good. I wanted to apologize."

"For what?"

"Not going fishing with you and Ethan. I've been a bit of a jerk."

"A bit?" Caleb's voice held a high pitch.

"Okay, maybe more. It's not easy being the oldest. A lot of pressure."

"Yeah, I get it. Matt's practically combusted over these expectations at some point. I can only imagine what it's done to you."

"It would have taken you down, too, if you hadn't run off to Maine."

"Maybe I'm the smart one."

"Yeah, seems so. Congratulations on your new son. I'm happy for you. And for…"

"Jake. His name is Jake."

"For Jake. I'd like to hang out with him the next time you're back in Connecticut."

"Sure. Congratulations to you, too, Teddy. About the baby."

"Yeah, it's great news. A lot going on."

"I know about Zach, Teddy."

"You know?"

"I know. No one else does. Zach needed to talk to someone. The stress and frustration over his actions ate away at him."

"It should have. To do that to his own brother?"

"Maybe he had extenuating circumstances," Caleb said.

"I know. Drunk. Trying to do something I couldn't do. Sarah wanted me to be happy. I don't relish being a fool. A cuckold."

"It'll take time. But with Matt in rehab and Ethan so sick… we have to stick together."

"I will think about it." Teddy shut his eyes.

"Good. I can't wait to see what you do with this new career in painting."

"You'll experience it soon enough. I've got a surprise for everyone."

* * *

Olivia and Teddy, as the two co-signers for Ben's shares of the firm, arrived at the office to execute the final agreement the next day. Upon walking through the frosted glass doors into the lobby and noticing the newest addition to the offices, an immediate and overwhelming flood of warmth filled Olivia's body. On the cream-colored walls behind the reception area were a series of paintings depicting several scenes of Ben interacting with his family. A commemorative plaque positioned above them read:

In memory of Benjamin Glass, loving husband, father, friend, and colleague to all whom he inspired, taught, and mentored over the years.

Olivia's eyes traveled across the paintings noticing how Ben grew older in each successive print, culminating in a final one where he sat at the desk in the study enjoying a glass of bourbon with a smile at his fully-grown sons who surrounded him.

"I could not be any prouder of you than I am at this moment. You have given us a beautiful gift as we close one chapter in this family's legacy, and we look forward to whatever our future holds in a life without your father right beside us. He may be gone, but he could never be forgotten with these incredible portraits you've given us. I can't understand how I've never seen any of your paintings before." Her eyes welled, and she dabbed a handkerchief to catch the tears before they ruined her makeup.

Teddy watched his mother's gaze remain fixed on his painting. "Mom, I'm not as strong as you. I miss Dad so much and wish he could be here to support my decision to sell. I talk to him sometimes, and I know he listens. I believe he would understand this decision."

"He would, but I'm only as strong as my family allows me to be. I'm bracing for the next few weeks as Ethan slips away from us." Olivia paused to formulate her response. "You're already going to lose one brother. Are you willing to lose Zachary too?"

"No, Mom. I don't want to lose Zach. I will speak to him and find a way to accept everything, and not because it's what you or Dad would tell me to do. Because it's what I want to do."

* * *

After a few weeks, Sarah and Teddy addressed the tension still growing between them. Sarah conveyed her doubts and concerns when she had learned that he was the reason they experienced such a hard time getting pregnant, fearing conception would never happen for them. Recognizing some of the anger he felt toward himself, Teddy committed to meeting with a marriage counselor to figure out how to move forward and to focus on the blessings the new baby would bring. After several weeks of therapy and a positive breakthrough one afternoon while wrapped in one another's arms in their bedroom, romance and intimacy returned to their relationship.

As he navigated her to the bed removing Sarah's clothes until she was naked, Teddy began pushing himself closer to his wife. "Are you sure we can do this?"

"Of course. I miss you." Sarah guided his waist on top of hers relaxing her body as he grew harder and pushed inside. "It's been months since we had any physical connection between us."

"Are you sure I won't hurt the baby?" Teddy's eyes pulled close together as the doubt grew on his face. "I'll be gentle."

Sarah pushed him back, so she could see his entire face, eager to convince him she'd never hurt him again. "Yes. I want to make love to you. I need to make love to you. It's right where I belong."

Teddy pulled her tighter against him and kissed her lips. As he pulled away, he said, "I trust you."

After Sarah assuaged his reservations, they made love for the first time in months, breathing in the warm, inviting lavender scent of the candles he'd lit, not because they tried to conceive a baby, but because their bodies finally wanted to be near each other.

Chapter 25 – Matt

After Matt confessed his addiction to anti-anxiety medication and amphetamines, the entire family regularly checked on him pitching in to babysit the girls, schedule his rehab appointments, and assure one another he would get better. They, too, wanted to put the entire mess behind them. Margaret was glad to have their assistance, as she had a hard time being a supportive wife once the whole situation had destroyed her sense of confidence.

"Matt, we need to talk," she said after everyone left one afternoon.

"Sure, what's up, doll?" His eyes blinked a few times, and he lowered his head.

"I need to tell my parents what's going on before they take the girls for the next few weeks while you get settled at the facility."

"We agreed you weren't going to tell them. I don't want them to think of me as a failure. It's bad enough I had to disappoint my own family. This is important to me."

"I understand, but I don't want to lie to them. If they ask me, I have to say something to them."

"They won't ask. They don't know anything." His voice strained with an elongated pleading, his fear rising to the surface.

Matt's wistful eyes and tempting dimples stole Margaret's attention. "Okay, but you must promise to focus on your recovery, Matt. You need to stick to the plan and keep me informed whenever you're struggling."

"I will. I promise to accept whatever the counselors request of me. I know I've caused this damage to our lives. I will fix it. I want to fix it."

Based on the first meeting with his counselor, Matt would be onsite at the rehabilitation facility for several weeks in September to complete a full detox process. He'd eventually phase into an outpatient treatment program for three months with a target to be ready to re-enter the workforce by the end of the year. Part of his recovery included time to remove any of the pressures he'd experienced in both his job and his family life.

For Matt, the first trigger point he needed to resolve involved tying up any loose ends at his job. Before attending the in-patient treatment program, Matt tried to partner with Teddy to close the remaining items for the firm's sale. He could tell Teddy was angry but couldn't break through his brother's closely-guarded barriers. Given he had his own problems to focus on, Matt ignored Teddy's irrational behavior and spoke directly with Wittleton and Davis himself. When both partners agreed he could re-join the firm, once he completed his rehab program and signed a separate agreement, Matt took a three-month leave of absence and expressed his gratitude for their patience and understanding. He even managed to avoid staring at Ms. Davis' chest despite the several occasions he swore she had intentionally teased him with her surreptitious glances and accidental touches.

* * *

Ira Rattenbury closed on Ben's personal estate and distributed the proceeds to the Glass family. Matt turned over their financial affairs to his wife, who agreed to organize everything while he recuperated at the rehabilitation facility. Olivia stopped by their house one morning for an early brunch. Margaret poured a cup of tea for Olivia as they took seats at the kitchen table prepared for a long overdue family conversation about money.

"I've been thinking about something for the last few weeks, but only realized I was ready to mention it after I spoke with your brother,

Zachary. He won his custody case to keep Anastasia and prevent that dreadful ex-girlfriend of his from hurting his child ever again. He's also accepted a new job and decided to move back to Brandywine, so that he can enroll Anastasia at the Madison Academy with Melanie," Olivia said.

"That's fantastic news," Margaret said. "It will be good to spend more time with him."

Matt nodded in agreement. "I'm glad we were able to pay off the debts and the girl's tuition with the inheritance Dad left me. It's given me a way to accept the entire situation I let impact my family."

"And you should have extra money coming to you from Teddy closing on the law firm," Margaret said.

"We should be on track in a couple of weeks, but not fully out of trouble," said Matt.

"I thought of a solution benefiting everyone," Olivia said.

A wishful glow overtook Matt's eyes, but he remembered nothing these days gave him hope beyond his own recovery. He struggled with forgiving himself for the damage he'd done to his family over the last few months and hoped therapy would provide relief.

Olivia explained her plan to address their situation, revealing she no longer wanted to sell the family home. She originally thought it would be best to sell the house where she and Ben had lived and raised their children, but as she'd gradually learned of the depth of the issues facing Ethan, Zachary, and Matthew, she'd changed her mind.

Olivia said, "If you sell your house and move into the family home, you'll earn a profit from all the renovations you started. You'll then have some extra money to support yourselves when the new baby arrives until Matthew returns to work."

Margaret nodded. "What about you, Olivia?"

"Diane and I have a few other plans in mind. I also need to find myself somewhere new away from the memories of the past. I want to keep some things, but I also need a fresh start. I need to adjust to all these changes in my life and figure out what comes next. If you're around, we'll have extra support for Ethan."

Margaret nodded at her husband, hoping to understand a sense of what drifted through his mind. She glanced back to Olivia. "It's considerate of you."

"Margaret, I know we've had a bit of a tenuous relationship between us in the past. I hope you don't interpret this as me controlling you, or as if you're being forced to move in with Matthew's family." Olivia reached a hand toward her daughter-in-law, smiling when it was received with a gentle squeeze.

"It's a brilliant plan, Matt," Margaret said. "It will give me help with the kids while you work on recovery. You'll get to spend more time with Ethan. The girls will love being around Anastasia. And your mother and I will learn how to work with one another for the sake of this family. It's a win for everyone."

"Let me consider it and talk to Margaret." Matt's voice held a sense of determination as if he knew every decision from this point forward impacted the critical path for his recovery. Matt told his mother he needed a few days to mull over the proposal and would let her know when she returned from her trip to visit Caleb and his new baby.

* * *

Margaret left to collect the girls from a babysitter. While she was away, Diane stopped by to check on Matt.

"Tomorrow's the big day, Matt. Are you ready to check yourself into rehab?"

Matt sat in the recliner in his living room rocking back and forth. "Yup. I'm a little nervous to leave Margaret alone, but she's been a good sport about the whole thing. I need to get better."

"You do, honey. This is quite a mess you got yourself into. It's been a long time since *you* did anything for *you*. So much of your time has been focused on helping Teddy at the firm, raising your daughters, and keeping up with Margaret's spending. The intervention was a necessary thing." She leaned forward and patted his knee. "I believe in you, Matt."

"Thanks. Should I sell my house and move in with Mom?" His mellow voice filled a few moments of silence.

"You won't be moving in with your momma. She and I are gonna be doing our own things... traveling... maybe find a smaller house together like when we were girls. We need time to figure out our futures without any husbands by our sides."

"Moving back home would be admitting I failed as if I let everyone tell me what to do because I can't hack it on my own." Matt's eyes focused on the floor unable to lock eyes with his aunt. He'd not shared these thoughts with anyone else yet.

Diane stopped his chair from rocking and reached a hand out to his chin, lifting his face until it met hers. "Matt, you listen to me now... you ain't no failure. A failure would have kept on taking those pills. A failure would have stayed hidden. You've admitted you got a problem. You're getting help. You're providing for your family. Think of it as an opportunity to fix your life. Temporary. Maybe you'll only stay at the house for a year or two, then you and Margaret can buy a new place again."

"It'd be nice to save money and not worry about that problem while I'm recovering."

"Exactly. Now your brain's functioning properly."

"What would my father say?"

"He'd tell you he's proud of you for doing the right thing. That's what he told Zach when he faced his problems."

Matt hugged his aunt. "Thank you. I needed to hear that."

* * *

On her way home from Matt's, Olivia's mind drifted to her impending meeting with Rowena. She'd already decided if Matthew were the baby Ben switched years ago, she would need to keep that secret until after he completed his recovery. Matthew had to focus on his own priorities, and learning his parents weren't who he thought they were could bring his rehabilitation to a grinding halt. As the head of the family, it was Olivia's responsibility to ensure everyone had the right support, love, and focus to move toward the future. She wrote him a note, telling him to open it on his first night at the rehab facility, and letting him know how proud she was of him for admitting his problem and seeking treatment. She assured him she would take care of his family while he healed and would work with Margaret to sell their house.

* * *

A few days after Margaret and the girls settled into the house, Olivia asked Margaret to join her for a cup of tea in Ben's study.

"I'm glad you moved in, Margaret. You've built a strong routine here watching over of the girls, the house, even helping Emma take care of Ethan." Olivia sat on the sofa motioning to Margaret to sit beside her. "It's time we had a private conversation."

"Certainly, Olivia. We should." She rubbed her stomach comforted by a few swift kicks from the baby.

"May I?" Olivia said as Margaret flinched at the last kick.

Margaret took Olivia's hand and placed it on her belly, and they both smiled when another one came.

"Olivia, I need to say something you may not want to hear."

Olivia nodded.

"You're a tough woman. I've tried hard to be a good wife and mother, to build a relationship with you and Ben… you're not that easy to…"

"To like?"

"I suppose that's what I'm saying. I mean, we've always been cordial to one another, but sometimes, you don't seem to like me very much."

"You're wrong, Margaret. I do. And I may not want to admit it, but you and I are an awful lot alike." Olivia sipped her tea and relaxed into the sofa.

Margaret's eyes widened. "How so?"

"We're both raising large families. We both enjoy excessive quality in whatever we choose. You went to school and quit working when the girls came along just as I did with my boys. We've been taking care of our husbands for years not quite realizing situations weren't always what they appeared to be."

Margaret blushed. "I never thought of it that way. I'd always assumed you believed I took Matt away from you."

"That's how things happen when children get older. You haven't really taken him away... you brought more love into his life, gave him the girls, and so many goals to anticipate in the future. I'm glad he has you. I won't always be around."

Margaret nodded at her mother-in-law thanking her for having an open and truthful conversation. "I should try to get closer to you, Olivia. Matt and I want you to be part of our lives. I hated fighting with him every time you tried to tell us how to raise the girls."

"I shouldn't have done that. I know better now. I want to fix this."

"You don't need to. Just, maybe, lighten up a little in the future. Maybe only tell me if I'm doing something wrong every once in a while."

Olivia laughed. "You never did anything wrong, Margaret. I need to control everyone sometimes, but the times are changing... and I'm getting a bit smarter about it. I'm going to suggest something if you don't mind."

Margaret's eyes narrowed almost fearful of what would come next. "It all depends on what you're about to say, Olivia."

"I've resigned from all the charities and organizations I've been running for the last few decades. It's time I let other women take charge. My friend, Betty, stepped in for most of them, but maybe you should take over some. It would get you out of the house a little. Every woman needs time away from her family where she can challenge herself, make a difference in the community. I want to nominate you for a few organizations, and it wouldn't consume too much of your time in the beginning."

"I have wanted to get back into the working world. Sometimes I fantasize about Matt staying home with the girls while I'm out earning a living."

Margaret and Olivia giggled over their newfound way to bond realizing they didn't need to fear one another. Margaret still worried Olivia said the words and wouldn't follow through, but she knew with Matt focusing on his recovery, it'd be good to be on the same side as her mother-in-law for once.

* * *

While Matt worked with his counselors, Ethan stopped in the rehab facility one afternoon to check on his brother's progress. As they spent time together talking about the reasons and the ways to go about getting healthier, how to handle the withdrawal symptoms, they once again grew closer. Ethan reduced the fears Matt had been experiencing over never eliminating the desire to self-medicate. Talking his brother through the situation enabled Ethan to temporarily forget his own impending health issues. Matt even let Teddy watch the Red Sox game, given the way the season concluded. The Yanks lost their last few games and fell to second place while the Red Sox clinched the division. They headed to the playoffs, leading Matt to congratulate Ethan on his win at one point in their conversation.

By late September, Matt completed his in-patient therapy and progressed with significant speed each day. He was due to be released to begin out-patient treatment that week and would be home in time for Ethan's wedding to Emma, something he anticipated almost as much as his own recovery. Matt knew it was time to heal before the next round of heartache the family would unfortunately experience when Ethan reached the end. After the final meeting where the counselor asked Margaret to share with Matt her fears and concerns, the two learned how to communicate more positively. As a congratulatory gift for completing the first part of his rehabilitation, Olivia rented a hotel room for Matt and Margaret to spend a weekend together before he came back to the family home.

While Margaret ordered room service, Matt drew a warm bubble bath for them to share. Matt removed his wife's clothes sliding off each article with delicate ease, kissing her neck, and rubbing her shoulders and back. He'd forgotten how sexy he found her when she was pregnant, admiring the beautiful round, growing belly as she started showing each month. He lit a few candles arranged along the edges of the tub and placed a few gardenia petals, her favorite, on the floor around them. Savoring the sweet and tangy smell of the flowers, Matt guided his wife into the warm water with one hand holding her fingers and the other placed on the small of her back. The candlelight shimmered against her silky skin in the mirror's reflection. Soft jazz music hummed in the background as he slid in next to her cradling her head against his chest and tickling the edges of her ears in gentle circles.

"Such an amazing sensation, Matt. Please don't stop."

"I love you, Margaret. And I'm so sorry for everything I've done. I've learned a lot more than I expected from therapy. None of this is your fault. I'm back in the game now."

"We'll fix it together, hon. I've no doubt in my mind. Yes, you are definitely back in my game now."

"Permission to proceed, captain?"

"Yes. It's been way too long. This field is all yours."

Chapter 26 – Ethan

Before they fell asleep the first night after moving into his childhood home, Emma and Ethan discussed the night he proposed. Her world had quickly changed after Ethan handed his great-grandmother's ring to her at Le Joliet giving her a choice to leave before he became too sick or to stay and marry him. She had begged him to leave the restaurant, as she didn't want to cry in public, and he ushered her back to their loft with an urgent desire to know her answer. When they arrived, she pulled him close.

"Yes, I will marry you, Ethan."

"Are you sure? I don't want to force you into it. I always anticipated you'd say yes, but part of me was scared you weren't strong enough to handle my disease."

"I had already made the decision years ago. When I first met you back in Boston, I knew you were the one. It had never crossed my mind we'd be apart. I thought it would be for our entire lifetime. I never realized it would be so short."

"We need to make it special. If we only have two or three months left together, we need to do everything, so it's perfect."

"Yes. I'm going to put my teaching job on hold. And we should put a plan together."

"Yes, but first, we need to pretend none of this happened. None of it except I asked you to marry me. And you said yes. We need to make love and forget about everything else but you and me right now."

"*I wish I could forget, Ethan. Tomorrow, I will do that. But tonight, I need to let out all the pain and fear, so it's gone forever. I want to make the most of what time we have left. I can't cry every time we're together, devastated by the reality that will hit me when you're taken away.*"

"*Okay. Anything. I'll do anything you want. Ask me any questions.*"

"*How long have you known?*

"*A few weeks.*"

"*Are you scared?*"

"*Yes.*"

Emma's eyes lost their strength, and tears poured from them for hours as Ethan explained everything he'd been through the last few weeks. She had learned to accept at a young age that life was not always what it should be. Some women had forty years with their husbands. Some only had forty days. She would be one of those women, no matter how much she willed it to change.

* * *

The first decision Ethan made was when and where to marry Emma. Despite his objections, Emma had chosen not to invite her family telling them they hadn't planned a big wedding. She wanted a cozy affair, more of an event for Ethan and his family, rather than a typical show for the bride and her family. She wanted the next few months to be about Ethan since she had the rest of her life to live after he died. And while she couldn't yet consider being with anyone else, she was still young and might eventually change her mind. For now, it was a non-starter for conversations.

Her family understood but had visited beforehand to spend a few days with their daughter and say goodbye to Ethan before it was too late. Observing Emma with her family had been difficult for Ethan, who struggled with eating full meals and having lengthy conversations some days. Emma would be putting her life on hold to spend the next few months with him before he died. He wouldn't be around when she needed to focus on herself. She would undoubtedly need a support structure beyond her parents to recover from his death.

Ethan could tell she bottled her emotions and would eventually need someone to lean on despite the brave cover she hid under. One afternoon, he woke from a nap after they moved into his mother's house. He left the bedroom and walked toward the den where he'd left her a few hours earlier. Stopping short a few feet outside the door, he could hear her laughing. He hadn't heard her laugh since before he delivered his news. It had become a forced and fake chuckle, but this time, her natural gaiety shined through. As he listened in, she chatted with his brother. When Zach received a phone call, and it turned out to be the news he'd won his custody case, Ethan watched Emma and Zach interact. Ethan considered whether Zach might be the one to support Emma once he died. It comforted him to know Emma would have additional support from his family beyond his mother.

* * *

Ethan had been disappointed his other brothers couldn't attend the fishing trip he took with Caleb, but he reached out to them to build memories that would last well beyond his death. One afternoon, he called Teddy.

"Hey, Ethan. How are you doing?"

"I'm good. Just starting to have problems walking on my own if I'm on my feet for too long. I'm afraid it's going to get worse soon."

"Don't say that. Maybe you'll get better. Sometimes things work out." Teddy's voice was full of hope but still held a slight stammer.

"No, Teddy. You know it's not true. Don't get all wishful on me. I've already accepted it."

"How are you so brave? I'd be a mess if I were losing out on my future."

"That's where we're different. I already had everything I ever needed. I've got my family. Emma. I achieved great things at the hospital. I've had so many rewarding experiences."

"You deserve more time. This isn't fair." Teddy's voice grew hollow as his eyes dropped to the ground.

"Listen to me, brother. Dad's gone. I'll be gone soon. Matt's going through a lot right now. Caleb lives far away. Zach can't hold this family together by himself. You need to look beyond the surface of your own issues and worry about the future of this family."

"I know. It's my job. I'm the oldest."

"No. Not because it's your job but because you want to. Because you finally realize you can choose for yourself. You're going to be a painter. You're going to be a father. Your life is on an uphill turn. You should want to give back a little more."

"I do. I hear you."

"Promise me, Teddy. Promise me you will keep an open mind and find a way to be happier and get closer to everyone. We all miss you."

"I love you, Ethan. I'm wrecked that some outside force took control of our future, but I promise I will do better for you. For me."

* * *

After going back and forth a few times searching for a day when everyone could be around, Ethan and Emma settled on a day in late September when his brother would be home from rehab and for when a minister could come to the house and marry them. By the time his wedding day arrived, Ethan had become more distant and sleepy worrying he'd soon lose several of his essential motor skills. On some days, he could idle around on his own, but on other days the couch or the bed were his prison. He retained his mental capacities except for when the headaches became intolerable. When he felt too sick, he encouraged Emma to spend time with Zach, so they could both get a break from being caregivers. It was his Aunt Diane who noticed what he had been feverishly trying to do.

"Ethan, you need to be careful with that girl. She's not ready to focus on a future after you're gone," Diane bluntly stated one evening while they played a game of cards.

"I'm not sure what you mean, Aunt Diane." Ethan, in a weakened state, sat up in his bed.

"You're thinking Zach could comfort Emma. Maybe he could be the connection to you once you're no longer around for her. That could be dangerous. She needs to decide for herself if she wants to lean on someone or to move on in her own time."

"I want her to know it's okay to find someone else after me. She is too young, beautiful, smart, and caring never to find love again."

"Tell her. Don't push her toward anyone. Let it occur naturally if that's what'll happen."

"I know, you're right. I'm getting tired and don't know how much longer I'll be able to do anything on my own. I'm getting feebler as each day passes, too weak, too quickly. I need your help with something, Aunt Diane."

"Of course." She swallowed forcing the pain back inside where it could stay hidden.

Ethan handed her a sealed box. "Could you give this to my mother… when she needs… when she can't remember… I mean…" Tears fell from his eyes, and he looked away from his aunt unable to finish his thoughts.

"When she needs to connect with you in the future, and you're no longer around." Diane hugged her nephew promising she would look after his mother and telling him she hadn't seen him cry since revealing to everyone the news of his disease. "You've loosened the cords in my heart, and even though they've already been weakened by the many hits our family has taken this summer, I'll find a way to handle it. It's my job to be strong for everyone."

* * *

Ethan's physical and mental strength peaked on the day of his wedding ceremony. He wore a crisp new black Gucci suit with a double-breasted coat embellished with his father's gold cufflinks. Emma chose a simple, beautiful white Hermes wedding gown with the diamond earrings and necklace she'd worn on the night Ethan proposed. With family around him in the backyard garden, Ethan stood firm, on his own, having prepared his wedding vows. Emma wrote her own as well, speaking of the memories they had shared the previous few years. When the minister pronounced them husband and wife, they stole one of their last romantic and passionate embraces under the setting sun surrounded by his family.

Ethan led the first dance with his new bride followed by a few other traditional wedding activities. They fed one another slices of cake, listened to toasts from everyone in the family, and instead of tossing a bouquet, Emma and Ethan planted flowers in the garden to create a memory for the future. Before he became too tired, Ethan requested a brief dance with his mother choosing *"Wind Beneath My Wings"* by Bette Midler. It was her favorite. As she danced with her son for what she knew would be the last time, letting his body lean onto hers for support, Olivia burned the image into her mind, simply so she could remember it forever.

* * *

Early the next morning, Olivia walked to the back deck to watch the sunrise hoping it would lift her spirits. Upon arriving, she found Diane sitting in the chaise with her arms wrapped around her body.

Diane lifted her head. "You couldn't sleep either, Liv?"

"Not at all. When we were girls, my dreams were happy, wonderful thoughts about the future. Since becoming a widow, my dreams are always of the past. What does it mean?"

"That we're older and too focused on what's already happened?"

"Or we're smarter about the misery yet to come? I miss my innocence, Diane."

"We haven't been those girls for a long time."

"I remember the anticipation of hope. Being wishful. Wanting everything to happen sooner than it did. Marriage. Houses. Children. Grandchildren. I've had all those memories now."

"You're a lucky woman." Diane stared back at her sister. "Why did it keep you awake last night?"

"Because one by one, I'm losing them. And I'll never again have those innocent little dreams. I'll never be that little girl who imagines falling in love, stripping petals off a forget-me-not until the last one says, *he loves me so*. I won't ever get to dance in a magic that heals the world. And my heart knows what darkness lies in wait each night stealing a piece with every sun that sets and moon that rises." Olivia's eyes glistened from the stars yet to disappear across the morning sky. She couldn't cry anymore even if she wanted to. "Was I a good mother?"

"Yes, you were. Those boys grew into strong men who love you unconditionally."

"I know they love me. But will they remember me as a kind, generous, caring mother who nursed their wounds, blanketed them with kisses, and offered them the keys to the world. Or will they remember me as the tough, controlling, and impractical woman who simply gave birth to them?"

"They'll remember you as a woman who gave them life. A woman who taught them to believe in themselves and grab hold of their futures. A woman who survived many hardships and still found the courage and hope never to lose faith."

"I want to dream of the future again, Diane. I don't want to think about losing my husband or any more sons to the past. I want to have one more innocent wish for the days still to come. Not a cold and distant fading memory of everything I've lost."

After a minute of silence, Diane spoke. "Did you ever find those photographs, Liv?"

"No. They've disappeared… like so many other treasures in my life."

They sat in silence for enough time to earn the courage to carry forward. Diane went inside to brew coffee. Olivia wandered alone to the dark study where she grabbed a packet of matches from the drawer, lit a candle and took a seat at Ben's desk knowing she'd done everything she could to show her children in the last few weeks how to solve each of their problems. With one hand pressed against her chest rising with each labored breath, her other hand retrieved the envelope from the unlocked drawer. She sliced the envelope with Ben's silver opener, removed its contents, held the letter near the flame, and spoke aloud. "One more day before I'm supposed to meet you, Rowena. It's finally my turn to make a choice for our son's future."

Chapter 27 – Olivia & Rowena

After the first major argument she had with Ben, Olivia had sought solace in a nearby park a few miles away from their home. She'd long forgotten what they disagreed about, but always remembered she'd driven around that afternoon until she came across a magnificent weeping willow marking the entrance to a few acres of reserved parklands on the western tip of Brandywine. She'd rarely spent any time in that part of town and hadn't previously noticed the park's beauty. Over the years, it became her private respite, where she could mull over any problem and eventually settle on a course of action. With everything happening the last few months, she'd forgotten about Willoughby Park but felt certain it was where she needed to be that morning on the first day of October.

Olivia chose to drive herself, leaving the car in the lot a few blocks away and crossed over to the entrance noticing the transition from summer to autumn occurring around her. The town had planted orange and red mums in the planter boxes, and a few yellow leaves were scattered on the ground amongst the pine and giant oak trees. She walked first to the weeping willow and admired its beauty silently wishing she'd shown Ben the place that would comfort her when they had a tiff. She sat on an old wooden bench tucked into a corner near the back gates weathered from the rain and snow over the years. She was grateful for a quiet, early morning in the park and selected those set of benches, given a series of trees covered one side and the back of a stone building protected the other. It offered shelter from the breeze and slight chill in the air.

A sparrow landed on a nearby tree, its deft claws balanced on a brittle branch. A few gray squirrels playfully chased one another in competition over the acorn nuts falling to the ground beneath the oaks. Their rambunctious game of hide and seek had been so distracting, she failed to notice the woman walking toward her.

"Olivia?" said a quiet, hesitant voice standing a few feet away.

Olivia lifted her eyes noticing first the woman's black leather flats and sheer nylon stockings, sensing the battle for control begin over the next steps. Rowena Hector stood dressed in a simple gray skirt falling at her knees, a matching long-sleeve jacket, and cream-colored silk shirt. She'd fashioned a delicate woven red dress hat with black trim and a rose in the front atop shoulder-length, slightly curly steel-gray hair. Her deep-set eyes, bluish green in color, sparkled against pasty skin which held little makeup other than a pale shade of red lipstick and blush. Medium height. Thin waist. An ordinary woman who seemed to live an ordinary life.

Olivia rose from her bench as Rowena extended her hand, the balance of scales between them set at equal. Olivia's hand grasped Rowena's noticing it was even colder than her own. She tried to guess Rowena's age, but couldn't be certain as while she appeared in her forties, a kind and easy life may have prevented her from aging. Rowena was seventeen when she gave up her son, but Olivia's mind could no longer focus on the math. "Yes, and you must be Rowena Hector?"

Rowena nodded.

Olivia had worked out a plan in her mind, determined to be the one to drive the conversation, ensuring Rowena answered her questions. It was imperative Olivia took the driver's seat, not only to protect herself, but also to protect her son. Olivia knew less than nothing about the woman and couldn't let Rowena destroy the family Olivia had repaired with fervent force. She pulled her hand away and pointed toward the bench. Olivia's eyes focused on the woman she feared held all the cards once seeing her in person.

"Thank you. This is a lovely park. I enjoy the fall weather," Rowena said.

Olivia settled into the bench, her hands folded her lap, realizing Rowena still held a thick Scottish brogue. "It is beautiful. A quiet and calm place for you and me to meet. Hopefully, it's not too chilly for you."

"No, I'm fine. It's much colder back in Michigan. I looked forward to seeing this part of the country again. I haven't been back here since..." Her voice trailed off.

"Since you had the baby." Olivia got right to the point. Rowena had obviously wanted to connect with her past, given she'd come all this way.

"Aye, since I had the baby." She became quiet, eyes focused on her gloved hands.

"I appreciate you coming back here. I can't imagine it made for an easy decision." Olivia watched for any reactions hopeful the woman had no interest but a mere curiosity of her son.

"When Mr. Rattenbury called, I was surprised. It was a long time ago when I first arrived in America. I never forgot about the child, but I didn't have many options back then," Rowena said. Her voice was direct, containing little emotion. "I'm sorry I couldn't get here sooner. My husband had surgery recently, and I couldn't leave him alone."

Olivia nodded, understanding the delay, appreciative of the extra time it had given her with her son, yet worried it may have stolen time from Rowena. "Should I assume because you've come back, you're interested in meeting him?"

"Aye, I'd like to meet him. I have thought about him several times in the last few months. I don't have any other children." Rowena focused on the ground, her eyes absorbed by a diligent ant carrying a piece of dried fruit across the stone path.

Olivia's skin grew clammy upon learning Rowena had no other children, assuming it meant she'd want to get close to her son now. "May I ask why?"

Rowena smiled at Olivia. "Certainly. I had an accident shortly after I left Connecticut. While I recovered from it during that first year, it left me unable to bear any more children."

Guilt consumed Olivia, but she reminded herself she wasn't part of the decision—merely a victim of circumstance. Ben and Rowena had done this without Olivia's input. "I'm sorry."

Rowena nodded. "There is no need to be sorry. I've had a long and fulfilling life. My husband had a few children from a prior marriage. They're a bit older, and one girl is in the way of having a child of her own. My husband is several years older than me. How many kids do you have?"

"I have five sons in total." Olivia ensured she clearly included the one Rowena had given birth to as if it were still a battle for who could claim ownership over him.

"And does he know about me?"

"No, he does not. I didn't know until Ben died a few months ago."

Rowena tilted her toward her left side and leaned forward with her eyes open wide. "You didn't know? I don't understand."

Olivia realized Rowena knew little about what Ben had done. "I did not know. Ben must have arranged the switch with the nurse. I believed the baby was my son until Ben recently died. He left me a letter confessing he had switched the babies, as you had given up your son for adoption and mine died." Olivia grasped the bench at the word *died*, her knuckles turning an instant white.

Rowena attempted to reach for Olivia's hand but pulled back as though something stopped her at the last second. "It must have been such a shock for you to find out. I'm so sorry for your loss." Rowena paused and collected her thoughts. "For both of your losses. Ben was a decent and good man when I met him."

Olivia hated the enervation that crept throughout her body, but she needed to understand how this happened. "Could you tell me how you met my husband?"

"Aye, I should." Rowena stood and wrapped her hands across her arms walking in a pensive circle, each step in sync with her words.

"I had been looking for someone to adopt the baby as I was in this country on my own. I found a young couple anxious to have a child, but right before I was due, they decided not to move forward with the adoption. I was stuck here alone, about to have a baby, not a cent to my name, and a new job waiting for me in Michigan. I went into labor, and my neighbor brought me to the hospital. She stayed behind in the waiting room since I had no one else with me. A few hours after the baby was born, a man came to me."

She paused to give Olivia a chance to respond.

"And that's how you met Ben?"

"Yes. He met my neighbor who told him I had given birth to a child I was planning to give up for adoption. I could see the pain in his eyes as he told me his child just died. He asked if I would consider giving my baby to him, and I agreed. It seemed the best solution. The nurse agreed to switch the two babies born within a few hours of one another. I never asked her why she did it, but she did. Ben covered my hospital costs as I had no money. The official record shows I gave birth to a baby who died shortly after being born. I left the hospital the next day and took a train to Michigan. I never spoke with Ben again."

Olivia listened to Rowena's words experiencing many different emotions. Relief she had been allowed as much time with her son as she had but fear over Rowena's decision to return to Connecticut. "Why do you want to meet him now?"

Rowena stopped walking in circles, looked away from Olivia, and spoke with a timid voice. "When I heard about Ben's death, I knew I needed to talk to the woman who raised the baby as her own son. A powerful and overwhelming need to close the chapter, and that part of my life suddenly appeared. I'm planning a trip back to Scotland for the first time since I came to America. I never doubted my decision to give up the baby for adoption, but before my past and I are reacquainted, I need to know how it ended."

A connection developed with Rowena at that point, a bond between two women who shared a common element. Rowena was on her own quest to confront the past she'd left behind when she left Scotland.

Olivia knew it must have been difficult for Rowena to leave her family and homeland to come to America. "How did you know my husband would be a good father to your baby? Weren't you worried you knew nothing about him?"

"No. I have always been able to read people. I could tell he was a strong and honorable man who would provide a good home for my son." Rowena turned and stared at Olivia. "Besides, as soon as he told me he already had four boys, I knew it was the right decision."

Olivia's heart stopped beating, her mind keenly aware of the silence the vacuum brought with it. The wind shook a few acorns off its branch. Olivia's eyes followed their path to the shady ground below the tree. When they collided with the dirt, everything else fell quiet around her. She let out a warm, deep, and heavy breath. Steam poured from her mouth and rose past her distant eyes. The trembling when Rowena first approached her had disappeared. In its place, a giant pit opened leaving a sense of great despair as her mind processed Rowena's words.

"Ethan."

"What did you say?"

"Your son's name. Ethan."

Rowena smiled as she sat next to Olivia. "I told Ben the baby's father's name was Ethan."

Olivia's mind raced attempting to interpret what it all meant. She let out a brief sigh to regain her focus. Olivia stared at Rowena recognizing for the first time she and Ethan shared the same long and narrow nose, recalling all the clues hiding before her but had ignored every time. "Ben told me he wanted to name the baby Ethan. I never knew why he picked that name. Did the father know you gave up the baby for adoption?"

Rowena closed her eyes. "No, he never knew. He was a reporter I met back home one day while on a trip to Edinburgh. We dated for a few weeks when he received an assignment to cover the war in Bosnia. On the night before he left, we were together for our last time. The next day, he left Scotland and took up with a wee refugee camp to cover the war for the tele. We kept in contact for the first month, but one day he stopped responding to my messages. A few weeks went by without any correspondence, and I grew nervous. I tried to contact the news station, but they wouldn't give me any information as I was a minor... still seventeen years old. When I learned that I was with child, I panicked."

"That's awful. I'm so sorry." Olivia's stomach sank when realizing how scared Rowena must have been.

"My family knew nothing about the reporter, and he was several years older than me. I was forced to ask my father for help, and I begged him to call the station to find out what happened. My father was terribly upset with me but called them only to learn a bomb had gone off a few weeks prior killing several journalists and civilians. I was heartbroken. Eventually, my father threw me out of the house in disgrace. I stayed with a friend for a few months, but I couldn't stay forever. I decided to move to America on my eighteenth birthday when I was six months along with Ethan."

"You've been through a lot of pain, Rowena. Just as I have these last few months."

Rowena nodded. "Aye, but it was a long time ago. I know it will be difficult when I go back to Scotland in a few weeks. It's time I reconnected with my family back home. It's also the reason I wanted to meet with you. I wanted to hear what happened to my son and maybe meet him if he was open to learning who I am."

"He's a good son. I'm certain he'd want to meet you." The hollow words left a stinging, bitter taste on her lips.

"Tell me about him." Rowena's wistful eyes pleaded for information. "What was he like as a child?"

Olivia searched her memory for the story she needed to tell, confident she wanted to do justice to her baby before sharing the news of his illness. "My sister and I had taken him to New York City one afternoon to see *Spiderman* while his brothers were on a fishing trip with their father. Ethan was too young to go with them as they were already teenagers at that point. Before the show, we had stopped to buy sandwiches at a delicatessen near the theatre. As we walked Seventh Avenue, Ethan asked me about the men and women sleeping on the streets. He wanted to know where they lived. I tried to pull him away from them, afraid they'd be crazy or hurt him. Fear of others never even entered Ethan's mind. I told him they were homeless and lived on the streets. He asked me how they found meals. I didn't know what to tell him. But he'd already known. He'd opened his sandwich bag, roast beef, his favorite, and walked to an older couple on the corner and handed it to them. He told them we bought it for them. I knew my seven-year-old boy was the pinnacle of innocence and kindness. Ever since that trip, Ethan insisted we buy meals for the homeless on all the holidays. And every year, on the same day, he buys dozens of sandwiches and hands them out along Seventh Avenue."

"You raised him well, Olivia." Rowena smiled. "Tell me more."

Olivia knew she needed to tell her Ethan was dying. Information of that degree could not be denied to the woman. Forgetting about the entire situation and worrying about the implications of Ben's actions years before, Olivia found the courage to tell Rowena the truth. She proudly covered Ethan's decision to become a doctor and his marriage to Emma. She shared with Rowena a few more stories about Ethan's childhood and his genuinely good soul. She explained his illness and how he had only a few more weeks to live. Olivia waited for Rowena to speak, but she did not.

Two young children played in the grass a few feet away from where they sat. Rowena took a few moments before responding to Olivia.

An intense need for closure compelled Olivia to ask the question that could change the face of her family forever. While opening her purse with one hand, Olivia searched for the envelope with the other. Once found, she clasped it between her fingers and pulled it through the opening knowing it was time to relieve herself of the burden she'd been carrying for far too long. Relief soon appeared over choosing not to burn it the night of the wedding when her mind was weak and searched for the easiest solution.

Handing the envelope to Rowena, she spoke. "This belongs to you and Ethan."

Rowena accepted her husband's truly final communication to his son and pulled out the contents. Before she read it, she said, "Is this from Ben?"

Olivia nodded. "He wanted me to give it to Ethan once you had acknowledged you wanted to meet your son."

"Thank you." She smiled as if a great weight lifted when she held the letter in her hand.

"Would you want me to arrange a meeting with Ethan?" Olivia was unsure how to take that step, but recognized it was necessary.

"I need to think about everything you've told me." Rowena stood and walked toward the front entrance, glancing at the new buds forming on the mums on the side of the pathway and descending deep into thought.

Olivia called after her wanting to ask Rowena to pretend none of this ever happened but knowing it was not her choice. Instead, she said, "We don't have much time."

"A day to come seems longer than a year that's gone."

Olivia listened to Rowena's words, failing to comprehend what they meant. Her days had been long, the years already gone. "I'm not certain I understand."

"It's an old Scottish proverb, Olivia. Years may pass, but when you have something difficult to do, a decision around the corner, a minute, an hour, a day can seem an eternity. You can choose to think we never have enough time. Or you can choose to believe we are given just the amount we need."

"Time is never what you think it is, Rowena."

Rowena never turned but replied while walking away. "I will call you tomorrow, Olivia. I appreciate you letting me decide. I know how hard it must have been, and it takes a strong and determined woman... mother... who can put her own heartache aside for the benefit of her son."

Chapter 28 – Rowena

Rowena shuffled across the grassy path, her feet idling every few steps as she searched along the row to find the proper marker. Given she'd never been to the site before, and whoever answered her morning inquiry was not helpful, it was possible she'd already gotten lost. As her eyes swept by the numbers identifying each lot, a sense of confidence grew inside her. Once she arrived a bit closer, she was certain she'd found the place. Situated directly in front of her, freshly planted, stood the stone she was not yet ready to see. Her eyes focused on the words chiseled on its front plate.

Ethan Glass
(b) 13 January 1994
(d) 21 October 2017
Loving Son, Brother & Husband

Rowena recalled the moment she'd learned she was pregnant with him over twenty-four years ago. Alone and empty, she knew her baby's father had been killed in an explosion and her family would disown her. Her father couldn't even look at her for getting pregnant at such a young age without having been married. Her mother had been too scared to disagree and chose to support her husband's decision to kick out their daughter. Her younger brother had wanted to help, but there was nothing he could do, as he was barely a teenager himself.

Upon settling in Michigan shortly after falling prey to the accident which resulted in her inability to have more children, Rowena believed God had punished her for being an unwed mother who chose to abandon the baby. When she'd met her future husband, who didn't want any more children given he already had several from his prior marriage, Rowena closed the door on the chapter of her life involving motherhood, choosing not to tell her husband about the baby she'd given away back in Connecticut. Years passed, and they enjoyed a happy marriage with his children.

They'd been married for twenty years that summer, and her stepchildren had all moved out beginning their lives with their own families. She'd turned forty-two years old when reading the obituary that revealed her father had passed away back in Scotland. Not having spoken with her family since she'd left, Rowena reached out to her mother and brother who were anxious to reconnect. After a few phone calls, she'd decided to visit her family and planned a trip with her husband. A few days before they were scheduled to leave, her husband had a minor heart attack, and she postponed the trip to take care of him. That's when Ira Rattenbury had contacted her and revealed the man who had adopted her baby passed away.

Given her mind had been focused on so much of her past, Rowena interpreted it as a sign to take the opportunity to reconnect with her son, planning the trip to Brandywine after her husband had recovered, so that she could meet with Olivia. Before deciding to disrupt her son's life, she had wanted to meet with his adoptive mother to understand what type of a boy he was and whether he had even known about her.

Rowena was surprised to learn Ben never told Olivia about the switch, but she was utterly shocked to learn her son was so sick. After she'd left Olivia in the park, Rowena finally confessed the secret to her husband, who had easily understood why she'd never told him before. He'd known she had a falling out with her family resulting in her move to the United States, but not that she'd given birth to a child after arriving. They'd spent the next few days deciding what would be best for Ethan when Rowena had remembered the letter Olivia gave her.

On the night before she planned to leave for the rescheduled trip to Scotland, she finally opened and read the message Ben had left for his son. Once she'd read Ben's letter, her decision was clear. Rowena called Olivia to explain that she would be leaving for Scotland the next day to visit her family to rebuild the broken relationships she'd left behind. It would be too difficult to meet and say goodbye to her son within a matter of weeks. Though it would break her heart never to actually meet a piece of herself, Rowena could hear Olivia's relief on the phone when revealing the news.

During the next few weeks, Rowena visited her family in Scotland knowing Ethan would pass away while she was away. She preferred it happen that way since she made the decision not to meet him or to tell him she was his birth mother. The alternative path would savagely rip apart too many people's lives.

Rowena decided when she arrived back in the States from her trip to Scotland to finally visit the child she'd given up twice. She took a car from the airport, driving directly to the cemetery, and located his grave. Her eyes focused on the words *Loving Son*, as those were the ones affecting her heart, while she rested a hand on the headstone. She spoke aloud to him certain he could see and hear her from beyond.

"I hope you're not angry with me for choosing not to meet you when I had the chance, or angry with me because I chose to give ye away in the first place. It wasn't the easiest decision I ever made, but it was also not the hardest one. I may have given birth to you, but I can say with certainty, I am not your mother. Olivia is your mother."

She leaned against the stone and rummaged through her coat pocket searching for Ben's letter. She held it in her right hand looking closely at the handwritten passages. The silence in the cemetery comforted her, and she could smell the still fresh dirt beneath her feet. While looking around the immediate area, she noticed Ethan's was the only new grave amongst the rows and aisles nearby.

"When I found out I was with child, and I realized I would be raising you on my own, it wasn't fair to you. I was young. I was foolish. I could barely take care of myself. I wasn't capable of being a good mother to you, and I knew it. After my family threw me out, I no longer wanted to live in Scotland, and I came to America to find you a good home."

Rowena paused to plant the seeds she'd brought with her from her trip back home. She'd forgotten to bring a shovel and used her bare hands to push away enough dirt to bury them deep. Kneeling on a fresh grassy patch, she balanced her weight against the headstone and dropped the seeds into the empty hole. She signed the cross against her relaxed chest, said a brief prayer, and covered all her bases. When finished, Rowena lifted her petite frame off the ground, dusted debris from her knees and legs, and admired her work.

"I brought these with me so that you'd have a piece of Scotland with you now, as you probably never did when you were alive. After I arrived in America, I met Ben, your adoptive father, your real father. I never met his wife, your mother, until recently. When she told me about you, I did want to meet you. I thought perhaps you'd understand why I made the choices I made, but she told me you were dying. And I was faced with choosing to destroy the last few weeks of your life, maybe even resulting in you passing away sooner from the disappointment and shock. Maybe if I told you, you might find the strength to stay longer, but I knew it couldn't happen. That's when I read the letter your father intended for you. And I realized how much love he had for his son, despite the circumstances that led you to him. I couldn't take it away from him, from your mother, from your family. I couldn't hurt you with the truth when you had so wee time left.

"Your father's words were sincere, heartfelt, and from a man who already suffered enough. It wasn't appropriate to let you think your father was weak. I did not want you to question why he couldn't tell you himself in person. And I didn't want you to pass on from this world wondering who you were. Cause you already know who you are, Ethan. You're the son of two loving parents who deserved you, two parents who raised an intelligent, caring, and honorable man on a quest to become a doctor who could heal sick people in great pain. You're a brother who taught his siblings to live their lives to the fullest and forgive one another. You're a husband to a bonnie young girl who will always remember you and compare everyone else to you. But above all, to me, you are proof I made the right decision to let you go all those years ago."

Ethan stopped being Rowena's son the moment his father had died in Bosnia when all her hopes and dreams to marry her lover and raise the child with him had been stolen. Once she was alone, after every hope had been brutally pilfered from her, she had only been able to take comfort in the replacement of an opportunity for a new life in America where she could put the past behind her. Giving birth was merely a responsibility she had to bear. Giving the child up for adoption had been her duty to help someone else. Even when she'd handed him to Ben, Rowena's emotions laid dormant knowing he was no longer part of her.

As she cast her eyes upon the gravestone that was the only piece of him she'd had the privilege to see since the day he'd been born, Rowena read Ben's letter aloud:

To my son, Ethan,

The gift of life is unlike any other gift one can receive. To imagine two people come together, each bringing a requisite piece of the puzzle, defines magic to someone like me. When this happens, destinies and paths are set, hopes and dreams grow, and love takes its course.

When your mother and I learned we were expecting a fifth child, it came as quite a shock. We hadn't expected any more children… our family was already complete. But it wasn't something we could easily change without repercussions, especially ones neither of us wanted to address. We were blessed with the gift of another life to nurture, and as her pregnancy progressed, our hopes and dreams grew exponentially.

We loved your brothers more than we could express, but as each day passed, thinking about having another child in our lives, our desire to be even better parents increased. We wanted to provide our new baby with all we'd learned from being parents to Teddy, Matt, Caleb, and Zach. We realized we had a hole in our family, incomplete with just the four of them. We'd been waiting for you.

I wanted another chance to bring a perfect life into this world. We'd received this gift for a reason, and I yearned for it. I wanted it. I needed it. As your mother's due date grew closer, I found myself listing the activities I should do to be the best father I could be to you. I promised myself I'd work less and spend more time at home with you and your brothers. I vowed to listen to you and guide you to become the man you wanted to be instead of me dictating what that was.

In the hospital, the day you were born, your mother and I experienced the greatest joy when she gave birth to a fifth boy to complete our family. But fate quickly took it away from us when the child died a few hours after being born. Your mother had been sleeping when it happened and never knew the tragedy that came before us.

It destroyed me. In an instant, everything I'd come to love was suddenly ripped away. I was angry. I couldn't accept it. But fate tempted me with an alternative solution. I could switch the baby we lost with another baby being given up for adoption.

By now you know I made that choice, and I'd choose the same one again. From the instant I accepted what fate laid at my doorstep, I accepted it was the same gift I'd already been promised when your mother told me she was pregnant. It didn't matter you came from a different set of parents. It didn't matter our child had just died. It mattered that I had the opportunity to accept the gift into our lives and follow suit with many hopes and dreams.

I'd closed my mind to the little voice inside me saying I should have told your mother what I'd done. I'd closed my mind to the fears someone would find out. I'd closed my mind to the entire situation because it meant you were ours.

And for the last eighteen years, I pretended it never happened. But as you're graduating from high school and moving on with your life to become a doctor, I realized I needed to tell your mother and you what I'd done. Please don't hold her accountable for any of this, as she knew nothing but that she loved her son.

I should have chosen to tell you this in person since you're an adult, but I'm not ready to do so. I need a few more years to watch you achieve the goals you've set to become a doctor and save the world from its own devices. I hope to grow the courage to tell you this story in person, not via this letter, but that's not today.

I've left this with my attorney in case anything happens to me before I can bring myself to tell your mother and you the truth. I hope someday I'll be honest enough, so I can leave this planet knowing I was worthy of my gift... worthy of you.

With much love,

Your Father

"I must go back to my husband and my family, knowing you have been with yours all along." Rowena kicked away a few burnt orange leaves that had fallen onto the grave, pushed nimble fingers and stoic hands into a pair of warm gloves, and stepped back into the cemetery's main pathway. Time had come for her to return to the plentiful life she'd enjoyed the last twenty years, grateful for a moment to experience a glimpse of the one that could have been.

Chapter 29 – Olivia

After Rowena decided she didn't want to meet her son, the dark mist surrounding Olivia began to disappear. In its wake remained only a shadow of despair that could have been much worse. Olivia never understood why Rowena declined meeting Ethan but was thankful for the reprieve. Ethan's illness was already difficult enough and had one of the other boys been Rowena's son, everything would have been different. A reassuring certainty convinced Olivia the secret could stay permanently buried, as she'd done everything her husband had asked despite the obstacles thrown in her way.

Olivia forgave Ben for not letting her become a part of the decision to switch the two babies, but she still needed to understand why he would leave a letter revealing the truth instead of telling her in person. They had a stronger relationship than he'd shown her by choosing that approach. She was angry she'd never be able to ask him or understand how he came to the conclusion.

Ira Rattenbury stopped by to check on her several weeks after closing on Ben's estate. "Olivia, he was a distraught. His body shuddered every moment I spent with him that afternoon in my office. He had no other choice."

"I hear what you're saying, but after so much time together, I question everything he ever did." Olivia fixed her eyes on Ben's study as if she could see him sitting behind the desk. "I thought I knew him."

"You cannot hold a man accountable by just one action. You must judge him by a lifetime of memories. He loved you, Olivia, more than I'd ever seen another man love his wife."

"I loved him, but when I lie in bed each night, how do I convince myself it was the only secret he kept?"

"Because he told you the truth, even after his death. He could have kept it to himself. We are human, Olivia. We all bleed. We cry. We hurt. We scare. Ben was no different than you or me. You'll come to accept it in time."

"I wish I had one more moment with him."

"We all do."

Olivia thanked Ira for his dedicated service and shut the door after he left Ben's study. She went in search of her daughter-in-law to say her next goodbye. Emma had stayed with her husband's family for a few weeks after Ethan's death, but now it was time to go home.

As she stepped toward the taxi, Olivia hugged her daughter-in-law. "I'm so glad you've become part of our lives, Emma. No one else will ever miss Ethan as much as you and I do. I consider you my daughter as much as Ethan was my son."

Emma nodded. "I sense the connection with Ethan when I'm around his family. My heart lifts a little higher, and my eyes grow less weak and blind."

"Don't forget we're your family now, too. I know Zachary would prefer you to stick around longer. Do you have to leave today?"

"It's time. I want to sort through our things back in Boston and figure out how to move on with my life. I'm not ready to think about anything beyond the next few days, but in time, maybe I'd want to get to know Zach a little better." Emma pulled the taxi door shut and left Brandywine.

Olivia walked back inside and stood in Ben's study recalling all the invasive life changes throughout the last few months. It was time to call each of her sons before she prepared for her own next journey.

She reached Teddy first. "You sound so much calmer. You were right to sell your father's practice."

"Will you attend my art show next spring? I've got two paintings planned for the exhibit."

"Yes, I'd love to. How is Sarah doing?"

"She's good, just began the third trimester today. We're planning on drawing a mural on the ceiling of the baby's room."

Olivia listened to him describe the images of the design he had in his head, aware of the confidence in his casual and friendly voice over the decision to return to art school. "I'm so happy for you. Will you be able to forgive Sarah?"

"Yes. We've started marriage counseling every week, and she plans to change her hospital shift so that we can have a more normal routine in our lives."

"That's wonderful. And you're not going to find out the baby's gender beforehand?"

"No, but we're both hoping for a little girl. I've been spending more time with Matt's girls, and it's been an eye-opening experience."

"What about Zachary?"

"I called him. We've been getting along better lately. It'll be back to normal in a couple of months."

Talking with Zach had unlocked the final door Teddy needed to accept the abundance of changes in his life even encouraging him to stop eating gyros and potato chips for every meal. When he'd hit Zach, he realized how much his intrusive physical ticks had encouraged every one of his nasty thoughts. Zach had convinced Teddy to meet at the gym one day where Teddy soon noticed pull-ups and boxing gloves were idyllic substitutes for the negativity that had encircled his life. The sheer passion of exerting positive physical energy served as a palpable replacement, propelling him to stop clenching his jaw and cracking his knuckles over the tension he'd built up throughout all the years.

"I love you, Teddy. And I'll call you when the plane lands." Knowing one son was on the road to recovery, Olivia disconnected the phone and dialed another to check his progress since she'd last seen him. Matt and Margaret were back at their house doing a walkthrough before the closing. He answered after a few rings.

"You're on speaker, Mom. Margaret's here with me. The buyers just left. The match is set, and we can close this game with the bank tomorrow."

When Olivia heard his voice, back to its normal cheery and jovial manner, it was as though she could recognize his smile boyish shining through the phone. "It's so good to hear you both. Congratulations. How are you feeling, Margaret?"

"I'm great, full of energy. Different than it was with the girls. It must mean I'm having a boy this time," Margaret said.

Olivia brightened at the volume of her daughter-in-law's exuberance blasting through the phone.

"Nope, it's a girl, doll. I'm shooting for a whole female basketball team. At least two more girls. I just know it. Maybe afterward, we'll have a boy," Matt said.

"Olivia, please help me deal with your son. If he talks about another baby again, I swear I'm gonna leave him."

Olivia laughed. "I agree with her, Matthew. Give it a break, Margaret knows what she's talking about. It's time you let her run the day-to-day around here."

"She's always run the place, Mom. Just didn't realize it."

"Exactly. It's time more women took charge of the Glass family." Margaret giggled as she squeezed her husband's shoulder.

Matt told his mother he'd completed his onsite treatment at the rehabilitation facility and learned to appreciate spending more quality time with his daughters. He volunteered as class dad once Melanie had started school at the Madison Academy, especially after Margaret had started spending more time with the charity organizations that Olivia had transitioned to her.

"We're all going to visit Caleb and Jake later in the month while you're away, Mom. Thanksgiving will be in Maine this year. Will you make it?"

Olivia laughed and told them she hadn't decided where she would be for the holidays this year, needing some time to herself for a change. She disconnected with Matt and Margaret, calling Caleb just as he'd put the baby down for a nap.

"Are you hosting Thanksgiving this year?" Olivia said.

"Yes. Jake's decided he's doing all the cooking. He's turned into Mr. Mom."

"I believe it. He's a good man, honey. I can see how much you guys love each other."

"Thank you, Mom. I'm sorry we didn't talk sooner about everything. I guess I wasn't ready to tell everyone until now."

Olivia closed her eyes as she sat behind the desk in Ben's study. "Don't apologize. Everything happens for a reason. A lot has changed in the last few months, but your father would be proud of where we ended up."

"As would Ethan."

Olivia reflected on the day Caleb and Jake brought their new son to Brandywine to visit with the whole family as Ethan neared his final days. When Ethan had a few lucid hours, Caleb took advantage of the opportunity to put a smile on his brother's face. He placed his newborn son in his brother's arms while Olivia watched as her grandson fell asleep with one tiny hand holding onto the tube that delivered breaths of air to his uncle. Ethan joked he might die from lack of oxygen due to his nephew's steel grip before the brain tumor finally killed him.

"Yes, he would be proud, too. Are you sure you don't want to consider moving back to Brandywine? Jake might love it here, too."

Caleb laughed and quickly squelched her suggestion. He was determined to spend more time with his family, but he and Jake had been content with their home nestled in the mountains on the Maine coastline where they could raise their family in a way they had chosen.

After they hung up, Olivia left Ben's study and wandered to the attic bedroom to say goodbye to Zach. When she arrived, she entered a twilight zone. He'd cleaned the room and threw away most of the junk he'd formerly left around having previously told her the clutter helped him more clearly focus on his musical inspiration.

"Mom, I've matured this summer. I'm not going to turn into some stick-in-the-mud like Pickles or Matt, or maybe a version of who you used to be, but I'm making positive changes." He winced as she pinched his ear in response to his sarcasm.

Olivia was delighted over everything he'd accomplished lately and had grown excited he would be living back home so Anastasia could be around her family. Olivia studied her son's tattoos and asked him for the first time what they meant.

Zach rolled one sleeve and explained the history of the vine growing up his one arm. He pointed to the dice and the playing cards on his other arm. "I got those when Anastasia was born because it'd be a gamble on whether I'd be a good parent or not."

Olivia smiled. "You won big on that one."

"Yeah, maybe I did. How could it be any different with you and Dad as role models?"

Anastasia bounded up the stairs grasping a shiny object in her hands as if she'd found a lucky charm. When she got close enough, Olivia recognized it as a picture frame as her granddaughter turned it around. It was a photo of Ben.

"It's Grandpa. He's watching over us now."

Zach looked at his mother, and they both shook their heads in laughter. "Yes, baby girl, maybe he is watching over us."

With a final goodbye to almost all her sons completed, Olivia stepped out the front door and took a seat in the car next to her sister. As Victor pulled away from the curb for the last time, Olivia glanced out the window at the home she'd lived in for forty years considering everything she'd been through while living in the house, both the good and bad memories.

Victor took them first through Willoughby Park providing Olivia with one last moment in her favorite respite. He then drove to the cemetery stopping at Ethan's grave to say a final goodbye before

Olivia left Brandywine. Diane stayed behind in the car to let her sister have a few moments alone with her son.

Olivia walked to the grave. The early stages of a flowering heather bush grew in front of the headstone. She hoped if Rowena had visited Ethan's grave, it lent her the comfort over choosing not to tell him she was his mother.

Olivia missed Ethan since he'd passed away the prior month, more than she thought possible. She'd expected the same pain and loss she experienced when Ben died, but not the remorse of knowing she'd outlived a son. In the last few days of his life, the brain tumor took away most of his abilities to move or speak. He spent the last hours in bed sleeping with only a few moments of clarity, where he did his best to comfort his family before leaving them behind. Watching her child die had been the most difficult thing Olivia experienced in her life, especially knowing she'd held the secret from her child even in his death. Knowing she was with her son in the end and hearing his last words, she'd finally been able to accept his fate. On the morning he passed away, in the last few hours of his life, he looked at her and said, "It's gonna be okay, Mom. You gave me the best life a son would want. I couldn't have asked for a better mother."

As she stood at the grave running her fingers through the heather, enjoying the tickling sensation it delivered with each breeze, Olivia whispered a goodbye to the son who'd been the most unexpected gift she'd ever received in her life. The gift who taught her how to forgive and let go of the past, enabling her to find a heart ready for the future.

Olivia walked a few rows to Ben's grave remembering the man who'd been her partner for over forty years, the husband who took her to the opera every new season, and the father who raised five amazing sons with her. She stood in silence appreciating the wind's gentle whisper on her face. Drops of pure white snow cascaded across her husband's grave as she smelled the cold of winter settle in. When she settled on the grave, she noticed the newly engraved memorial sitting next to her husband's headstone, filling with instant relief and comfort.

In memory of the loved ones we lost, may they rest in peace. Mom and Dad.

Saying goodbye to her husband and son within months of each other had nearly killed Olivia, but she refused to fade away into the background. She'd put her family back on their own paths, exuding confidence in her decisions, and it was time for her to walk her own road. The journey she'd been on for most of her life hadn't ended when Ben and Ethan died. It opened up new directions where she could consciously choose to put the pain and the fears in the past and to embrace whatever destiny danced before her.

Deep within Olivia's soul, she knew it was time to leave. With one last glance at his grave, she rested shaky fingers atop his headstone. "I'm taking this trip for the both of us, Ben. You will always be in my heart. You were a good husband, and I can now say I understand what you did for me."

Olivia lingered a moment to let the falling snow land on her face enjoying the refreshing sensation as each flake melted on her skin, recalling a childhood where she similarly embarked on the prospect of a new life. She grasped the cold metal handle, opened the car's passenger door, and slid onto the leather seat next to her sister, who sat waiting in the vehicle's cozy warmth.

"I hope it gave you comfort with them today. Were you able to say everything you wanted to say, Liv?"

"I believe so." Olivia nodded at her sister. "Did you add the new stone to the grave?"

Diane smiled at her sister. "Yes. Just a brief message so you'll always have a reminder of both your sons. You needed to say goodbye not only to Ben and Ethan but to the child you lost, whom no one else will ever remember."

"It was Ethan. Ethan was the baby Ben switched."

The car remained silent for a few minutes, as they each thought of the secret haunting Ben when he died.

"I suspected it was him but didn't wanna ask," Diane said. "I knew you'd tell me when you were ready."

"When I met Rowena and learned which son was hers, I found peace and understood what Ben chose to do. I needed a little more time to accept his death and to find a way to say goodbye to him."

"Let's not say goodbye. We'll be back before the new grandkids are born. Ethan will live on in your first grandson."

"Yes, it's come full circle. My son, Ethan, was adopted. Caleb's adopted son's name is Ethan. I'm sure we'll be back to visit them, but right now, it's time to take control of our future and focus on our own lives."

"You're stronger than I thought." Diane reached into a large canvas bag on the floor of the car.

"I am stronger because of everything that's happened the last few months and because of you. You've protected me all my life, even though I'm supposed to be the older sister."

Diane handed a ten by twelve box wrapped in white tissue paper to her sister. "From Ethan. He asked me to give it to you when you were ready."

"And why do you think I am now?"

"Let's call it a sister's intuition and leave it at that." She smiled and winked at her sister.

Olivia slipped off the tissue paper as if it were the blanket she'd brought Ethan home in from the hospital and lifted the top of the wooden box with a delicate balance. Its weight comforted her. As she handed the lid to Diane, Olivia removed the gift from the box and opened the cover. On the first page read the words *The Glass Family*, and as she flipped through the remaining pages, pictures of Ben and Olivia, their parents, Diane, and all the sons and their families flooded Olivia's eyes. Ethan had collected hundreds of photos of the Glass family over the years assembling a picture book as a keepsake for his mother.

Olivia ingested each memory recalling the family camping trip to Yellowstone, the black and white Christmas photos, Grandma

Eleanor's eightieth birthday party, the game board Grandpa William carved with his own hands, and Ethan and Emma's wedding where the entire family took their final portrait. And in it, Olivia held a framed photo of Ben from their wedding day so that he could be part of the permanent memory. Sewn into the last few pages of the album were parchment scrolls that displayed a beautiful calligraphy, the Glass Family Tree—Ethan's passion serving as a tribute to the family he had loved his whole life. He even had time to add Jake and Emma, and his own namesake, his new nephew, Ethan.

As Olivia thumbed through each page, Diane's eyes watered, and this time, she was the sister who couldn't retain her composure in the car leaving the cemetery.

Olivia reached for Diane's hand and consoled her younger sister. "For the first time in a long time, I have my family back and no matter what fate throws at us, we will handle it together. But it's our turn now."

"Are you ready?" Diane brushed tears away from her eyes.

Olivia nodded and caught her driver's attention.

"Italy's *La Dolce Vita* waits for me, Victor... And for once, a day to come seems *shorter* than the year that's gone."

About the Author

James is my given name, but most folks call me Jay. I live in New York City, grew up on Long Island, and graduated from Moravian College with a degree in English literature. I spent fifteen years building a technology career in the retail, sports, media, and entertainment industries. I enjoyed my job, but a passion for books and stories had been missing far too long. I am a voracious reader in my favorite genres (thriller, suspense, contemporary, mystery, and historical fiction), as books transport me to a different world where I can immerse myself in so many fantastic cultures and places. I am an avid genealogist who hopes to visit all the German, Scottish, Irish, and British villages my ancestors emigrated from in the 18th and 19th centuries. I write a daily blog and publish book reviews on everything I read at *ThisIsMyTruth-Now* via WordPress. Most of my free time is spent with family, friends, my significant other and our Shiba inu dog, Ryder, who even has his own *Facebook* page.

Writing has been a part of my life as much as my heart, my mind, and my body. I decided to pursue my passion by dusting off the creativity inside my head and drafting outlines for several novels. I suddenly realized I was back in my element, growing happier and more excited with life each day. When I completed the first book, *Watching Glass Shatter*, I knew I'd stumbled upon my passion again, suddenly dreaming up characters, plots, and settings all day long. I chose my second novel, *Father Figure*, through a poll on my blog where I let everyone vote for their favorite plot and character summaries. My goal in writing is to connect with readers who want to be part of great stories and who enjoy interacting with authors. To get a strong picture of who I am, check out my author website or my blog where the *365 Daily Challenge* reveals something about my personality every day. It's full of humor and eccentricity, sharing connections with everyone I follow, all in the hope of building a network of friends across the world.

Websites & Blog
Website: https://jamesjcudney.com/
Blog: https://thisismytruthnow.com/

Social Media Links
Twitter: https://twitter.com/jamescudney4
Facebook: https://www.facebook.com/JamesJCudneyIVAuthor/
Pinterest: https://www.pinterest.com/jamescudney4/
Instagram: https://www.instagram.com/jamescudney4/
Goodreads: https://www.goodreads.com/jamescudney4
LinkedIn: https://www.linkedin.com/in/jamescudney4

Dear reader,

Thank you for taking time to read *Watching Glass Shatter*. Word of mouth is an author's best friend and much appreciated. If you enjoyed it, please consider supporting this author:

- Leave a book review on Amazon US, Amazon (also your own country if different), Goodreads, BookBub and any other book site you use to help market and promote this book

- Tell your friends, family and colleagues all about this author and his books

- Share brief posts on your social media platforms and tag (#WatchingGlassShatter) the book or author (#JamesJCudney) on Twitter, Facebook, Instagram, Pinterest, LinkedIn, WordPress, Google+, Tumblr, YouTube, Bloglovin, and SnapChat

- Suggest the book for book clubs, to book stores or to any libraries you know

You can discover more books by James J. Cudney at https://www.nextchapter.pub/authors/james-j-cudney
    Want to know when one of our books is free or discounted for Kindle? Join the newsletter at http://eepurl.com/bqqB3H
    Best regards,

James J. Cudney and the Next Chapter Team

You might also like:
Academic Curveball by James J. Cudney

To read the first chapter for free, head to:
https://www.nextchapter.pub/books/academic-curveball

Made in the USA
Columbia, SC
24 April 2020

94092196R00178